CLEMENT BALOUP
VIETNAMESE MEMORIES
BOOK 1: LEAVING SAIGON

Life Drawn

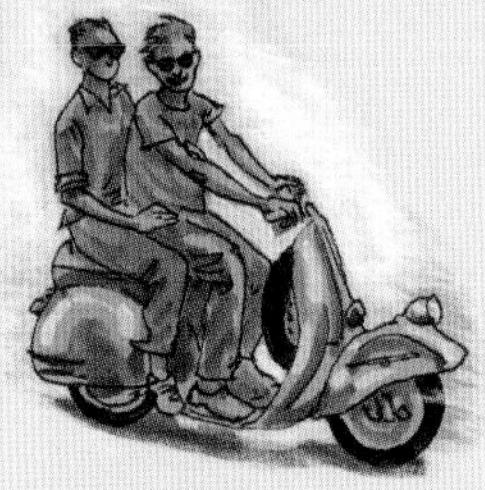

CLEMENT BALOUP
Story & Art

PIERRE DAUM
Linh Tho, original story

*

ALEX DONOGHUE
& FABRICE SAPOLSKY
U.S. Edition Editors

VINCENT HENRY
Original Edition Editor

JERRY FRISSEN
Senior Art Director

FABRICE GIGER
Publisher

Rights & Licensing - licensing@humanoids.com
Press and Social Media - pr@humanoids.com

*

"To my daughter Bianca, may she knows her roots." - Clément Baloup

This book was translated and edited as part of the University of East Anglia (UEA) project for professional development in literary translation MADE in TRANSLATION, run by the School of Politics, Philosophy, Language and Communication Studies (PPL) in collaboration with the School of Literature, Drama and Creative Writing (LDC) and funded by the UEA Alumni Fund.

VIETNAMESE MEMORIES Book 1 : LEAVING SAIGON was translated by Naomi Alice Botting, Chester Bowerman, Ruby Louise Gwynne-Evans, Jennifer Helena Karlsson and Francesca Montemagno and edited by Olivia Hanks.

MADE in TRANSLATION is a project created by Cristina Alonso Punter and supported by Claire Cuminatto and this translation project was coordinated by Ilse Renaudie.

VIETNAMESE MEMORIES Book 1: LEAVING SAIGON
This title is a publication of Humanoids, Inc. 8033 Sunset Blvd. #628, Los Angeles, CA 90046.

Life Drawn is an imprint of Humanoids, Inc.

First published in France under the title "Mémoires de Viet kieu: Quitter Saigon" and "Mémoires de Viet Kieu : Les Linh Tho, immigrés de force."

FOREWORD

As a child of the Vietnam War, Clément Baloup did not start off being a historian. He was 20 years old when he sat down in his father's kitchen in Aix-en-Provence during the mundane act of learning how to make coconut curry shrimp, and heard what he had never heard as a child growing up in the West: the story of a Vietnamese immigrant — his father.

In previous visits to his motherland, including as a 22-year-old studying at Fine Arts College in Hanoi, Clement had absorbed the intense color, heat, smells, and sensibilities of Vietnam. As he heard his father that day in the kitchen, he felt compelled to bring embodiment and attention to the experiences of a person whose voice, like so many in history, was lost under the goings-on of world and military leaders.

Clément's father, like my parents, came from a generation where after so many people had suffered, it was felt that no one needed to talk about what they went through because it wasn't special. During a national catastrophe, pretty much everyone suffered or was impacted by traumatic events. They "protected" us, the next generation, by keeping us ignorant. They held those painful experiences inside until a moment came in our adulthood, when they trusted us enough to tell us. Clément shares with us, in gorgeous reds and greens and moody blues, that moment as it occurred for him.

Clément felt the fire to put his father's story on paper and quickly got his 10-page *bande dessinée* (Franco-Belgian comics) published in *La Maison Qui Pue* (or Smelly House in English), a comics magazine.

"*It felt like a drop in the bucket when there's an ocean of stories. I felt so frustrated. I had to do so much more. It was an act to support the free speech of the people I interviewed,*" Clement told me recently from his home in Marseille.

Many people read the short piece, including Vincent Henry, the future editor of the first French edition of this book, originally entitled *Quitter Saigon*. Henry, publisher of the French graphic novel publishing house *La Boite à Bulles*, asked Clément if he would do more. For Clément, there was no choice *but* to do more.

Clément's sense of urgency sent images flying from his memory onto paper with ink and color. He worked frenetically, knowing that if no one records these personal stories, they will disappear. History is mostly told by the privileged and powerful, and rarely by those who are most affected. The danger is that, when all the participants are long gone, that what will be left of the Vietnam War will be old news magazines written by foreign journalists, a Wikipedia entry and textbooks based on third hand information, Hollywood films focused on the experience of American soldiers, or, at best, documentaries by Ken Burns (whose *Vietnam War* series will appear in his oeuvre next to *Jazz* and *Baseball*) or a Kennedy scion, obfuscating her family's role in the war.

While I was working on my 2007 documentary film, *Oh, Saigon*, about the division of my family in the Vietnam War and our escape on the last civilian helicopter out of Saigon, I spoke to an American woman, supposedly educated, about my work and the work of other Vietnamese artists. She said, "*Well, there are already Vietnam War movies like* The Deer Hunter, Full Metal Jacket *and* Apocalypse Now. *Why do you need to make anything else? Hasn't it all been said before?*" The sentiment from Oliver Stone's *Platoon*, that Vietnam was a place where America lost its innocence highlights how we Vietnamese are seen as side characters in our own civil war, falling dominoes in the struggles of more important countries.

To the West, we of the Vietnamese diaspora were peasants, prostitutes, traitors, and pawns. And casually, many of us were called "boat people". We were cruelly and often inaccurately given the name and identity of a last-ditch method of escape for a number of refugees (many of whom were killed or raped in the process). Here is an opportunity to see beyond these caricatures.

This book you hold in your hands took 6 years to come to fruition.

Clément did not coolly and rationally decide to work on books about immigration and the aftermath of colonialism and war, subjects in which he is now considered an "expert." His project began with his conscience, ignited amid a kitchen table talk with his father. Clément uncovered and animated with passion these stories of the Vietnamese diaspora, finding his own identity both as a Frenchman and as a son of a Vietnamese immigrant. He filled in gaps not only in the history of those from Vietnam, but the history of France, the US and other countries who were a part of the Cold War.

Here in this sumptuously beautiful and important graphic novel, you will intimately bear witness to what so few in the world have been privy to. May it make you, like many other readers, closer to what may be hidden in your own families and hidden in the history of your own country.

— Đoan Hoàng, Los Angeles, 2017

Đoan Hoàng is an award-winning director, producer, and screenwriter. Her documentary *Oh, Saigon* explored divisions in her family, both political and personal, after her parents escaped with her at the end of the Vietnam War on the last helicopter taking civilians out of Saigon, while leaving her sister behind. *Oh, Saigon* garnered a number of international film prizes, including a Sundance documentary award, aired on PBS, Netflix, Amazon & Hulu and has been screened and broadcast in 16 countries. Doan traveled with *Oh, Saigon* throughout Spain and Vietnam for the U. S. Department of State and has lectured at institutions such as the Museum of Modern Art (MoMA), Yale, Columbia University, USC, and Centre de Cultura Contemporània de Barcelona. She lives with her husband and family in Los Angeles.

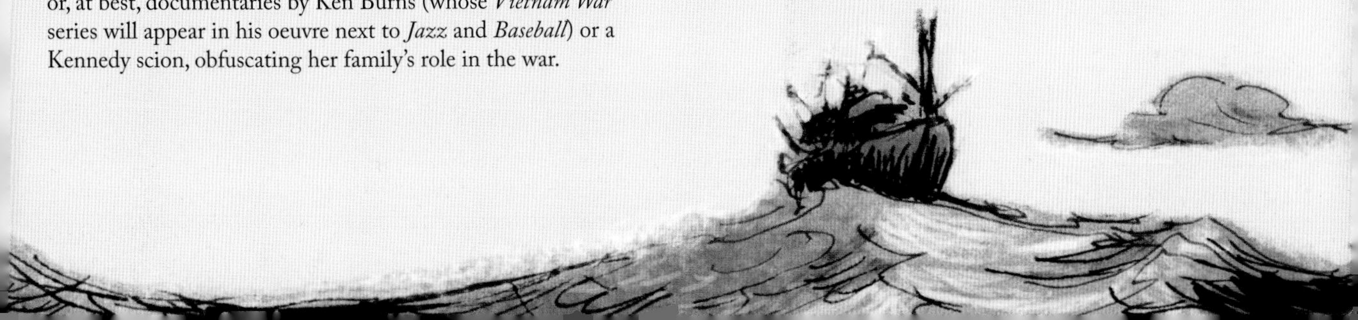

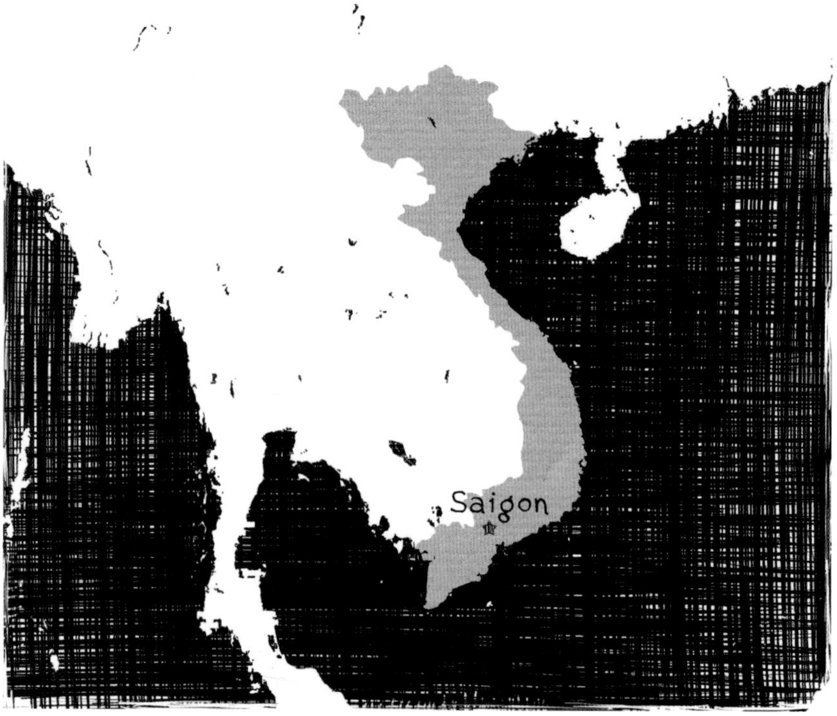
Saigon

TRÀNG BÀNG, SOUTH VIETNAM, SUMMER 1972.

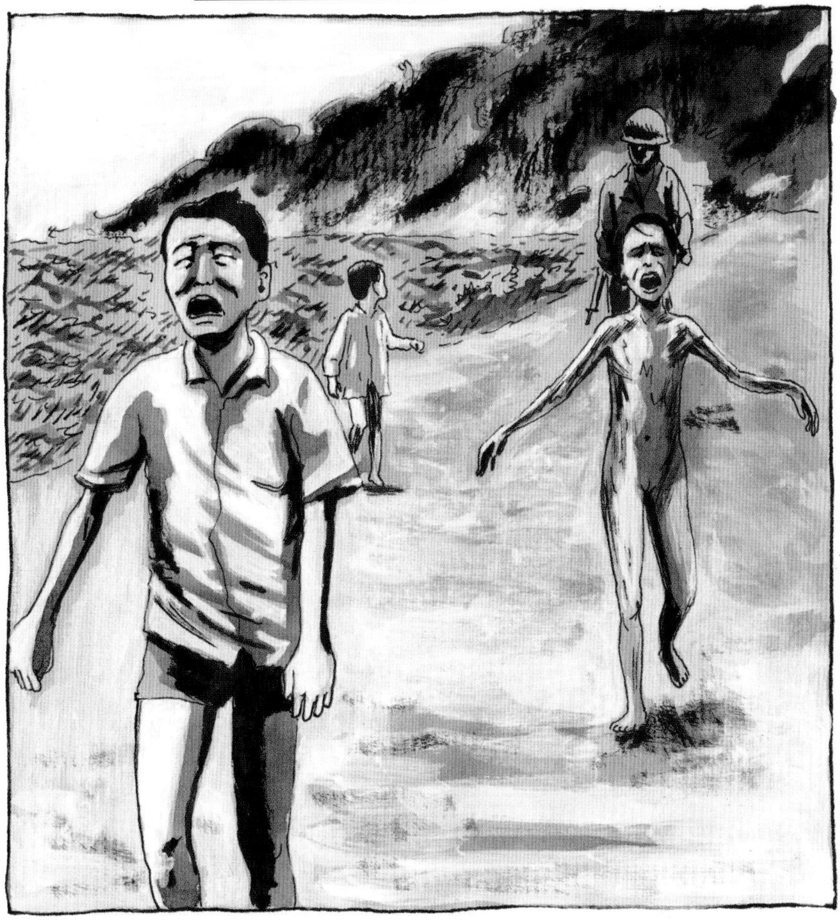

THERE IS NOT A SINGLE IMAGE FROM THE VIETNAM WAR MORE INTERNATIONALLY RECOGNIZED THAN THAT OF THESE CHILDREN RUNNING FROM THEIR VILLAGE TO ESCAPE THE BURNING NAPALM.

THIS PHOTO WAS AWARDED WITH THE 1972 PULITZER PRIZE, AFFECTING THE WORLD'S ATTITUDE TOWARDS THE WAR. AT THE TIME, PROTESTS AGAINST THE WAR TOOK PLACE IN CAPITAL CITIES ACROSS THE GLOBE.

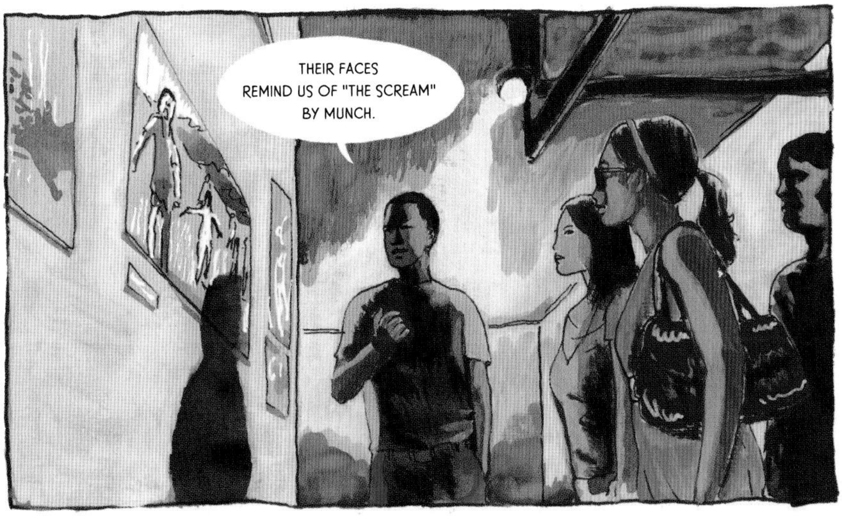
THEIR FACES REMIND US OF "THE SCREAM" BY MUNCH.

THE WAR REMNANTS MUSEUM, MODERN-DAY HO CHI MINH CITY (FORMERLY SAIGON).

WHAT ELSE DO WE KNOW ABOUT THIS WAR? WE ALL REMEMBER OPERATION ROLLING THUNDER, LED BY B52s
AND OTHER AMERICAN WAR PLANES, DURING WHICH TWICE AS MANY BOMBS WERE DROPPED OVER VIETNAM
AS WERE DEPLOYED ALL OVER THE WORLD THROUGHOUT THE ENTIRE SECOND WORLD WAR.

AT THE WAR REMNANTS MUSEUM WE FIND GLASS JARS CONTAINING HORRIFYING
RELICS OF THE WAR. AGENT ORANGE, A DEADLY DEFOLIANT, CONTINUES TO CLAIM VICTIMS
TO THIS DAY. BABIES ARE BORN WITH DEFORMITIES, OR OFTEN STILLBORN, WHILST THE
UNITED STATES AND MONSANTO, THE INVENTOR OF THE CHEMICAL, DENY ALL RESPONSIBILITY.

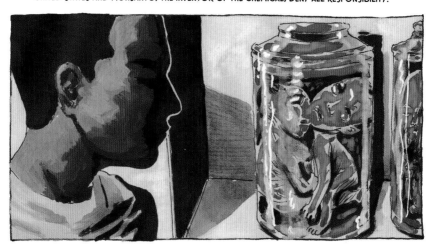

HOLLYWOOD MOVIES HAVE SHOWN US THE NIGHTMARE THE GIs HAD TO EXPERIENCE.
THE DEFEAT OF THE POWERFUL CAPITALIST ARMY AT THE HANDS OF THE COMMUNIST
VILLAGERS IS ALMOST A MODERN-DAY VERSION OF DAVID AND GOLIATH. YET THESE HORRIFIC
IMAGES SHOW US MERELY A SMALL PART OF VIETNAM'S VIOLENT HISTORY IN MODERN TIMES.

IT ALL BEGAN IN THE SECOND HALF OF THE NINETEENTH CENTURY WITH FRANCE'S COLONISATION OF VIETNAM AND THE CREATION OF FRENCH INDOCHINA. IN SPITE OF PROTEST MOVEMENTS AND REBELLIONS, THE FRENCH EMPIRE'S CONTROL WAS SOLIDIFIED AND THE FRENCH SETTLED COMFORTABLY IN VIETNAM.

THEN CAME THE SECOND WORLD WAR. JAPANESE TROOPS LAUNCHED A MASSIVE STRIKE ON ASIA AND THE PACIFIC. IT SEEMED NOTHING CAN WITHSTAND THE MIKADO'S ARMY.

THEY QUICKLY BROUGHT THE FRENCH ARMY TO ITS KNEES AND SEIZED CONTROL OF INDOCHINA.

THIS DID NOT LAST LONG, HOWEVER, AS THE ATOMIC BOMBS DROPPED ON HIROSHIMA AND NAGASAKI ON THE 6TH AND 9TH OF AUGUST 1945 FORCED THE JAPANESE INTO UNCONDITIONAL SURRENDER BY SEPTEMBER.

THE FRENCH AUTHORITIES SAW FIT TO RETURN AND SENT THE FRENCH FAR EAST EXPEDITIONARY CORPS TO REGAIN CONTROL.

YET THE VIETNAMESE FREEDOM FIGHTERS HAD LEARNED A VALUABLE LESSON: THE FRENCH COULD BE DEFEATED AND DRIVEN OUT OF THE COUNTRY. IN 1945, THE "INDOCHINA WAR" -- AS IT IS REFERRED TO NOW -- BEGAN. IT CAME TO AN END IN 1954 WITH THE BATTLE OF DIEN BIEN PHU. THE FRENCH COLONY DISSOLVED, LEAVING BEHIND A NATION DIVIDED IN TWO BUT DESTINED TO BE REUNIFIED WITHIN TWO YEARS.

THE AMERICANS IMMEDIATELY INTERVENED, SENDING MILITARY ADVISORS WITH THE OFFICIAL PURPOSE OF AIDING THE SOUTHERN REGIME. THE AMERICANS' TRUE MOTIVE, HOWEVER, WAS TO COUNTER THE COMMUNIST INFLUENCE GRADUALLY SPREADING THROUGHOUT ASIA. THEY BACKED THE ESTABLISHMENT OF A CAPITALIST PUPPET REGIME IN THE SOUTH AND PLUNGED THEMSELVES INTO THE "NAM" WAR, A CONFLICT WHICH LASTED UNTIL 1975.

THIRTY YEARS OF WAR RESULTED IN A HORRIFYING NUMBER OF DEATHS, LEAVING A COUNTRY BLED DRY AND A VIETNAMESE POPULATION TORN IN TWO: NORTH AND SOUTH.

DURING AND AFTER THESE CONFLICTS -- TO ESCAPE THE WAR AND DEPRIVATION OR IN SEARCH OF A BETTER FUTURE -- MORE THAN TWO MILLION VIETNAMESE SOUGHT TO FLEE THEIR COUNTRY.

FATE LAID MANY TRYING ORDEALS IN THE PATHS OF THE EXILED, BUT THEY ALL SHARED THE BURDEN OF LEAVING EVERYTHING BEHIND THEM.

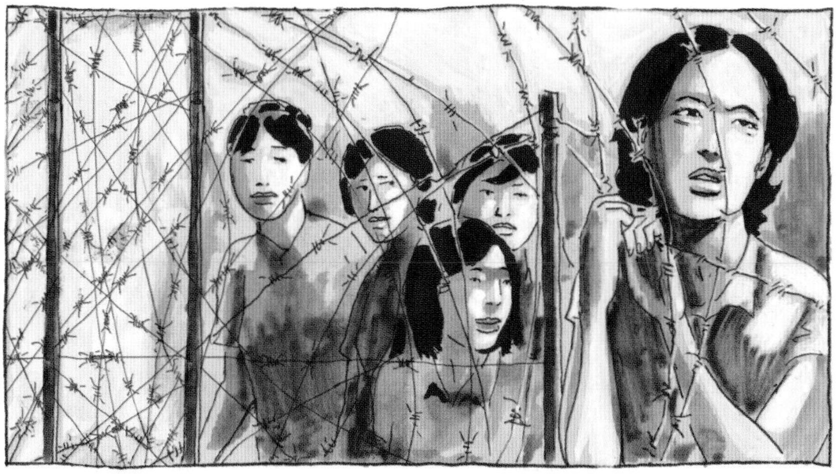

ONE OF THE MOST TRAGIC EPISODES OF THIS EXODUS, STILL STRONGLY ANCHORED IN OUR MEMORY, WAS THE DEPARTURE OF THE "BOAT PEOPLE," PREPARED TO PUT THEIR LIVES AT RISK IN THE MOST PRECARIOUS OF CONDITIONS FOR FEAR OF REPRESSION FOLLOWING THE ESTABLISHMENT OF COMMUNISM IN 1975.

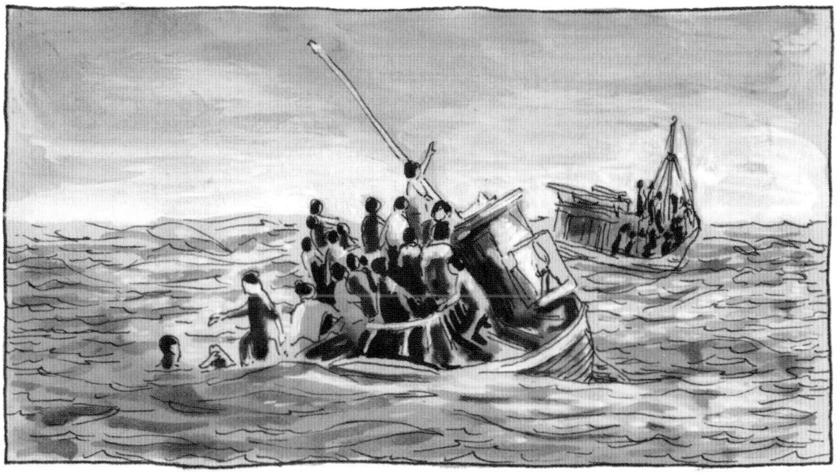

TODAY, OUTSIDE OF VIETNAM, THEY MAKE UP AN ACTIVE DIASPORA MAINLY SETTLED IN THE USA, FRANCE, CANADA AND AUSTRALIA BUT ALSO PRESENT ACROSS EUROPE AND ASIA.

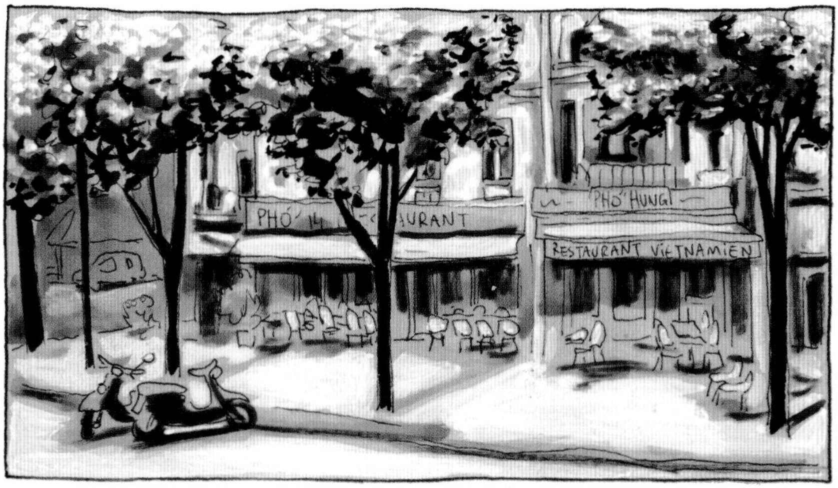
PHỞ 14
AURANT
PHỞ HUNG
RESTAURANT VIETNAMIEN

THESE VIETNAMESE LIVING OVERSEAS HAVE BEEN NICKNAMED: THE VIET KIEU... HERE ARE SOME OF THEIR STORIES.

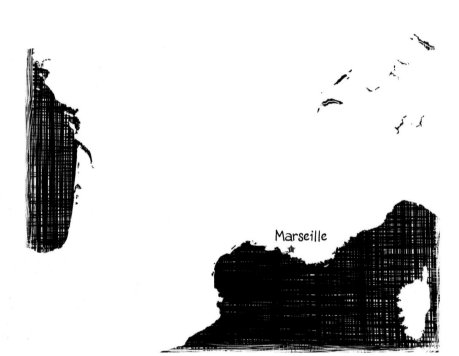
Marseille

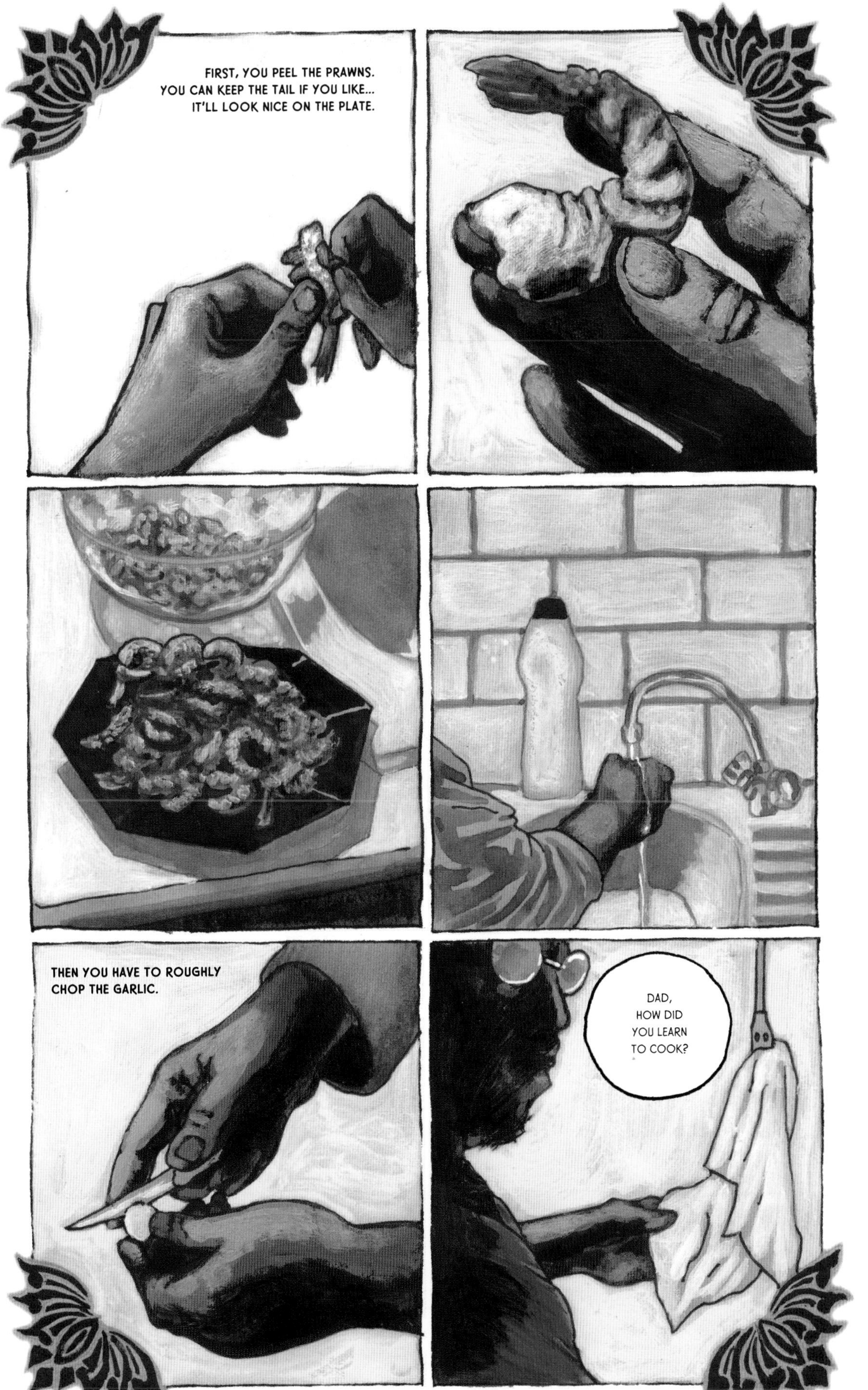
FIRST, YOU PEEL THE PRAWNS. YOU CAN KEEP THE TAIL IF YOU LIKE... IT'LL LOOK NICE ON THE PLATE.
THEN YOU HAVE TO ROUGHLY CHOP THE GARLIC.
DAD, HOW DID YOU LEARN TO COOK?

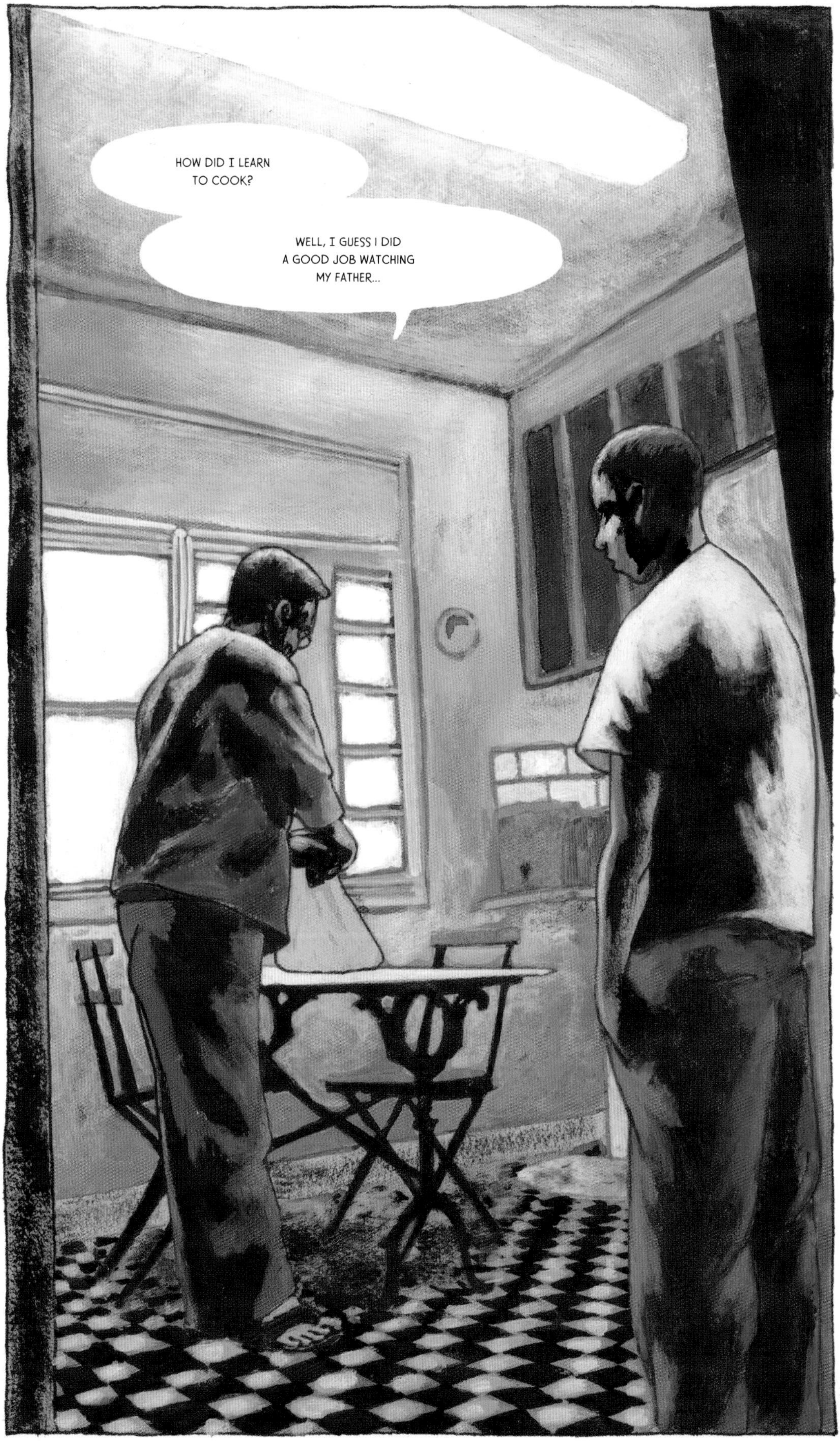
HOW DID I LEARN TO COOK?
WELL, I GUESS I DID A GOOD JOB WATCHING MY FATHER...

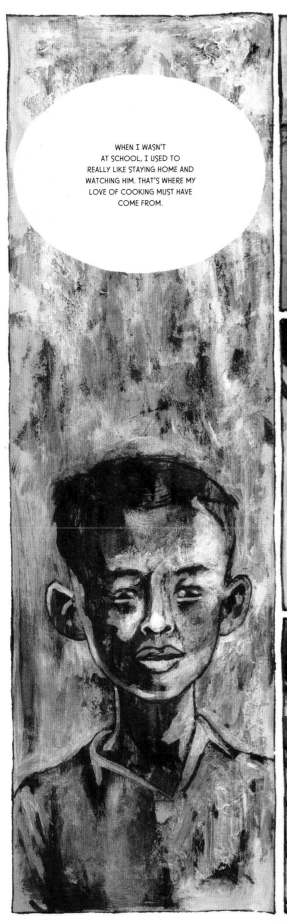

WHEN I WASN'T AT SCHOOL, I USED TO REALLY LIKE STAYING HOME AND WATCHING HIM. THAT'S WHERE MY LOVE OF COOKING MUST HAVE COME FROM.

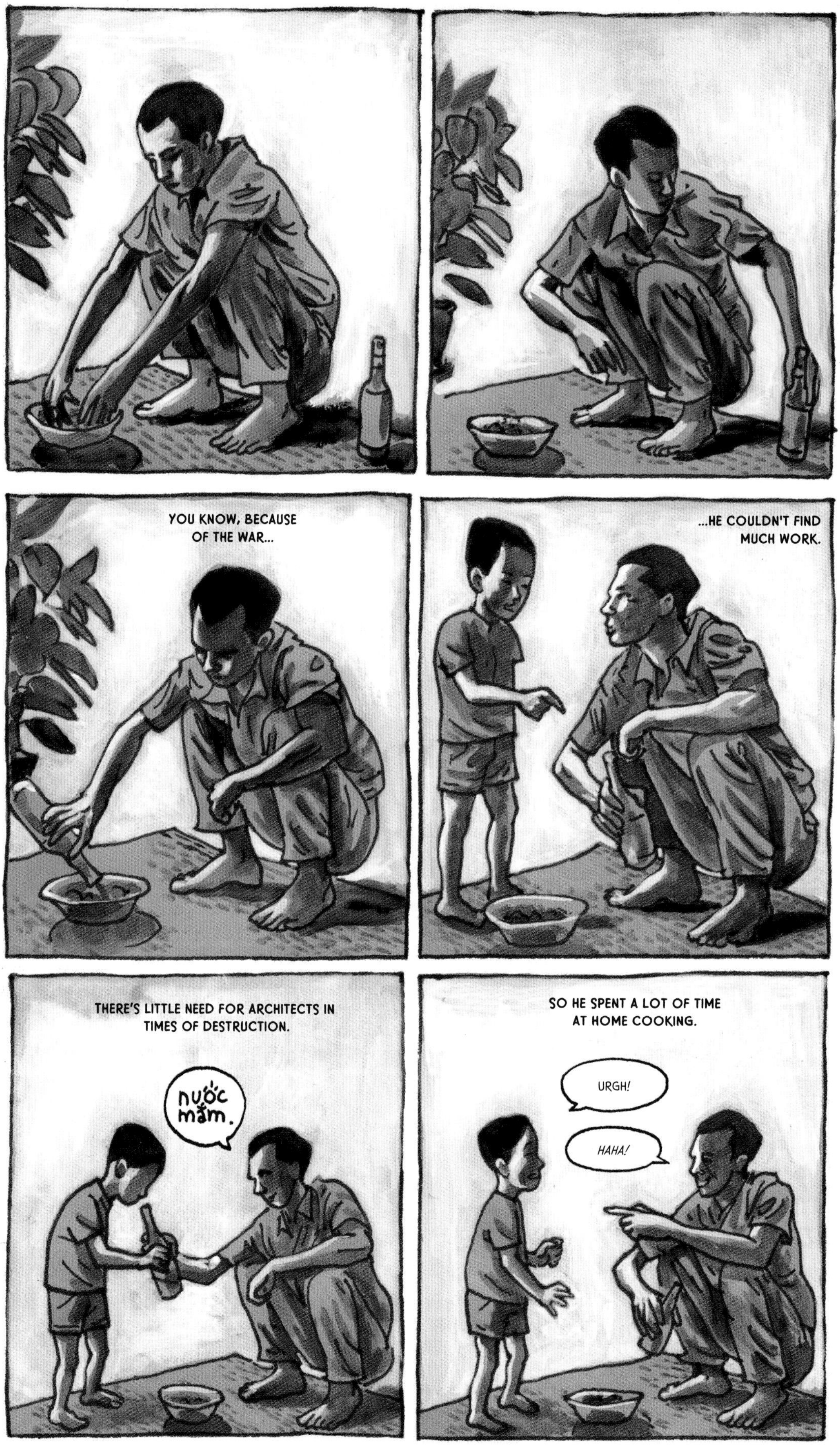
YOU KNOW, BECAUSE OF THE WAR...
...HE COULDN'T FIND MUCH WORK.
THERE'S LITTLE NEED FOR ARCHITECTS IN TIMES OF DESTRUCTION.
nước mắm.
SO HE SPENT A LOT OF TIME AT HOME COOKING.
URGH!
HAHA!

YOU FRY THE GARLIC IN THE OIL UNTIL IT BROWNS.

THEN YOU ADD THE PRAWNS, SEARING THEM A LITTLE.

ALWAYS OVER A LOW FLAME...

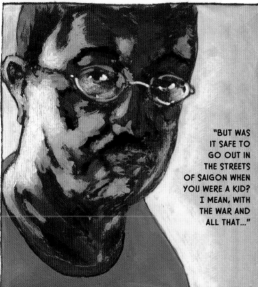

"BUT WAS IT SAFE TO GO OUT IN THE STREETS OF SAIGON WHEN YOU WERE A KID? I MEAN, WITH THE WAR AND ALL THAT..."

OH YES, WE OFTEN PLAYED IN THE STREETS.

THERE WERE GIs EVERYWHERE. WE USED TO COLLECT THE CARTRIDGES THEY WERE ALWAYS DROPPING...

...THEN WE'D WHACK THEM TO MAKE THEM EXPLODE. THEY'D GO OFF LIKE FIRECRACKERS!

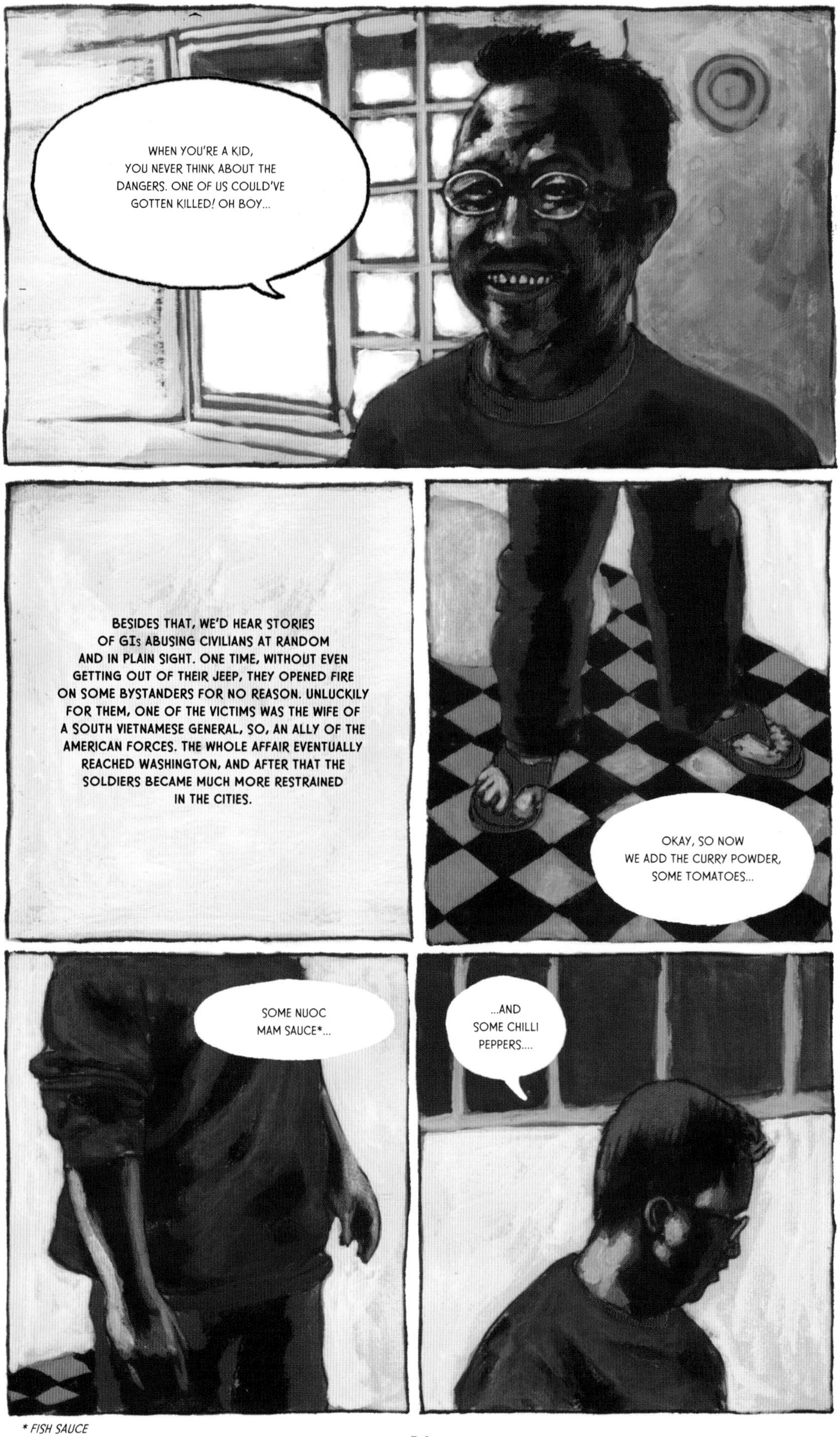
WHEN YOU'RE A KID, YOU NEVER THINK ABOUT THE DANGERS. ONE OF US COULD'VE GOTTEN KILLED! OH BOY...
BESIDES THAT, WE'D HEAR STORIES OF GIs ABUSING CIVILIANS AT RANDOM AND IN PLAIN SIGHT. ONE TIME, WITHOUT EVEN GETTING OUT OF THEIR JEEP, THEY OPENED FIRE ON SOME BYSTANDERS FOR NO REASON. UNLUCKILY FOR THEM, ONE OF THE VICTIMS WAS THE WIFE OF A SOUTH VIETNAMESE GENERAL, SO, AN ALLY OF THE AMERICAN FORCES. THE WHOLE AFFAIR EVENTUALLY REACHED WASHINGTON, AND AFTER THAT THE SOLDIERS BECAME MUCH MORE RESTRAINED IN THE CITIES.
OKAY, SO NOW WE ADD THE CURRY POWDER, SOME TOMATOES...
SOME NUOC MAM SAUCE*...
...AND SOME CHILLI PEPPERS....

* FISH SAUCE

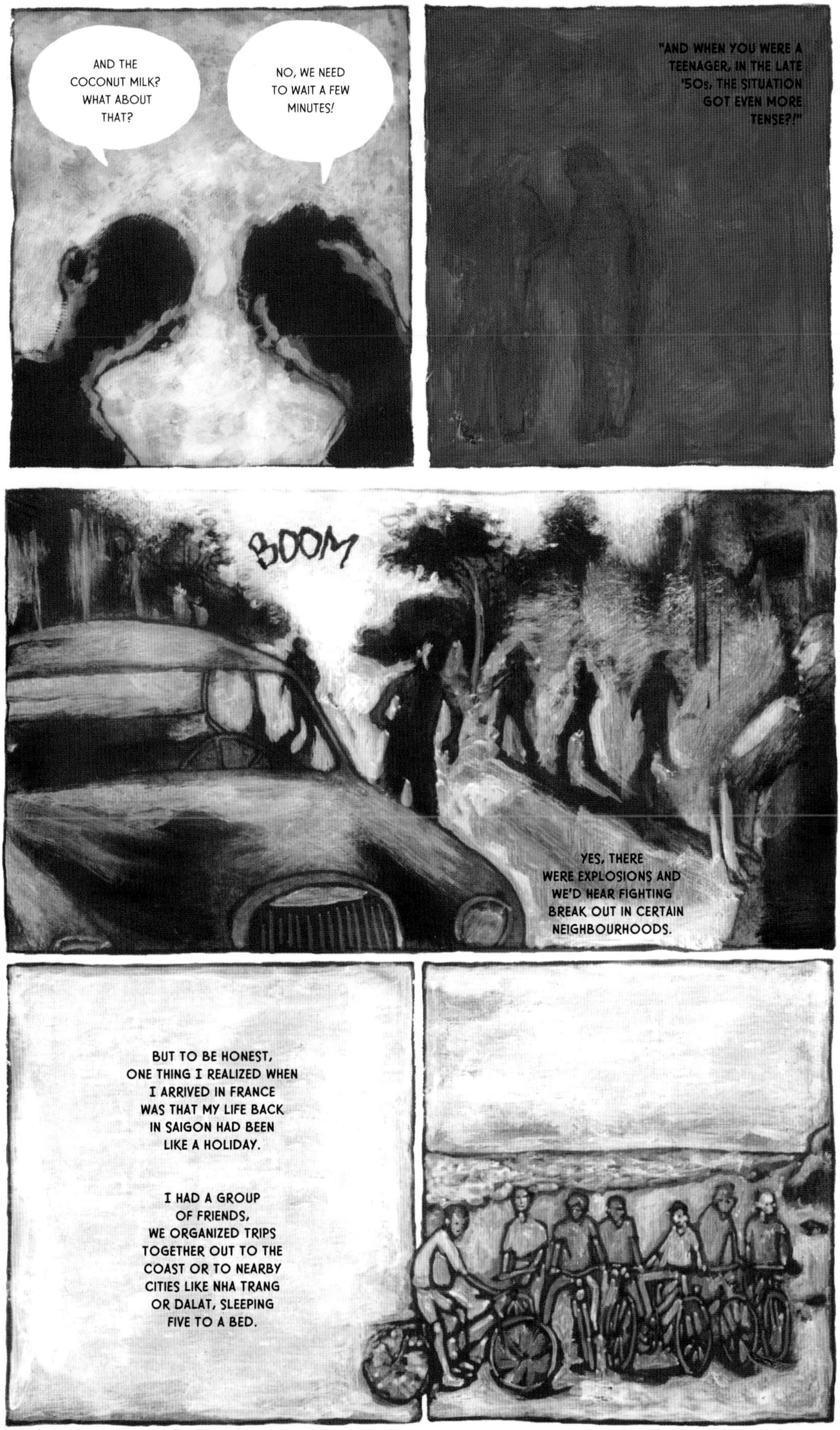
AND THE COCONUT MILK? WHAT ABOUT THAT?
NO, WE NEED TO WAIT A FEW MINUTES!
"AND WHEN YOU WERE A TEENAGER, IN THE LATE '50s, THE SITUATION GOT EVEN MORE TENSE?!"
BOOM
YES, THERE WERE EXPLOSIONS AND WE'D HEAR FIGHTING BREAK OUT IN CERTAIN NEIGHBOURHOODS.
BUT TO BE HONEST, ONE THING I REALIZED WHEN I ARRIVED IN FRANCE WAS THAT MY LIFE BACK IN SAIGON HAD BEEN LIKE A HOLIDAY.
I HAD A GROUP OF FRIENDS, WE ORGANIZED TRIPS TOGETHER OUT TO THE COAST OR TO NEARBY CITIES LIKE NHA TRANG OR DALAT, SLEEPING FIVE TO A BED.

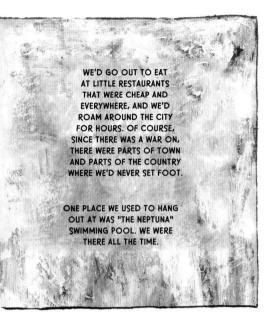

WE'D GO OUT TO EAT AT LITTLE RESTAURANTS THAT WERE CHEAP AND EVERYWHERE, AND WE'D ROAM AROUND THE CITY FOR HOURS. OF COURSE, SINCE THERE WAS A WAR ON, THERE WERE PARTS OF TOWN AND PARTS OF THE COUNTRY WHERE WE'D NEVER SET FOOT.

ONE PLACE WE USED TO HANG OUT AT WAS "THE NEPTUNA" SWIMMING POOL. WE WERE THERE ALL THE TIME.

TIME TO ADD THE COCONUT MILK! *VOILA!*

TWO MINUTES AND IT'LL BE READY!

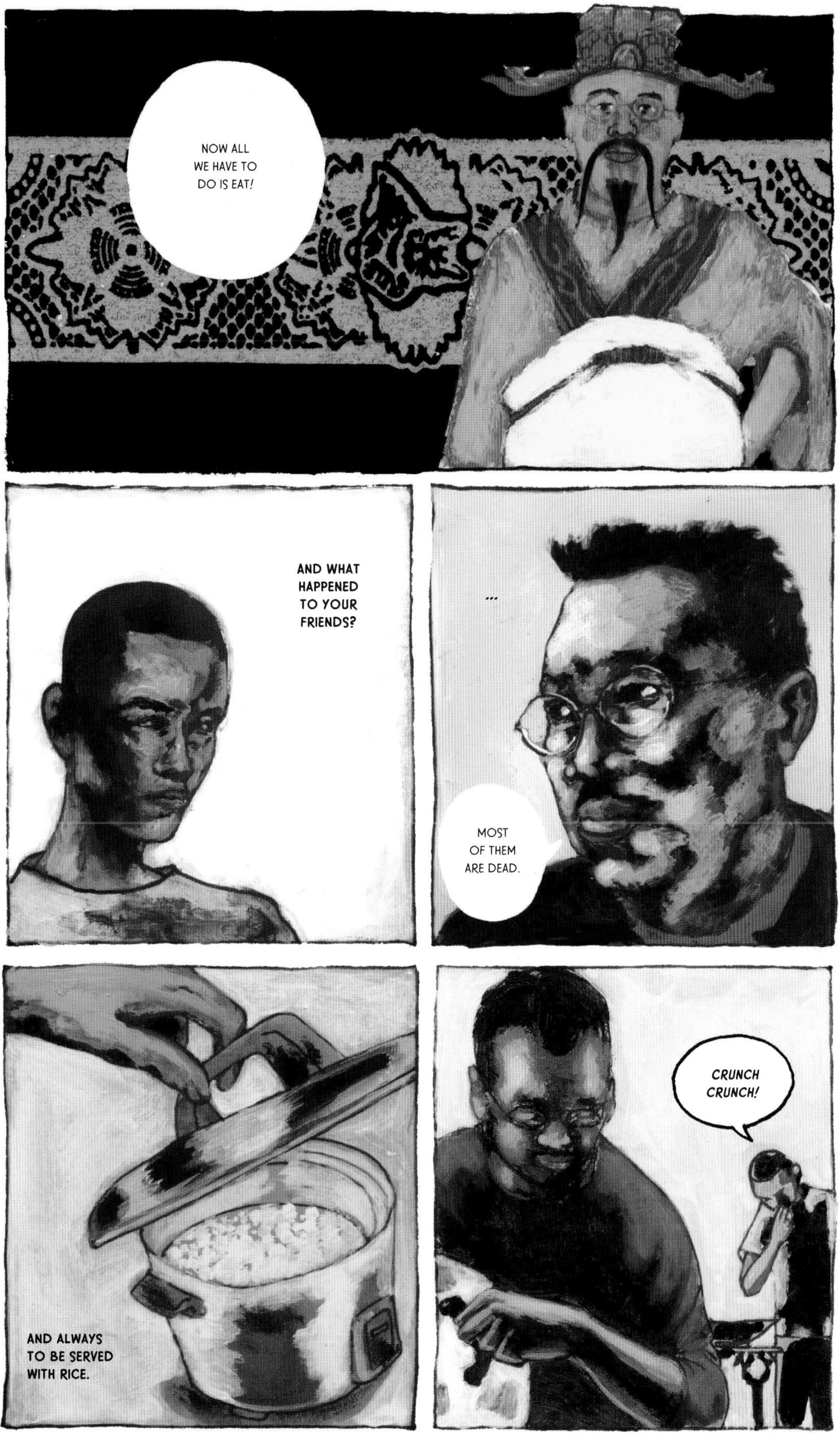
NOW ALL WE HAVE TO DO IS EAT!
AND WHAT HAPPENED TO YOUR FRIENDS?
...
MOST OF THEM ARE DEAD.
AND ALWAYS TO BE SERVED WITH RICE.
CRUNCH CRUNCH!

DON'T PICK AT THE FOOD!

AND ER...WHAT WAS IT LIKE WHEN YOU ARRIVED IN FRANCE?

WELL, IT WAS PRETTY GOOD ACTUALLY...

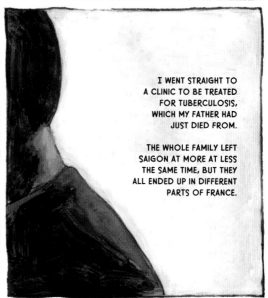

I WENT STRAIGHT TO A CLINIC TO BE TREATED FOR TUBERCULOSIS, WHICH MY FATHER HAD JUST DIED FROM.

THE WHOLE FAMILY LEFT SAIGON AT MORE AT LESS THE SAME TIME, BUT THEY ALL ENDED UP IN DIFFERENT PARTS OF FRANCE.

AS I WAS SAYING, I SOON FOUND MYSELF IN GRENOBLE WHERE I WAS TREATED.

I LOVED BEING IN THE MOUNTAINS.

SICK, ALONE AND FAR FROM HOME...

...AND YOU'RE SAYING THAT WAS *GOOD?!*

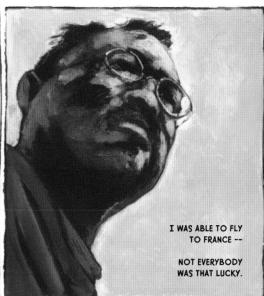

I WAS ABLE TO FLY TO FRANCE --

NOT EVERYBODY WAS THAT LUCKY.

AND BESIDES, I WASN'T ALONE: THERE WERE A FEW OTHER VIETNAMESE PEOPLE IN THE SAME SITUATION AS ME IN THE CLINIC.

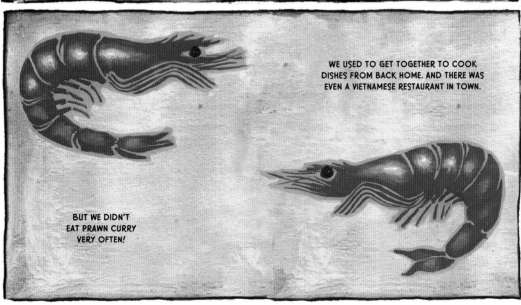

WE USED TO GET TOGETHER TO COOK DISHES FROM BACK HOME. AND THERE WAS EVEN A VIETNAMESE RESTAURANT IN TOWN.

BUT WE DIDN'T EAT PRAWN CURRY VERY OFTEN!

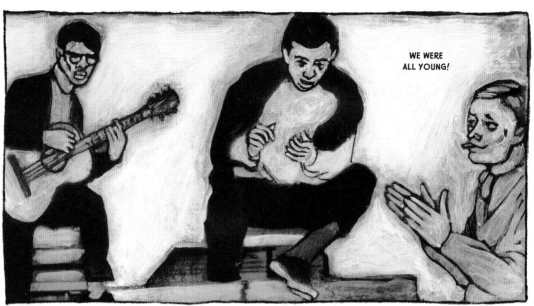

WE WERE ALL YOUNG!

IT WAS A NICE ATMOSPHERE.

I WENT BACK TO MY STUDIES, BUT I WAS STILL RECEIVING TREATMENT AND THEY GAVE ME PILLS WHICH MADE ME SEE EVERYTHING IN BLUE.

CAN YOU PLEASE SET THE TABLE?

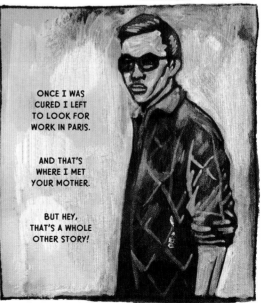

ONCE I WAS CURED I LEFT TO LOOK FOR WORK IN PARIS.

AND THAT'S WHERE I MET YOUR MOTHER.

BUT HEY, THAT'S A WHOLE OTHER STORY!

Aix-en-Provence
★

HERE YOU ARE.

THANKS.

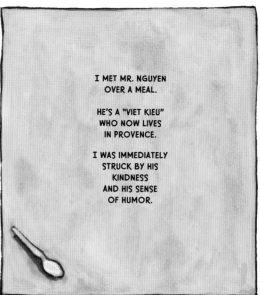

I MET MR. NGUYEN OVER A MEAL.

HE'S A "VIET KIEU" WHO NOW LIVES IN PROVENCE.

I WAS IMMEDIATELY STRUCK BY HIS KINDNESS AND HIS SENSE OF HUMOR.

SO, YOUR FOOD WASN'T AS NICE AS THIS WHEN YOU WERE IN THE CAMP, *RIGHT?!*

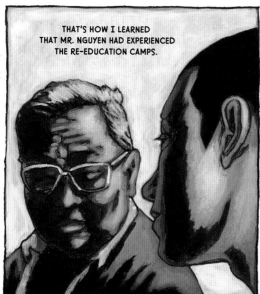

THAT'S HOW I LEARNED THAT MR. NGUYEN HAD EXPERIENCED THE RE-EDUCATION CAMPS.

WELL, IN THE MORNINGS WE'D HAVE BACON AND EGGS, AND FOR LUNCH, STEAKS AN INCH THICK!

HAHAHAHA!

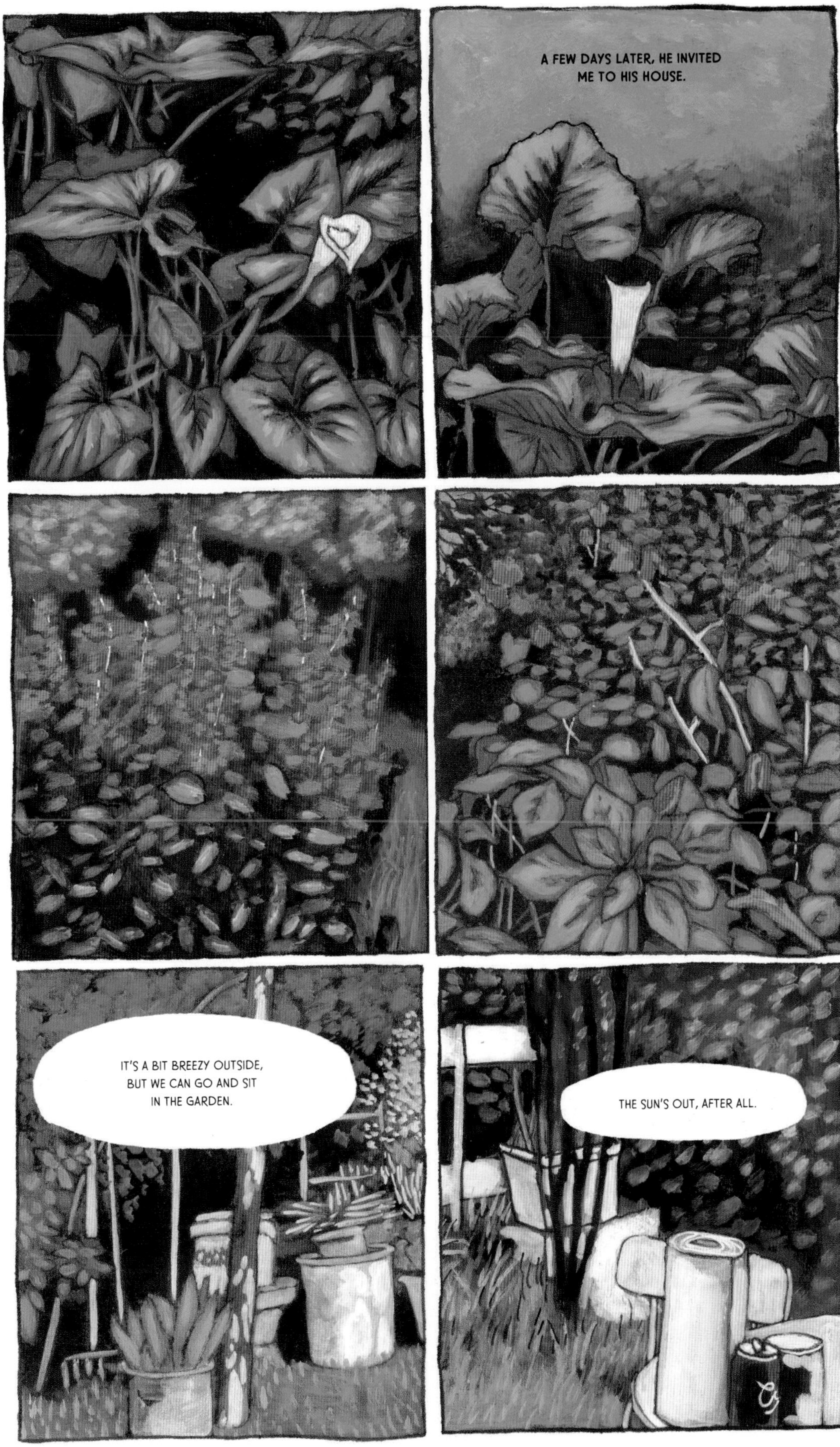
A FEW DAYS LATER, HE INVITED ME TO HIS HOUSE.
IT'S A BIT BREEZY OUTSIDE, BUT WE CAN GO AND SIT IN THE GARDEN.
THE SUN'S OUT, AFTER ALL.

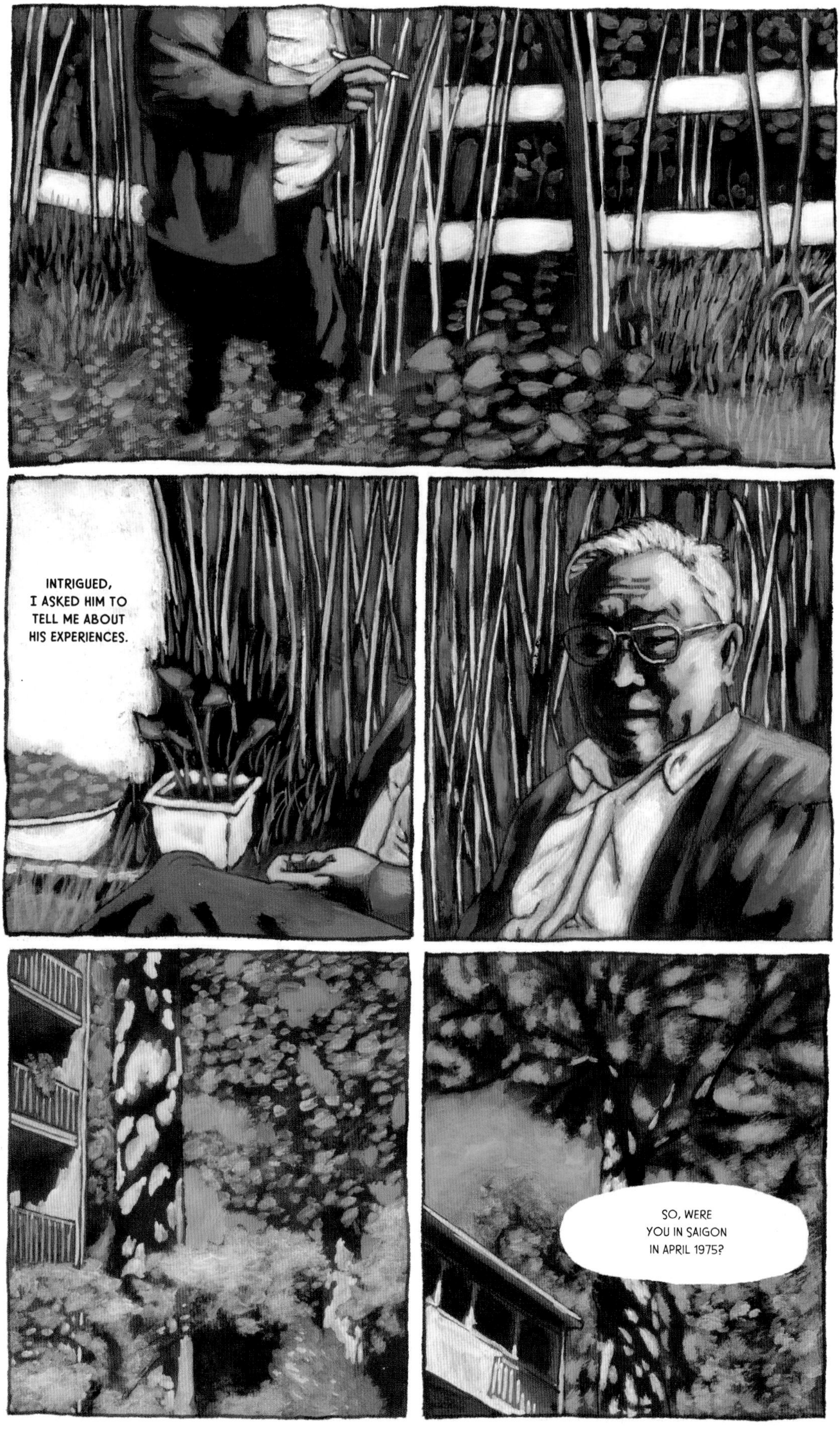
INTRIGUED, I ASKED HIM TO TELL ME ABOUT HIS EXPERIENCES.
SO, WERE YOU IN SAIGON IN APRIL 1975?

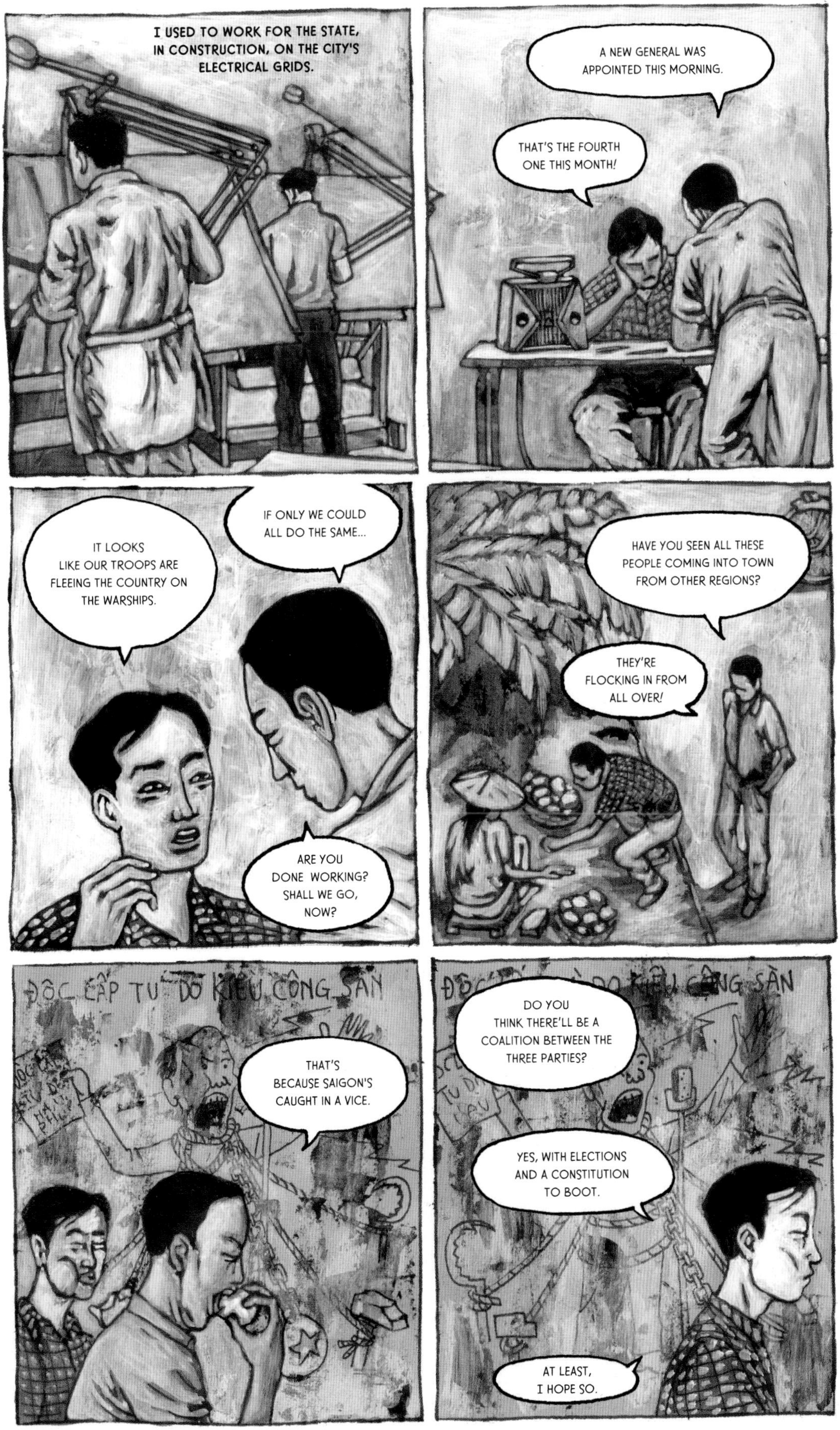
I USED TO WORK FOR THE STATE, IN CONSTRUCTION, ON THE CITY'S ELECTRICAL GRIDS.
A NEW GENERAL WAS APPOINTED THIS MORNING.
THAT'S THE FOURTH ONE THIS MONTH!
IT LOOKS LIKE OUR TROOPS ARE FLEEING THE COUNTRY ON THE WARSHIPS.
IF ONLY WE COULD ALL DO THE SAME...
ARE YOU DONE WORKING? SHALL WE GO, NOW?
HAVE YOU SEEN ALL THESE PEOPLE COMING INTO TOWN FROM OTHER REGIONS?
THEY'RE FLOCKING IN FROM ALL OVER!
THAT'S BECAUSE SAIGON'S CAUGHT IN A VICE.
DO YOU THINK THERE'LL BE A COALITION BETWEEN THE THREE PARTIES?
YES, WITH ELECTIONS AND A CONSTITUTION TO BOOT.
AT LEAST, I HOPE SO.

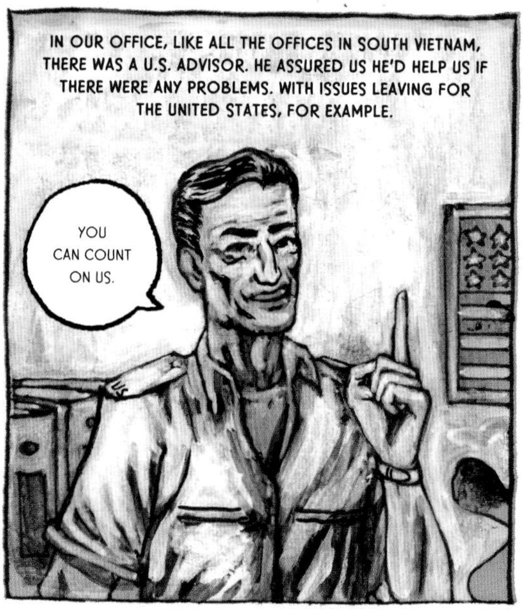
IN OUR OFFICE, LIKE ALL THE OFFICES IN SOUTH VIETNAM, THERE WAS A U.S. ADVISOR. HE ASSURED US HE'D HELP US IF THERE WERE ANY PROBLEMS. WITH ISSUES LEAVING FOR THE UNITED STATES, FOR EXAMPLE.
YOU CAN COUNT ON US.

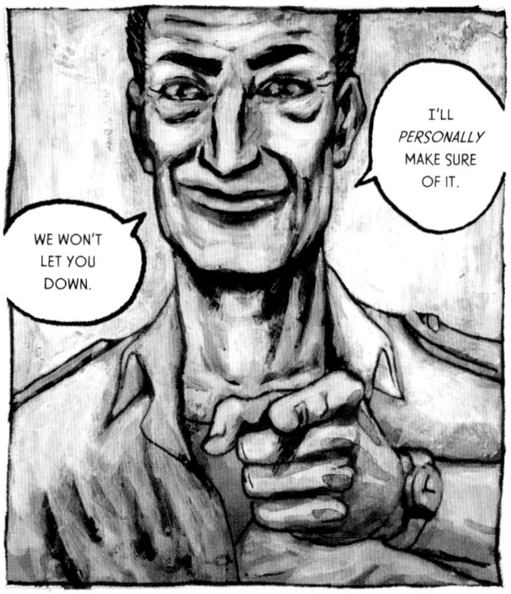
I'LL *PERSONALLY* MAKE SURE OF IT.
WE WON'T LET YOU DOWN.

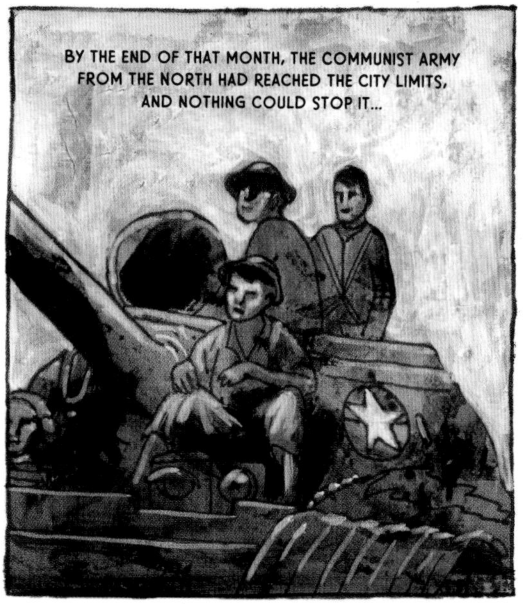
BY THE END OF THAT MONTH, THE COMMUNIST ARMY FROM THE NORTH HAD REACHED THE CITY LIMITS, AND NOTHING COULD STOP IT...

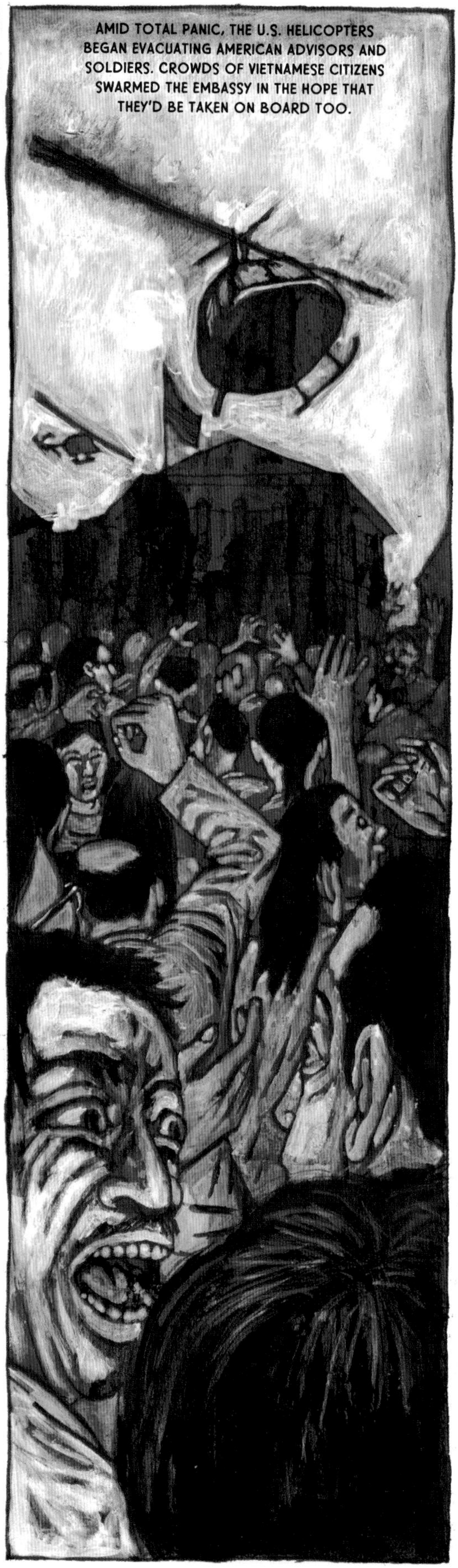
AMID TOTAL PANIC, THE U.S. HELICOPTERS BEGAN EVACUATING AMERICAN ADVISORS AND SOLDIERS. CROWDS OF VIETNAMESE CITIZENS SWARMED THE EMBASSY IN THE HOPE THAT THEY'D BE TAKEN ON BOARD TOO.

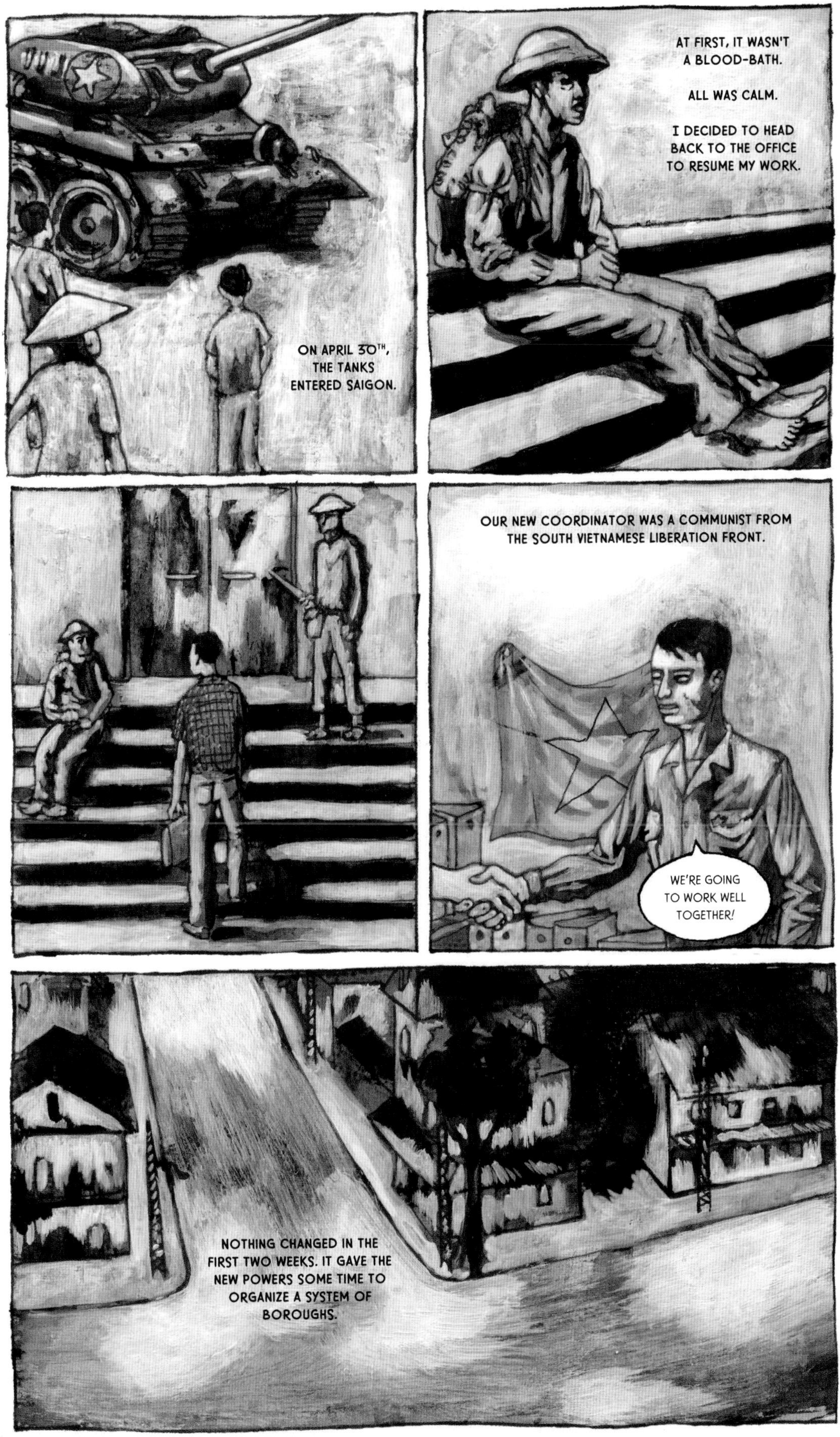
ON APRIL 30TH, THE TANKS ENTERED SAIGON.
AT FIRST, IT WASN'T A BLOOD-BATH.
ALL WAS CALM.
I DECIDED TO HEAD BACK TO THE OFFICE TO RESUME MY WORK.
OUR NEW COORDINATOR WAS A COMMUNIST FROM THE SOUTH VIETNAMESE LIBERATION FRONT.
WE'RE GOING TO WORK WELL TOGETHER!
NOTHING CHANGED IN THE FIRST TWO WEEKS. IT GAVE THE NEW POWERS SOME TIME TO ORGANIZE A SYSTEM OF BOROUGHS.

THEN...

...THE HOUSES OF THOSE WHO LEFT WERE REQUISITIONED, THEIR OWNERS DISPOSSESSED ACCORDING TO THE NEW POLICY OF "ONE HOUSE PER FAMILY."

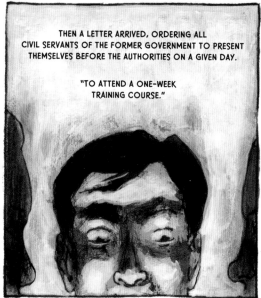

THEN A LETTER ARRIVED, ORDERING ALL CIVIL SERVANTS OF THE FORMER GOVERNMENT TO PRESENT THEMSELVES BEFORE THE AUTHORITIES ON A GIVEN DAY.

"TO ATTEND A ONE-WEEK TRAINING COURSE."

OH MY GOD! THEY'RE GOING TO DO THE SAME AS IN RUSSIA!

WE'RE JUST WORKERS! WHAT DO THEY *WANT* FROM US?

OUR COORDINATOR TRIED TO REASSURE US.

THEY'RE WAITING FOR YOU.

IN ANY EVENT, I COULDN'T HIDE. ONE OF MY NEIGHBORS HAD TAKEN IT UPON HIMSELF TO REPORT ME TO THE NEW POLICE ORDER.

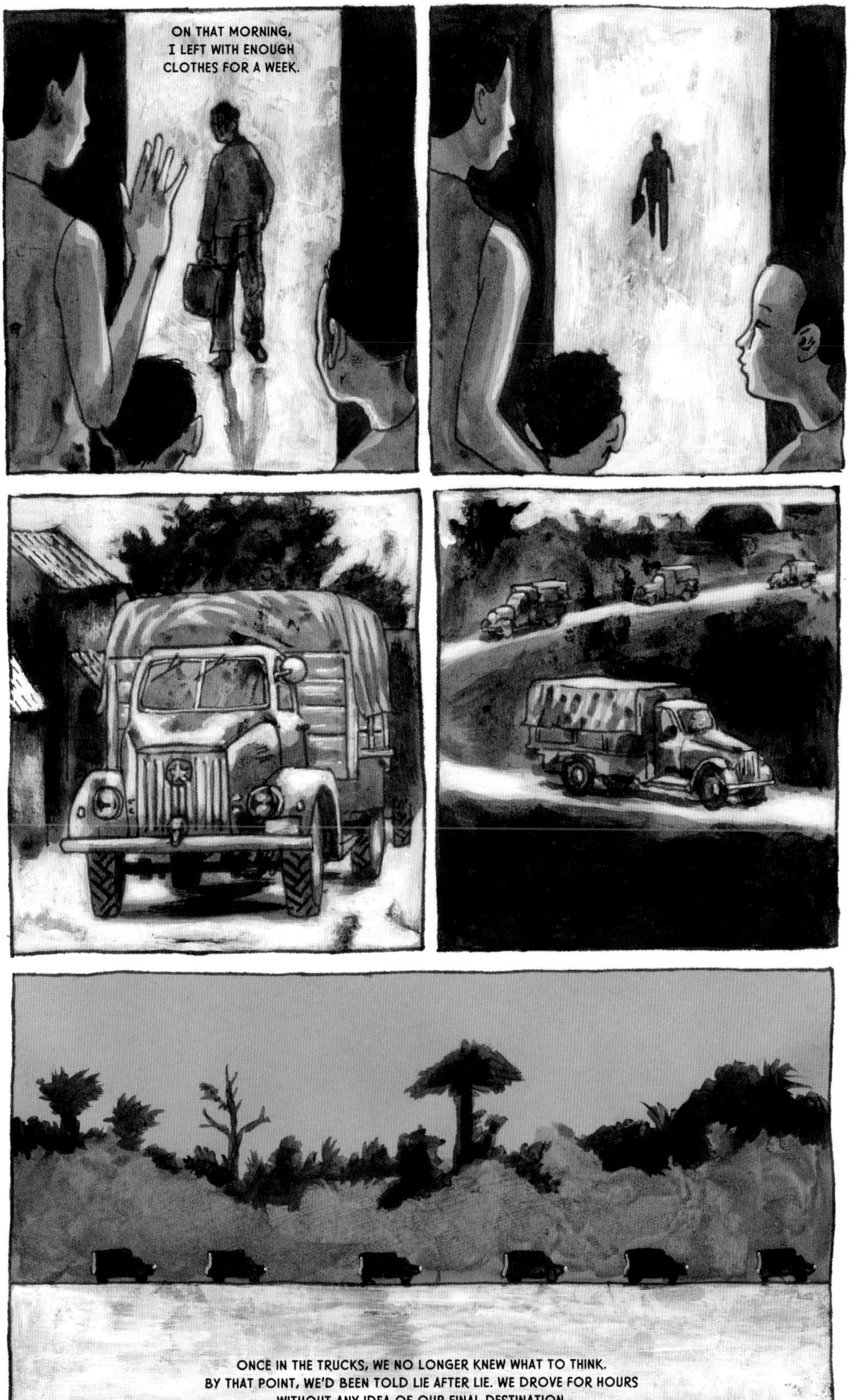
ON THAT MORNING, I LEFT WITH ENOUGH CLOTHES FOR A WEEK.
ONCE IN THE TRUCKS, WE NO LONGER KNEW WHAT TO THINK. BY THAT POINT, WE'D BEEN TOLD LIE AFTER LIE. WE DROVE FOR HOURS WITHOUT ANY IDEA OF OUR FINAL DESTINATION.

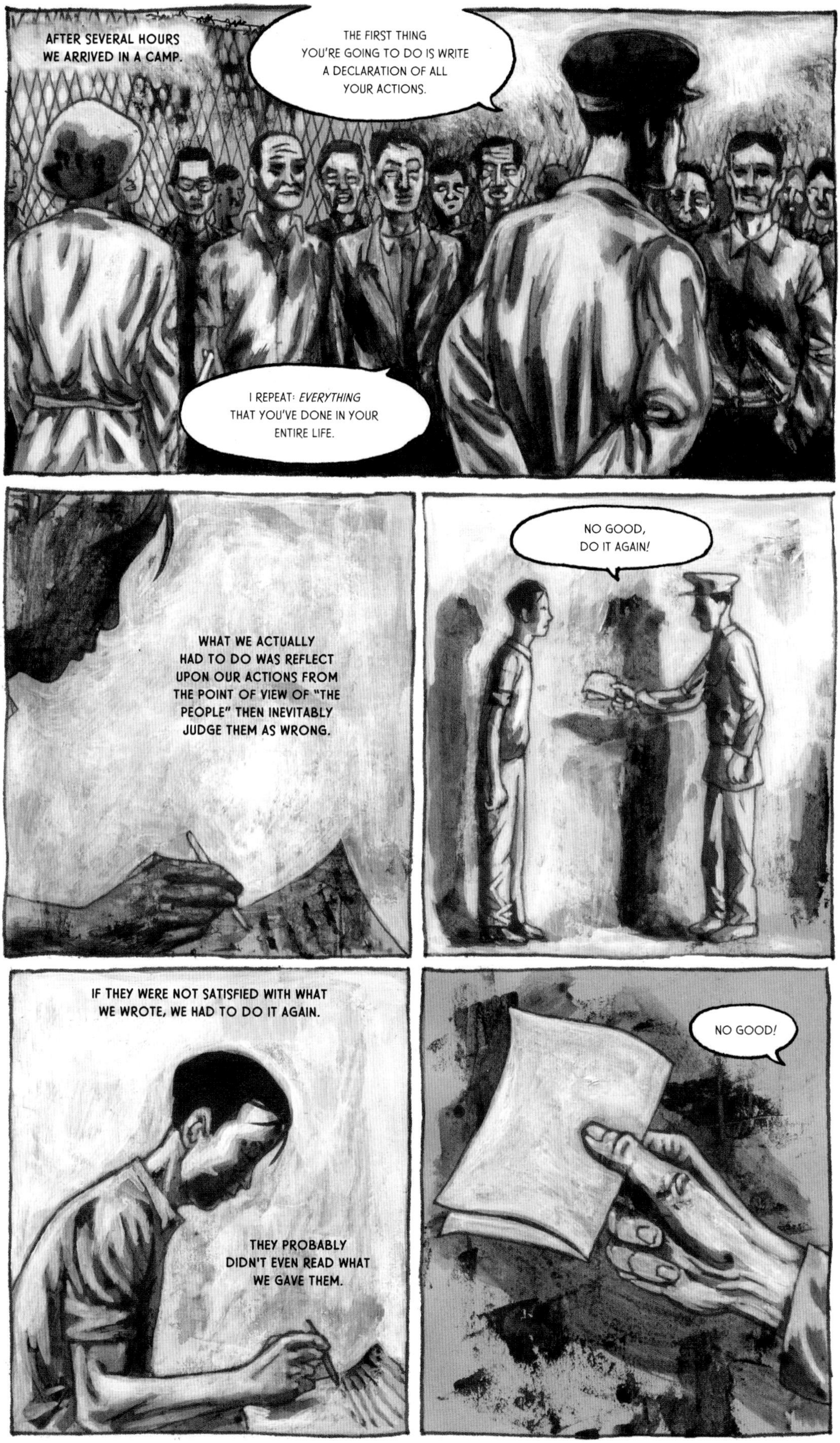
AFTER SEVERAL HOURS WE ARRIVED IN A CAMP.
THE FIRST THING YOU'RE GOING TO DO IS WRITE A DECLARATION OF ALL YOUR ACTIONS.
I REPEAT: *EVERYTHING* THAT YOU'VE DONE IN YOUR ENTIRE LIFE.
WHAT WE ACTUALLY HAD TO DO WAS REFLECT UPON OUR ACTIONS FROM THE POINT OF VIEW OF "THE PEOPLE" THEN INEVITABLY JUDGE THEM AS WRONG.
NO GOOD, DO IT AGAIN!
IF THEY WERE NOT SATISFIED WITH WHAT WE WROTE, WE HAD TO DO IT AGAIN.
THEY PROBABLY DIDN'T EVEN READ WHAT WE GAVE THEM.
NO GOOD!

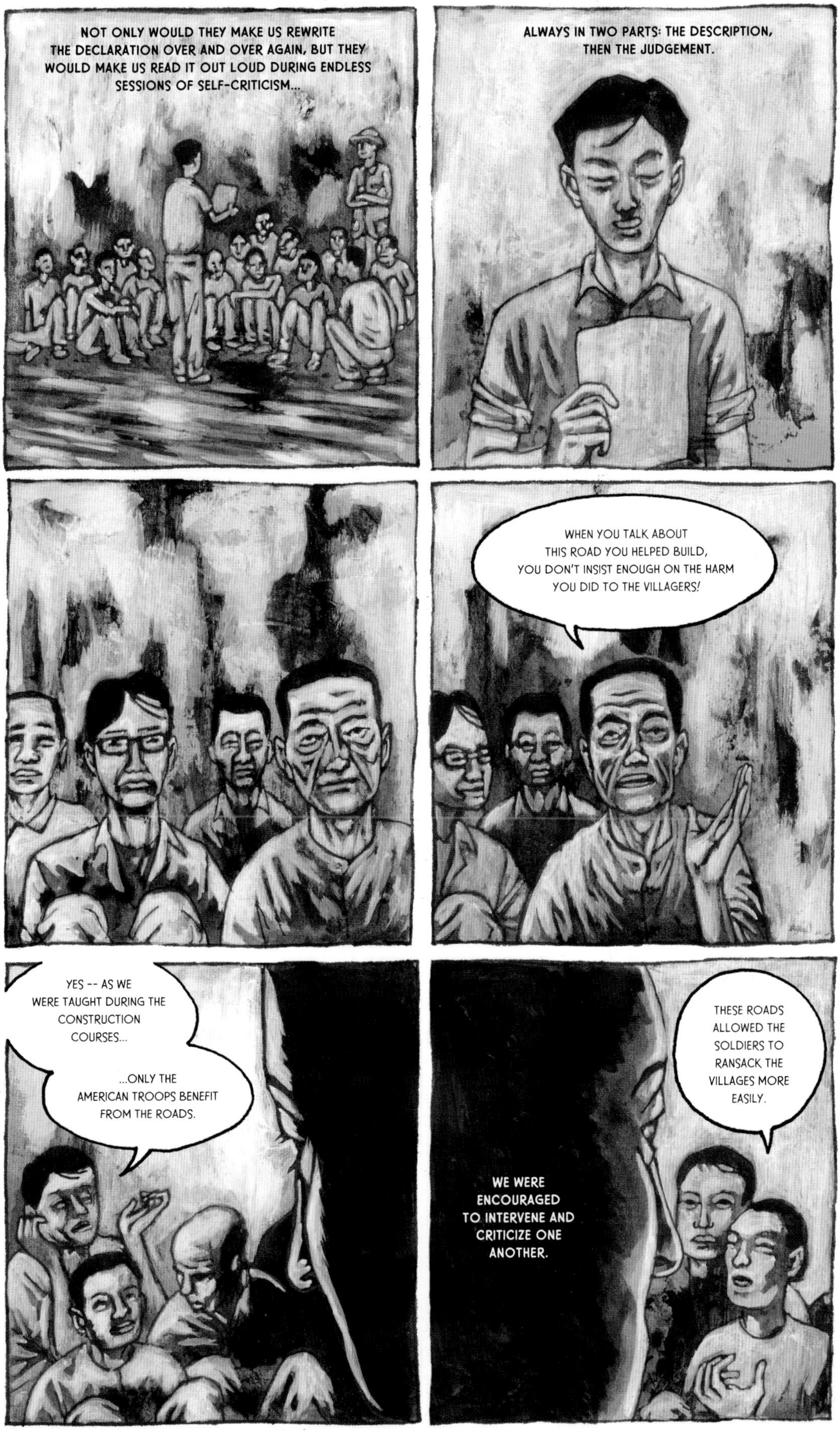

NOT ONLY WOULD THEY MAKE US REWRITE THE DECLARATION OVER AND OVER AGAIN, BUT THEY WOULD MAKE US READ IT OUT LOUD DURING ENDLESS SESSIONS OF SELF-CRITICISM...
ALWAYS IN TWO PARTS: THE DESCRIPTION, THEN THE JUDGEMENT.
WHEN YOU TALK ABOUT THIS ROAD YOU HELPED BUILD, YOU DON'T INSIST ENOUGH ON THE HARM YOU DID TO THE VILLAGERS!
YES -- AS WE WERE TAUGHT DURING THE CONSTRUCTION COURSES...
...ONLY THE AMERICAN TROOPS BENEFIT FROM THE ROADS.
WE WERE ENCOURAGED TO INTERVENE AND CRITICIZE ONE ANOTHER.
THESE ROADS ALLOWED THE SOLDIERS TO RANSACK THE VILLAGES MORE EASILY.

BEFORE WORKING ON THE CITY'S ELECTRICAL SYSTEM, I HAD HELPED IN THE CONSTRUCTION OF A ROAD THAT CONNECTED ISOLATED VILLAGES. WHERE I HAD SEEN A MEANS TO ENDING THE ISOLATION AND PROVIDING BETTER ACCESS TO HEALTHCARE AND COMMUNICATION, THEY MADE US SEE SOMETHING NEGATIVE, SOMETHING WHICH ONLY SERVED THE PURPOSES OF THE AMERICAN INVADERS...

IT WAS DEEMED THAT MY WORK ON THE GRIDS HAD ALSO BENEFITED THE FORMER SOUTHERN REGIME AND ITS AMERICAN ALLY, TO THE DETRIMENT OF THE PEOPLE.

MY PRESENCE IN THE CAMP WAS JUSTIFIED BY THE NEED TO ACKNOWLEDGE AND CONFESS JUST HOW BAD MY BEHAVIOR HAD BEEN.

ONCE WE WERE DONE WITH OUR SELF-CRITICISM, IT WAS THEN SOMEBODY ELSE'S TURN TO DO THEIRS, WHILE WE WOULD TAKE THEIR PLACE.

JUDGED, THEN JUDGE. WE ALL HAD TO DO IT.

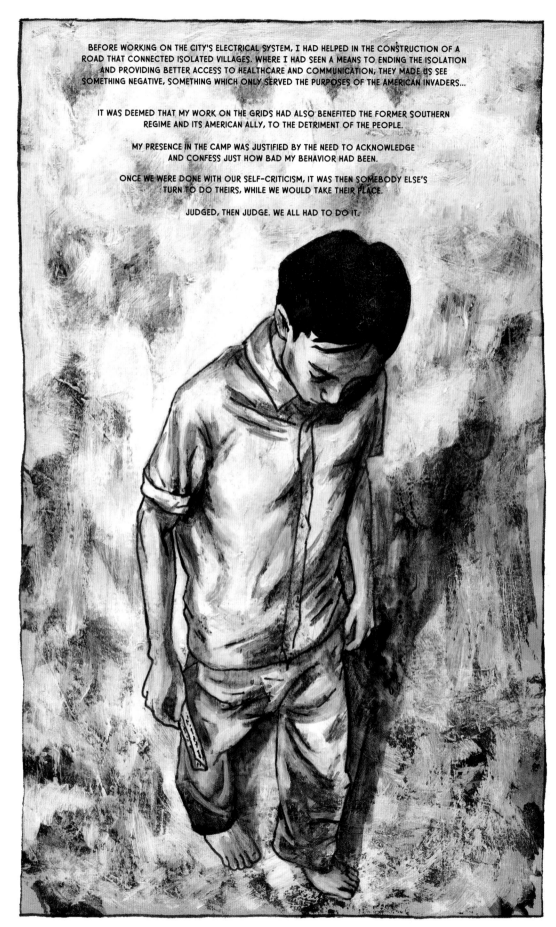

WE WERE ALLOWED VERY LITTLE SLEEP.

WE WERE CONTINUALLY GIVEN LECTURES TO INDOCTRINATE US WITH THE COMMUNIST IDEOLOGY. OFTEN IN THE MIDDLE OF THE NIGHT.

THEY WOULD TALK TO US NONSTOP, BUILDING UP A HOPE FOR FREEDOM. A FREEDOM THAT WAS ONLY ATTAINABLE IF WE WERE TO START THINKING "THE RIGHT WAY."

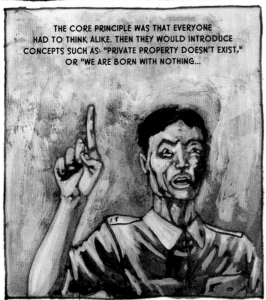

THE CORE PRINCIPLE WAS THAT EVERYONE HAD TO THINK ALIKE. THEN THEY WOULD INTRODUCE CONCEPTS SUCH AS: "PRIVATE PROPERTY DOESN'T EXIST," OR "WE ARE BORN WITH NOTHING...

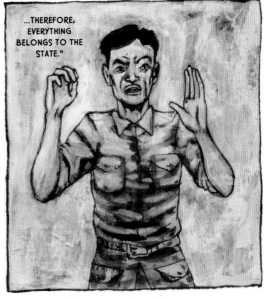

...THEREFORE, EVERYTHING BELONGS TO THE STATE."

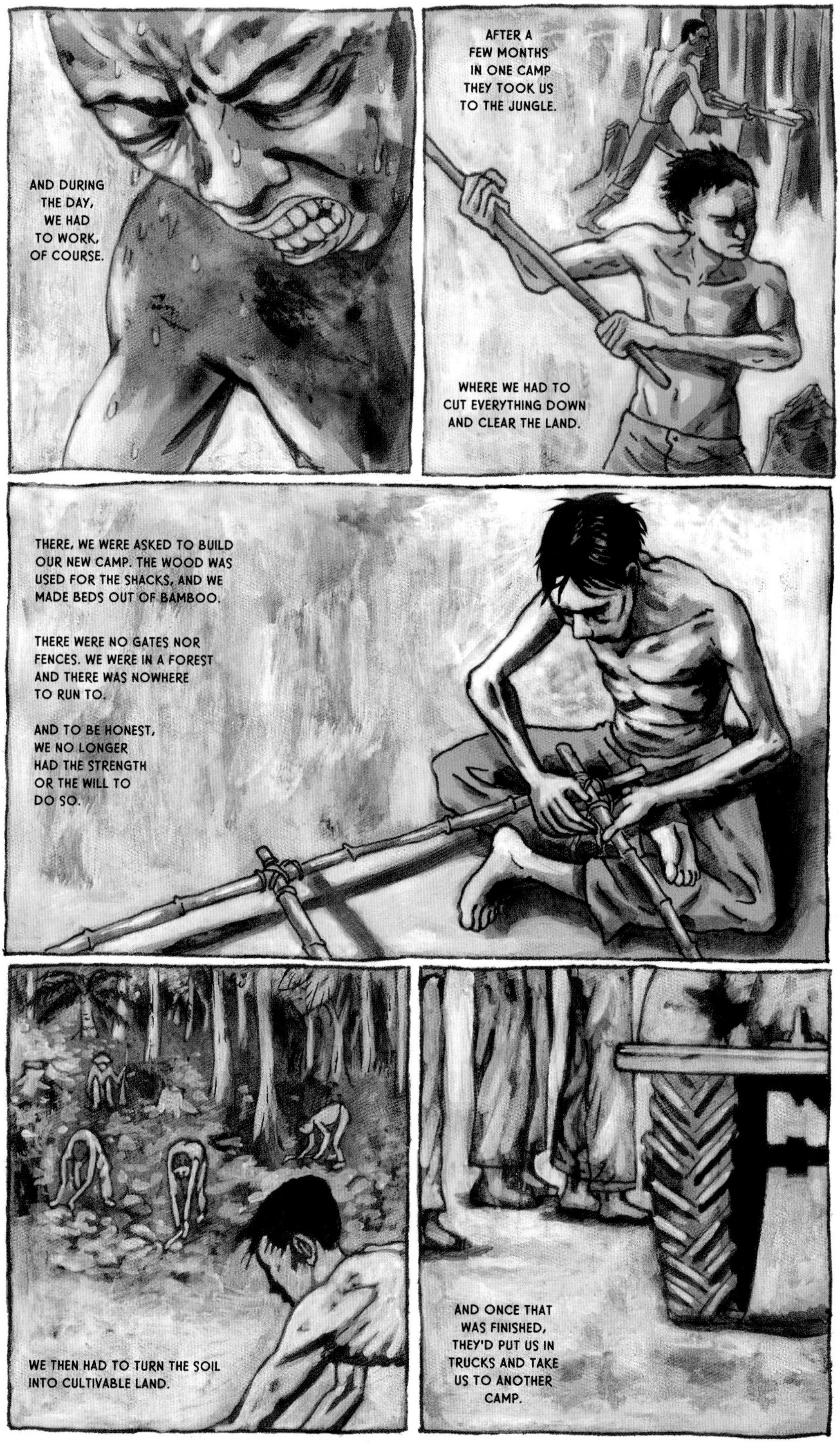
AND DURING THE DAY, WE HAD TO WORK, OF COURSE.
AFTER A FEW MONTHS IN ONE CAMP THEY TOOK US TO THE JUNGLE.
WHERE WE HAD TO CUT EVERYTHING DOWN AND CLEAR THE LAND.
THERE, WE WERE ASKED TO BUILD OUR NEW CAMP. THE WOOD WAS USED FOR THE SHACKS, AND WE MADE BEDS OUT OF BAMBOO.
THERE WERE NO GATES NOR FENCES. WE WERE IN A FOREST AND THERE WAS NOWHERE TO RUN TO.
AND TO BE HONEST, WE NO LONGER HAD THE STRENGTH OR THE WILL TO DO SO.
WE THEN HAD TO TURN THE SOIL INTO CULTIVABLE LAND.
AND ONCE THAT WAS FINISHED, THEY'D PUT US IN TRUCKS AND TAKE US TO ANOTHER CAMP.

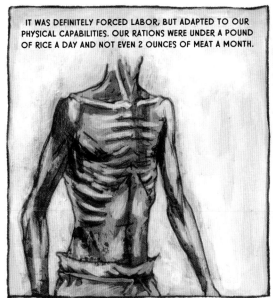

IT WAS DEFINITELY FORCED LABOR, BUT ADAPTED TO OUR PHYSICAL CAPABILITIES. OUR RATIONS WERE UNDER A POUND OF RICE A DAY AND NOT EVEN 2 OUNCES OF MEAT A MONTH.

MANY DIED.

OF STARVATION OR FROM SICKNESS.

FORTUNATELY, WE COULD GET MAIL EVERY THREE MONTHS.

WE COULD BOTH SEND AND RECEIVE IT.

WE WERE GIVEN A TINY PIECE OF PAPER WHERE WE'D SQUEEZE IN AS MUCH TEXT AS POSSIBLE.

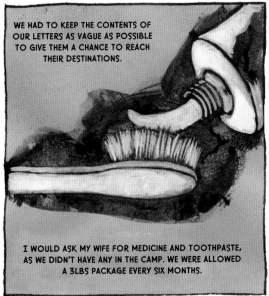

WE HAD TO KEEP THE CONTENTS OF OUR LETTERS AS VAGUE AS POSSIBLE TO GIVE THEM A CHANCE TO REACH THEIR DESTINATIONS.

I WOULD ASK MY WIFE FOR MEDICINE AND TOOTHPASTE, AS WE DIDN'T HAVE ANY IN THE CAMP. WE WERE ALLOWED A 3LBS PACKAGE EVERY SIX MONTHS.

I CLUNG TO THE HOPE OF LEAVING THE CAMP AND EVENTUALLY LEAVING THE COUNTRY. A RUMOR BEGAN TO CIRCULATE THAT THE WORKERS DEEMED USEFUL WOULD BE LIBERATED. SO I REPEATED RED WHEN THEY SAID RED, EVEN WHEN I COULD SEE IT WAS BLACK. ALTHOUGH MY MOUTH WAS NOT FIGHTING THEM, MY SPIRIT STAYED STRONG.

I WAS LUCKIER THAN OTHERS AROUND ME WHO BEGAN BREAKING DOWN.

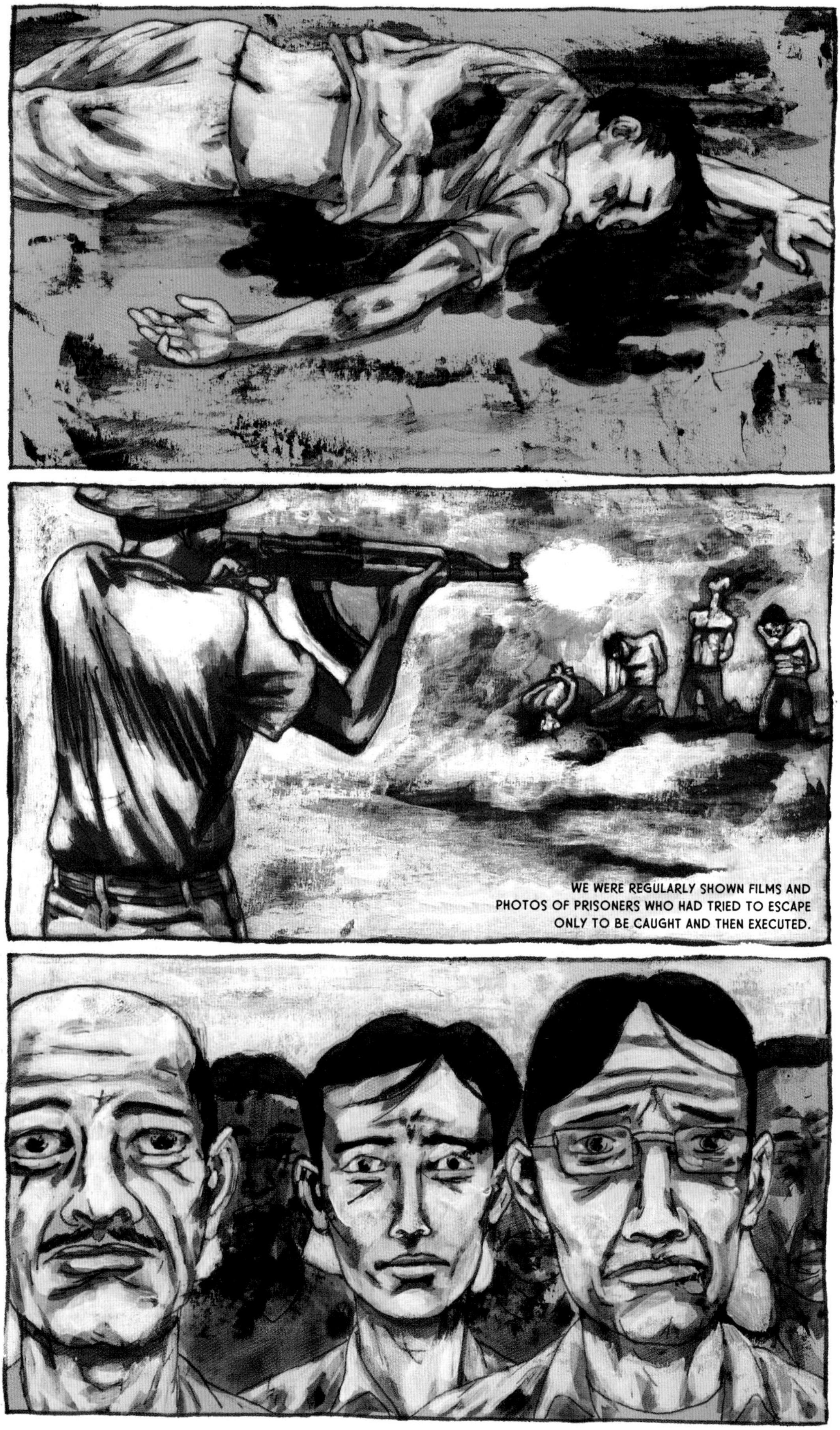
WE WERE REGULARLY SHOWN FILMS AND PHOTOS OF PRISONERS WHO HAD TRIED TO ESCAPE ONLY TO BE CAUGHT AND THEN EXECUTED.

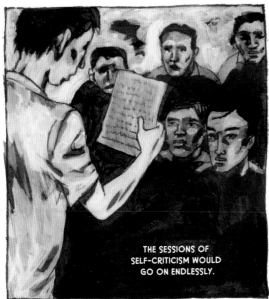

THE SESSIONS OF
SELF-CRITICISM WOULD
GO ON ENDLESSLY.

I PLAYED THE GAME,
LIKE EVERYONE ELSE.

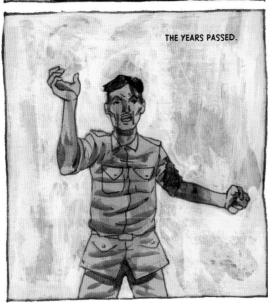

THE YEARS PASSED.

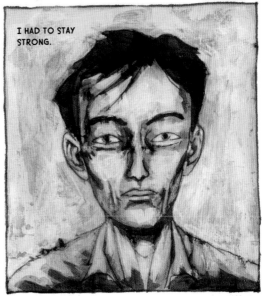

I HAD TO STAY
STRONG.

THE CAMP BECAME A ROUTINE OF ITS OWN.

WE GOT USED TO IT.

ONE NIGHT THE GUARDS CALLED OUT EIGHT NAMES, INCLUDING MINE.

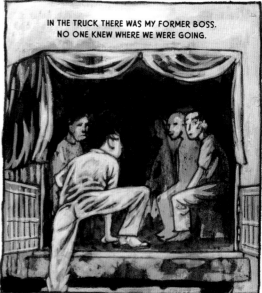

IN THE TRUCK THERE WAS MY FORMER BOSS. NO ONE KNEW WHERE WE WERE GOING.

WHEN THE TRUCK FINALLY STOPPED, WE WERE BACK IN SAIGON.

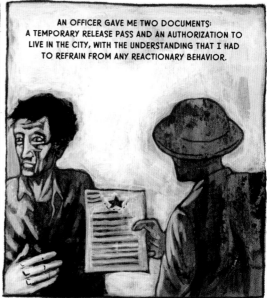

AN OFFICER GAVE ME TWO DOCUMENTS: A TEMPORARY RELEASE PASS AND AN AUTHORIZATION TO LIVE IN THE CITY, WITH THE UNDERSTANDING THAT I HAD TO REFRAIN FROM ANY REACTIONARY BEHAVIOR.

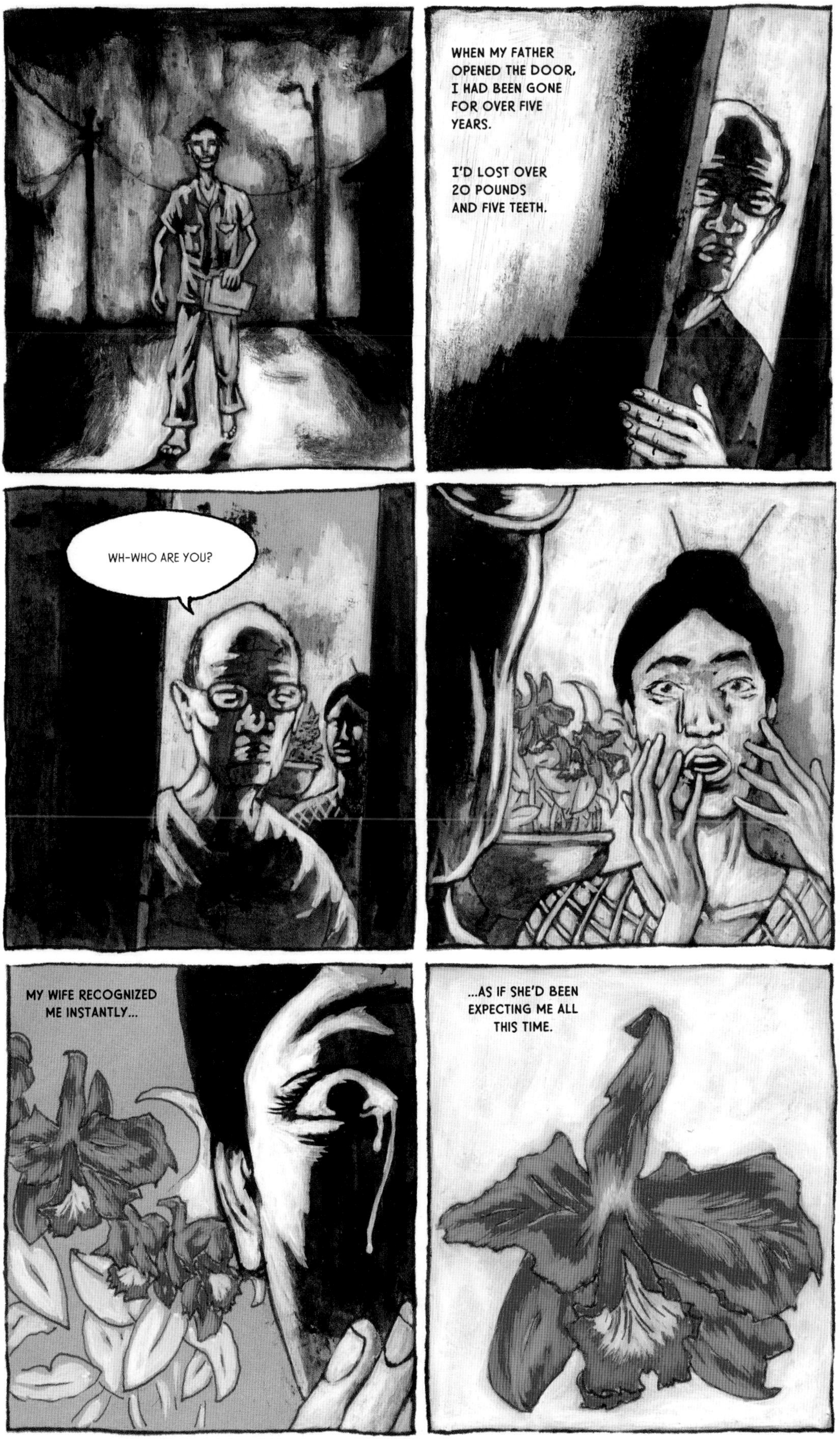
WHEN MY FATHER OPENED THE DOOR, I HAD BEEN GONE FOR OVER FIVE YEARS.
I'D LOST OVER 20 POUNDS AND FIVE TEETH.
WH-WHO ARE YOU?
MY WIFE RECOGNIZED ME INSTANTLY...
...AS IF SHE'D BEEN EXPECTING ME ALL THIS TIME.

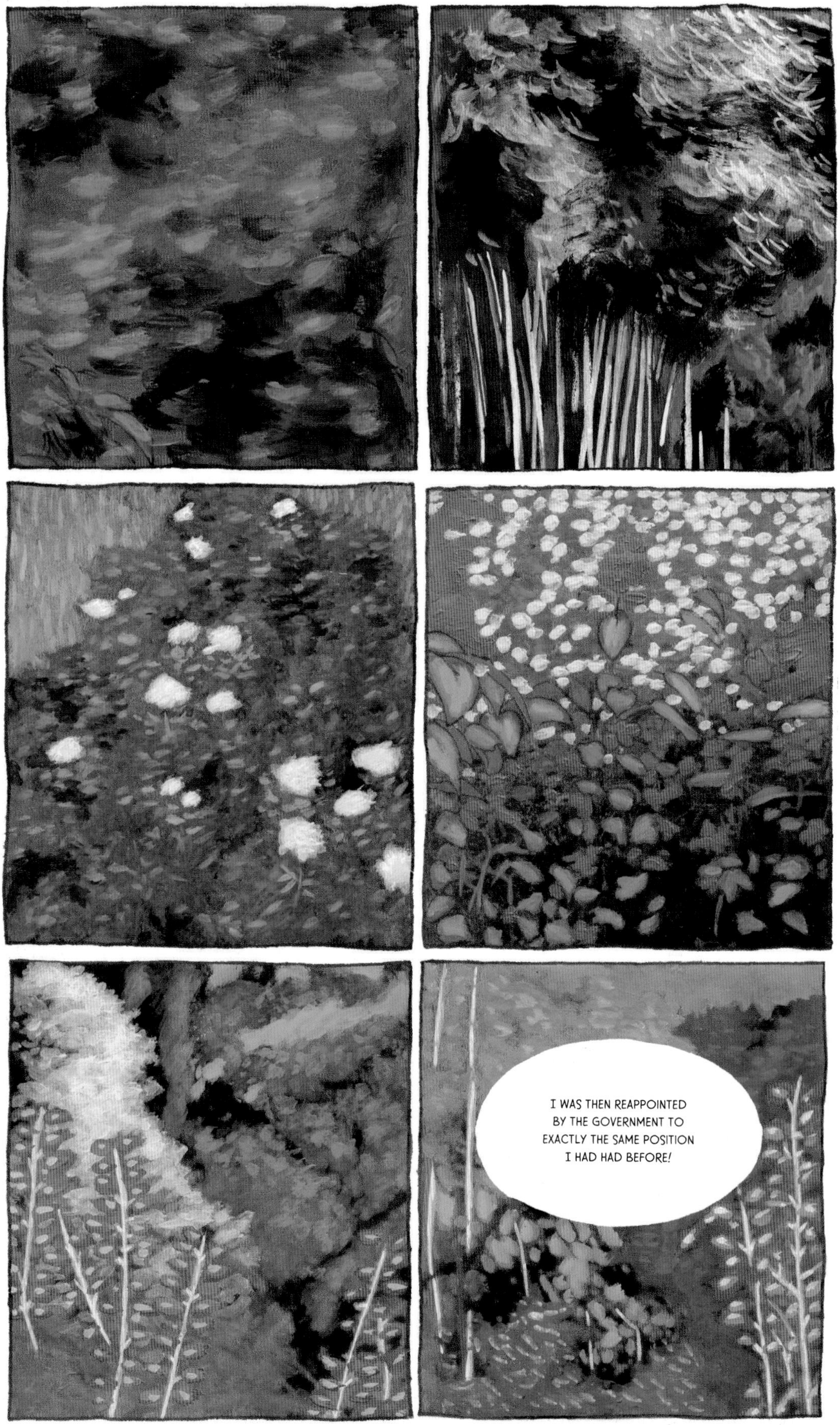
I WAS THEN REAPPOINTED BY THE GOVERNMENT TO EXACTLY THE SAME POSITION I HAD HAD BEFORE!

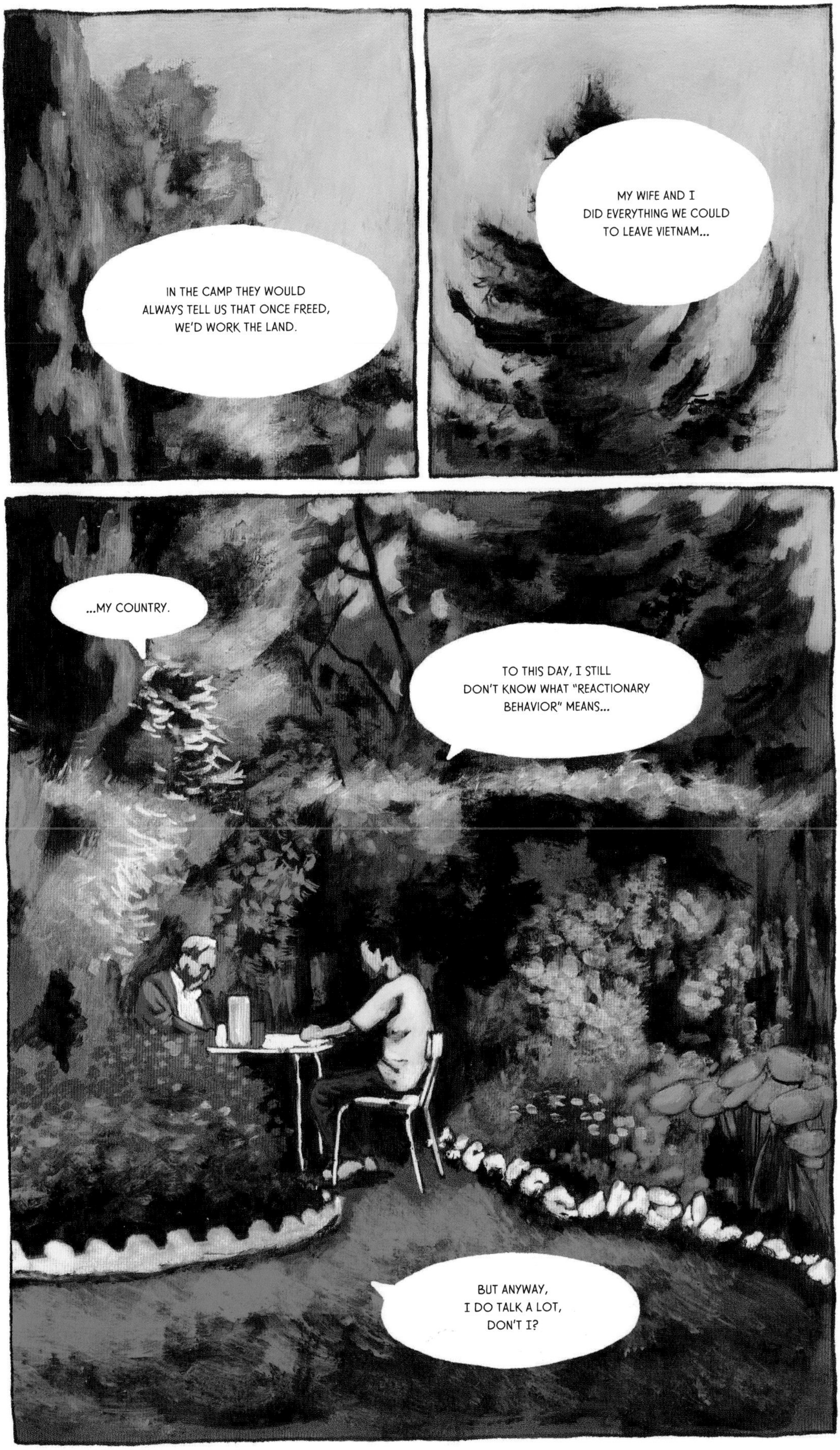
IN THE CAMP THEY WOULD ALWAYS TELL US THAT ONCE FREED, WE'D WORK THE LAND.
MY WIFE AND I DID EVERYTHING WE COULD TO LEAVE VIETNAM...
...MY COUNTRY.
TO THIS DAY, I STILL DON'T KNOW WHAT "REACTIONARY BEHAVIOR" MEANS...
BUT ANYWAY, I DO TALK A LOT, DON'T I?

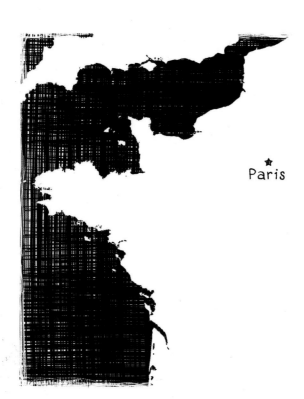

Paris

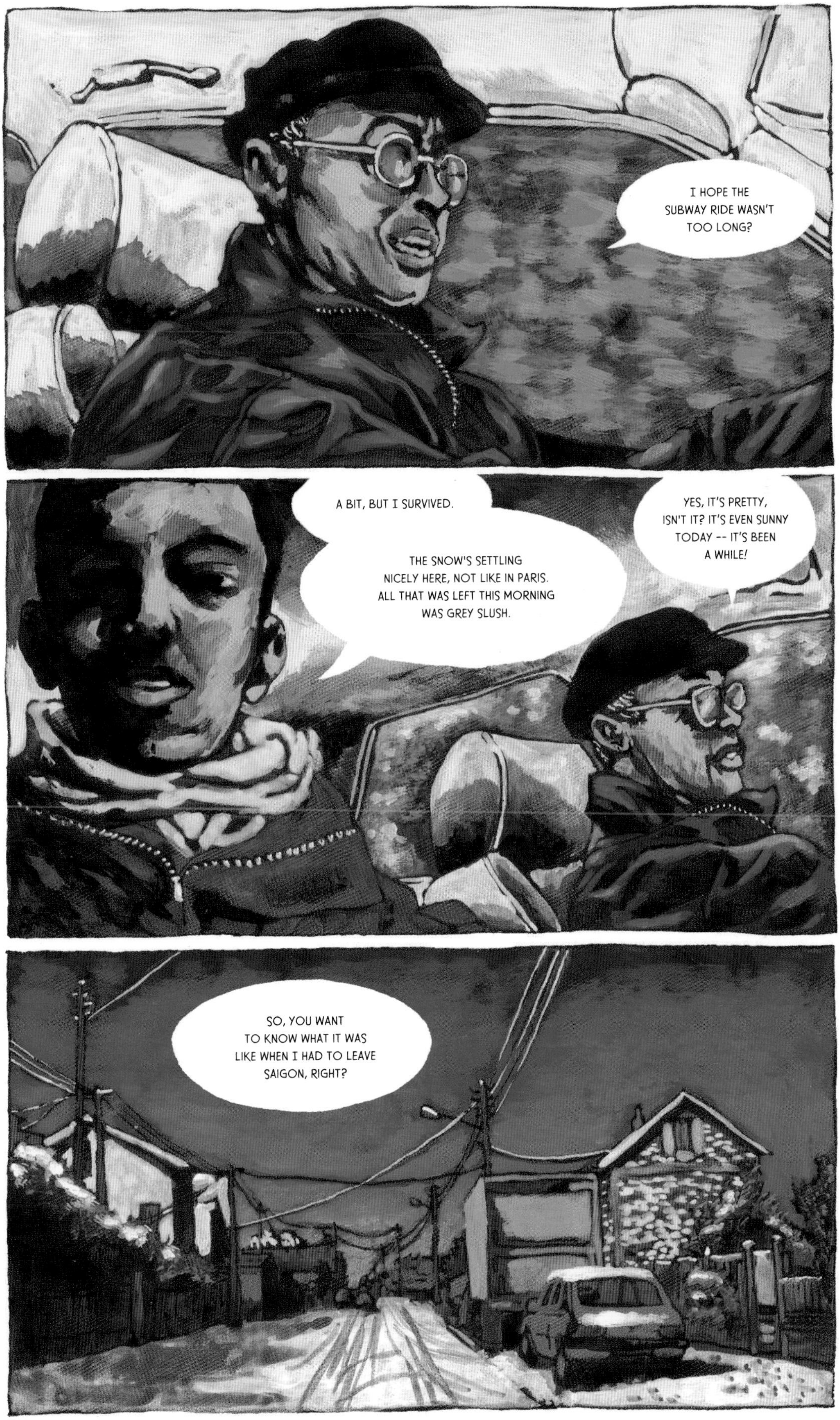
I HOPE THE SUBWAY RIDE WASN'T TOO LONG?
A BIT, BUT I SURVIVED.
THE SNOW'S SETTLING NICELY HERE, NOT LIKE IN PARIS. ALL THAT WAS LEFT THIS MORNING WAS GREY SLUSH.
YES, IT'S PRETTY, ISN'T IT? IT'S EVEN SUNNY TODAY -- IT'S BEEN A WHILE!
SO, YOU WANT TO KNOW WHAT IT WAS LIKE WHEN I HAD TO LEAVE SAIGON, RIGHT?

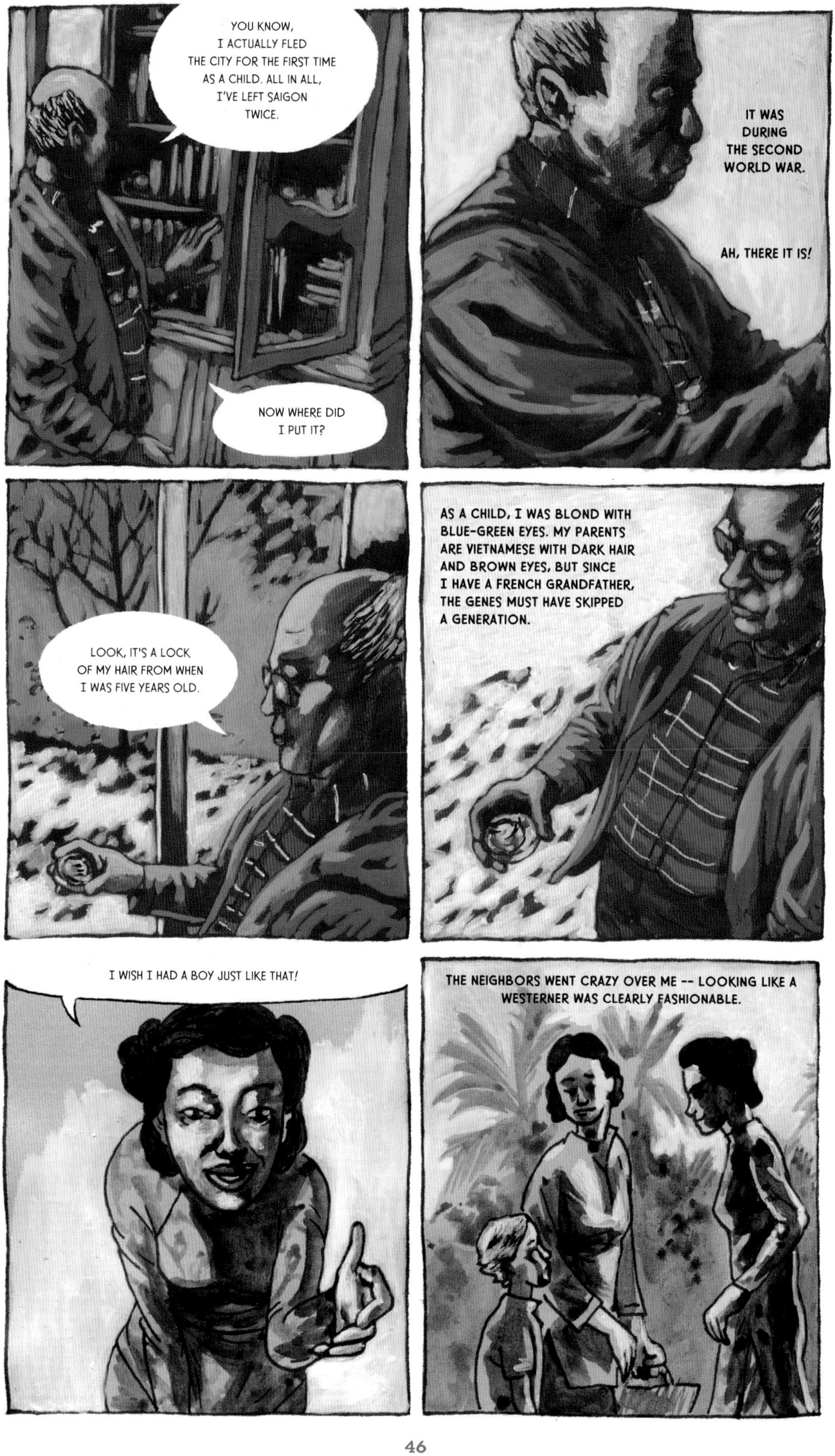
YOU KNOW, I ACTUALLY FLED THE CITY FOR THE FIRST TIME AS A CHILD. ALL IN ALL, I'VE LEFT SAIGON TWICE.
NOW WHERE DID I PUT IT?
IT WAS DURING THE SECOND WORLD WAR.
AH, THERE IT IS!
LOOK, IT'S A LOCK OF MY HAIR FROM WHEN I WAS FIVE YEARS OLD.
AS A CHILD, I WAS BLOND WITH BLUE-GREEN EYES. MY PARENTS ARE VIETNAMESE WITH DARK HAIR AND BROWN EYES, BUT SINCE I HAVE A FRENCH GRANDFATHER, THE GENES MUST HAVE SKIPPED A GENERATION.
I WISH I HAD A BOY JUST LIKE THAT!
THE NEIGHBORS WENT CRAZY OVER ME -- LOOKING LIKE A WESTERNER WAS CLEARLY FASHIONABLE.

BYE BYE.
ER...
WHAT'S THE MATTER, ANDRÉ?
MOM, COULD YOU PLEASE CUT MY HAIR? PEOPLE SAY I LOOK LIKE A GIRL!
DON'T LISTEN TO THEM, THEY'RE TALKING NONSENSE!
MY BLOND HAIR WAS MY MOTHER'S PRIDE AND JOY. SO SHE LET IT GROW, AND ALL I COULD DO WAS TO ACCEPT IT.
IT'S BECAUSE OF THIS HAIR THAT I RAN INTO TROUBLE WITH THE JAPANESE.
THE JAPANESE BACK THEN WERE NOT AS NICE AS THEY ARE NOW.
THEY WERE HARSH PEOPLE.

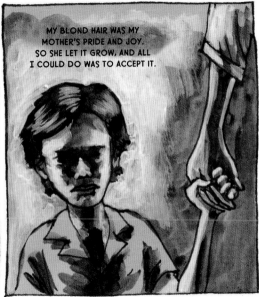

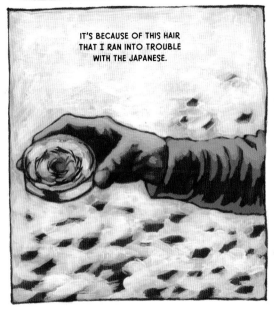

IN 1943, THE JAPANESE INVASION OF INDOCHINA BEGAN...

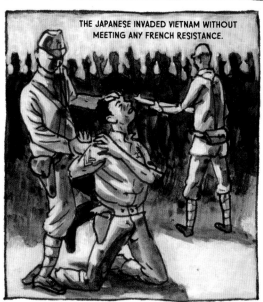

THE JAPANESE INVADED VIETNAM WITHOUT MEETING ANY FRENCH RESISTANCE.

THEY PUT ALL THE FRENCH -- AND ANY WESTERNERS -- THEY FOUND INTO PRISON CAMPS.

MY DAD WAS REQUISITIONED TO MANUFACTURE SHIPS AND FUEL TANKS FOR THE PLANES.

I CAN'T DO THAT!

I DON'T HAVE THE SKILLS!

ARCHITECT, ENGINEER, *SAME THING!* YOU DESIGN AND YOU BUILD! **UNDERSTOOD?!**

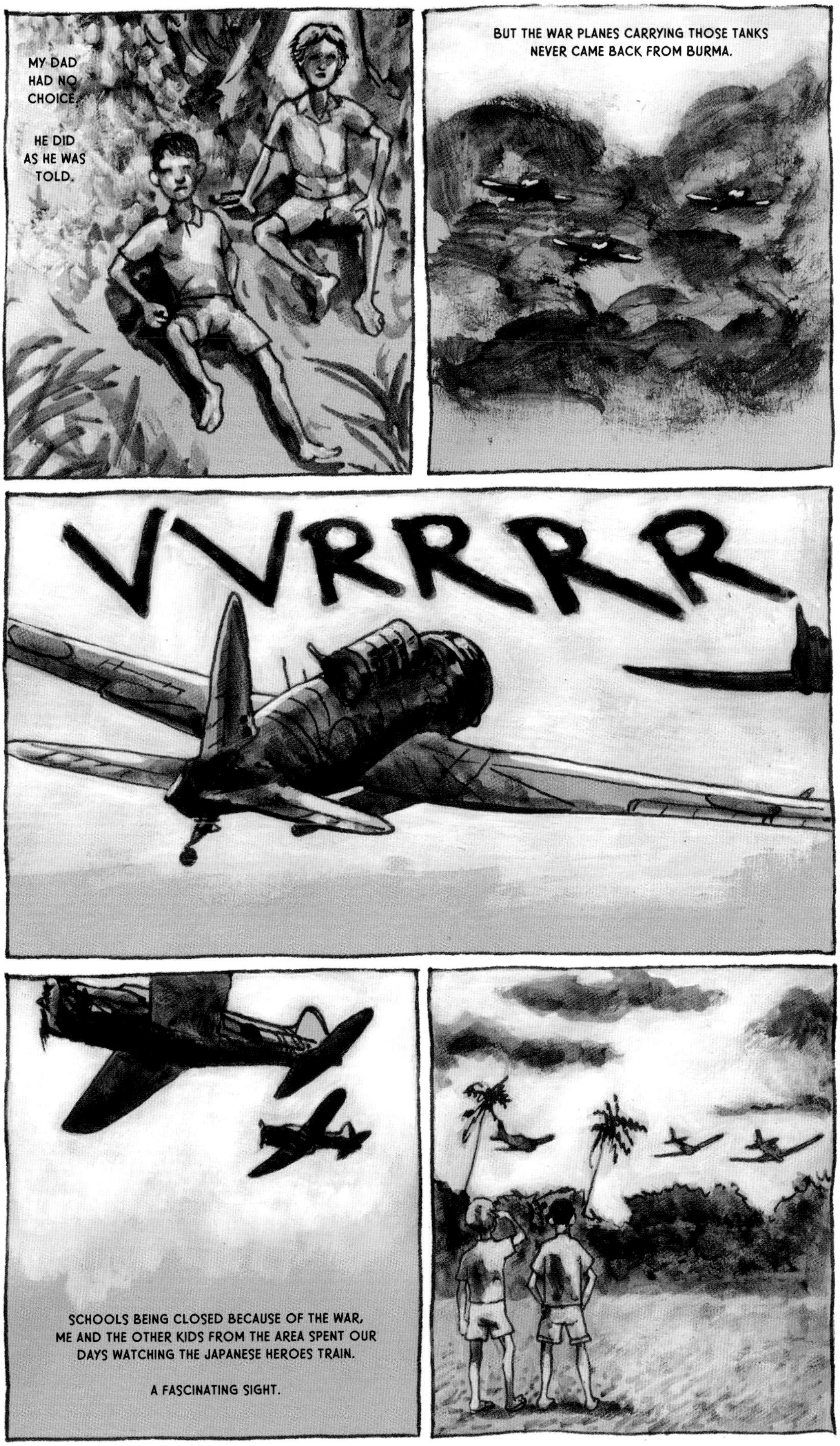
MY DAD HAD NO CHOICE.
HE DID AS HE WAS TOLD.
BUT THE WAR PLANES CARRYING THOSE TANKS NEVER CAME BACK FROM BURMA.
VVRRRR
SCHOOLS BEING CLOSED BECAUSE OF THE WAR, ME AND THE OTHER KIDS FROM THE AREA SPENT OUR DAYS WATCHING THE JAPANESE HEROES TRAIN.
A FASCINATING SIGHT.

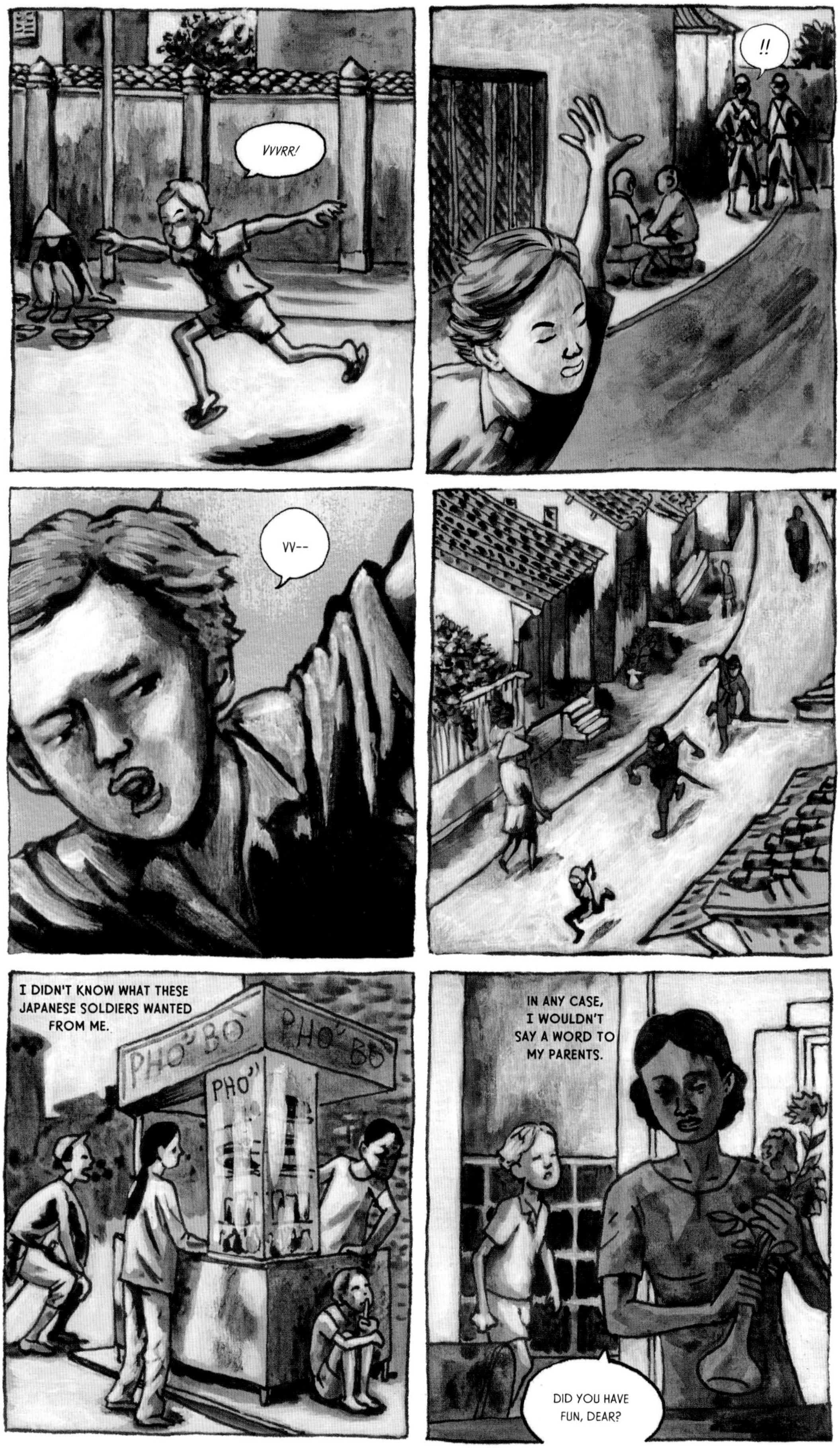
VVVRR!
!!
VV--
I DIDN'T KNOW WHAT THESE JAPANESE SOLDIERS WANTED FROM ME.
PHỞ BÒ
PHỞ BÒ
PHỞ
IN ANY CASE, I WOULDN'T SAY A WORD TO MY PARENTS.
DID YOU HAVE FUN, DEAR?

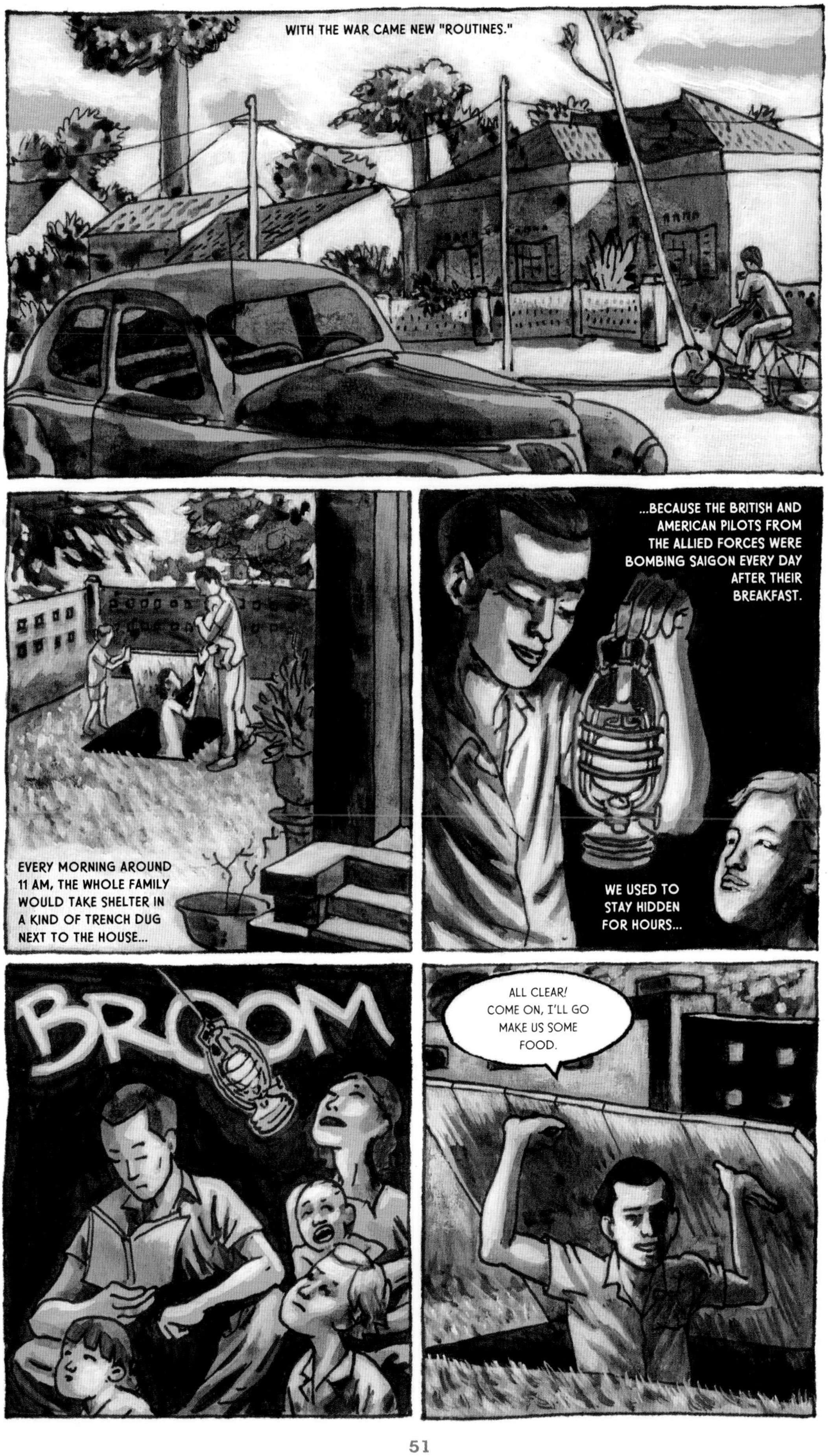
WITH THE WAR CAME NEW "ROUTINES."
EVERY MORNING AROUND 11 AM, THE WHOLE FAMILY WOULD TAKE SHELTER IN A KIND OF TRENCH DUG NEXT TO THE HOUSE...
...BECAUSE THE BRITISH AND AMERICAN PILOTS FROM THE ALLIED FORCES WERE BOMBING SAIGON EVERY DAY AFTER THEIR BREAKFAST.
WE USED TO STAY HIDDEN FOR HOURS...
BROOM
ALL CLEAR! COME ON, I'LL GO MAKE US SOME FOOD.

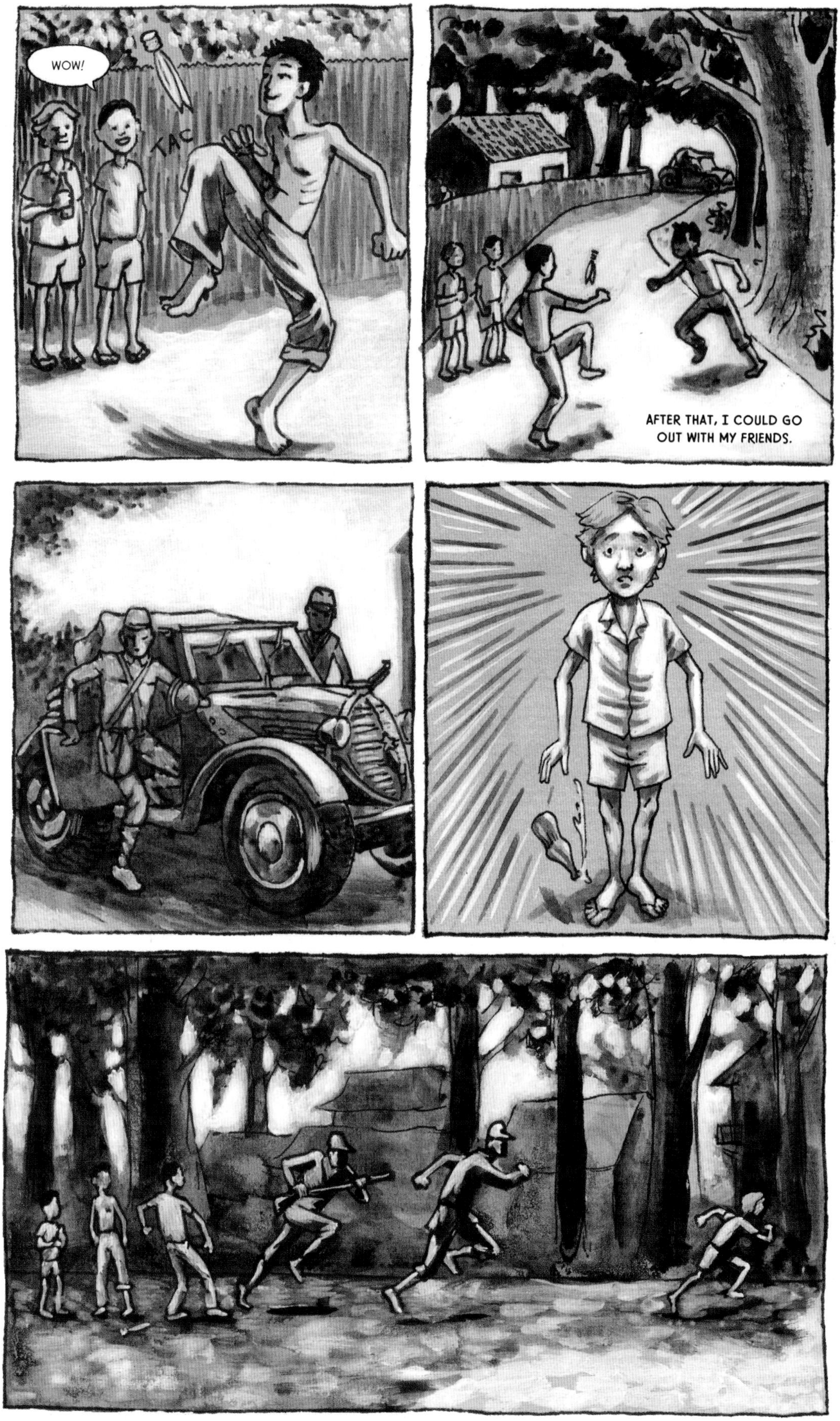
WOW!
TAC
AFTER THAT, I COULD GO OUT WITH MY FRIENDS.

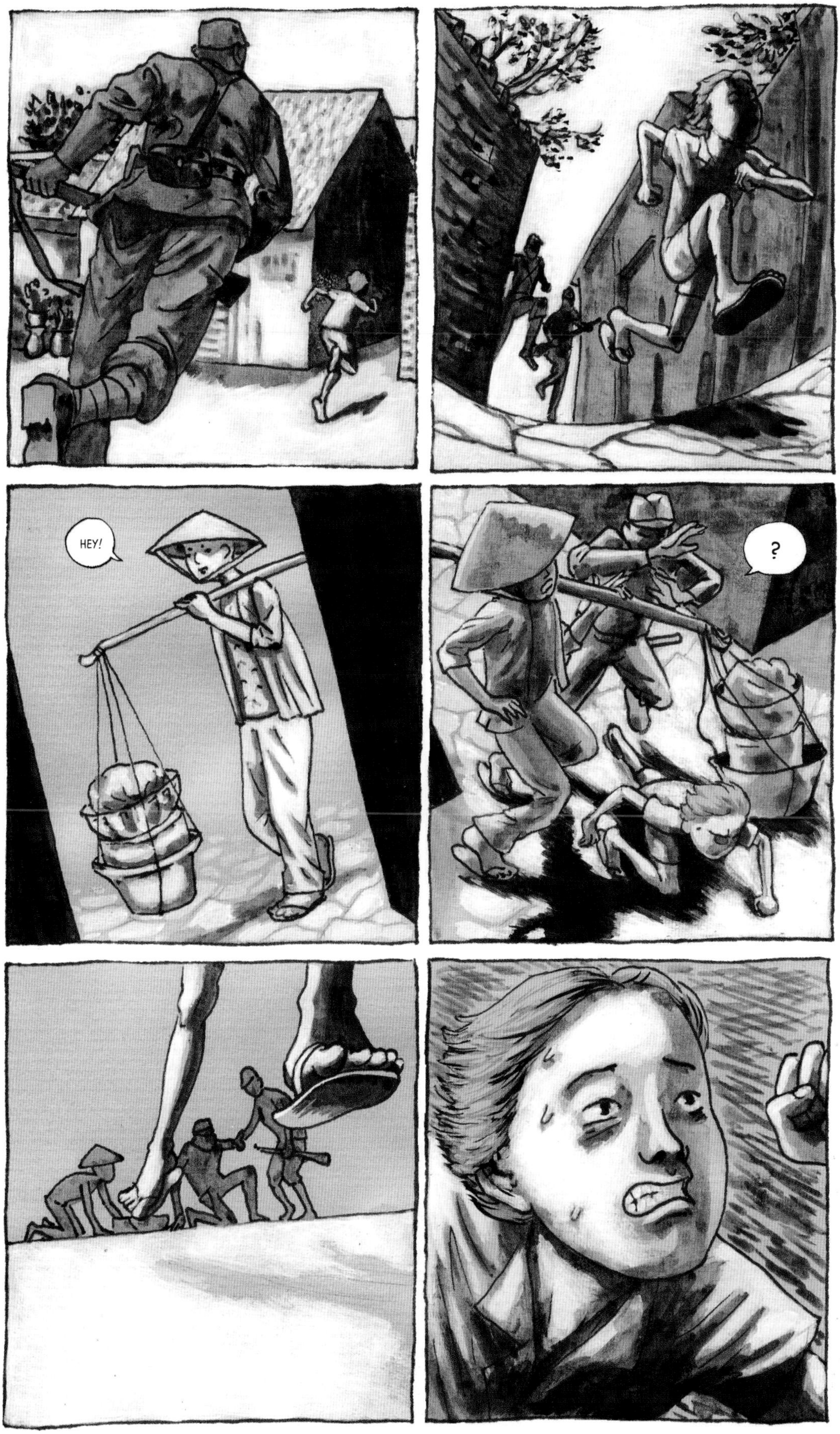
HEY!
?

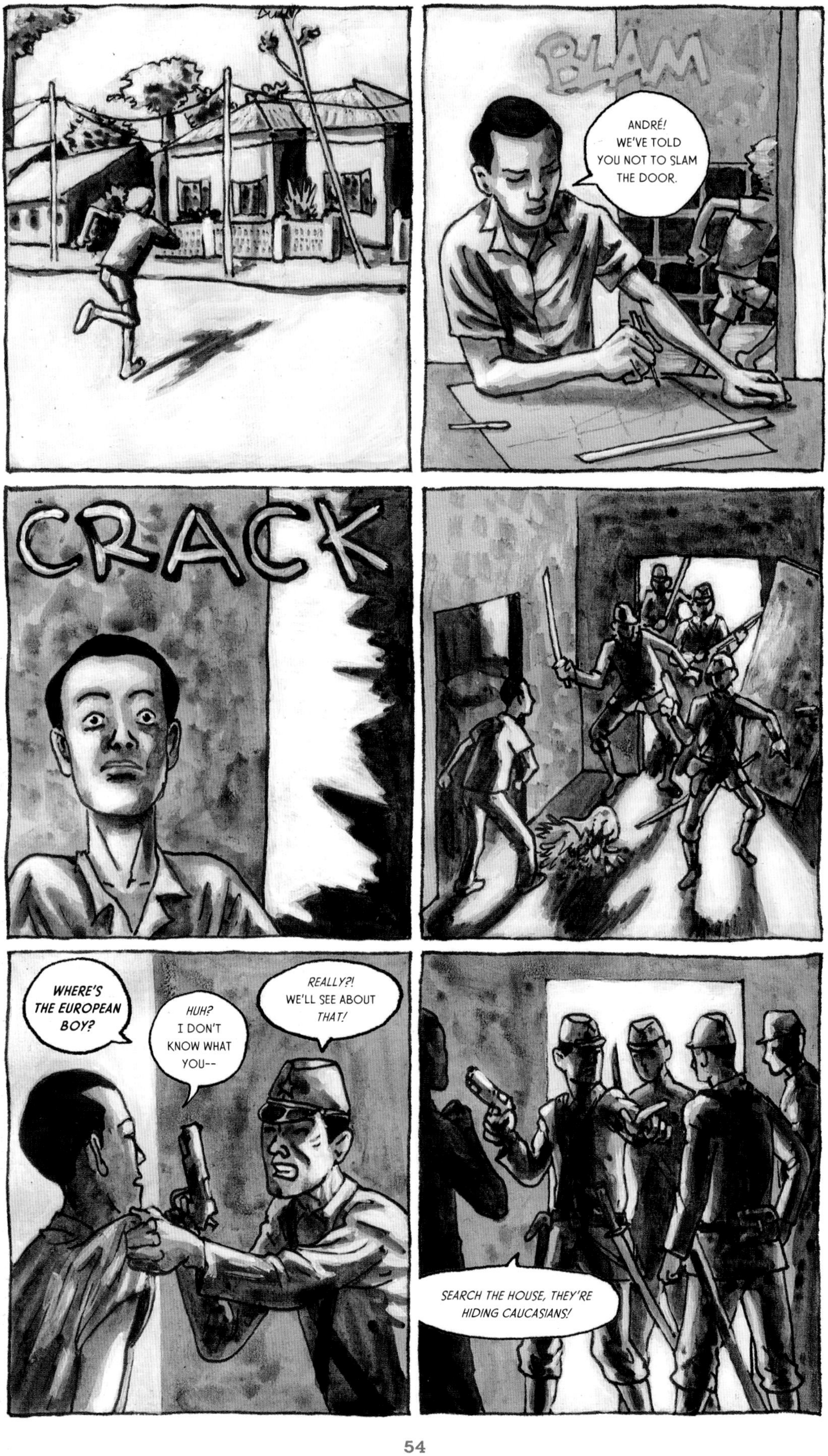
BLAM
ANDRÉ! WE'VE TOLD YOU NOT TO SLAM THE DOOR.
CRACK
WHERE'S THE EUROPEAN BOY?
HUH? I DON'T KNOW WHAT YOU--
REALLY?! WE'LL SEE ABOUT THAT!
SEARCH THE HOUSE, THEY'RE HIDING CAUCASIANS!

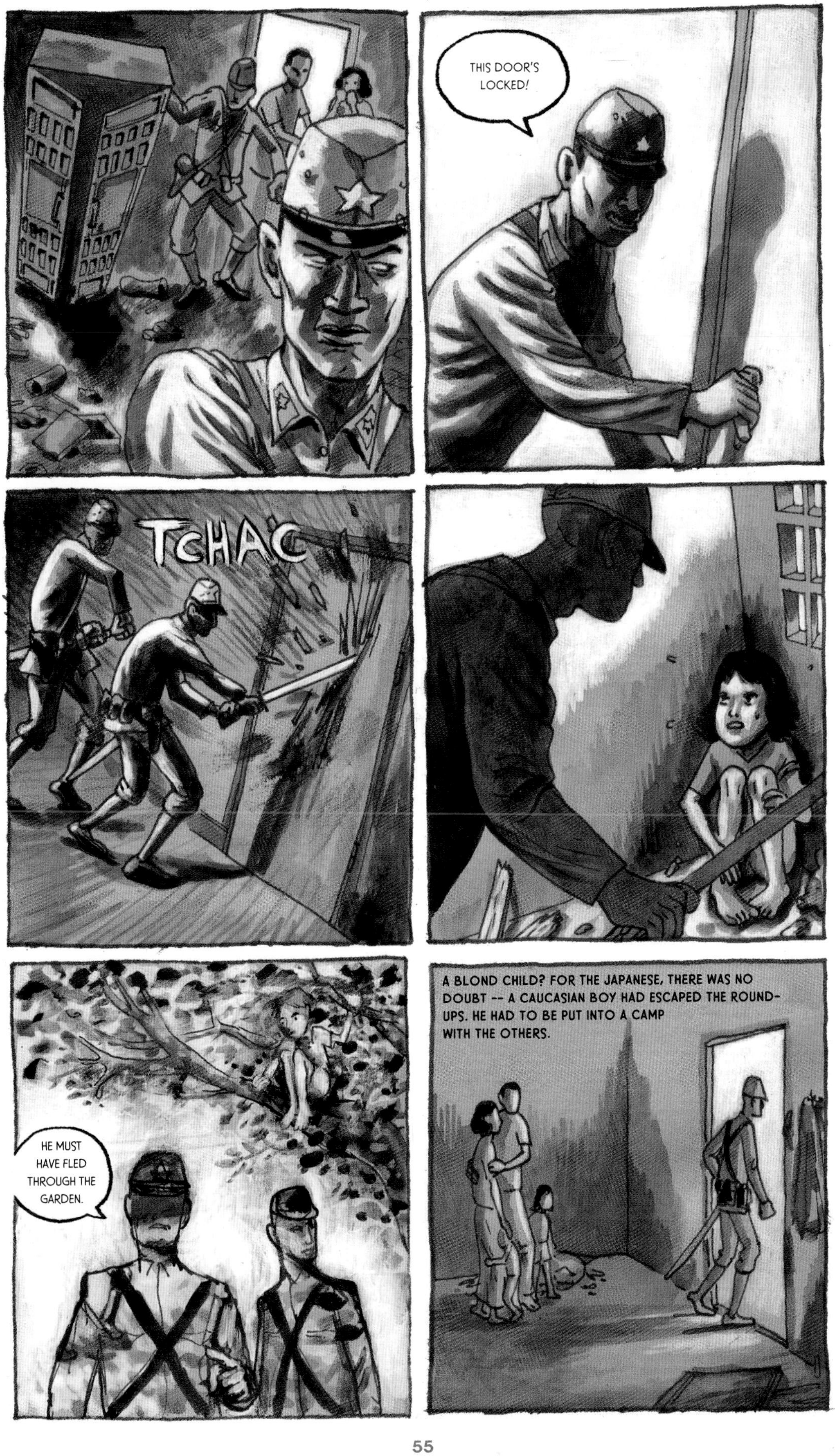
THIS DOOR'S LOCKED!
TCHAC
HE MUST HAVE FLED THROUGH THE GARDEN.
A BLOND CHILD? FOR THE JAPANESE, THERE WAS NO DOUBT -- A CAUCASIAN BOY HAD ESCAPED THE ROUND-UPS. HE HAD TO BE PUT INTO A CAMP WITH THE OTHERS.

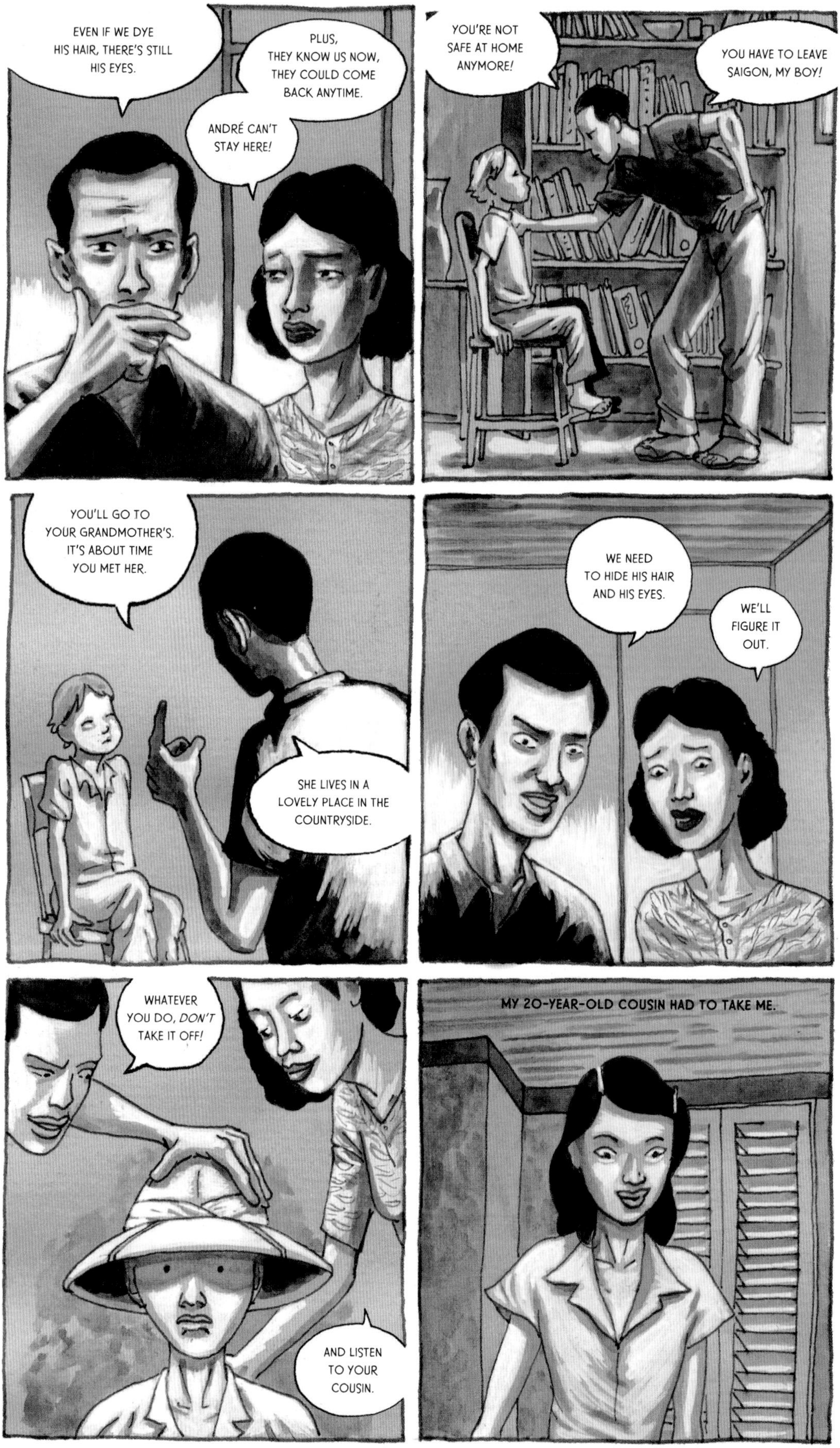
EVEN IF WE DYE HIS HAIR, THERE'S STILL HIS EYES.
PLUS, THEY KNOW US NOW, THEY COULD COME BACK ANYTIME.
ANDRÉ CAN'T STAY HERE!
YOU'RE NOT SAFE AT HOME ANYMORE!
YOU HAVE TO LEAVE SAIGON, MY BOY!
YOU'LL GO TO YOUR GRANDMOTHER'S. IT'S ABOUT TIME YOU MET HER.
SHE LIVES IN A LOVELY PLACE IN THE COUNTRYSIDE.
WE NEED TO HIDE HIS HAIR AND HIS EYES.
WE'LL FIGURE IT OUT.
WHATEVER YOU DO, *DON'T* TAKE IT OFF!
AND LISTEN TO YOUR COUSIN.
MY 20-YEAR-OLD COUSIN HAD TO TAKE ME.

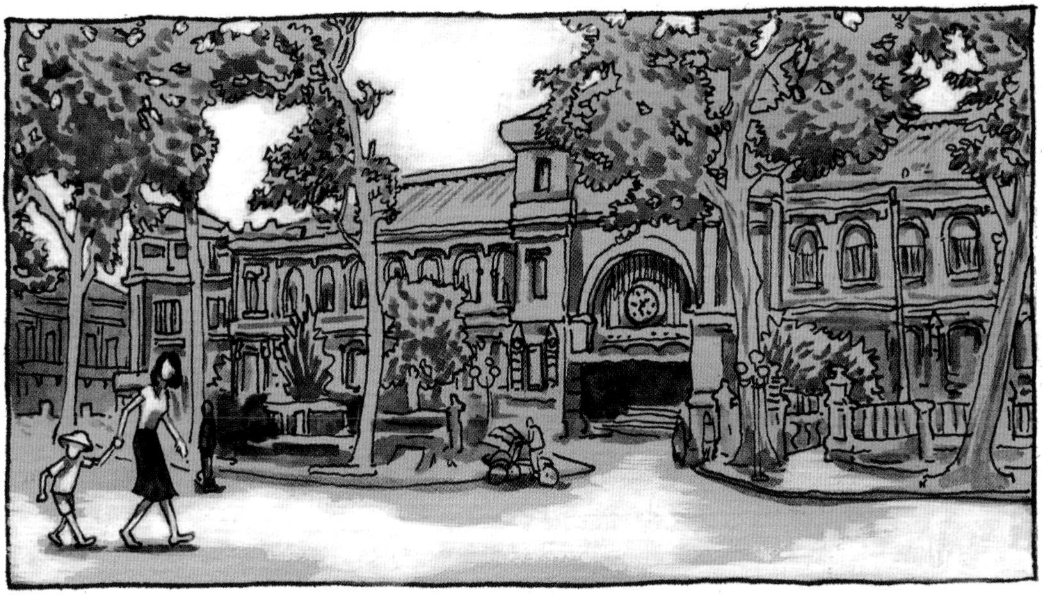

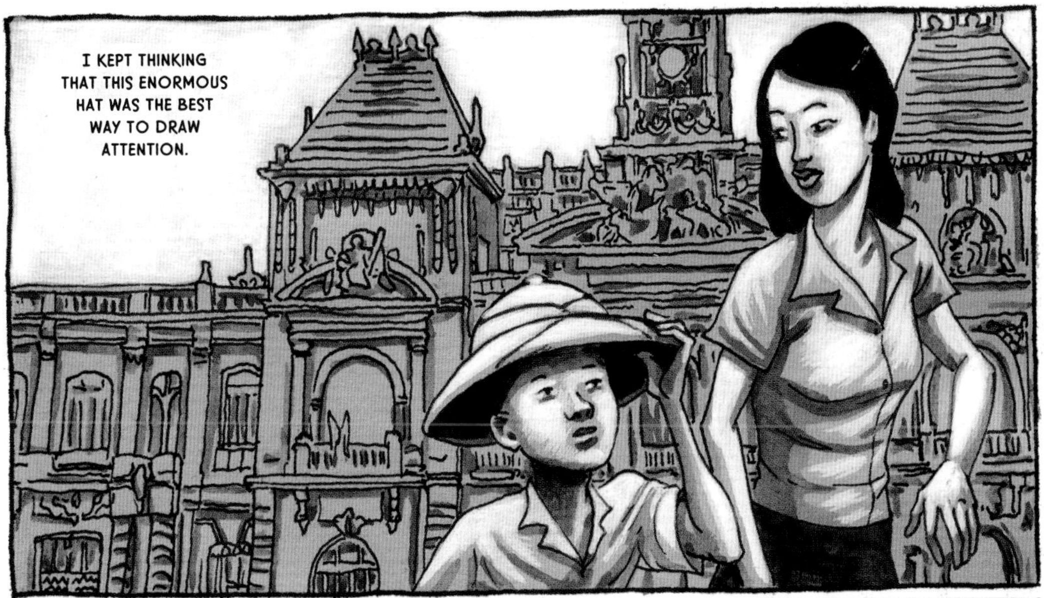
I KEPT THINKING THAT THIS ENORMOUS HAT WAS THE BEST WAY TO DRAW ATTENTION.

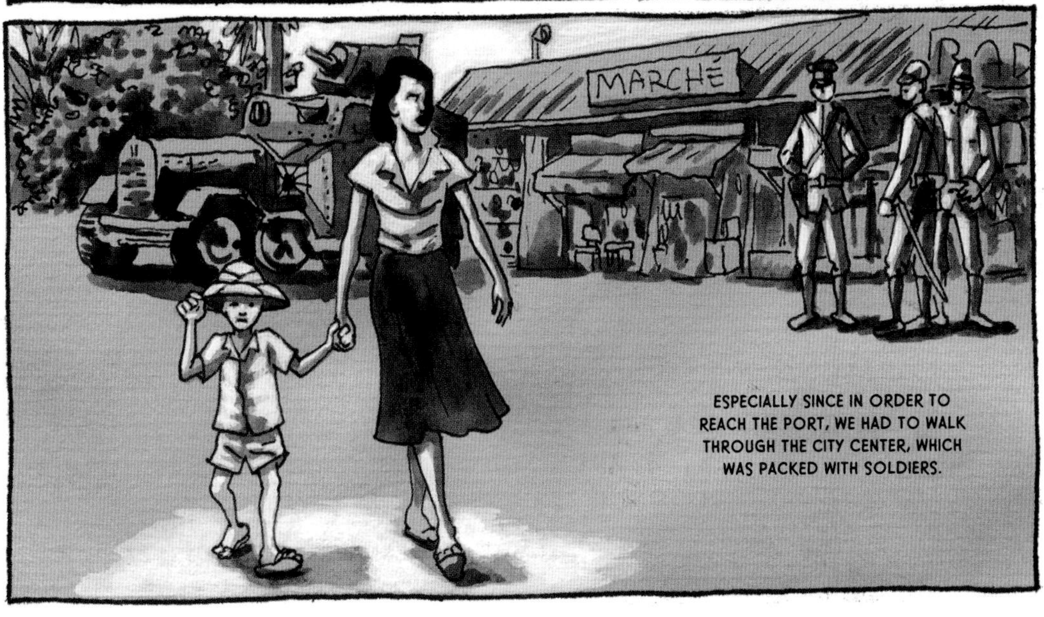
MARCHÉ
ESPECIALLY SINCE IN ORDER TO REACH THE PORT, WE HAD TO WALK THROUGH THE CITY CENTER, WHICH WAS PACKED WITH SOLDIERS.

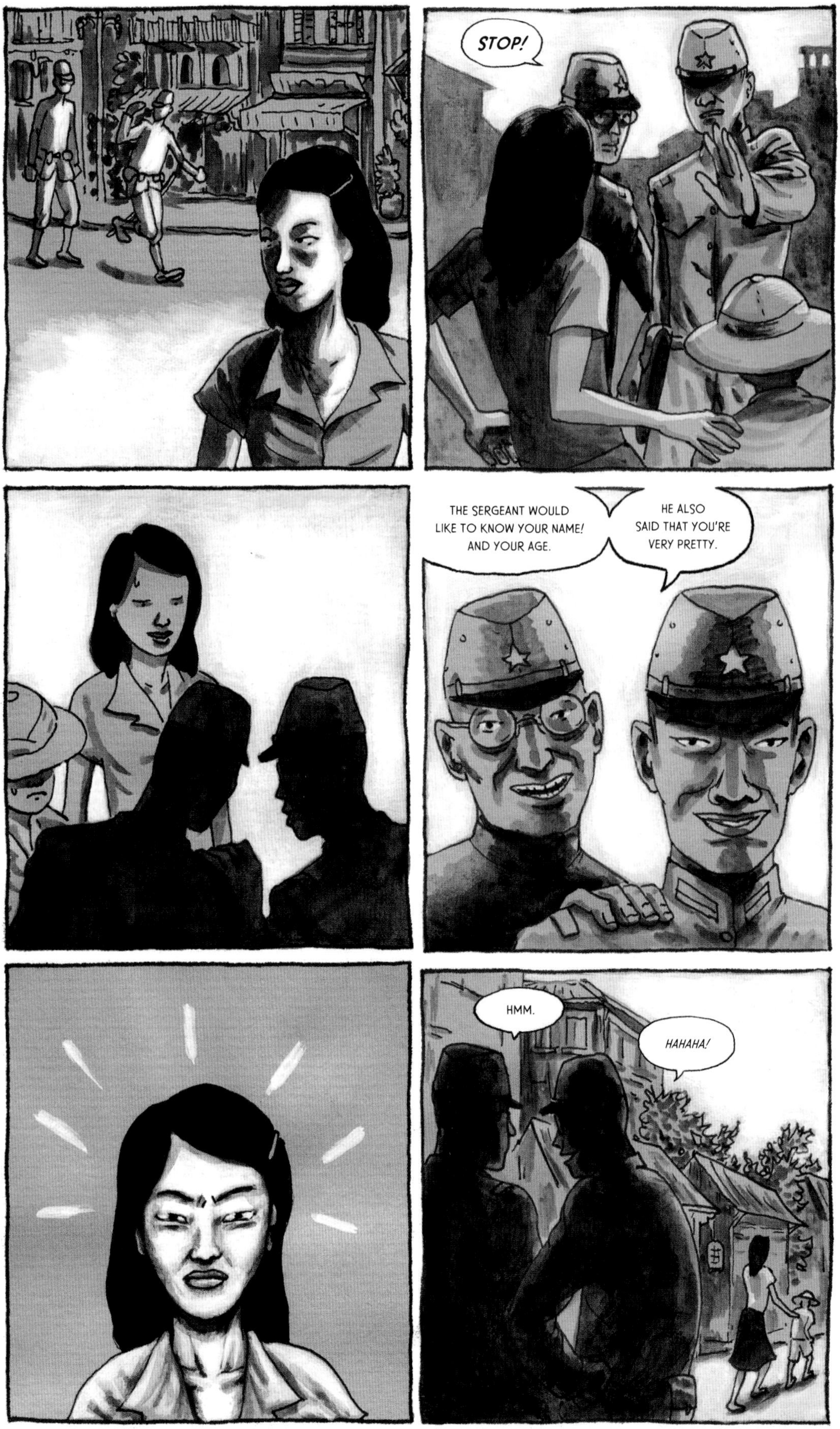
STOP!
THE SERGEANT WOULD LIKE TO KNOW YOUR NAME! AND YOUR AGE.
HE ALSO SAID THAT YOU'RE VERY PRETTY.
HMM.
HAHAHA!

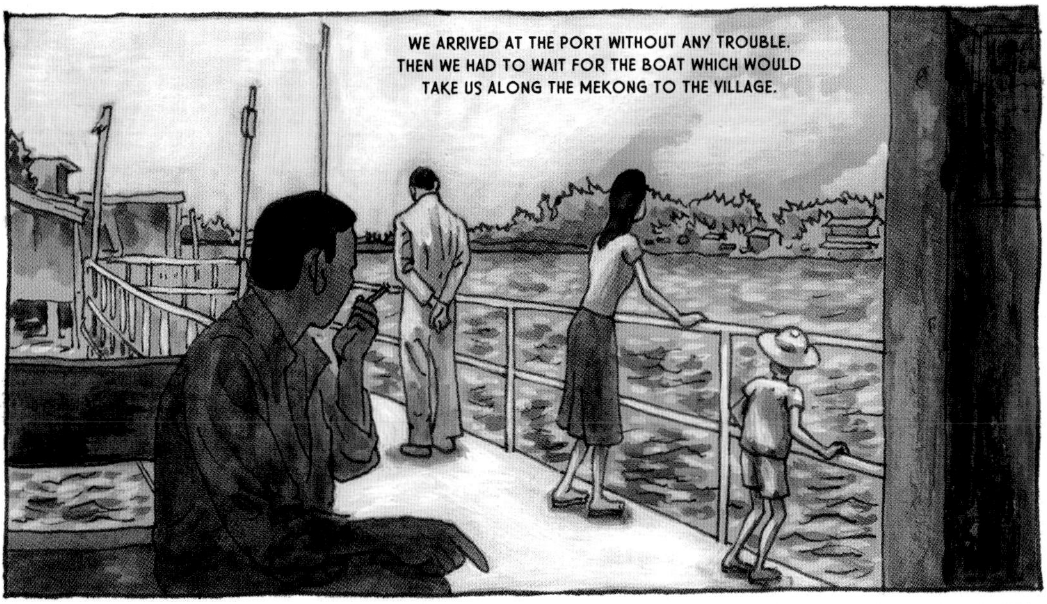
WE ARRIVED AT THE PORT WITHOUT ANY TROUBLE.
THEN WE HAD TO WAIT FOR THE BOAT WHICH WOULD
TAKE US ALONG THE MEKONG TO THE VILLAGE.

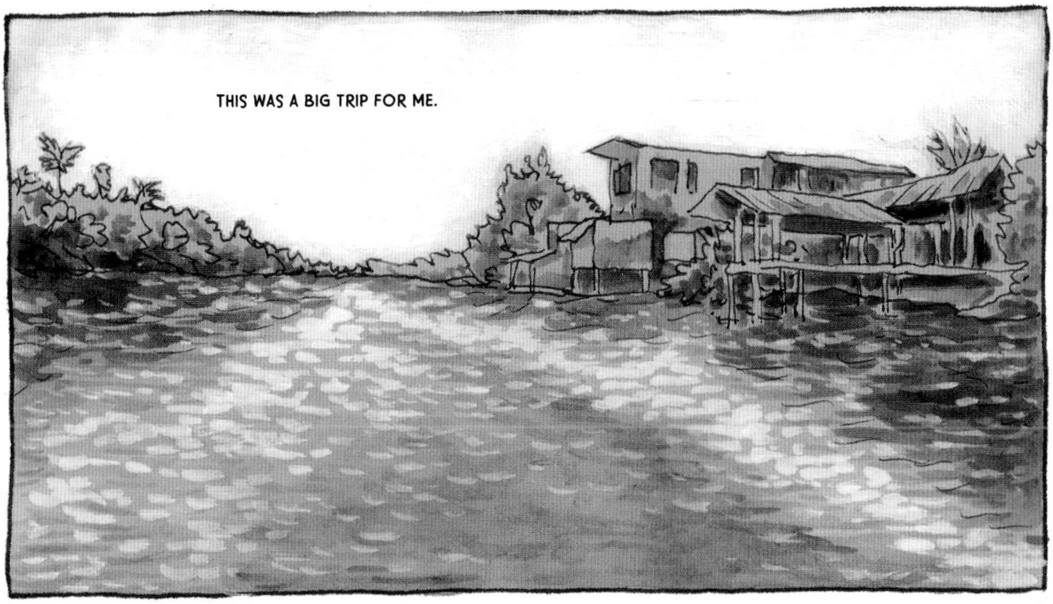
THIS WAS A BIG TRIP FOR ME.

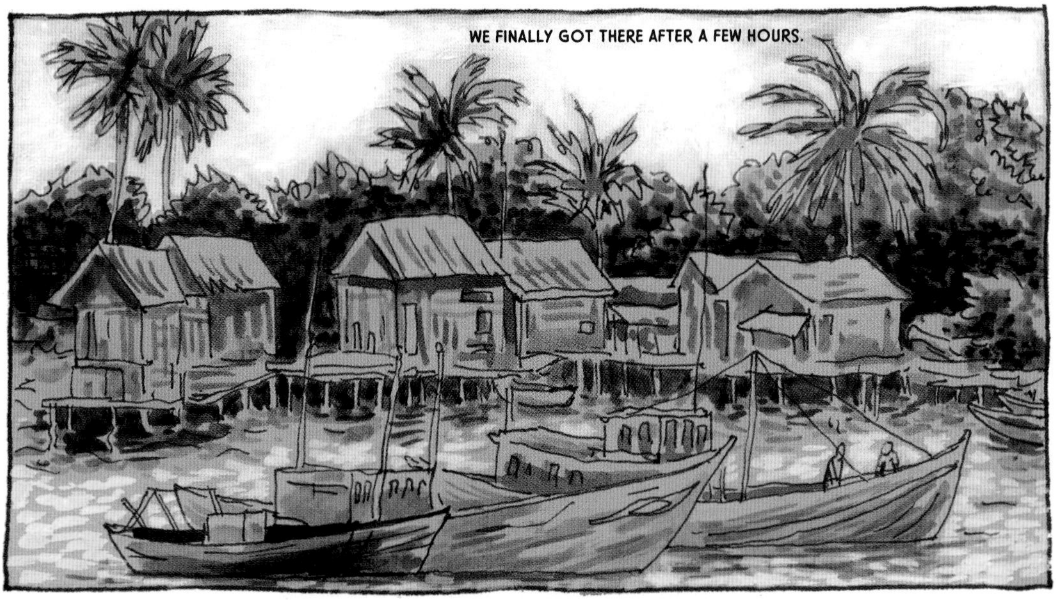
WE FINALLY GOT THERE AFTER A FEW HOURS.

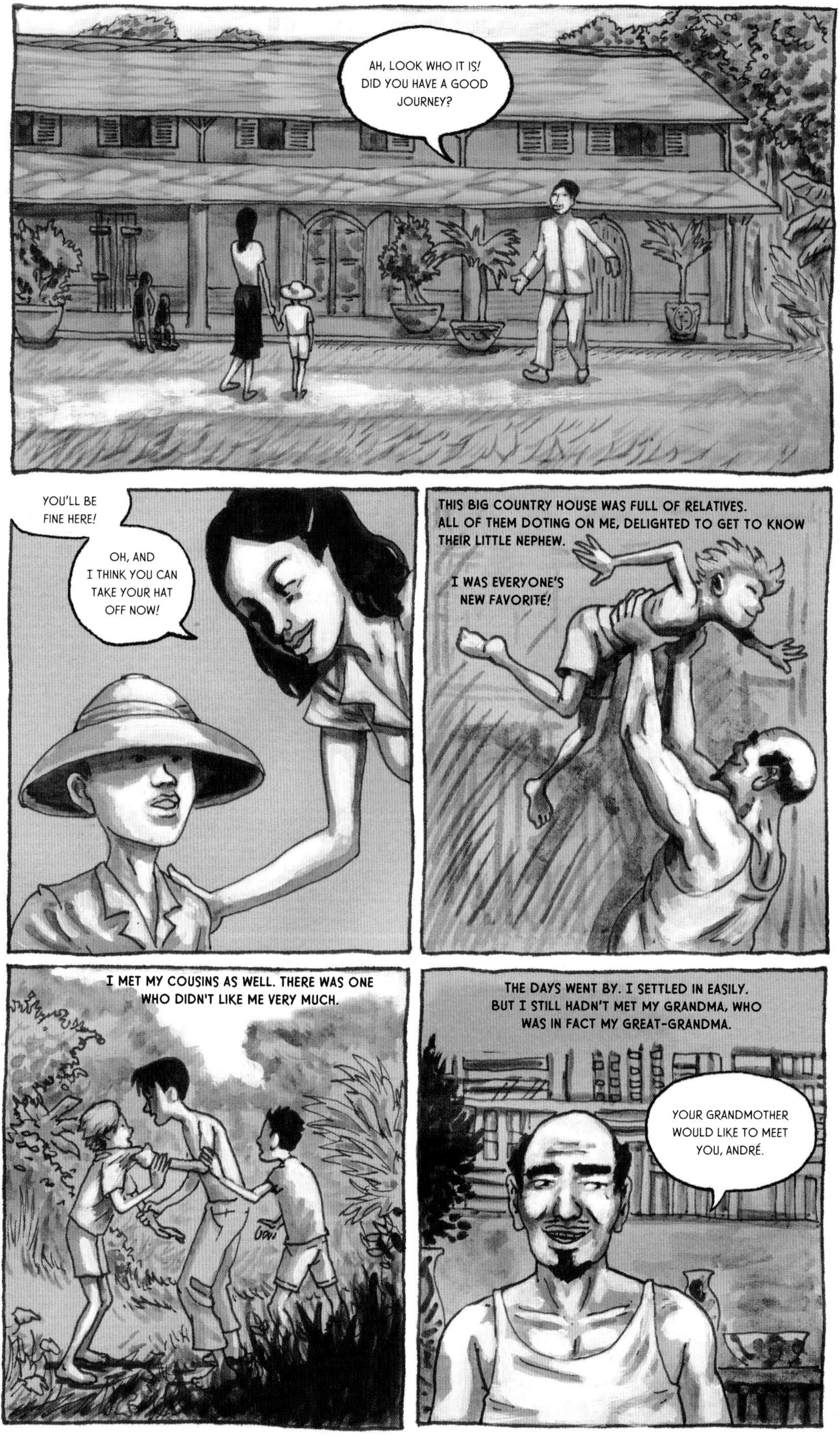
AH, LOOK WHO IT IS! DID YOU HAVE A GOOD JOURNEY?
YOU'LL BE FINE HERE!
OH, AND I THINK YOU CAN TAKE YOUR HAT OFF NOW!
THIS BIG COUNTRY HOUSE WAS FULL OF RELATIVES. ALL OF THEM DOTING ON ME, DELIGHTED TO GET TO KNOW THEIR LITTLE NEPHEW.
I WAS EVERYONE'S NEW FAVORITE!
I MET MY COUSINS AS WELL. THERE WAS ONE WHO DIDN'T LIKE ME VERY MUCH.
THE DAYS WENT BY. I SETTLED IN EASILY. BUT I STILL HADN'T MET MY GRANDMA, WHO WAS IN FACT MY GREAT-GRANDMA.
YOUR GRANDMOTHER WOULD LIKE TO MEET YOU, ANDRÉ.

FOR A LITTLE BOY LIKE ME, THE HOUSE FELT ENORMOUS, THE ROOMS BREATHTAKING.

THE FIRST THING I SAW IN THE ROOM WAS A COFFIN...

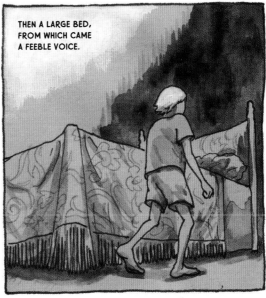

THEN A LARGE BED, FROM WHICH CAME A FEEBLE VOICE.

IT'S THE ONLY MEMORY I HAVE OF MY GRANDMOTHER: A VAGUE SHAPE.

I REMEMBER OUR FISHING TRIPS TO THE RIVER MUCH MORE VIVIDLY.

TRADITION HAS IT THAT THE COFFIN IS CHOSEN BY THE PERSON WHO WILL OCCUPY IT. AND SINCE GRANDMA COULD NO LONGER GET UP, THE COFFIN HAD BEEN BROUGHT INTO THE ROOM.

WITH THE END OF THE WAR, I WAS ABLE TO RETURN HOME TO SAIGON.

THE JAPANESE HAD LEFT.

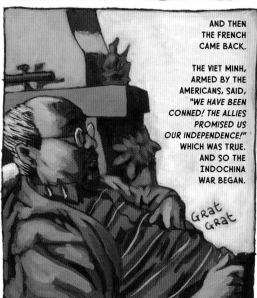

AND THEN THE FRENCH CAME BACK.

THE VIET MINH, ARMED BY THE AMERICANS, SAID, *"WE HAVE BEEN CONNED! THE ALLIES PROMISED US OUR INDEPENDENCE!"* WHICH WAS TRUE. AND SO THE INDOCHINA WAR BEGAN.

Grat Grat

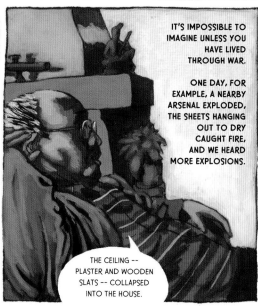

IT'S IMPOSSIBLE TO IMAGINE UNLESS YOU HAVE LIVED THROUGH WAR.

ONE DAY, FOR EXAMPLE, A NEARBY ARSENAL EXPLODED, THE SHEETS HANGING OUT TO DRY CAUGHT FIRE, AND WE HEARD MORE EXPLOSIONS.

THE CEILING -- PLASTER AND WOODEN SLATS -- COLLAPSED INTO THE HOUSE.

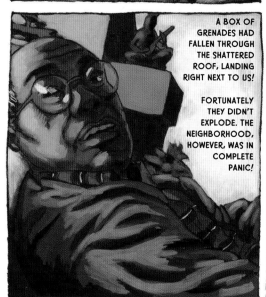

A BOX OF GRENADES HAD FALLEN THROUGH THE SHATTERED ROOF, LANDING RIGHT NEXT TO US!

FORTUNATELY THEY DIDN'T EXPLODE. THE NEIGHBORHOOD, HOWEVER, WAS IN COMPLETE PANIC!

SO, WHICH YEAR DID YOU LEAVE VIETNAM TO COME TO FRANCE?

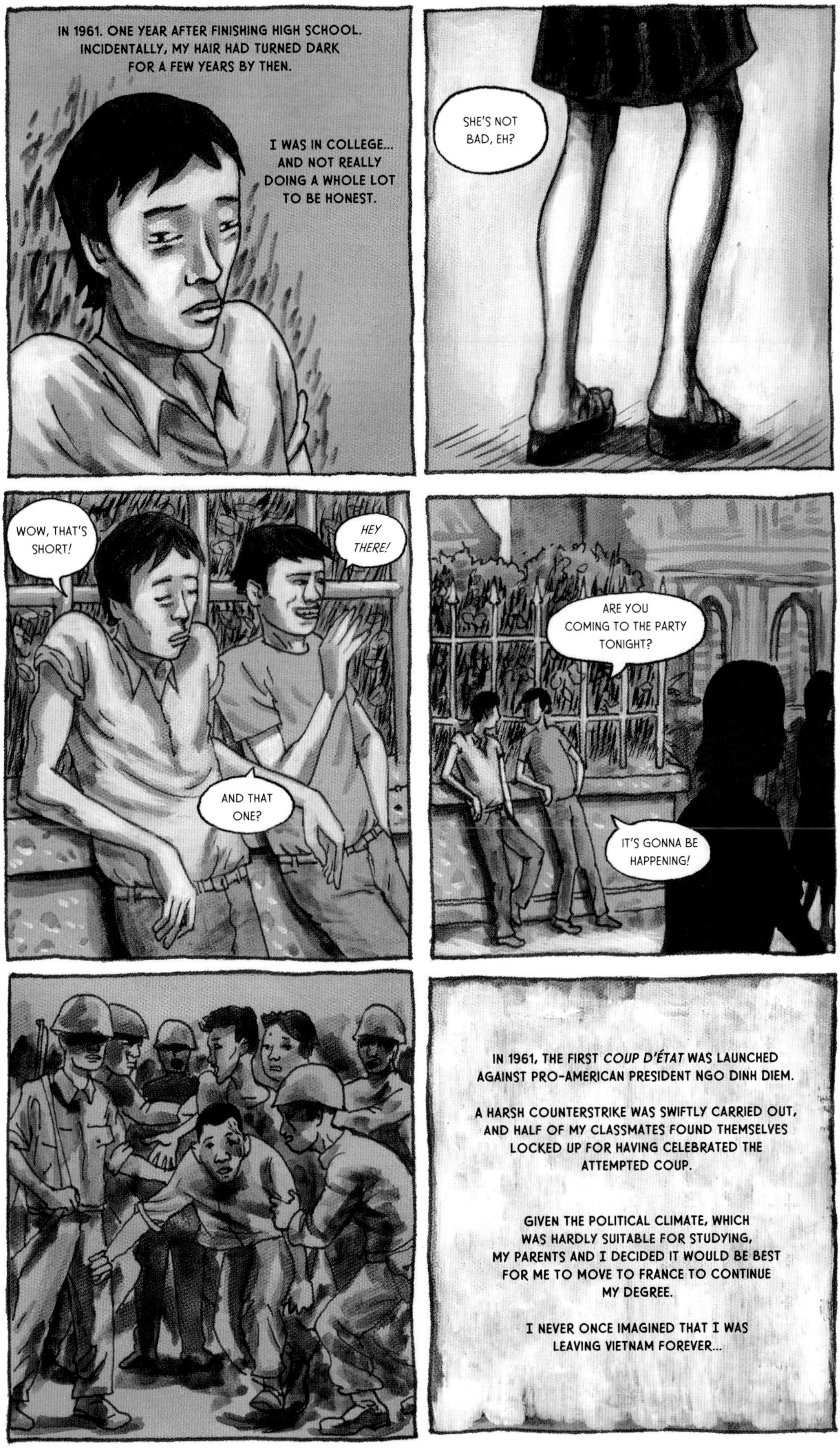
IN 1961. ONE YEAR AFTER FINISHING HIGH SCHOOL. INCIDENTALLY, MY HAIR HAD TURNED DARK FOR A FEW YEARS BY THEN.
I WAS IN COLLEGE... AND NOT REALLY DOING A WHOLE LOT TO BE HONEST.
SHE'S NOT BAD, EH?
WOW, THAT'S SHORT!
HEY THERE!
AND THAT ONE?
ARE YOU COMING TO THE PARTY TONIGHT?
IT'S GONNA BE HAPPENING!
IN 1961, THE FIRST *COUP D'ÉTAT* WAS LAUNCHED AGAINST PRO-AMERICAN PRESIDENT NGO DINH DIEM.
A HARSH COUNTERSTRIKE WAS SWIFTLY CARRIED OUT, AND HALF OF MY CLASSMATES FOUND THEMSELVES LOCKED UP FOR HAVING CELEBRATED THE ATTEMPTED COUP.
GIVEN THE POLITICAL CLIMATE, WHICH WAS HARDLY SUITABLE FOR STUDYING, MY PARENTS AND I DECIDED IT WOULD BE BEST FOR ME TO MOVE TO FRANCE TO CONTINUE MY DEGREE.
I NEVER ONCE IMAGINED THAT I WAS LEAVING VIETNAM FOREVER...

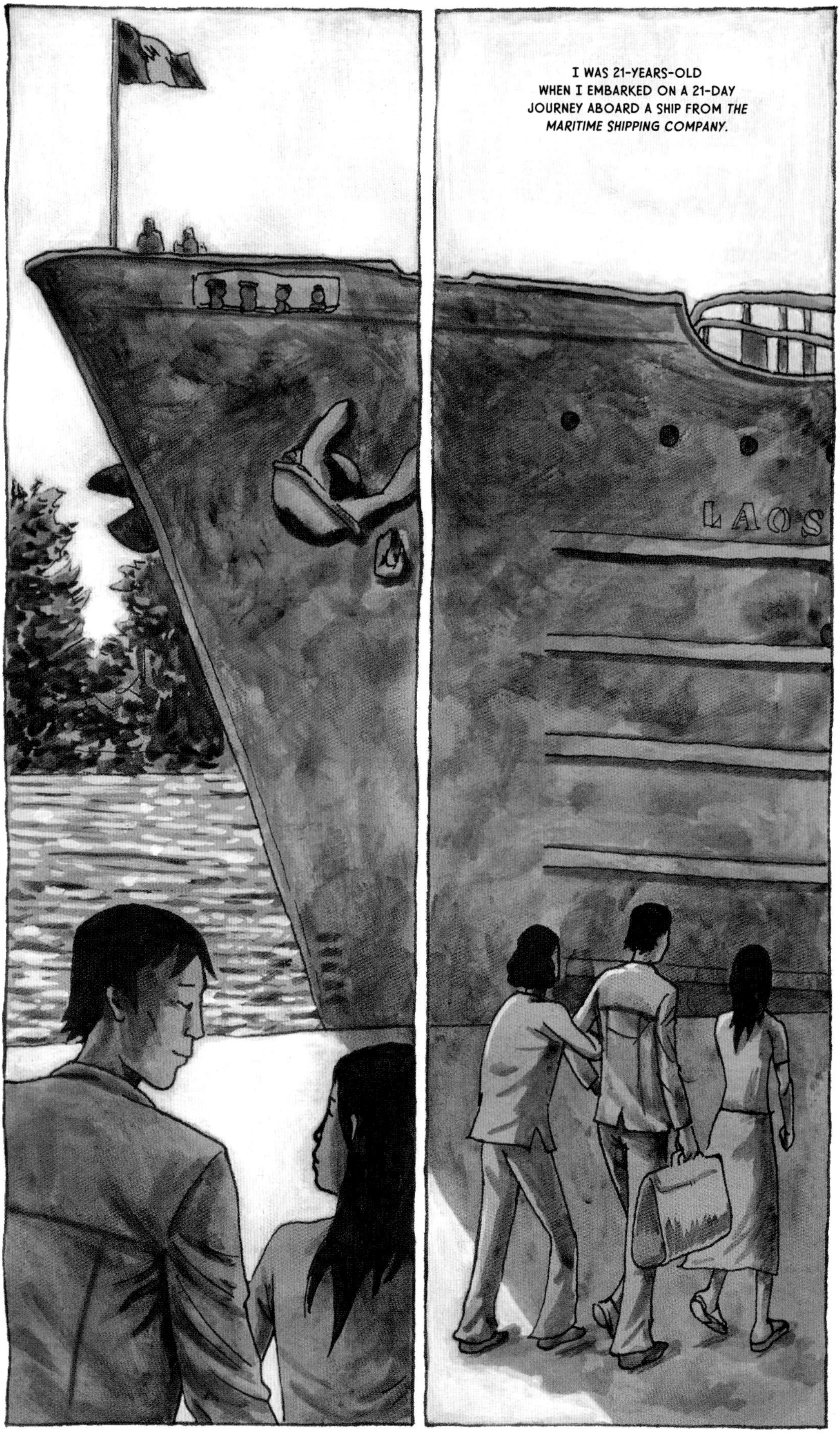
I WAS 21-YEARS-OLD
WHEN I EMBARKED ON A 21-DAY
JOURNEY ABOARD A SHIP FROM *THE
MARITIME SHIPPING COMPANY*.
LAOS

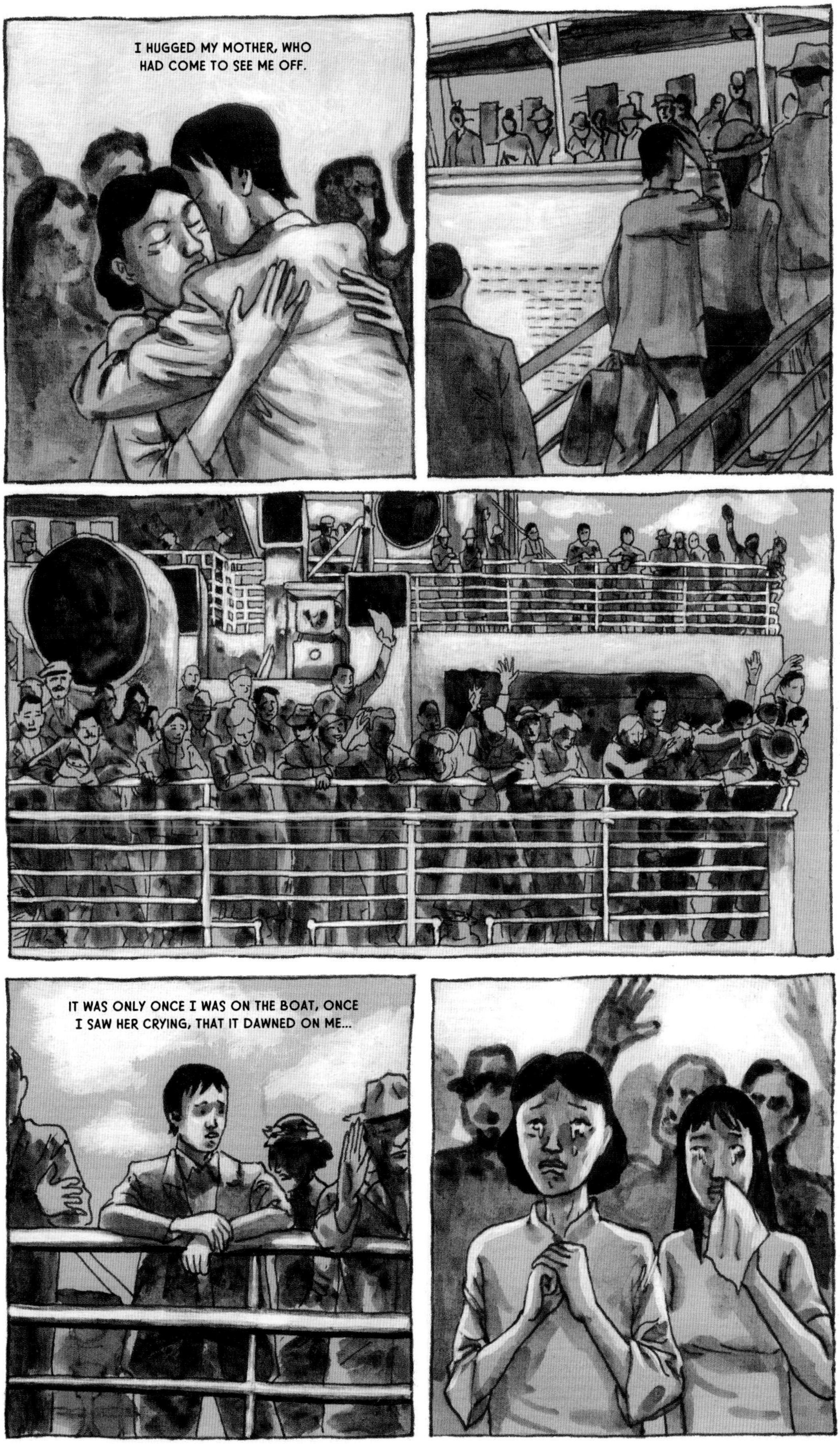
I HUGGED MY MOTHER, WHO HAD COME TO SEE ME OFF.
IT WAS ONLY ONCE I WAS ON THE BOAT, ONCE I SAW HER CRYING, THAT IT DAWNED ON ME...

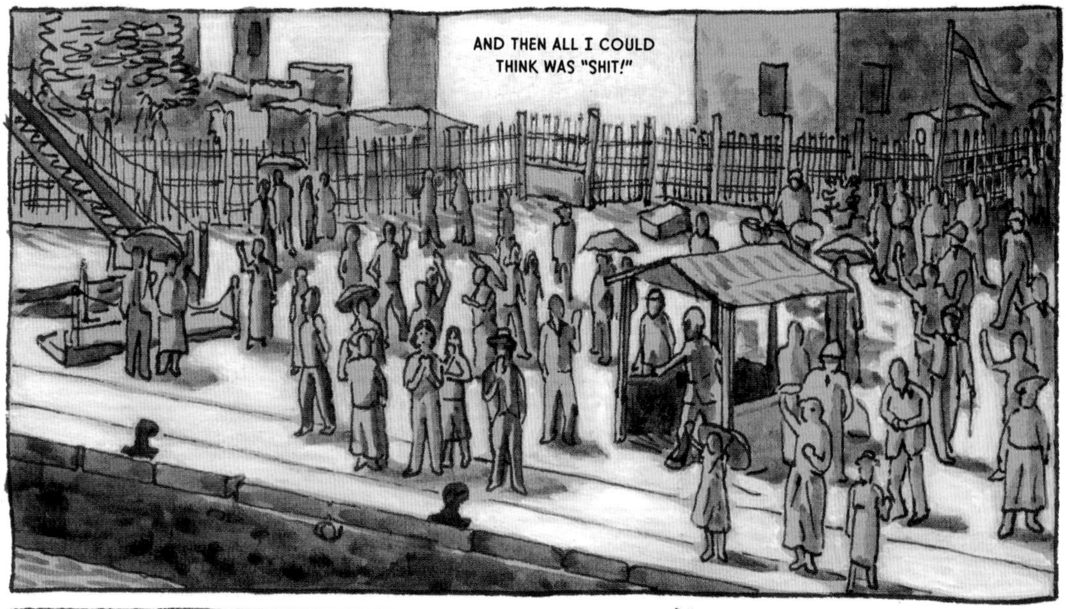
AND THEN ALL I COULD THINK WAS "SHIT!"

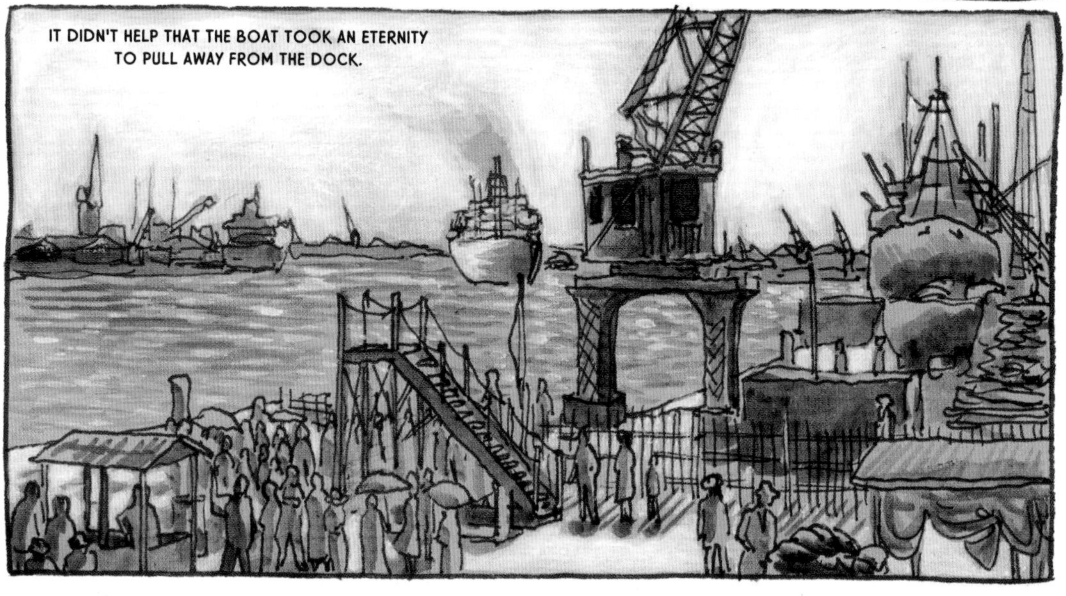
IT DIDN'T HELP THAT THE BOAT TOOK AN ETERNITY TO PULL AWAY FROM THE DOCK.

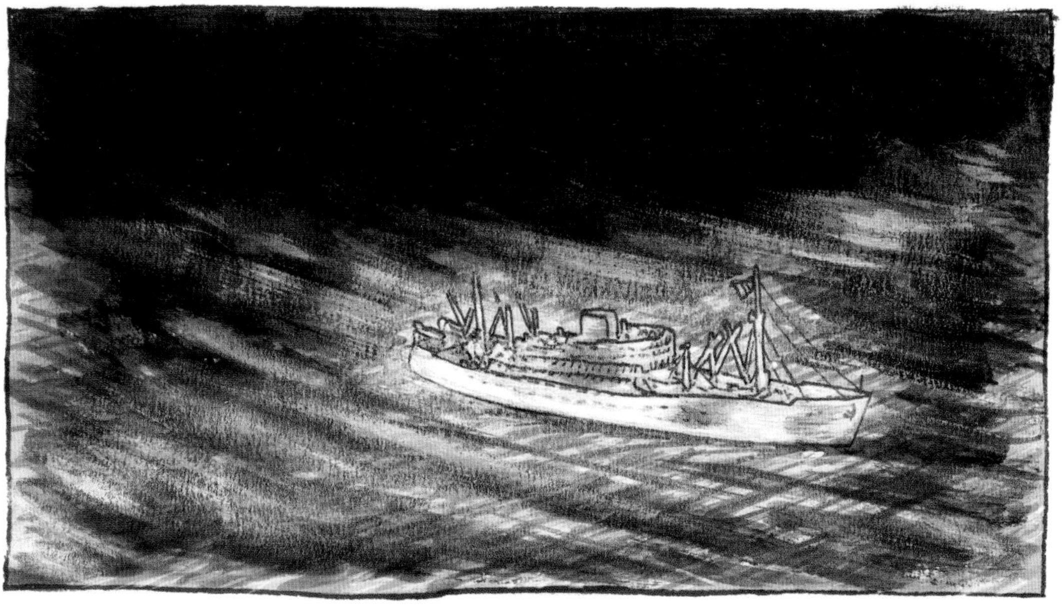

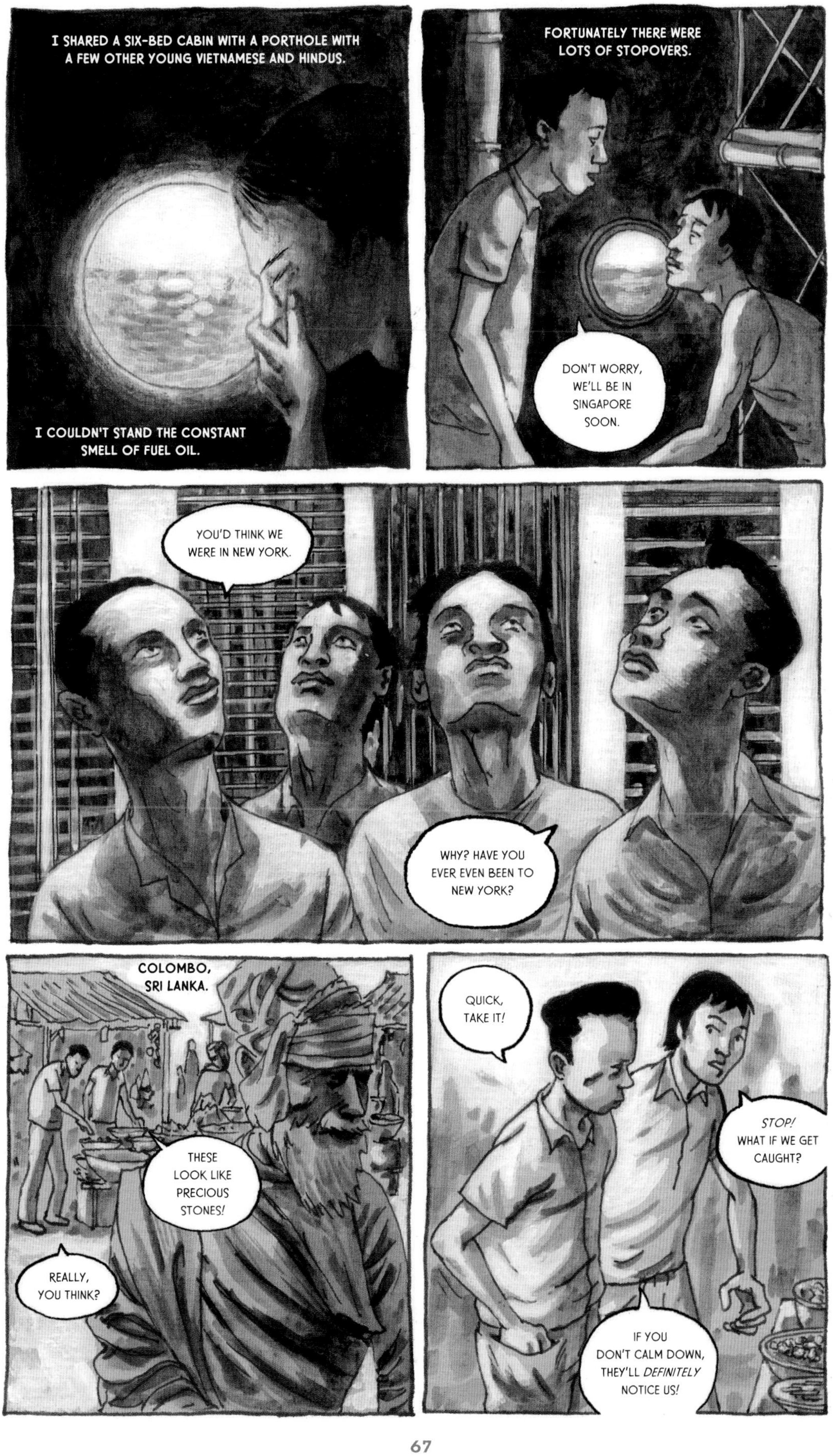

I SHARED A SIX-BED CABIN WITH A PORTHOLE WITH A FEW OTHER YOUNG VIETNAMESE AND HINDUS.
I COULDN'T STAND THE CONSTANT SMELL OF FUEL OIL.
FORTUNATELY THERE WERE LOTS OF STOPOVERS.
DON'T WORRY, WE'LL BE IN SINGAPORE SOON.
YOU'D THINK WE WERE IN NEW YORK.
WHY? HAVE YOU EVER EVEN BEEN TO NEW YORK?
COLOMBO, SRI LANKA.
THESE LOOK LIKE PRECIOUS STONES!
REALLY, YOU THINK?
QUICK, TAKE IT!
STOP! WHAT IF WE GET CAUGHT?
IF YOU DON'T CALM DOWN, THEY'LL *DEFINITELY* NOTICE US!

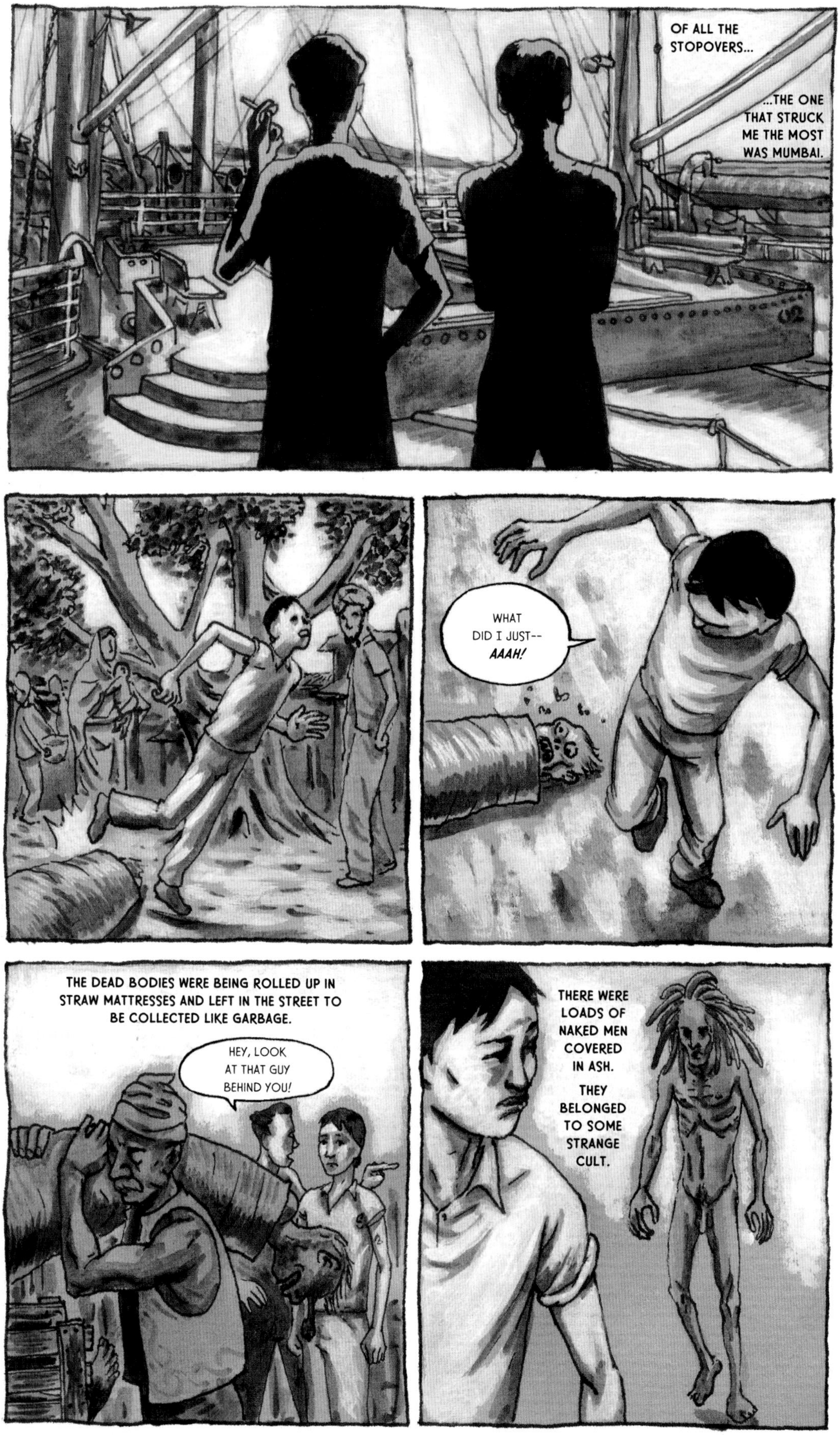

OF ALL THE STOPOVERS...
...THE ONE THAT STRUCK ME THE MOST WAS MUMBAI.
WHAT DID I JUST-- AAAH!
THE DEAD BODIES WERE BEING ROLLED UP IN STRAW MATTRESSES AND LEFT IN THE STREET TO BE COLLECTED LIKE GARBAGE.
HEY, LOOK AT THAT GUY BEHIND YOU!
THERE WERE LOADS OF NAKED MEN COVERED IN ASH.
THEY BELONGED TO SOME STRANGE CULT.

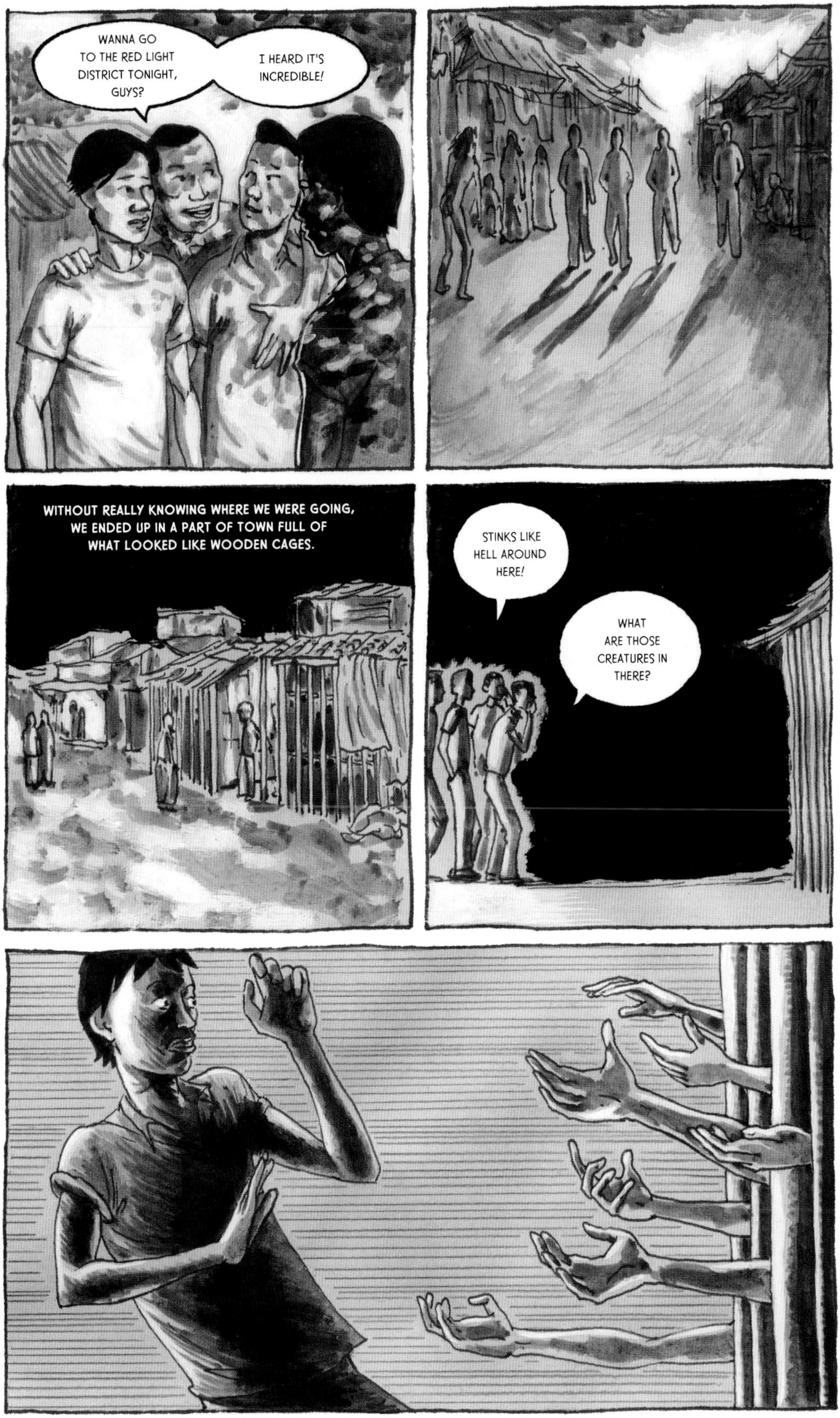
WANNA GO TO THE RED LIGHT DISTRICT TONIGHT, GUYS?
I HEARD IT'S INCREDIBLE!
WITHOUT REALLY KNOWING WHERE WE WERE GOING, WE ENDED UP IN A PART OF TOWN FULL OF WHAT LOOKED LIKE WOODEN CAGES.
STINKS LIKE HELL AROUND HERE!
WHAT ARE THOSE CREATURES IN THERE?

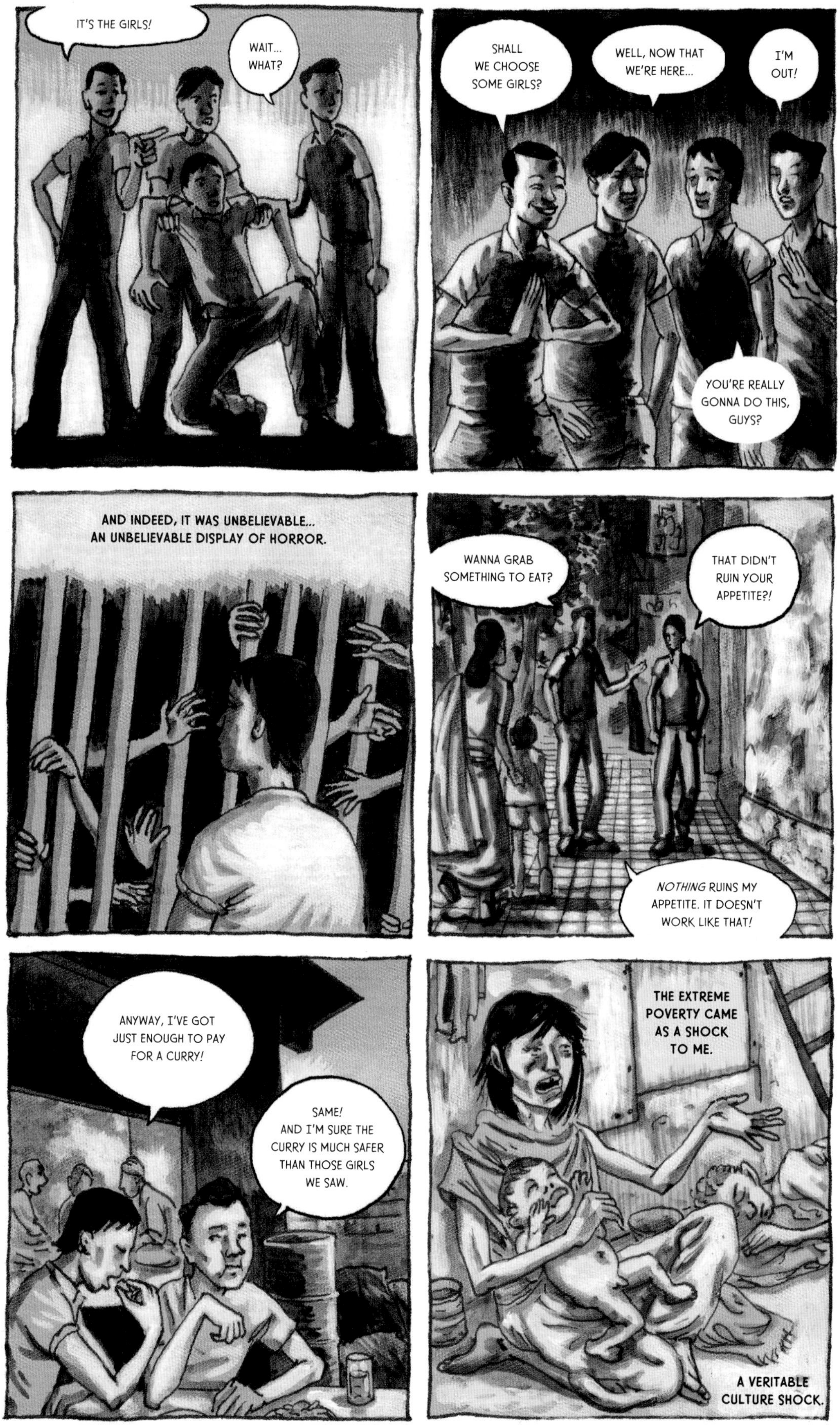
IT'S THE GIRLS!
WAIT... WHAT?
SHALL WE CHOOSE SOME GIRLS?
WELL, NOW THAT WE'RE HERE...
I'M OUT!
YOU'RE REALLY GONNA DO THIS, GUYS?
AND INDEED, IT WAS UNBELIEVABLE... AN UNBELIEVABLE DISPLAY OF HORROR.
WANNA GRAB SOMETHING TO EAT?
THAT DIDN'T RUIN YOUR APPETITE?!
NOTHING RUINS MY APPETITE. IT DOESN'T WORK LIKE THAT!
ANYWAY, I'VE GOT JUST ENOUGH TO PAY FOR A CURRY!
SAME! AND I'M SURE THE CURRY IS MUCH SAFER THAN THOSE GIRLS WE SAW.
THE EXTREME POVERTY CAME AS A SHOCK TO ME.
A VERITABLE CULTURE SHOCK.

AFTER MUMBAI, THE OTHER STOPS WEREN'T NEARLY AS TRAUMATISING.

EXCEPT FOR THE HEAT ON THE RED SEA.

WHEN WE STOPPED IN DJIBOUTI, IT MUST HAVE BEEN BETWEEN 100 AND 120 DEGREES

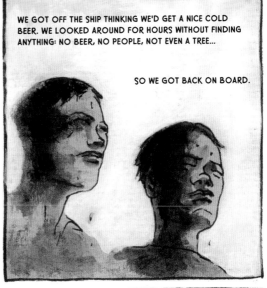

WE GOT OFF THE SHIP THINKING WE'D GET A NICE COLD BEER. WE LOOKED AROUND FOR HOURS WITHOUT FINDING ANYTHING: NO BEER, NO PEOPLE, NOT EVEN A TREE...

SO WE GOT BACK ON BOARD.

LOOK AT THAT ONE, IT'S HUGE!

WE WATCHED THE SHARKS AS THEY CIRCLED THE SHIP.

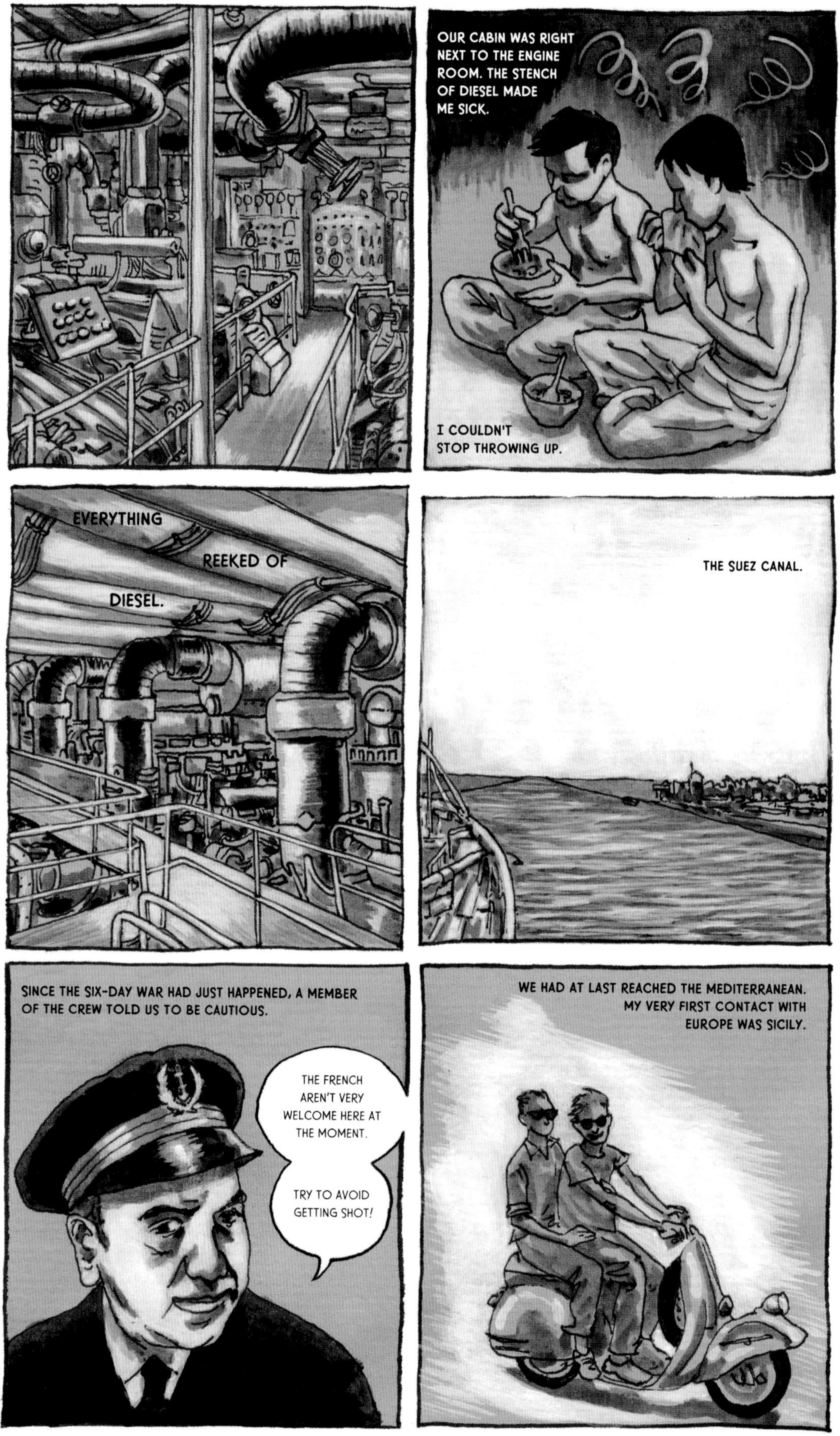
OUR CABIN WAS RIGHT NEXT TO THE ENGINE ROOM. THE STENCH OF DIESEL MADE ME SICK.
I COULDN'T STOP THROWING UP.
EVERYTHING
REEKED OF
DIESEL.
THE SUEZ CANAL.
SINCE THE SIX-DAY WAR HAD JUST HAPPENED, A MEMBER OF THE CREW TOLD US TO BE CAUTIOUS.
THE FRENCH AREN'T VERY WELCOME HERE AT THE MOMENT.
TRY TO AVOID GETTING SHOT!
WE HAD AT LAST REACHED THE MEDITERRANEAN. MY VERY FIRST CONTACT WITH EUROPE WAS SICILY.

FINALLY, WE ARRIVED IN MARSEILLE.

I WAS NOT TOO WORRIED, BECAUSE A FRIEND OF MY DAD WAS SUPPOSED TO COME AND GREET ME.

HOW WAS YOUR JOURNEY?

I WILL NEVER SET FOOT ON A SHIP EVER AGAIN!

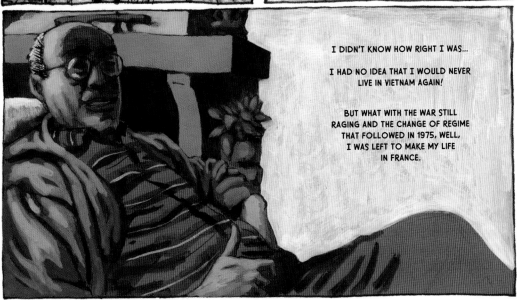

I DIDN'T KNOW HOW RIGHT I WAS...

I HAD NO IDEA THAT I WOULD NEVER LIVE IN VIETNAM AGAIN!

BUT WHAT WITH THE WAR STILL RAGING AND THE CHANGE OF REGIME THAT FOLLOWED IN 1975, WELL, I WAS LEFT TO MAKE MY LIFE IN FRANCE.

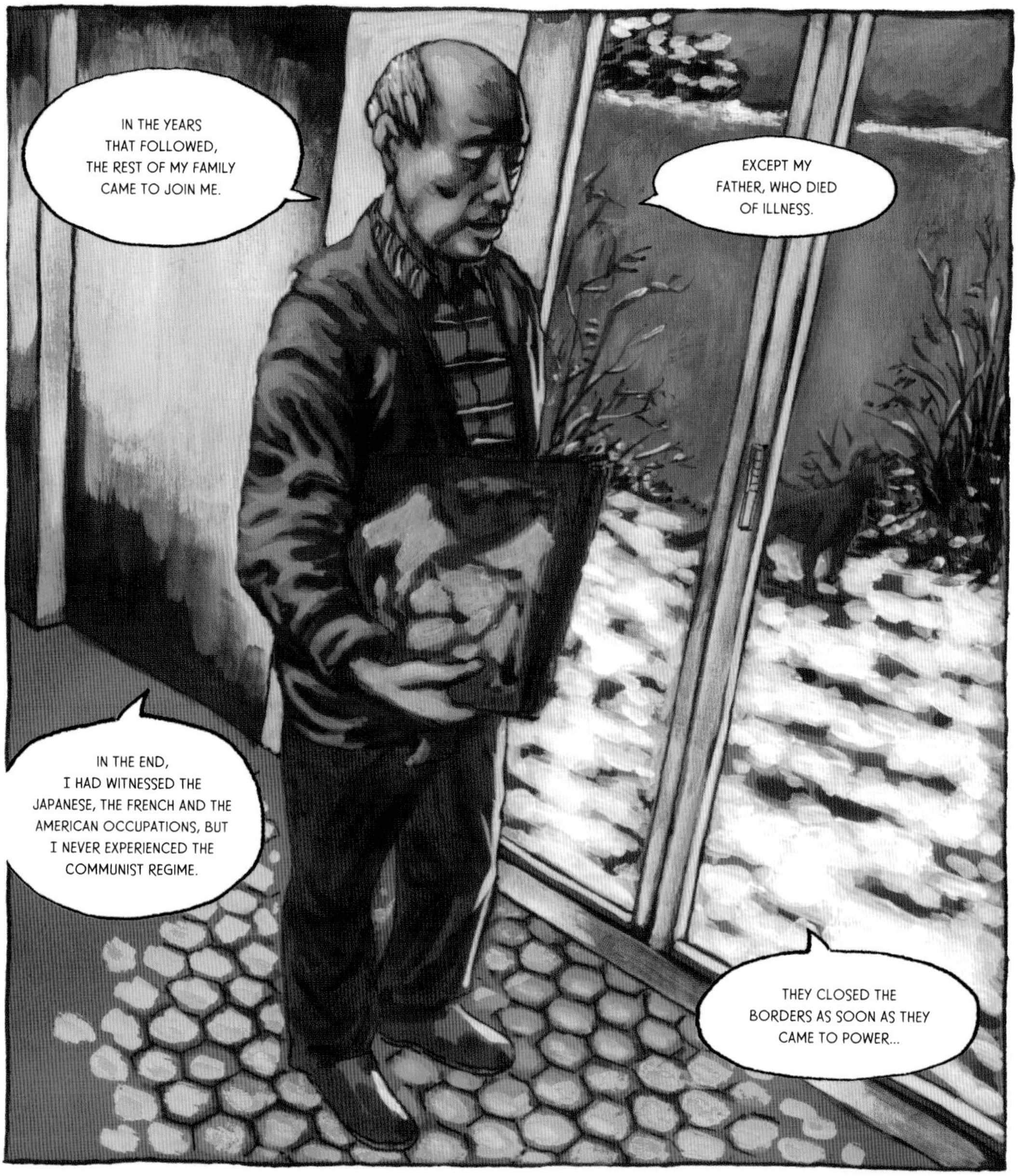
IN THE YEARS THAT FOLLOWED, THE REST OF MY FAMILY CAME TO JOIN ME.
EXCEPT MY FATHER, WHO DIED OF ILLNESS.
IN THE END, I HAD WITNESSED THE JAPANESE, THE FRENCH AND THE AMERICAN OCCUPATIONS, BUT I NEVER EXPERIENCED THE COMMUNIST REGIME.
THEY CLOSED THE BORDERS AS SOON AS THEY CAME TO POWER...

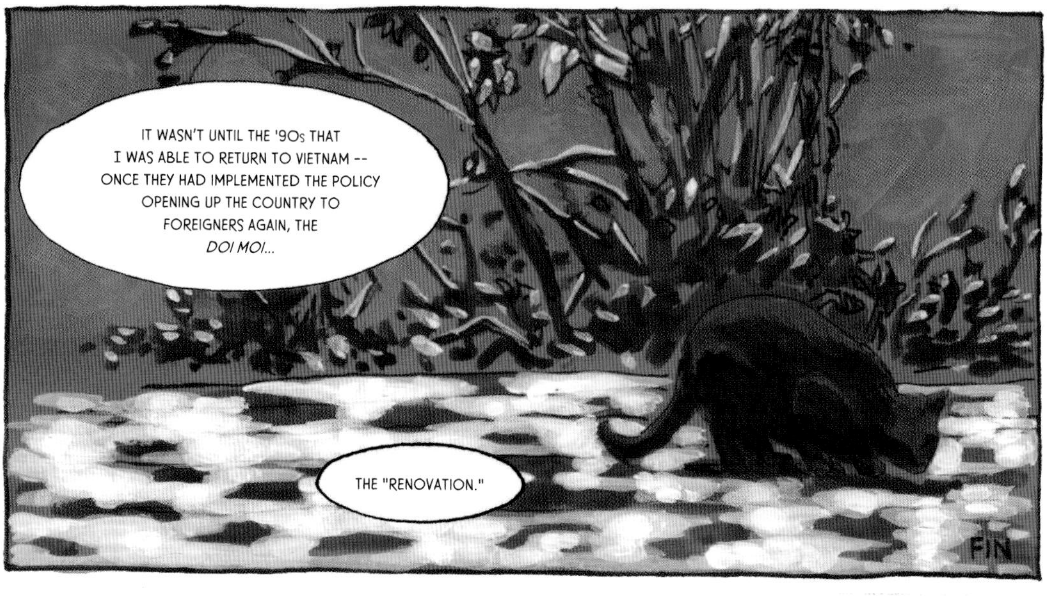
IT WASN'T UNTIL THE '90s THAT I WAS ABLE TO RETURN TO VIETNAM -- ONCE THEY HAD IMPLEMENTED THE POLICY OPENING UP THE COUNTRY TO FOREIGNERS AGAIN, THE *DOI MOI*...
THE "RENOVATION."
FIN

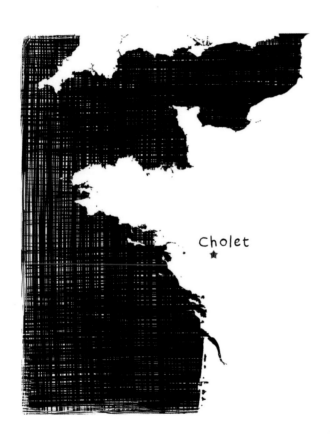

Cholet

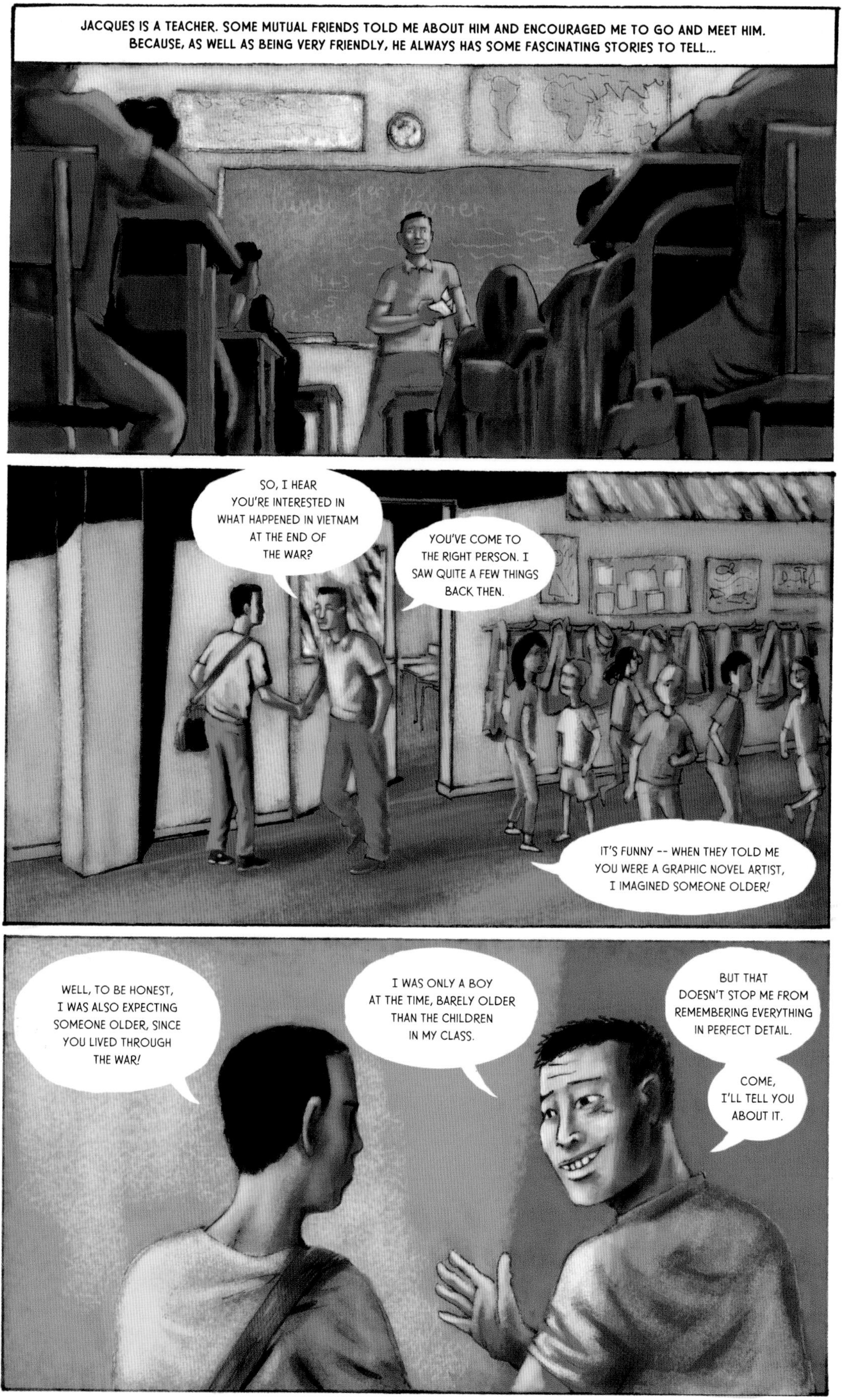
JACQUES IS A TEACHER. SOME MUTUAL FRIENDS TOLD ME ABOUT HIM AND ENCOURAGED ME TO GO AND MEET HIM. BECAUSE, AS WELL AS BEING VERY FRIENDLY, HE ALWAYS HAS SOME FASCINATING STORIES TO TELL...
SO, I HEAR YOU'RE INTERESTED IN WHAT HAPPENED IN VIETNAM AT THE END OF THE WAR?
YOU'VE COME TO THE RIGHT PERSON. I SAW QUITE A FEW THINGS BACK THEN.
IT'S FUNNY -- WHEN THEY TOLD ME YOU WERE A GRAPHIC NOVEL ARTIST, I IMAGINED SOMEONE OLDER!
WELL, TO BE HONEST, I WAS ALSO EXPECTING SOMEONE OLDER, SINCE YOU LIVED THROUGH THE WAR!
I WAS ONLY A BOY AT THE TIME, BARELY OLDER THAN THE CHILDREN IN MY CLASS.
BUT THAT DOESN'T STOP ME FROM REMEMBERING EVERYTHING IN PERFECT DETAIL.
COME, I'LL TELL YOU ABOUT IT.

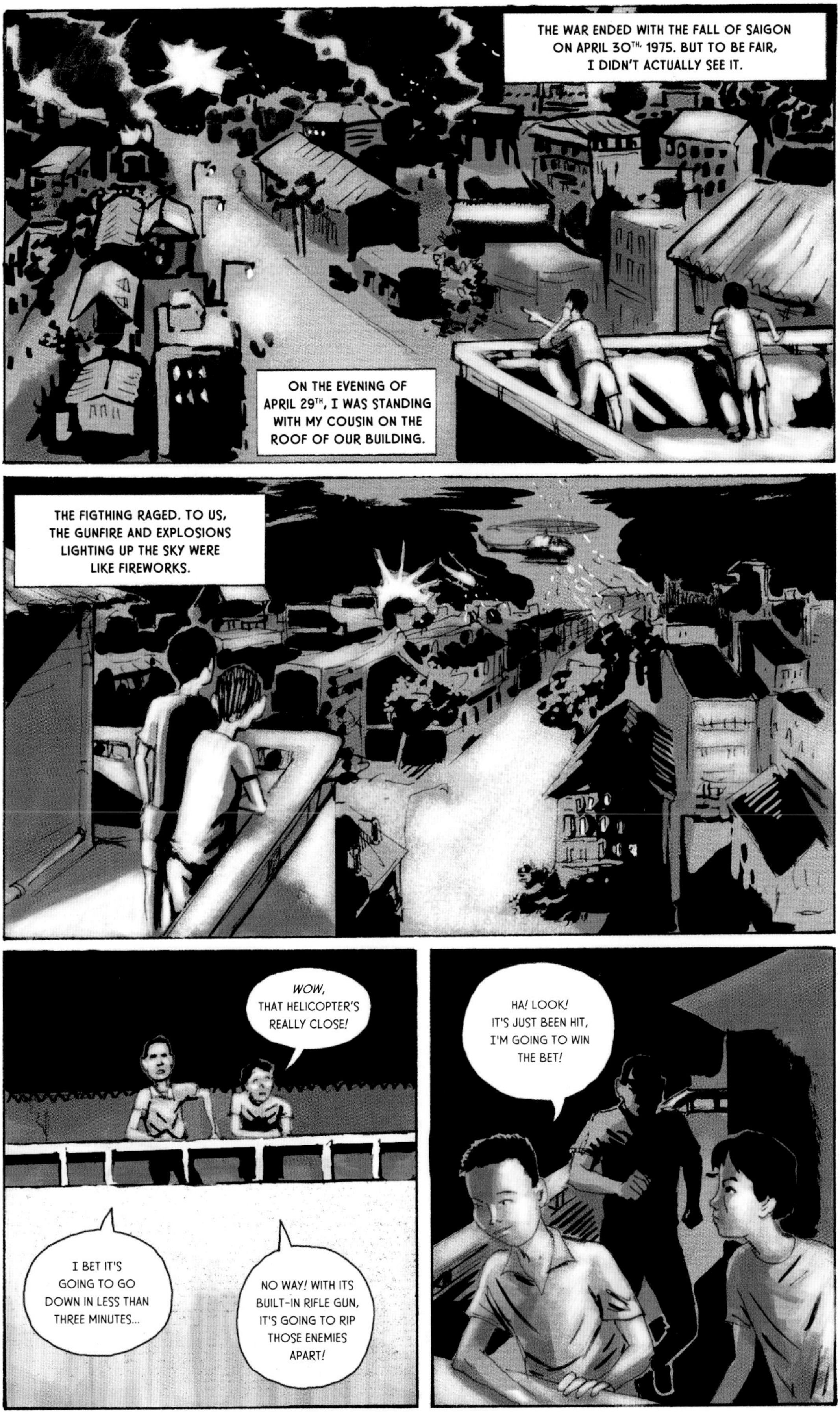
THE WAR ENDED WITH THE FALL OF SAIGON ON APRIL 30TH, 1975. BUT TO BE FAIR, I DIDN'T ACTUALLY SEE IT.
ON THE EVENING OF APRIL 29TH, I WAS STANDING WITH MY COUSIN ON THE ROOF OF OUR BUILDING.
THE FIGTHING RAGED. TO US, THE GUNFIRE AND EXPLOSIONS LIGHTING UP THE SKY WERE LIKE FIREWORKS.
WOW, THAT HELICOPTER'S REALLY CLOSE!
I BET IT'S GOING TO GO DOWN IN LESS THAN THREE MINUTES...
NO WAY! WITH ITS BUILT-IN RIFLE GUN, IT'S GOING TO RIP THOSE ENEMIES APART!
HA! LOOK! IT'S JUST BEEN HIT, I'M GOING TO WIN THE BET!

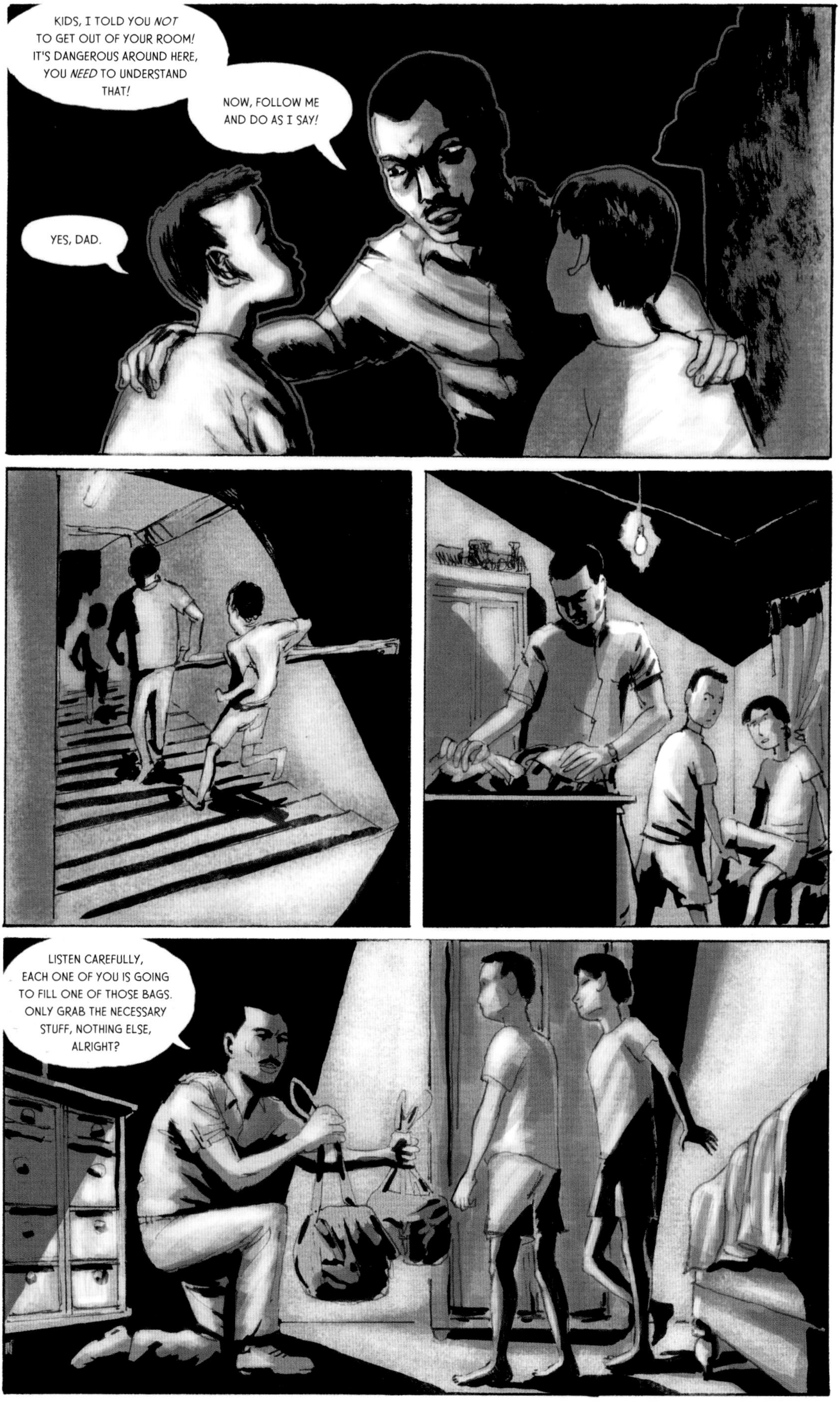
KIDS, I TOLD YOU *NOT* TO GET OUT OF YOUR ROOM! IT'S DANGEROUS AROUND HERE, YOU *NEED* TO UNDERSTAND THAT!
NOW, FOLLOW ME AND DO AS I SAY!
YES, DAD.
LISTEN CAREFULLY, EACH ONE OF YOU IS GOING TO FILL ONE OF THOSE BAGS. ONLY GRAB THE NECESSARY STUFF, NOTHING ELSE, ALRIGHT?

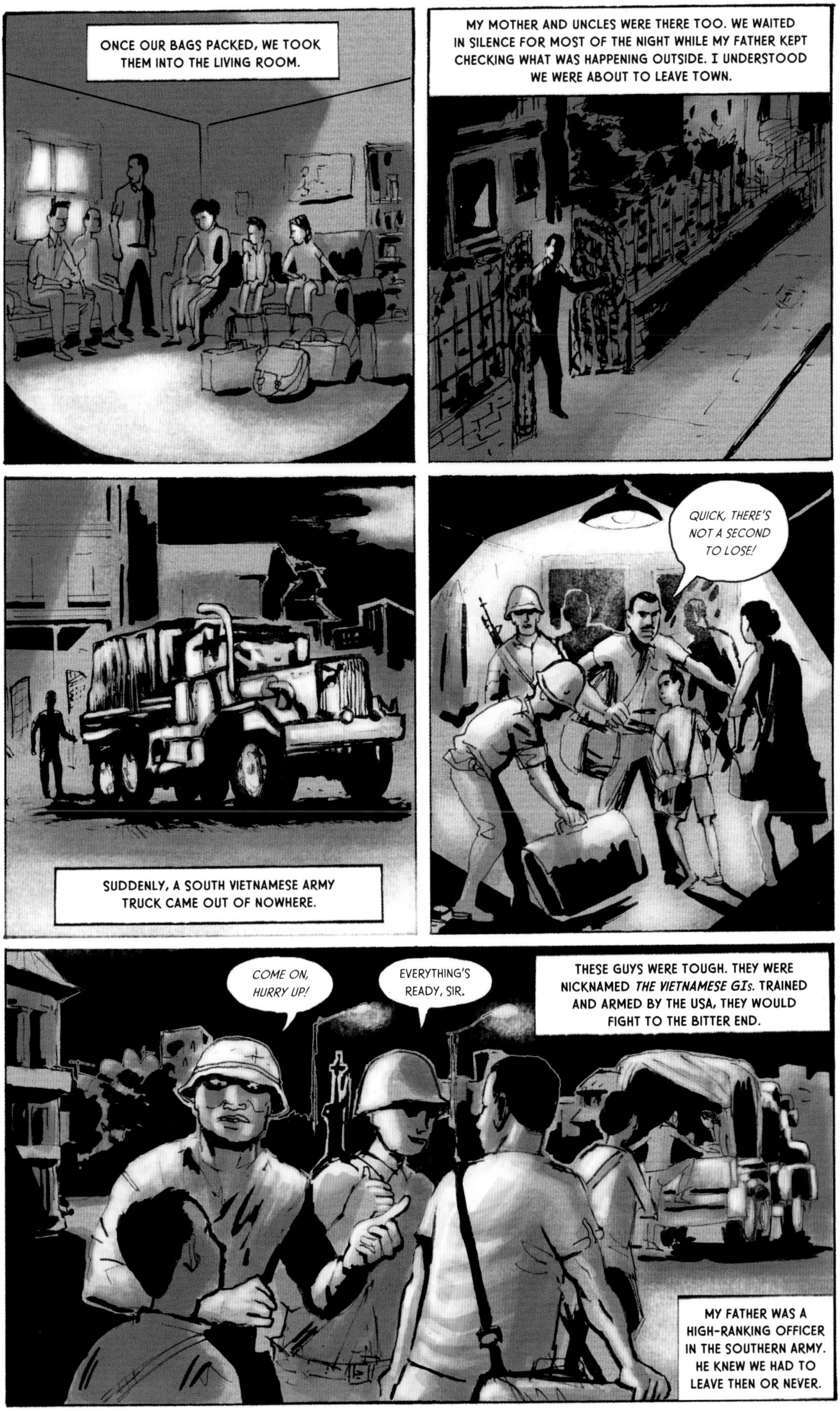
ONCE OUR BAGS PACKED, WE TOOK THEM INTO THE LIVING ROOM.
MY MOTHER AND UNCLES WERE THERE TOO. WE WAITED IN SILENCE FOR MOST OF THE NIGHT WHILE MY FATHER KEPT CHECKING WHAT WAS HAPPENING OUTSIDE. I UNDERSTOOD WE WERE ABOUT TO LEAVE TOWN.
SUDDENLY, A SOUTH VIETNAMESE ARMY TRUCK CAME OUT OF NOWHERE.
QUICK, THERE'S NOT A SECOND TO LOSE!
COME ON, HURRY UP!
EVERYTHING'S READY, SIR.
THESE GUYS WERE TOUGH. THEY WERE NICKNAMED *THE VIETNAMESE GIs*. TRAINED AND ARMED BY THE USA, THEY WOULD FIGHT TO THE BITTER END.
MY FATHER WAS A HIGH-RANKING OFFICER IN THE SOUTHERN ARMY. HE KNEW WE HAD TO LEAVE THEN OR NEVER.

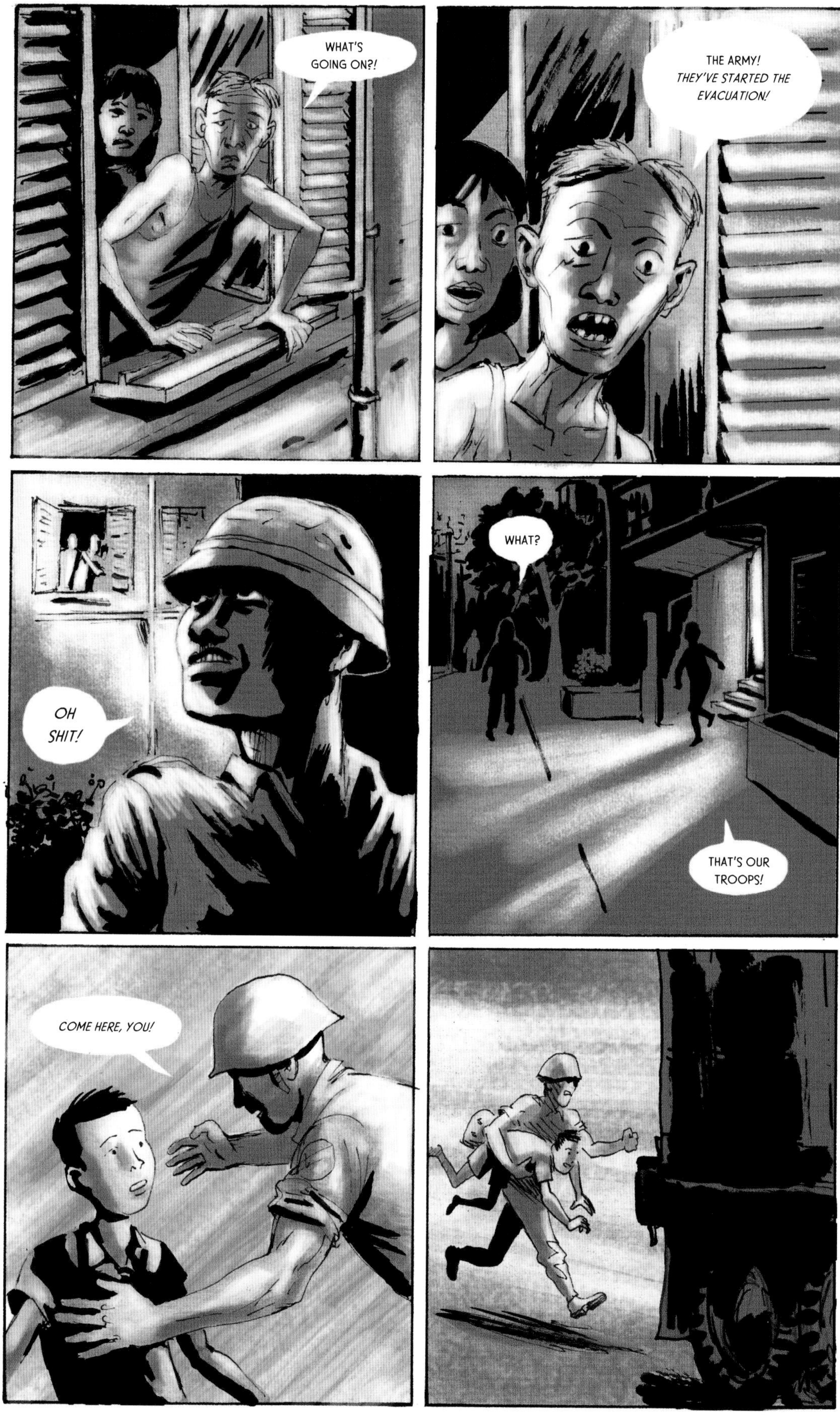
WHAT'S GOING ON?!
THE ARMY! THEY'VE STARTED THE EVACUATION!
OH SHIT!
WHAT?
THAT'S OUR TROOPS!
COME HERE, YOU!

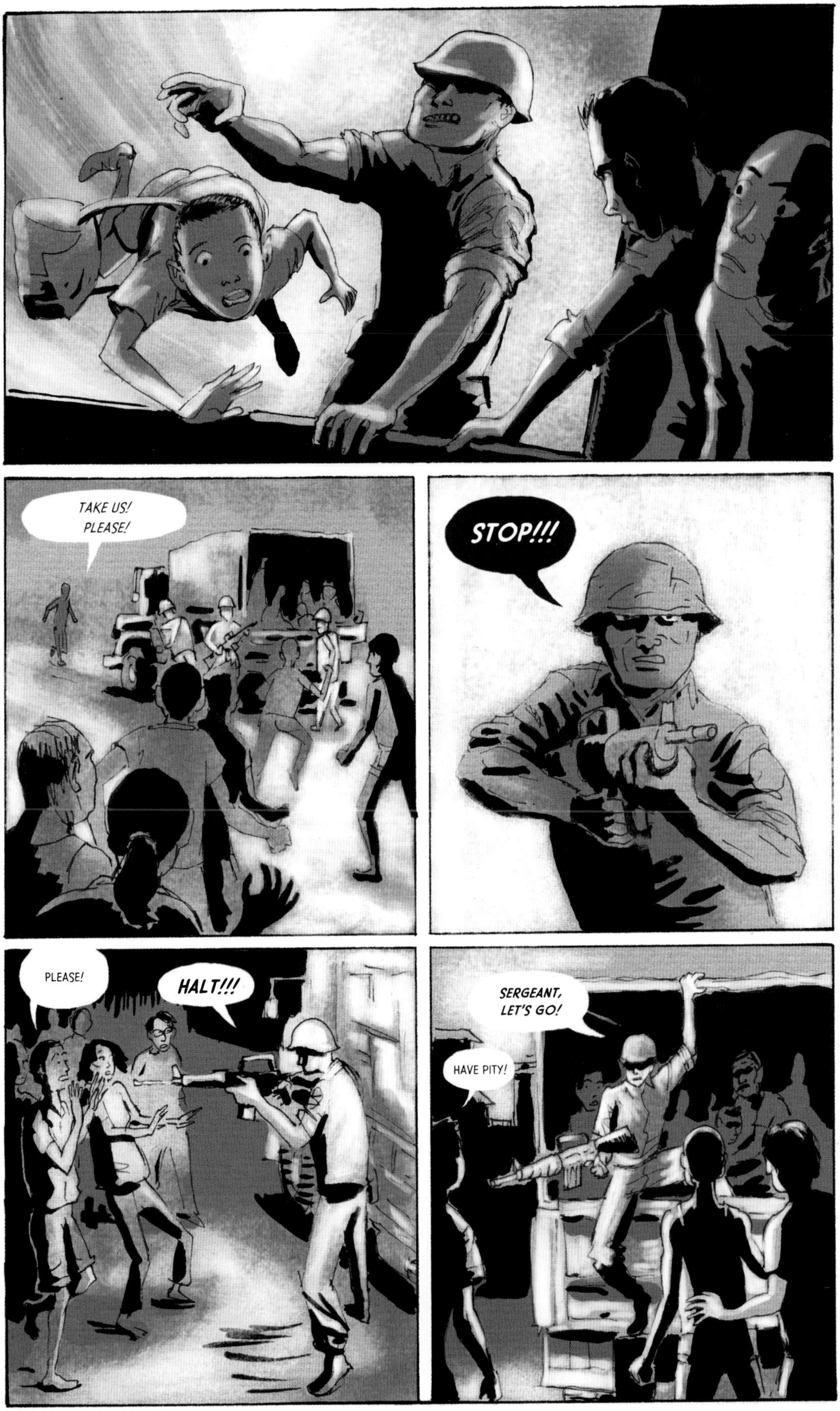
TAKE US! PLEASE!
STOP!!!
PLEASE!
HALT!!!
SERGEANT, LET'S GO!
HAVE PITY!

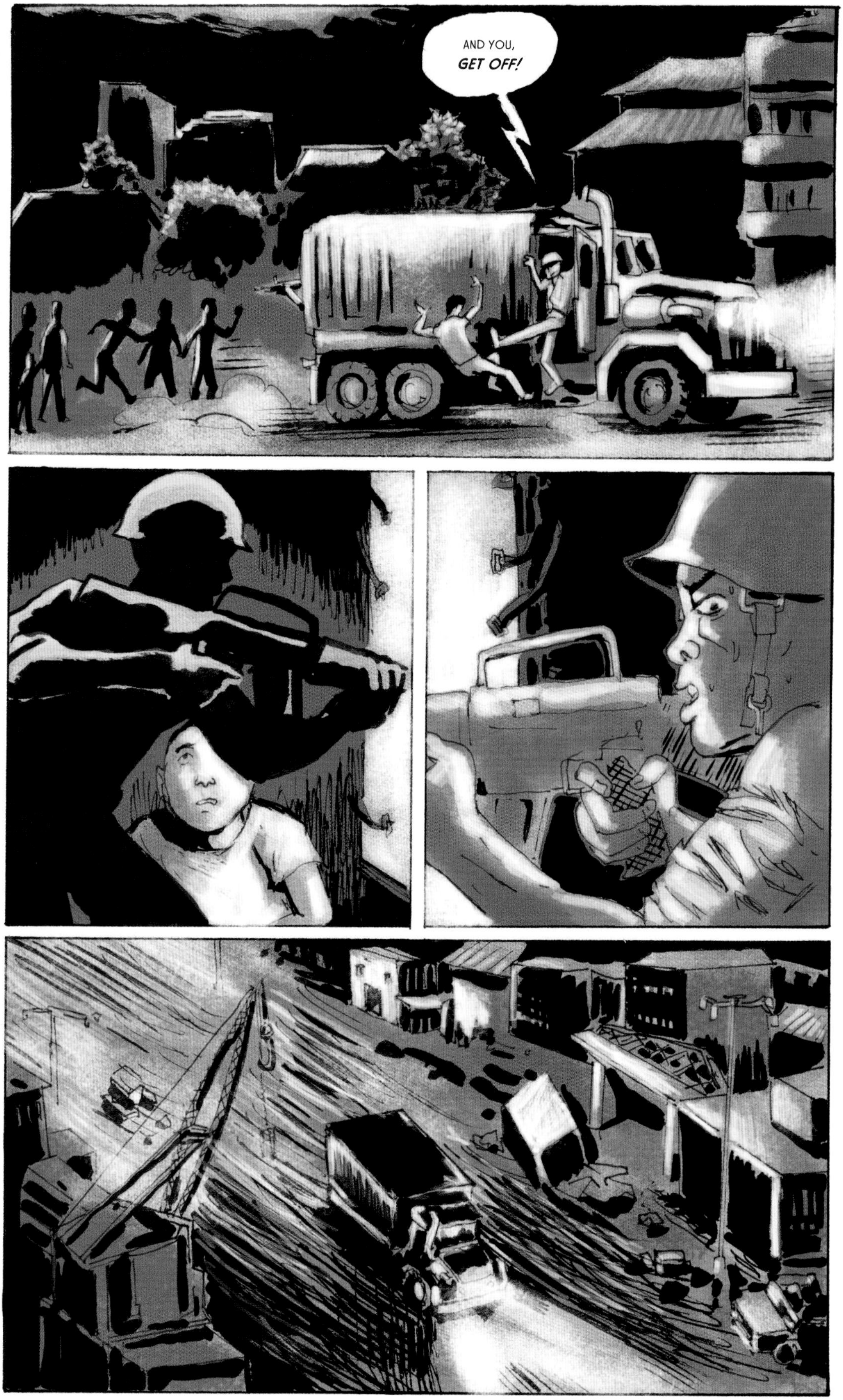
AND YOU,
GET OFF!

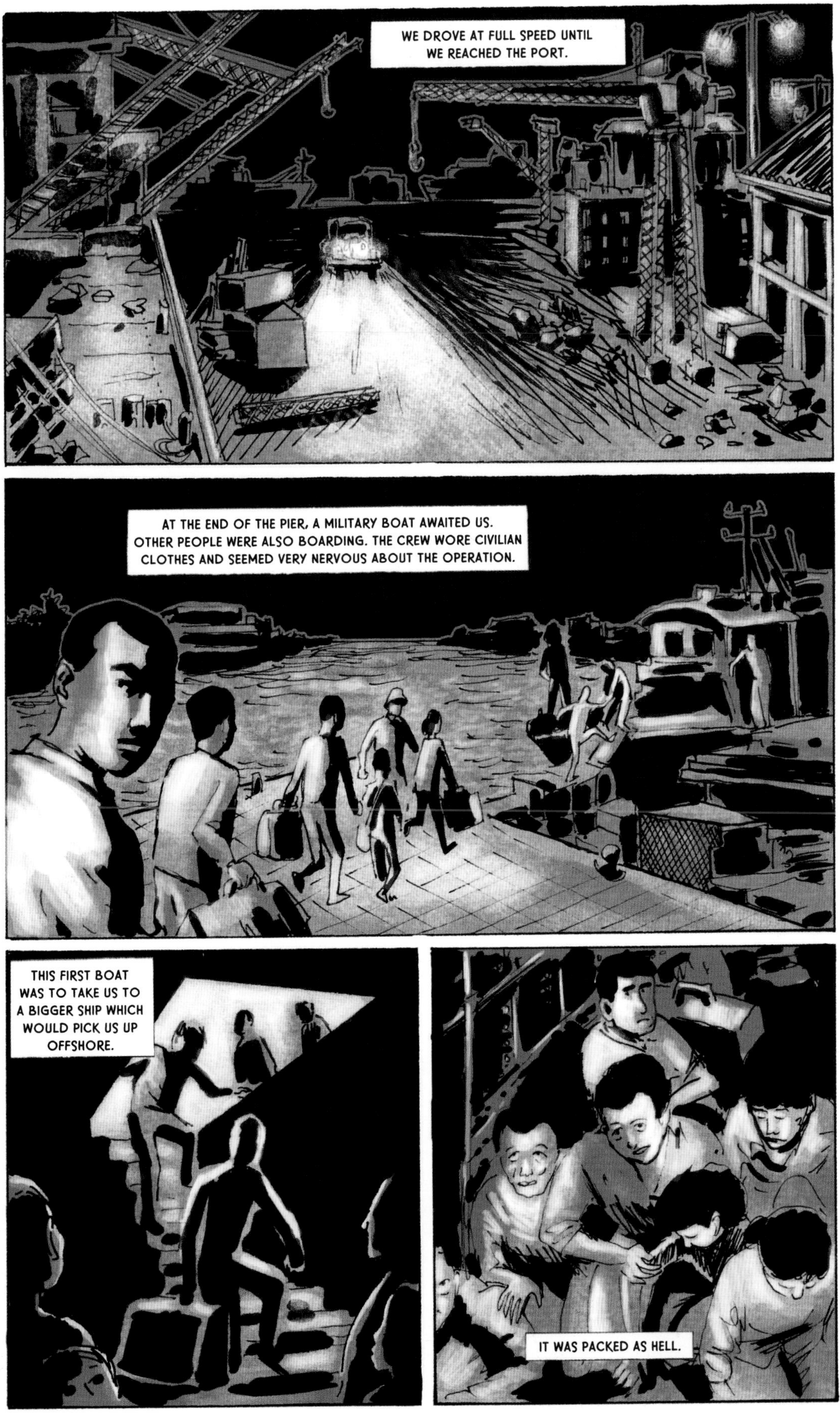
WE DROVE AT FULL SPEED UNTIL WE REACHED THE PORT.
AT THE END OF THE PIER, A MILITARY BOAT AWAITED US. OTHER PEOPLE WERE ALSO BOARDING. THE CREW WORE CIVILIAN CLOTHES AND SEEMED VERY NERVOUS ABOUT THE OPERATION.
THIS FIRST BOAT WAS TO TAKE US TO A BIGGER SHIP WHICH WOULD PICK US UP OFFSHORE.
IT WAS PACKED AS HELL.

WE WENT DOWN THE MEKONG AND REACHED THE OPEN SEA WITHOUT ANY TROUBLE.

BUT THE FOLLOWING DAY THERE WAS NO OTHER BOAT AT THE MEETING POINT.

IT'S BEEN OVER FIFTEEN HOURS NOW! WE CAN'T STAY HERE FOREVER -- IF THE COMMUNISTS FIND US THEY'LL OPEN FIRE WITHOUT WARNING.

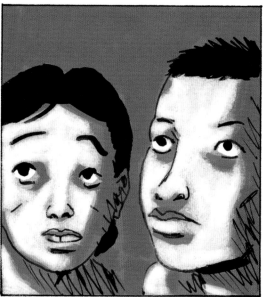

WE WERE TOLD THAT IT WAS TOO DANGEROUS TO REMAIN ON BOARD. THAT IT WAS TOO EASY TO SPOT, BUT THAT WE HAD TO NONETHELES WAIT FOR THE LARGER SHIP.

THE SOLUTION WAS TO TRANSFER US TO A KIND OF RESCUE RAFT, A FLOATING BARGE WHICH WOULD ORDINARILY BE USED FOR TRANSPORTING CARGO.

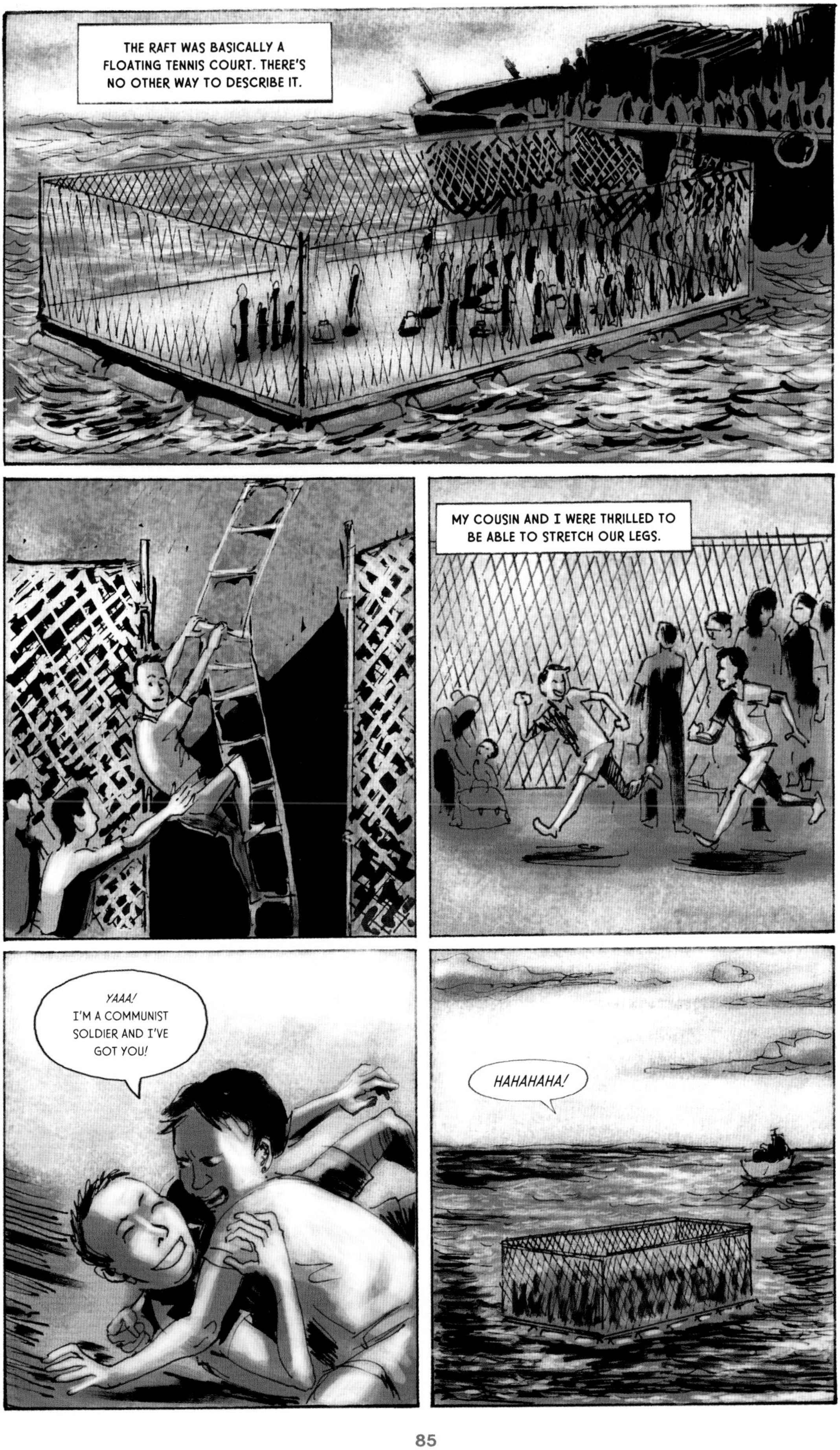
THE RAFT WAS BASICALLY A FLOATING TENNIS COURT. THERE'S NO OTHER WAY TO DESCRIBE IT.
MY COUSIN AND I WERE THRILLED TO BE ABLE TO STRETCH OUR LEGS.
YAAA! I'M A COMMUNIST SOLDIER AND I'VE GOT YOU!
HAHAHAHA!

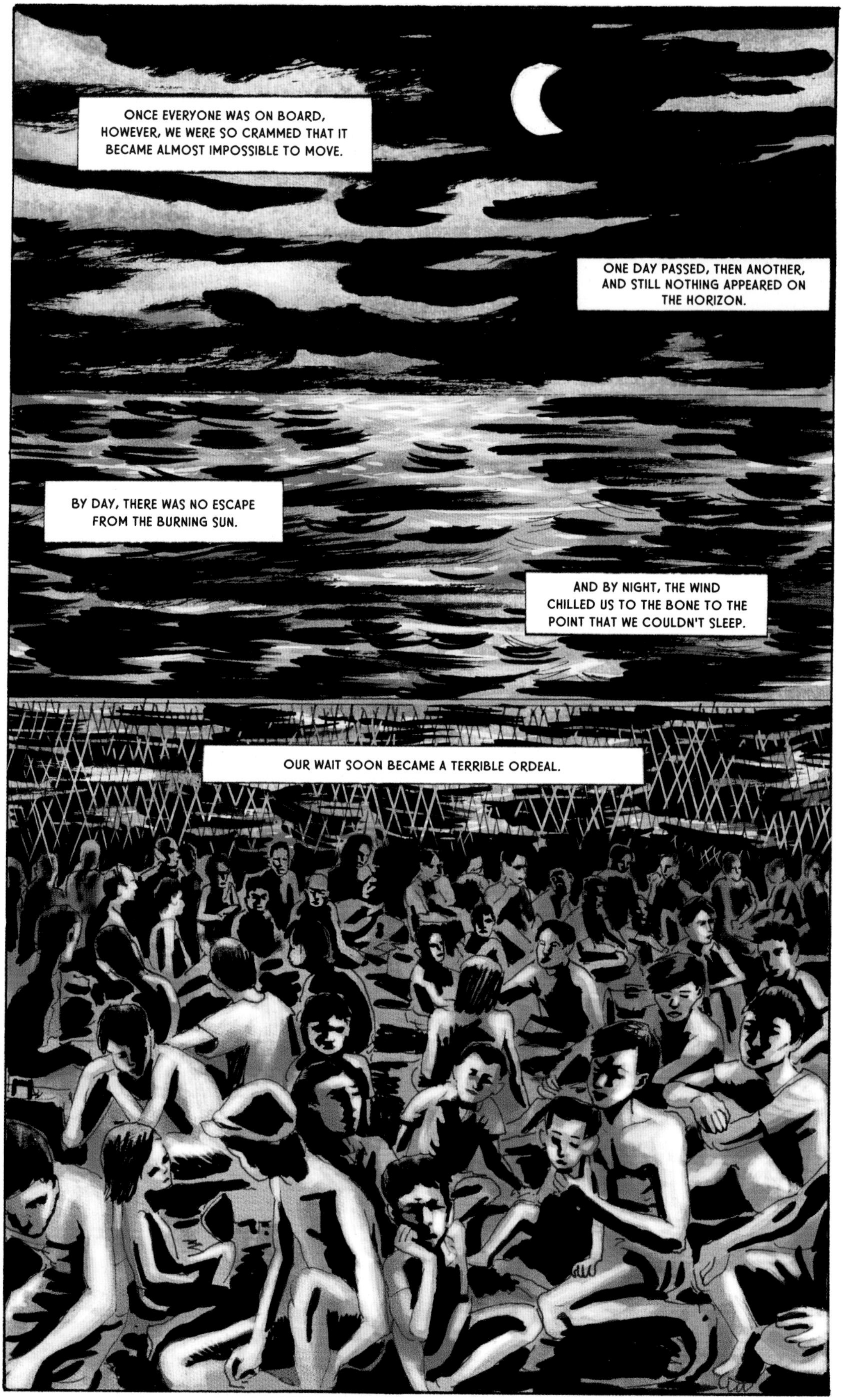
ONCE EVERYONE WAS ON BOARD, HOWEVER, WE WERE SO CRAMMED THAT IT BECAME ALMOST IMPOSSIBLE TO MOVE.
ONE DAY PASSED, THEN ANOTHER, AND STILL NOTHING APPEARED ON THE HORIZON.
BY DAY, THERE WAS NO ESCAPE FROM THE BURNING SUN.
AND BY NIGHT, THE WIND CHILLED US TO THE BONE TO THE POINT THAT WE COULDN'T SLEEP.
OUR WAIT SOON BECAME A TERRIBLE ORDEAL.

FOOD AND WATER EVENTUALLY RAN OUT.

WE COULDN'T EVEN MOVE. NO CHOICE BUT TO PEE OURSELVES.

SOME PEOPLE DIED FROM HEATSTROKE, BUT I WAS SO DISORIENTATED THAT I BARELY EVEN NOTICED. THE CRYING AND THE SCREAMING EVENTUALLY GREW FAINT AND DISTANT.

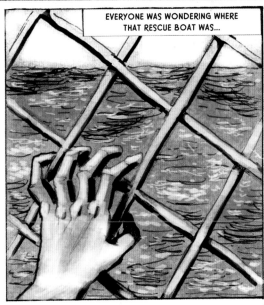

EVERYONE WAS WONDERING WHERE THAT RESCUE BOAT WAS...

WHAT WOULD HAPPEN IF THE COMMUNISTS FOUND US FIRST?

OR PIRATES?

HEY! OVER THERE!

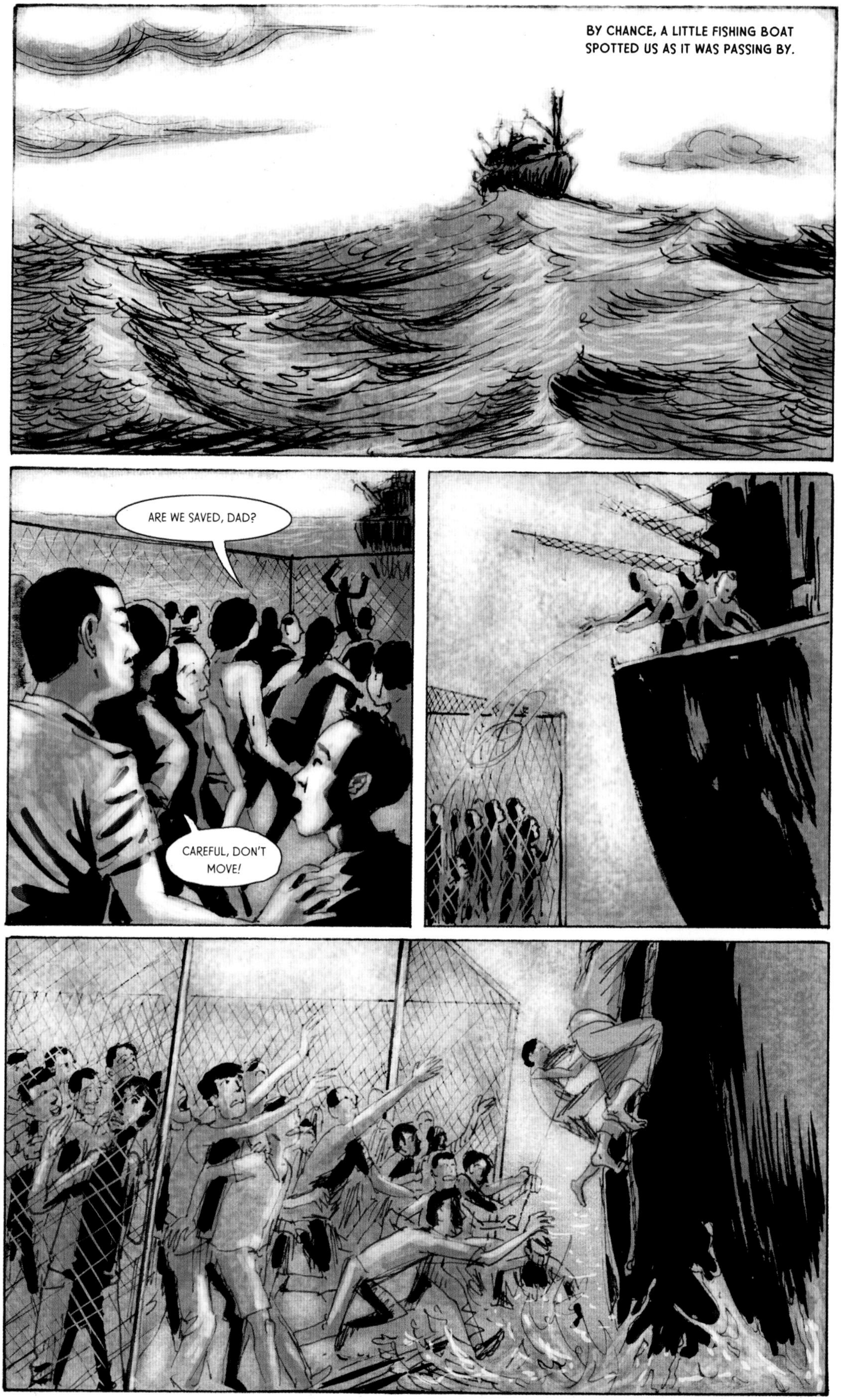
BY CHANCE, A LITTLE FISHING BOAT SPOTTED US AS IT WAS PASSING BY.
ARE WE SAVED, DAD?
CAREFUL, DON'T MOVE!

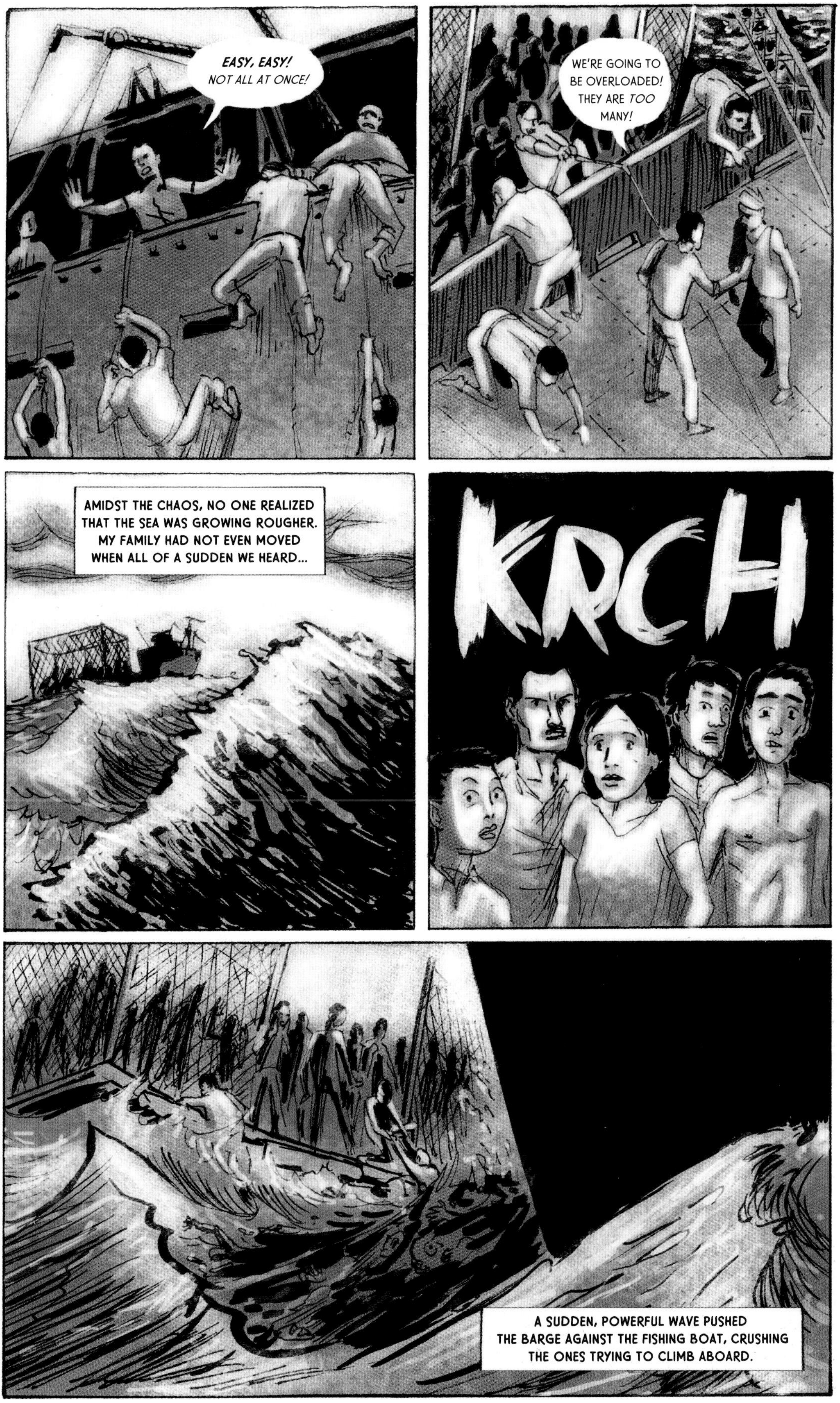
EASY, EASY!
NOT ALL AT ONCE!
WE'RE GOING TO BE OVERLOADED! THEY ARE TOO MANY!
AMIDST THE CHAOS, NO ONE REALIZED THAT THE SEA WAS GROWING ROUGHER. MY FAMILY HAD NOT EVEN MOVED WHEN ALL OF A SUDDEN WE HEARD...
KRCH
A SUDDEN, POWERFUL WAVE PUSHED THE BARGE AGAINST THE FISHING BOAT, CRUSHING THE ONES TRYING TO CLIMB ABOARD.

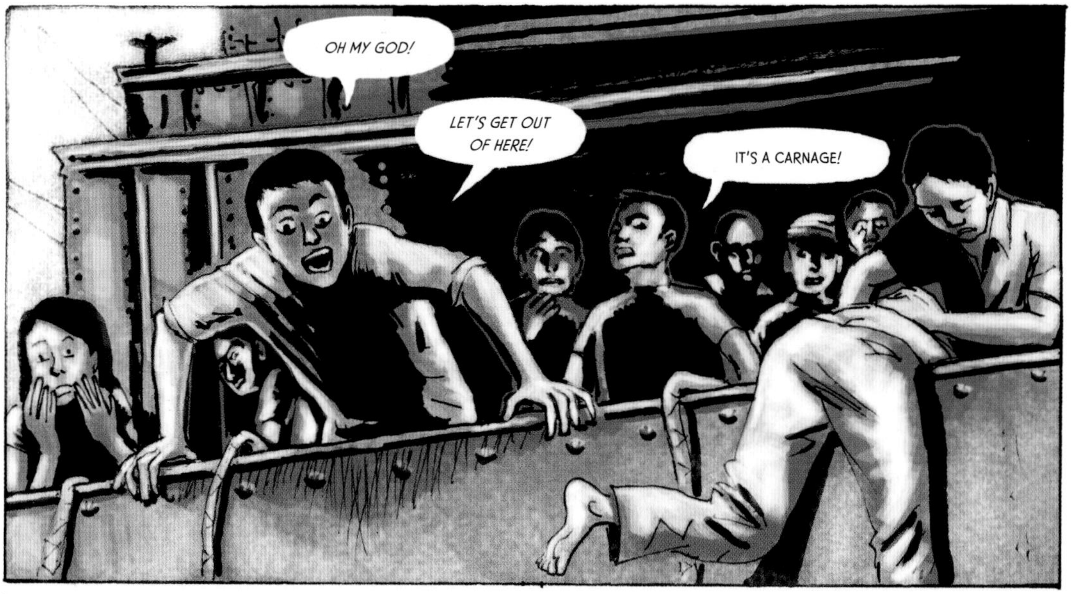
OH MY GOD!
LET'S GET OUT OF HERE!
IT'S A CARNAGE!

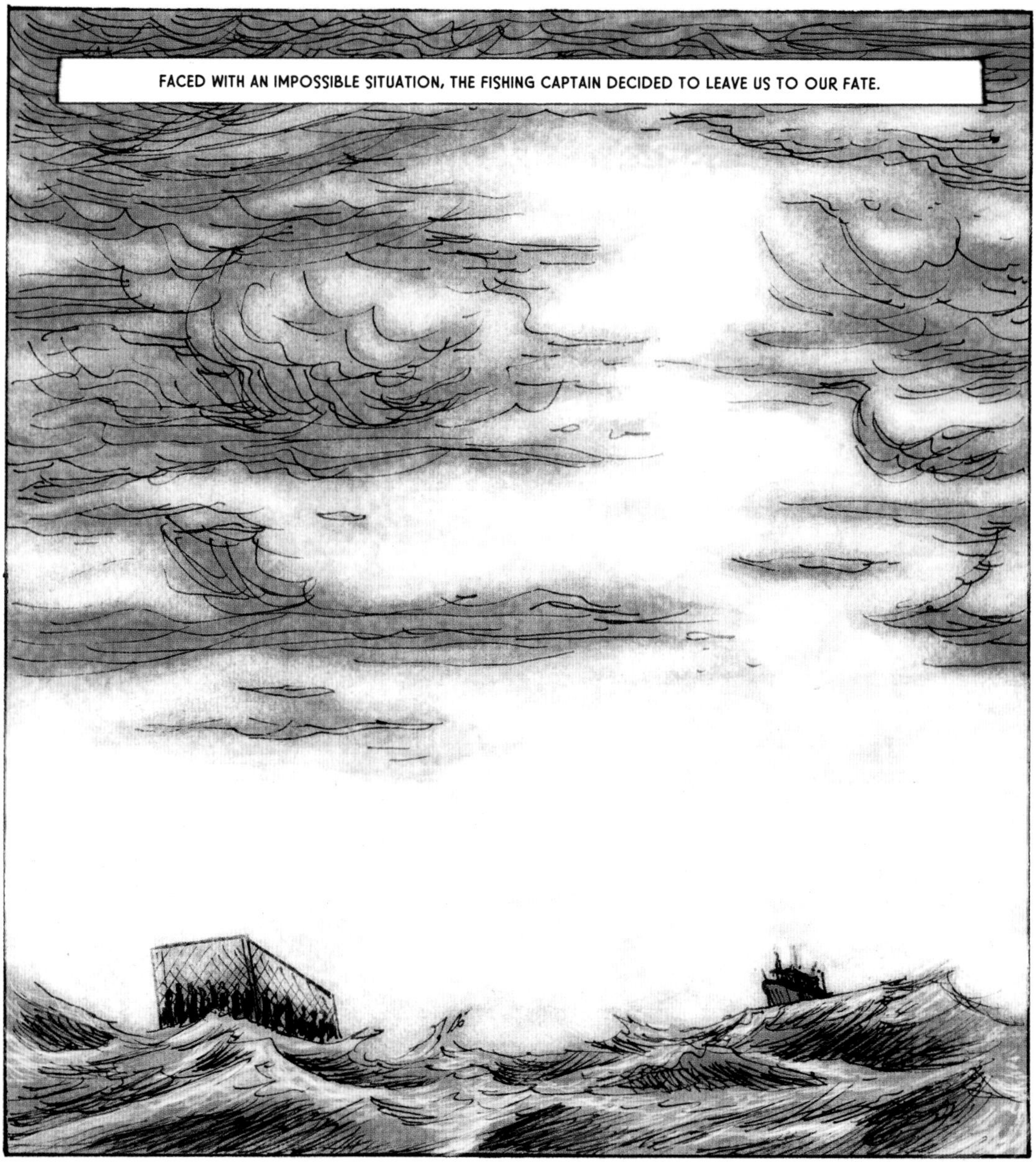
FACED WITH AN IMPOSSIBLE SITUATION, THE FISHING CAPTAIN DECIDED TO LEAVE US TO OUR FATE.

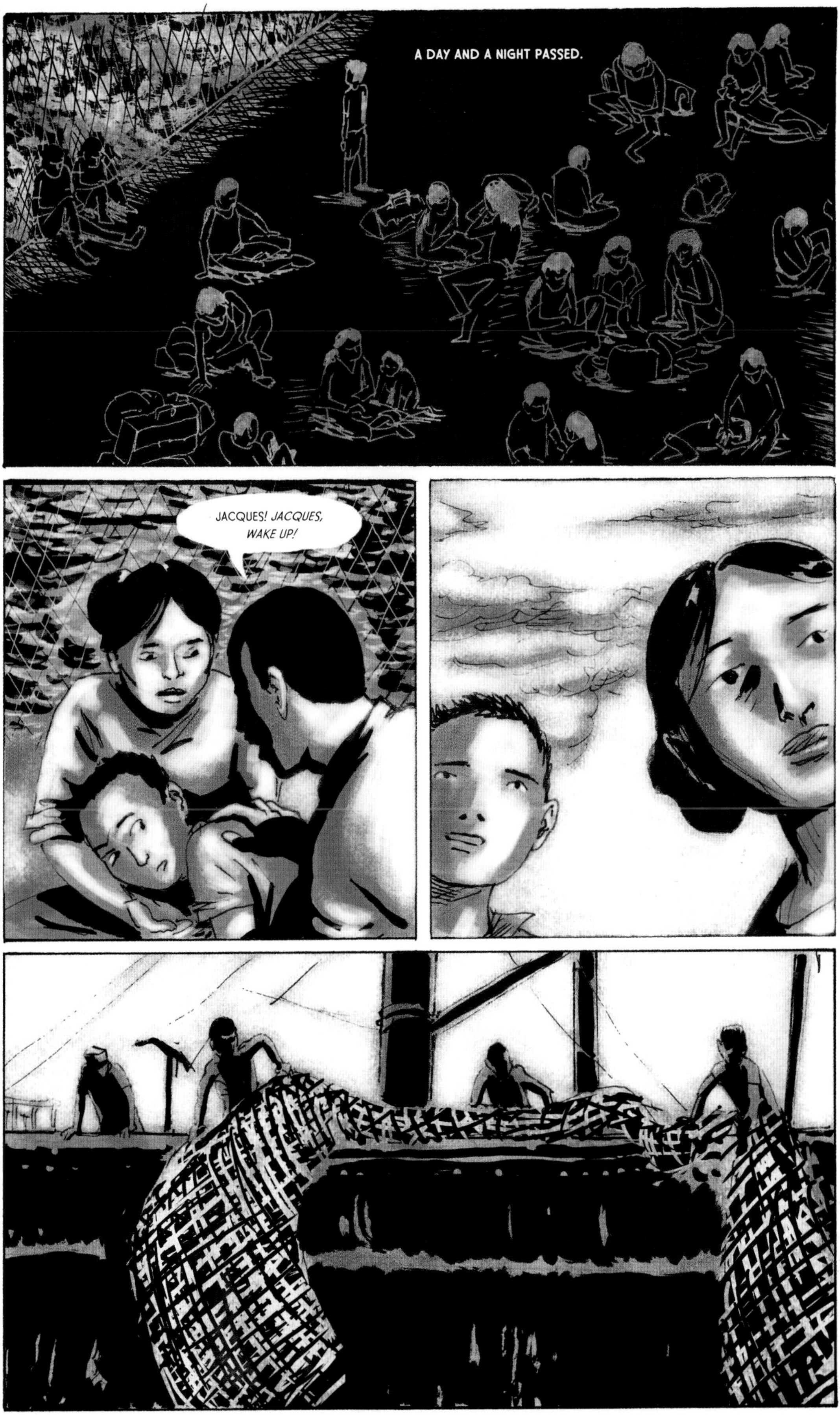
A DAY AND A NIGHT PASSED.
JACQUES! JACQUES, WAKE UP!

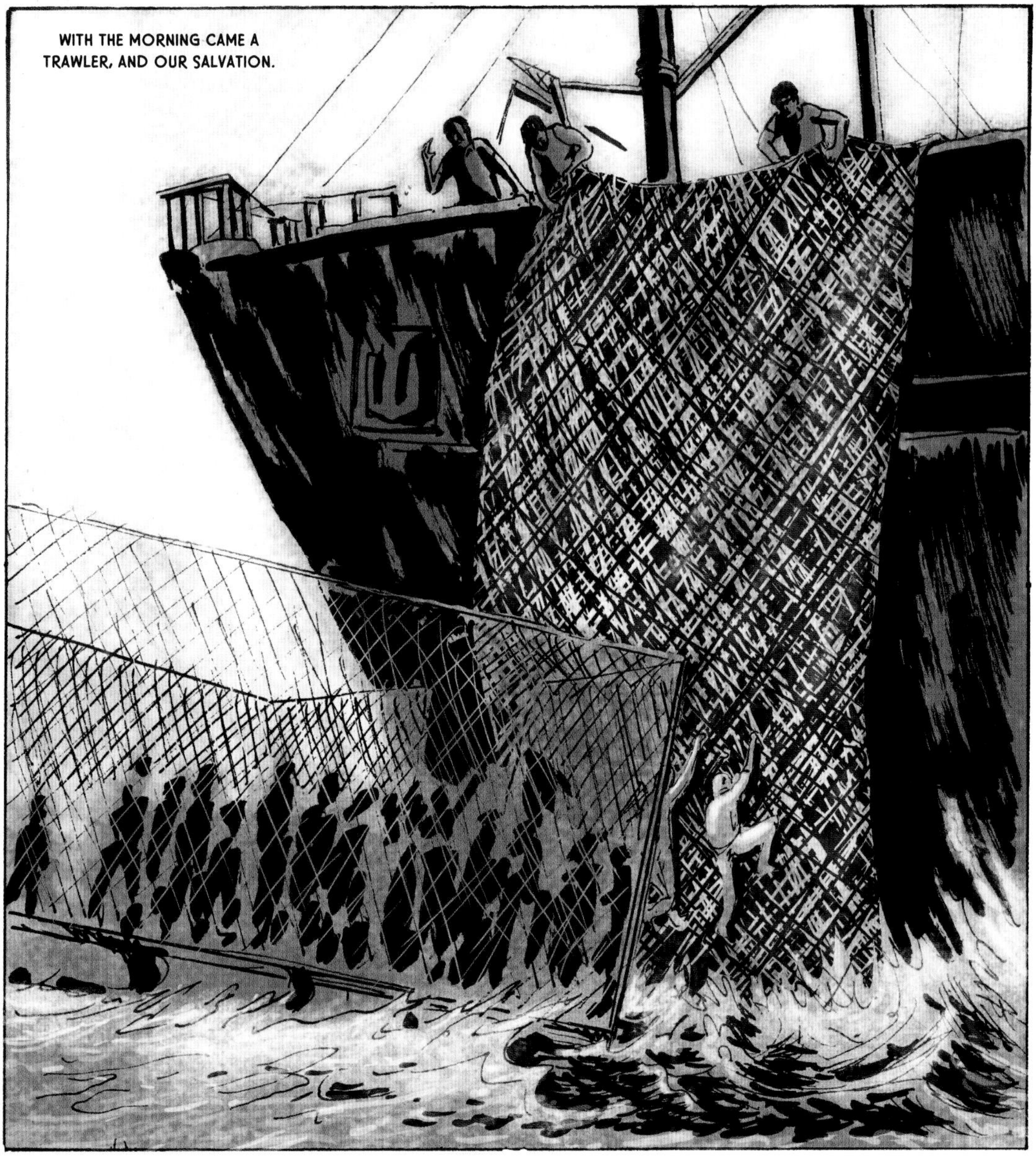
WITH THE MORNING CAME A TRAWLER, AND OUR SALVATION.

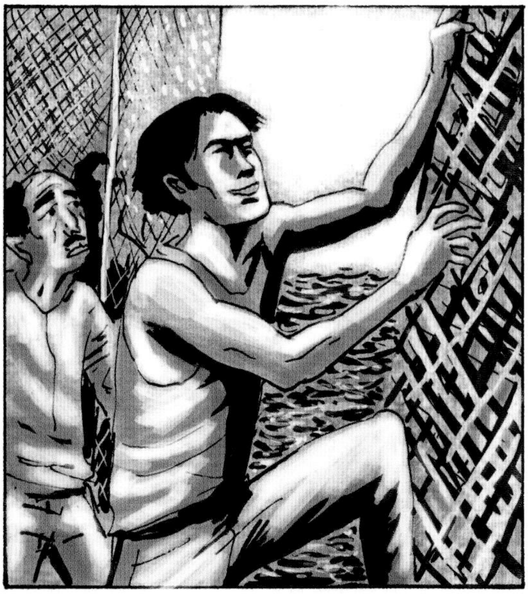

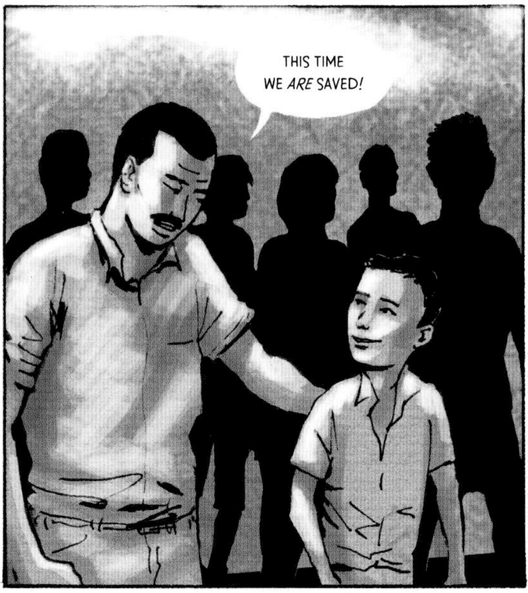
THIS TIME WE *ARE* SAVED!

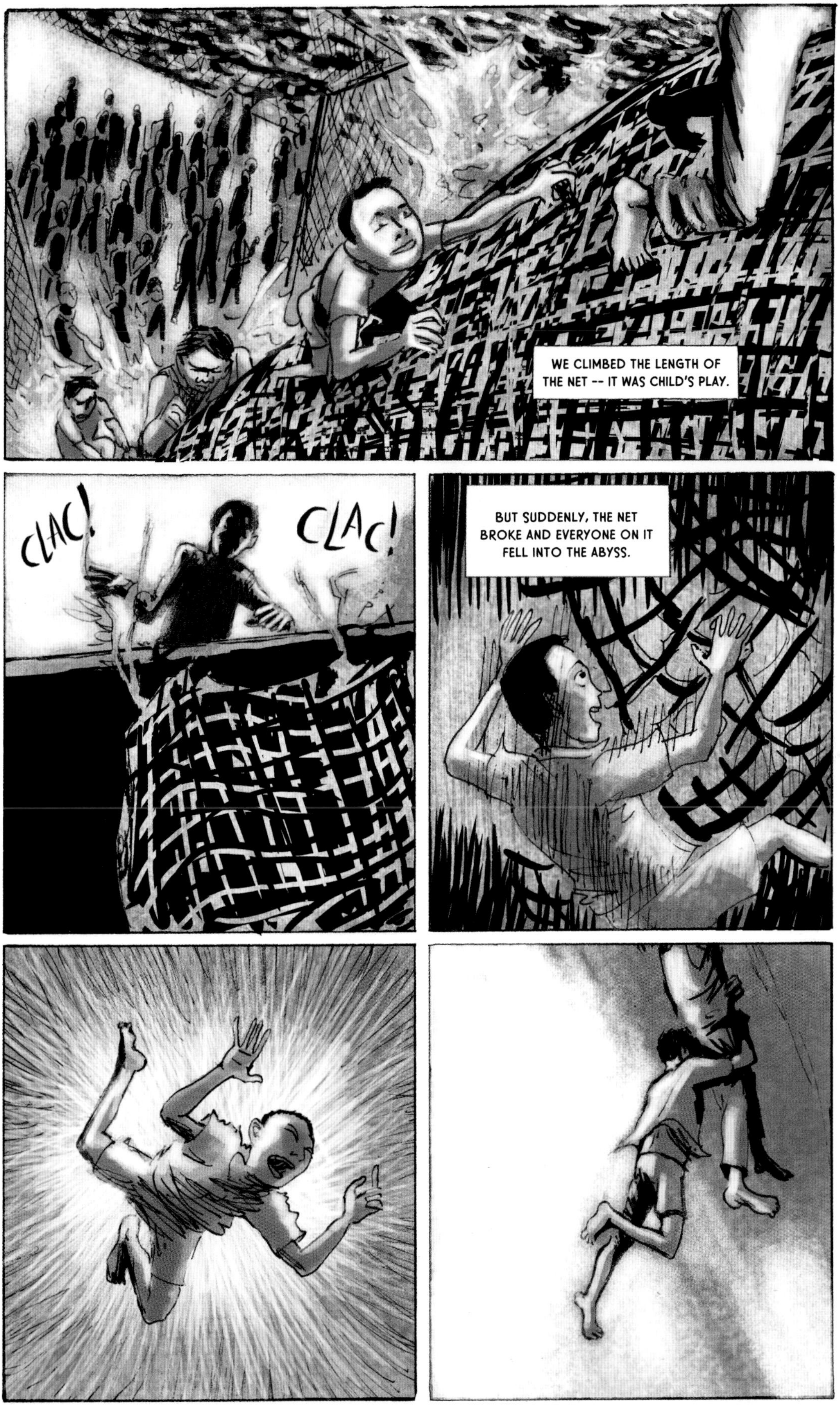
WE CLIMBED THE LENGTH OF THE NET -- IT WAS CHILD'S PLAY.
CLAC!
CLAC!
BUT SUDDENLY, THE NET BROKE AND EVERYONE ON IT FELL INTO THE ABYSS.

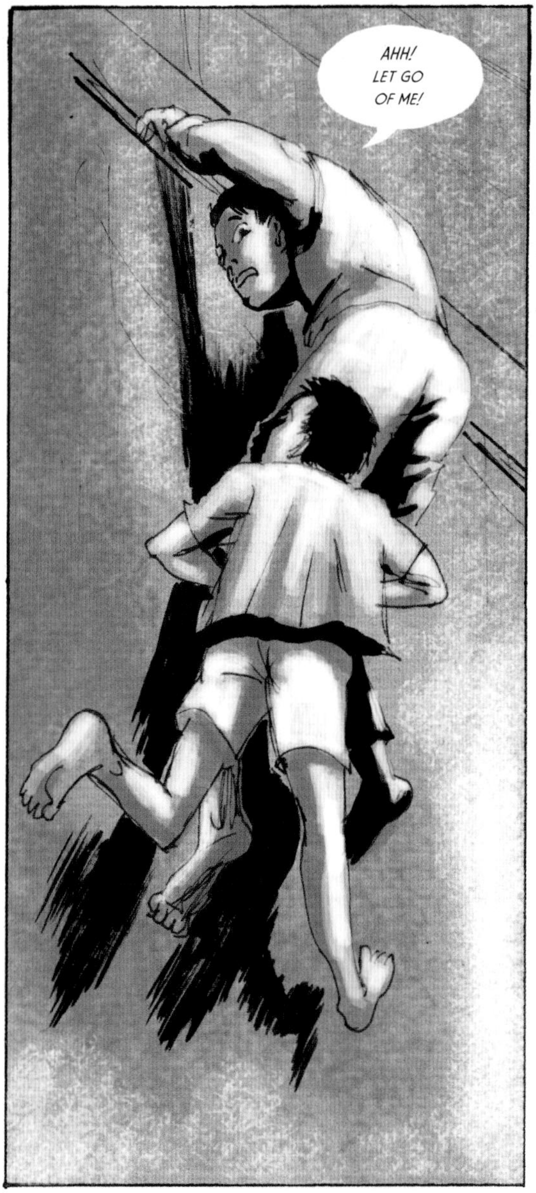
AHH! LET GO OF ME!
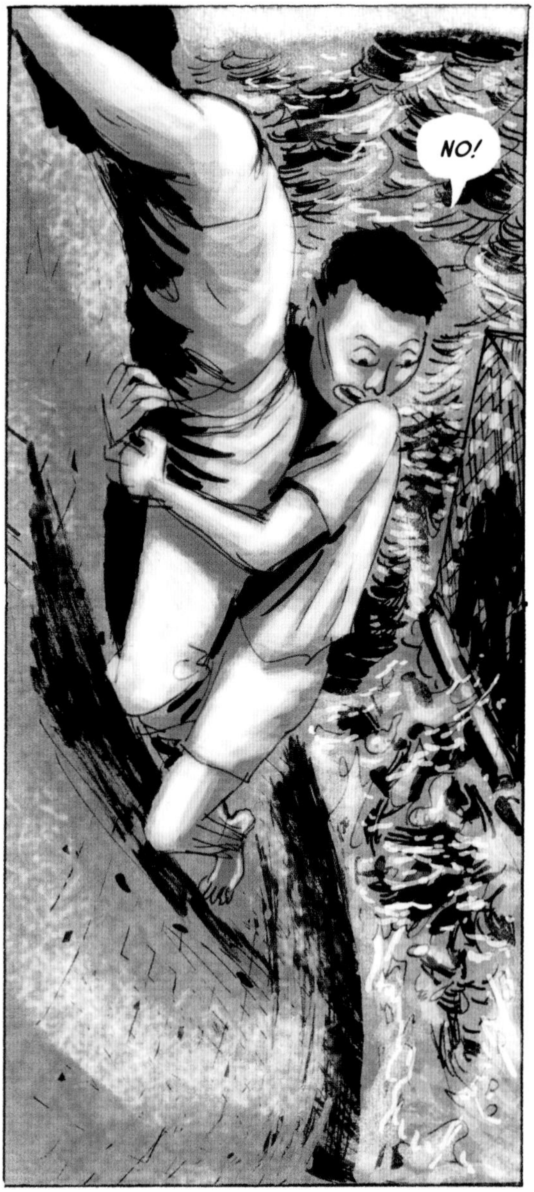
NO!
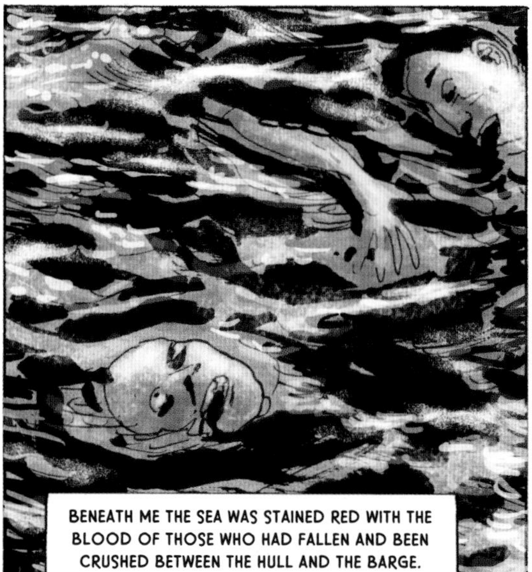
BENEATH ME THE SEA WAS STAINED RED WITH THE BLOOD OF THOSE WHO HAD FALLEN AND BEEN CRUSHED BETWEEN THE HULL AND THE BARGE.
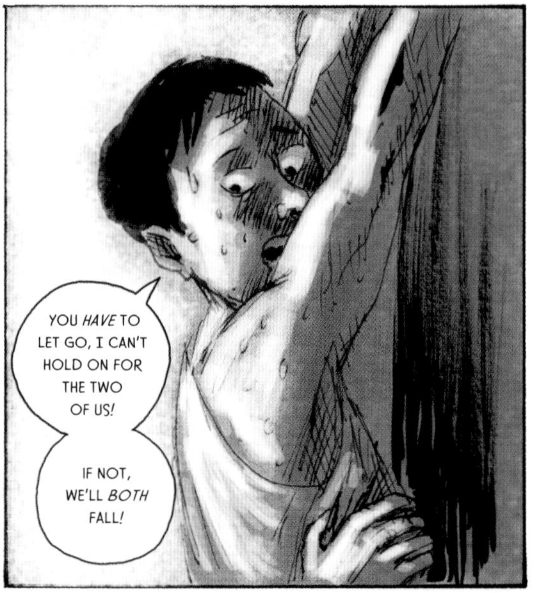
YOU *HAVE* TO LET GO, I CAN'T HOLD ON FOR THE TWO OF US!
IF NOT, WE'LL *BOTH* FALL!

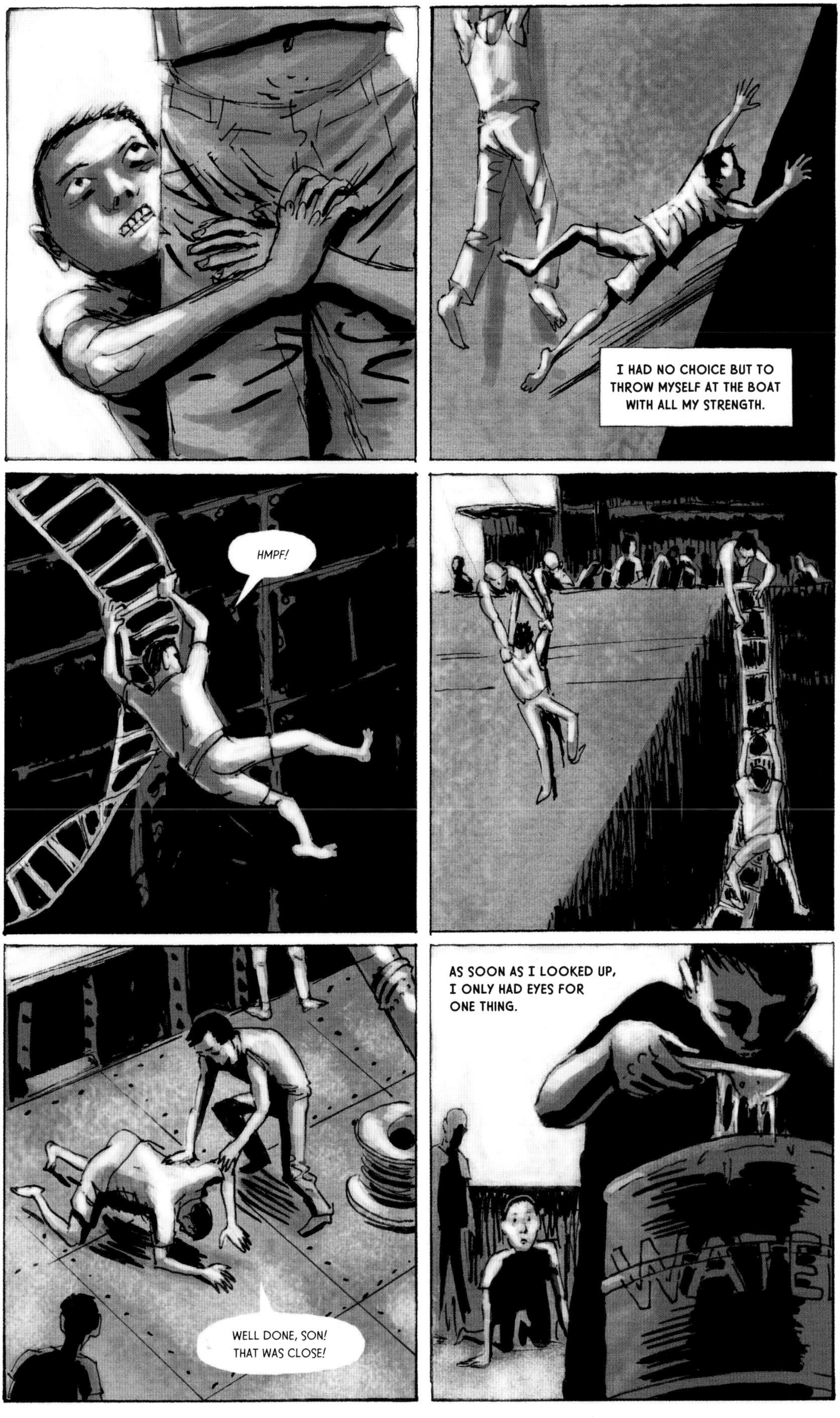
I HAD NO CHOICE BUT TO THROW MYSELF AT THE BOAT WITH ALL MY STRENGTH.
HMPF!
WELL DONE, SON! THAT WAS CLOSE!
AS SOON AS I LOOKED UP, I ONLY HAD EYES FOR ONE THING.
WATE

WATER!

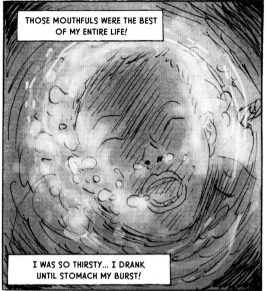

THOSE MOUTHFULS WERE THE BEST OF MY ENTIRE LIFE!

I WAS SO THIRSTY... I DRANK UNTIL STOMACH MY BURST!

SOON ENOUGH, EVERYONE MADE IT ON BOARD. THANKS TO MY FATHER'S MILITARY CONNECTIONS WE WERE ABLE TO MOVE TO CALIFORNIA. BUT HE DIDN'T REALLY LIKE THE U.S., SO IN THE END, MY FAMILY CAME TO SETTLE IN FRANCE!

AS FOR ME... IN MY HEART, I'VE ALWAYS WANTED TO GO BACK AND LIVE IN MY HOME COUNTRY. EVEN AFTER ALL THIS TIME!

BUT I'VE MADE MY LIFE HERE. MY CHILDREN ARE FRENCH...

... AND VIETNAM HAS CHANGED A LOT.

IT'S NOT THE COUNTRY I KNEW AS A CHILD...

AND WHILE I STILL LOVE IT, I KNOW I WON'T EVER LIVE THERE AGAIN.

Sainte-Livrade-sur-Lot

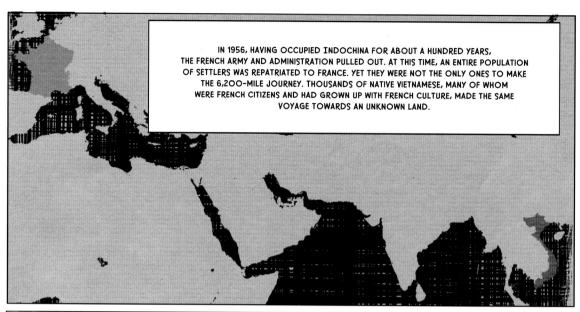

IN 1956, HAVING OCCUPIED INDOCHINA FOR ABOUT A HUNDRED YEARS, THE FRENCH ARMY AND ADMINISTRATION PULLED OUT. AT THIS TIME, AN ENTIRE POPULATION OF SETTLERS WAS REPATRIATED TO FRANCE. YET THEY WERE NOT THE ONLY ONES TO MAKE THE 6,200-MILE JOURNEY. THOUSANDS OF NATIVE VIETNAMESE, MANY OF WHOM WERE FRENCH CITIZENS AND HAD GROWN UP WITH FRENCH CULTURE, MADE THE SAME VOYAGE TOWARDS AN UNKNOWN LAND.

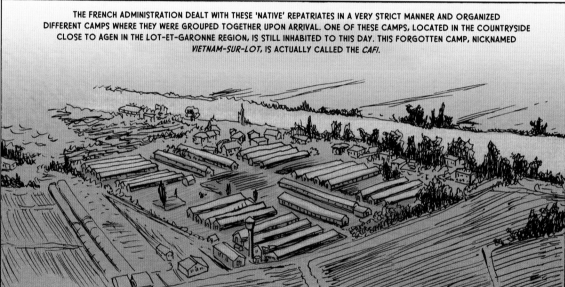

THE FRENCH ADMINISTRATION DEALT WITH THESE 'NATIVE' REPATRIATES IN A VERY STRICT MANNER AND ORGANIZED DIFFERENT CAMPS WHERE THEY WERE GROUPED TOGETHER UPON ARRIVAL. ONE OF THESE CAMPS, LOCATED IN THE COUNTRYSIDE CLOSE TO AGEN IN THE LOT-ET-GARONNE REGION, IS STILL INHABITED TO THIS DAY. THIS FORGOTTEN CAMP, NICKNAMED *VIETNAM-SUR-LOT*, IS ACTUALLY CALLED THE *CAFI*.

I HAVE SO MANY MEMORIES OF THIS PLACE. IT WAS MY WHOLE YOUTH.

THE CAFI HAS NOW BEEN HOME TO THREE GENERATIONS.

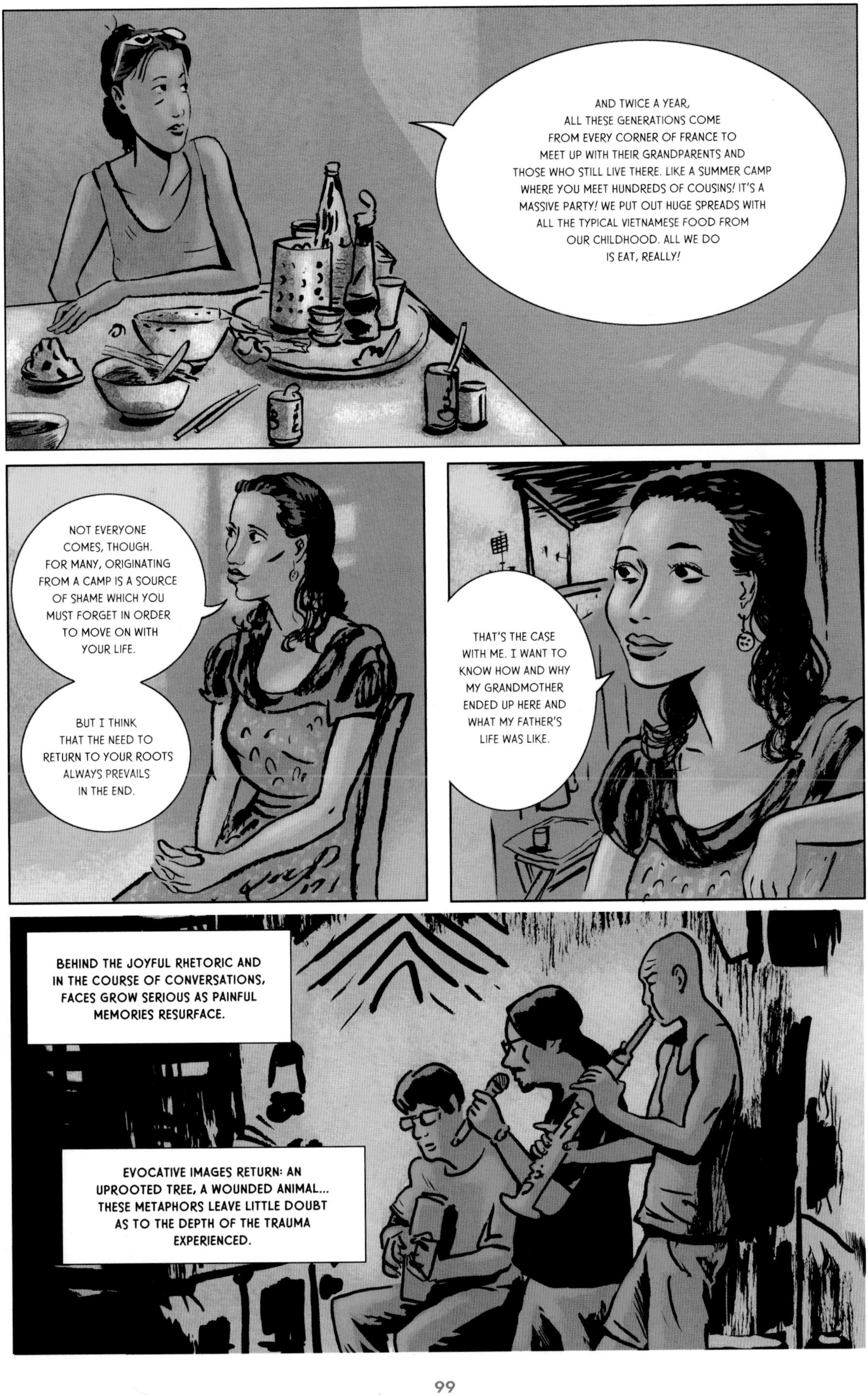
AND TWICE A YEAR, ALL THESE GENERATIONS COME FROM EVERY CORNER OF FRANCE TO MEET UP WITH THEIR GRANDPARENTS AND THOSE WHO STILL LIVE THERE. LIKE A SUMMER CAMP WHERE YOU MEET HUNDREDS OF COUSINS! IT'S A MASSIVE PARTY! WE PUT OUT HUGE SPREADS WITH ALL THE TYPICAL VIETNAMESE FOOD FROM OUR CHILDHOOD. ALL WE DO IS EAT, REALLY!
NOT EVERYONE COMES, THOUGH. FOR MANY, ORIGINATING FROM A CAMP IS A SOURCE OF SHAME WHICH YOU MUST FORGET IN ORDER TO MOVE ON WITH YOUR LIFE.
BUT I THINK THAT THE NEED TO RETURN TO YOUR ROOTS ALWAYS PREVAILS IN THE END.
THAT'S THE CASE WITH ME. I WANT TO KNOW HOW AND WHY MY GRANDMOTHER ENDED UP HERE AND WHAT MY FATHER'S LIFE WAS LIKE.
BEHIND THE JOYFUL RHETORIC AND IN THE COURSE OF CONVERSATIONS, FACES GROW SERIOUS AS PAINFUL MEMORIES RESURFACE.
EVOCATIVE IMAGES RETURN: AN UPROOTED TREE, A WOUNDED ANIMAL... THESE METAPHORS LEAVE LITTLE DOUBT AS TO THE DEPTH OF THE TRAUMA EXPERIENCED.

THE CAZES FAMILY IS ONE OF THE CAMP'S MOST PROMINENT ONES. MADAME CAZES, AN ELDERLY LADY, AND HER DAUGHTERS, ARE BUSY AT THE STOVE IN PREPARATION FOR THE SUMMER FESTIVITIES. THEY'LL COOK SEVERAL HUNDREDS OF MEALS OVER JUST A FEW DAYS.

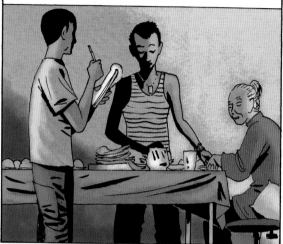

EVERY YEAR, ON AUGUST 15TH, THE LARGEST CAFI GATHERING TAKES PLACE. THE FESTIVITIES INCLUDE KARAOKE, CONCERTS, BUFFETS, AND PRAYER MEETINGS.

MADAME CAZES IS A PRIESTESS. SHE ENSURES THE PASSING-DOWN OF BÀ-ĐÔNG WORSHIP, ORIGINATING FROM VIETNAM, LINKED TO BUDDHISM AND TO ANCESTRAL TRADITIONS.

TELL ME -- YOU'RE A HANDSOME BOY, ARE YOU MARRIED? DO YOU HAVE ANY CHILDREN?

UH NO... AND NO I DON'T.

HERE, THE CULTURE AND CUSTOMS ARE RATHER DIFFERENT.

WHY DO YOU ASK?

WELL, WE COULD FIND SOMEONE TO YOUR LIKING IF YOU WANT.

HOW DOES THAT SOUND?

AH NO, NO THANK YOU. IT'S VERY KIND OF YOU, BUT I'LL TRY AND MAKE DO ON MY OWN!

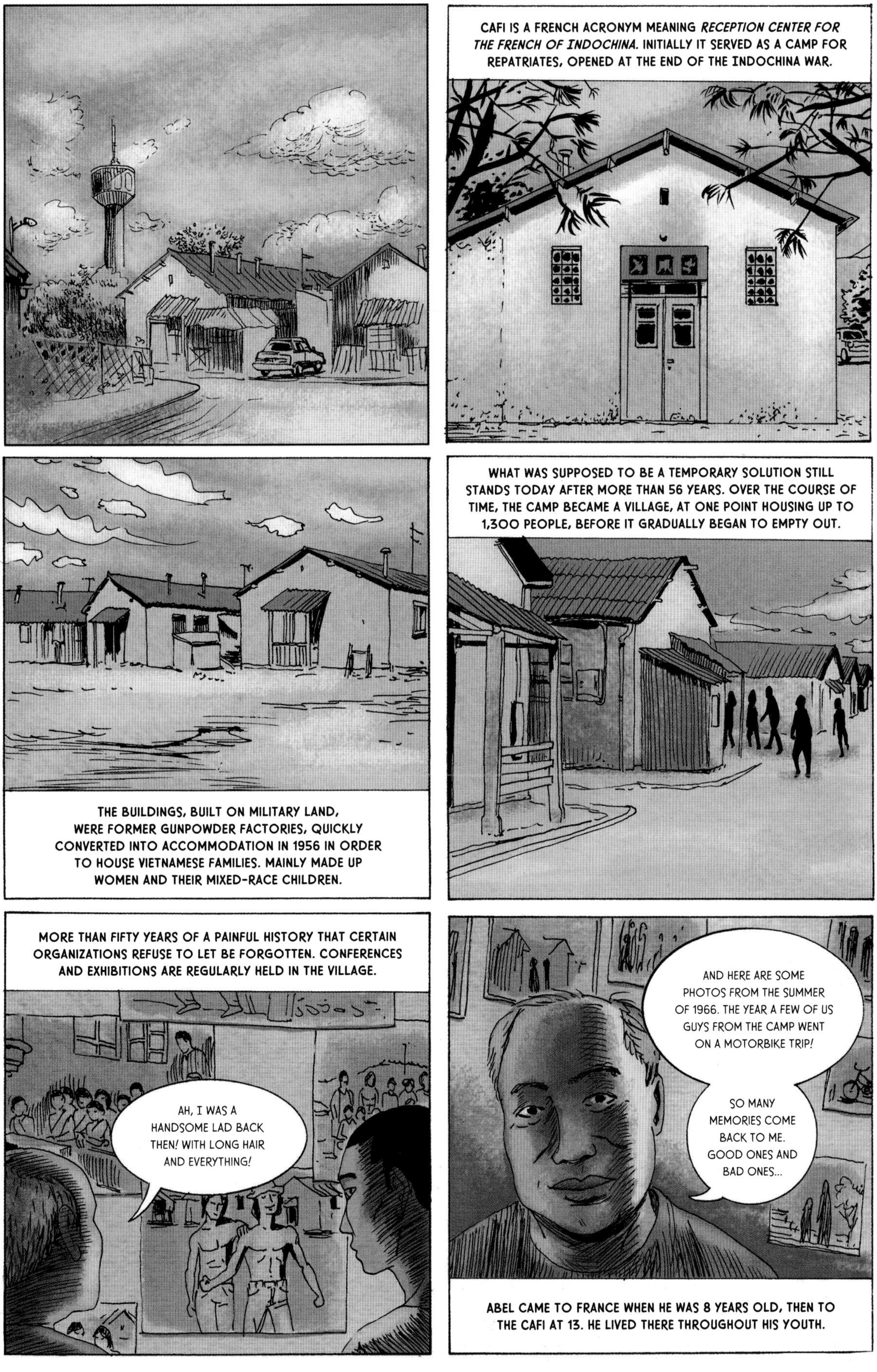
CAFI IS A FRENCH ACRONYM MEANING *RECEPTION CENTER FOR THE FRENCH OF INDOCHINA*. INITIALLY IT SERVED AS A CAMP FOR REPATRIATES, OPENED AT THE END OF THE INDOCHINA WAR.
THE BUILDINGS, BUILT ON MILITARY LAND, WERE FORMER GUNPOWDER FACTORIES, QUICKLY CONVERTED INTO ACCOMMODATION IN 1956 IN ORDER TO HOUSE VIETNAMESE FAMILIES. MAINLY MADE UP WOMEN AND THEIR MIXED-RACE CHILDREN.
WHAT WAS SUPPOSED TO BE A TEMPORARY SOLUTION STILL STANDS TODAY AFTER MORE THAN 56 YEARS. OVER THE COURSE OF TIME, THE CAMP BECAME A VILLAGE, AT ONE POINT HOUSING UP TO 1,300 PEOPLE, BEFORE IT GRADUALLY BEGAN TO EMPTY OUT.
MORE THAN FIFTY YEARS OF A PAINFUL HISTORY THAT CERTAIN ORGANIZATIONS REFUSE TO LET BE FORGOTTEN. CONFERENCES AND EXHIBITIONS ARE REGULARLY HELD IN THE VILLAGE.
AH, I WAS A HANDSOME LAD BACK THEN! WITH LONG HAIR AND EVERYTHING!
AND HERE ARE SOME PHOTOS FROM THE SUMMER OF 1966. THE YEAR A FEW OF US GUYS FROM THE CAMP WENT ON A MOTORBIKE TRIP!
SO MANY MEMORIES COME BACK TO ME. GOOD ONES AND BAD ONES...
ABEL CAME TO FRANCE WHEN HE WAS 8 YEARS OLD, THEN TO THE CAFI AT 13. HE LIVED THERE THROUGHOUT HIS YOUTH.

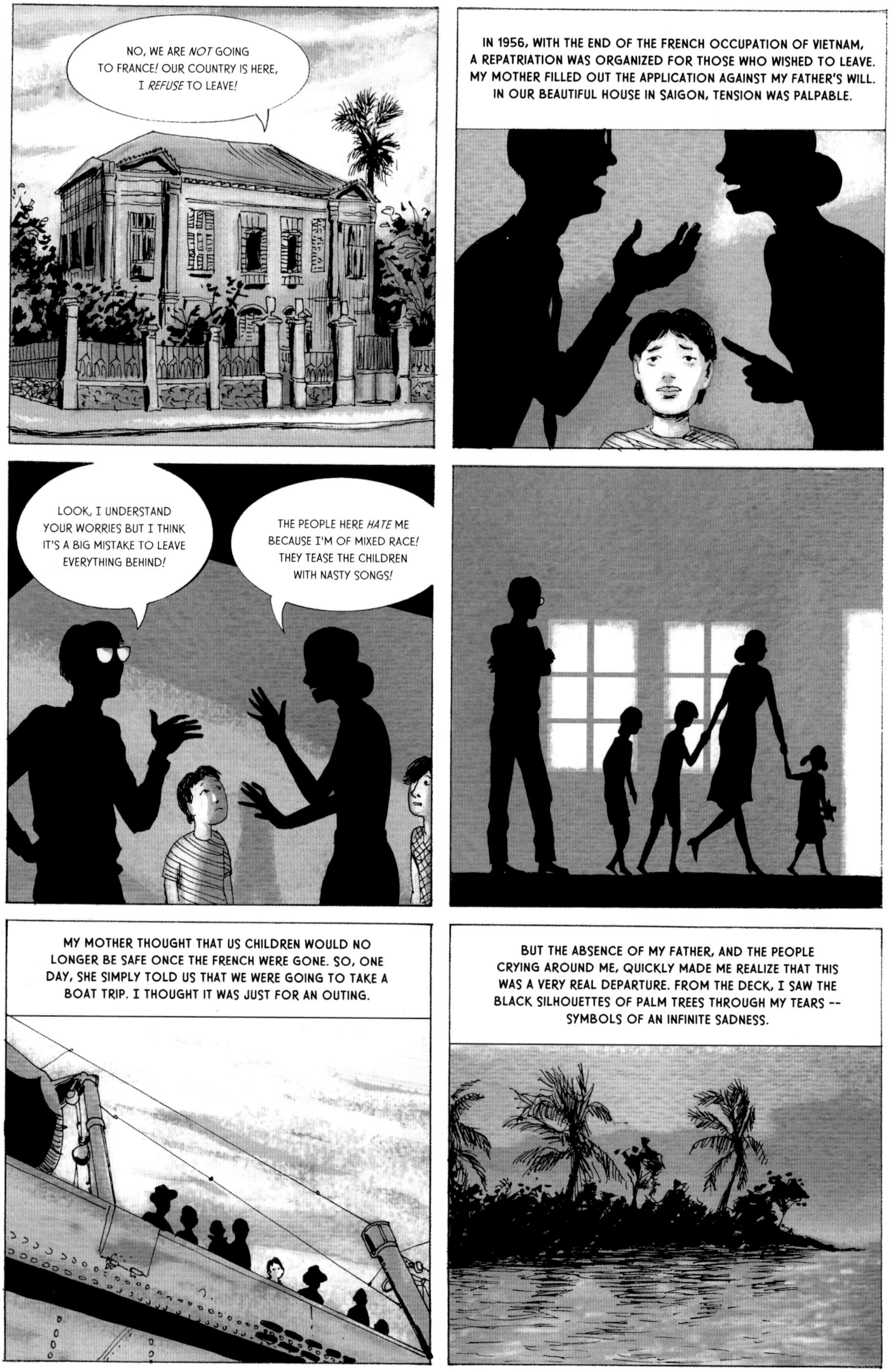
NO, WE ARE NOT GOING TO FRANCE! OUR COUNTRY IS HERE, I REFUSE TO LEAVE!
IN 1956, WITH THE END OF THE FRENCH OCCUPATION OF VIETNAM, A REPATRIATION WAS ORGANIZED FOR THOSE WHO WISHED TO LEAVE. MY MOTHER FILLED OUT THE APPLICATION AGAINST MY FATHER'S WILL. IN OUR BEAUTIFUL HOUSE IN SAIGON, TENSION WAS PALPABLE.
LOOK, I UNDERSTAND YOUR WORRIES BUT I THINK IT'S A BIG MISTAKE TO LEAVE EVERYTHING BEHIND!
THE PEOPLE HERE HATE ME BECAUSE I'M OF MIXED RACE! THEY TEASE THE CHILDREN WITH NASTY SONGS!
MY MOTHER THOUGHT THAT US CHILDREN WOULD NO LONGER BE SAFE ONCE THE FRENCH WERE GONE. SO, ONE DAY, SHE SIMPLY TOLD US THAT WE WERE GOING TO TAKE A BOAT TRIP. I THOUGHT IT WAS JUST FOR AN OUTING.
BUT THE ABSENCE OF MY FATHER, AND THE PEOPLE CRYING AROUND ME, QUICKLY MADE ME REALIZE THAT THIS WAS A VERY REAL DEPARTURE. FROM THE DECK, I SAW THE BLACK SILHOUETTES OF PALM TREES THROUGH MY TEARS -- SYMBOLS OF AN INFINITE SADNESS.

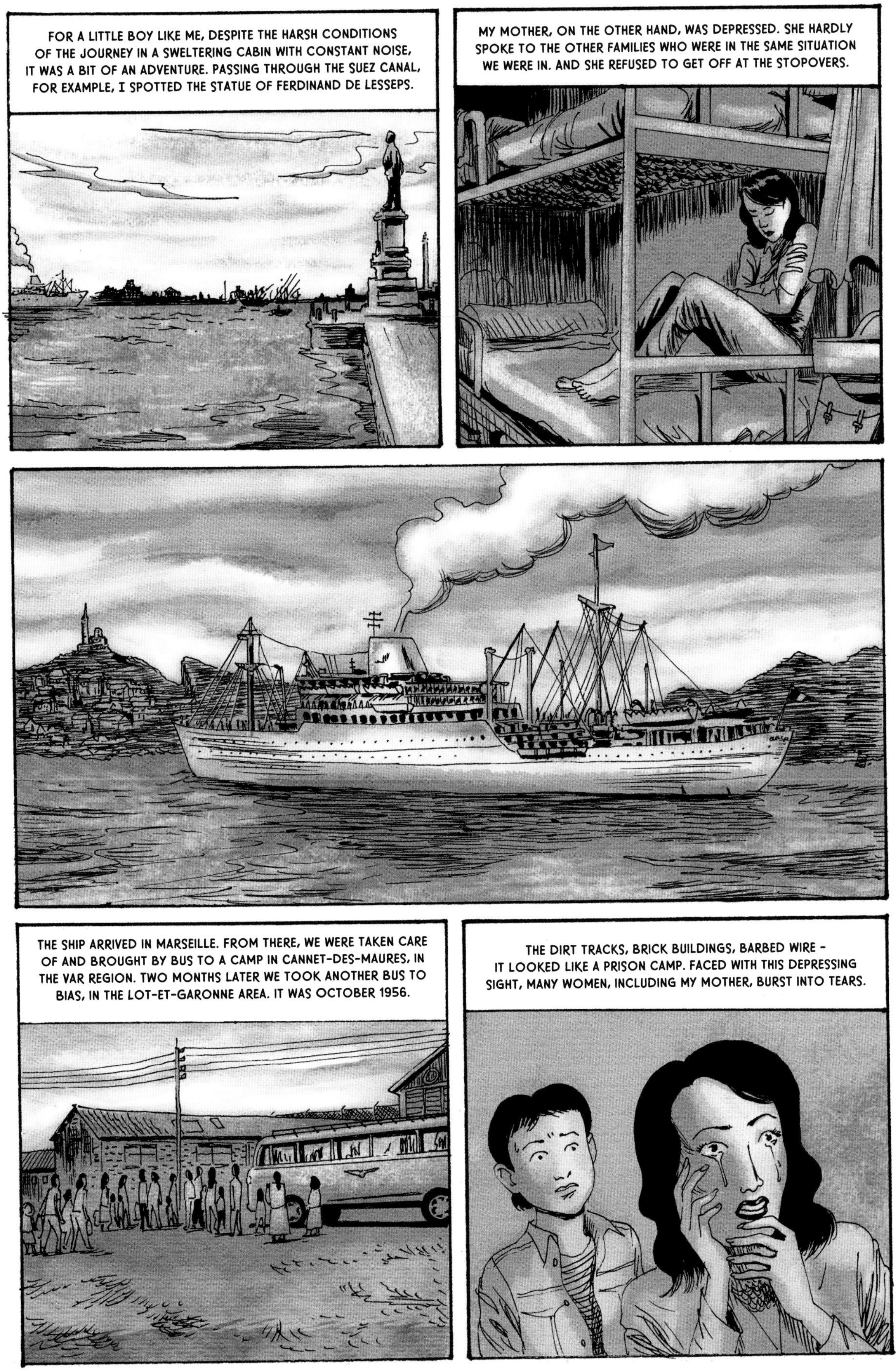
FOR A LITTLE BOY LIKE ME, DESPITE THE HARSH CONDITIONS OF THE JOURNEY IN A SWELTERING CABIN WITH CONSTANT NOISE, IT WAS A BIT OF AN ADVENTURE. PASSING THROUGH THE SUEZ CANAL, FOR EXAMPLE, I SPOTTED THE STATUE OF FERDINAND DE LESSEPS.
MY MOTHER, ON THE OTHER HAND, WAS DEPRESSED. SHE HARDLY SPOKE TO THE OTHER FAMILIES WHO WERE IN THE SAME SITUATION WE WERE IN. AND SHE REFUSED TO GET OFF AT THE STOPOVERS.
THE SHIP ARRIVED IN MARSEILLE. FROM THERE, WE WERE TAKEN CARE OF AND BROUGHT BY BUS TO A CAMP IN CANNET-DES-MAURES, IN THE VAR REGION. TWO MONTHS LATER WE TOOK ANOTHER BUS TO BIAS, IN THE LOT-ET-GARONNE AREA. IT WAS OCTOBER 1956.
THE DIRT TRACKS, BRICK BUILDINGS, BARBED WIRE - IT LOOKED LIKE A PRISON CAMP. FACED WITH THIS DEPRESSING SIGHT, MANY WOMEN, INCLUDING MY MOTHER, BURST INTO TEARS.

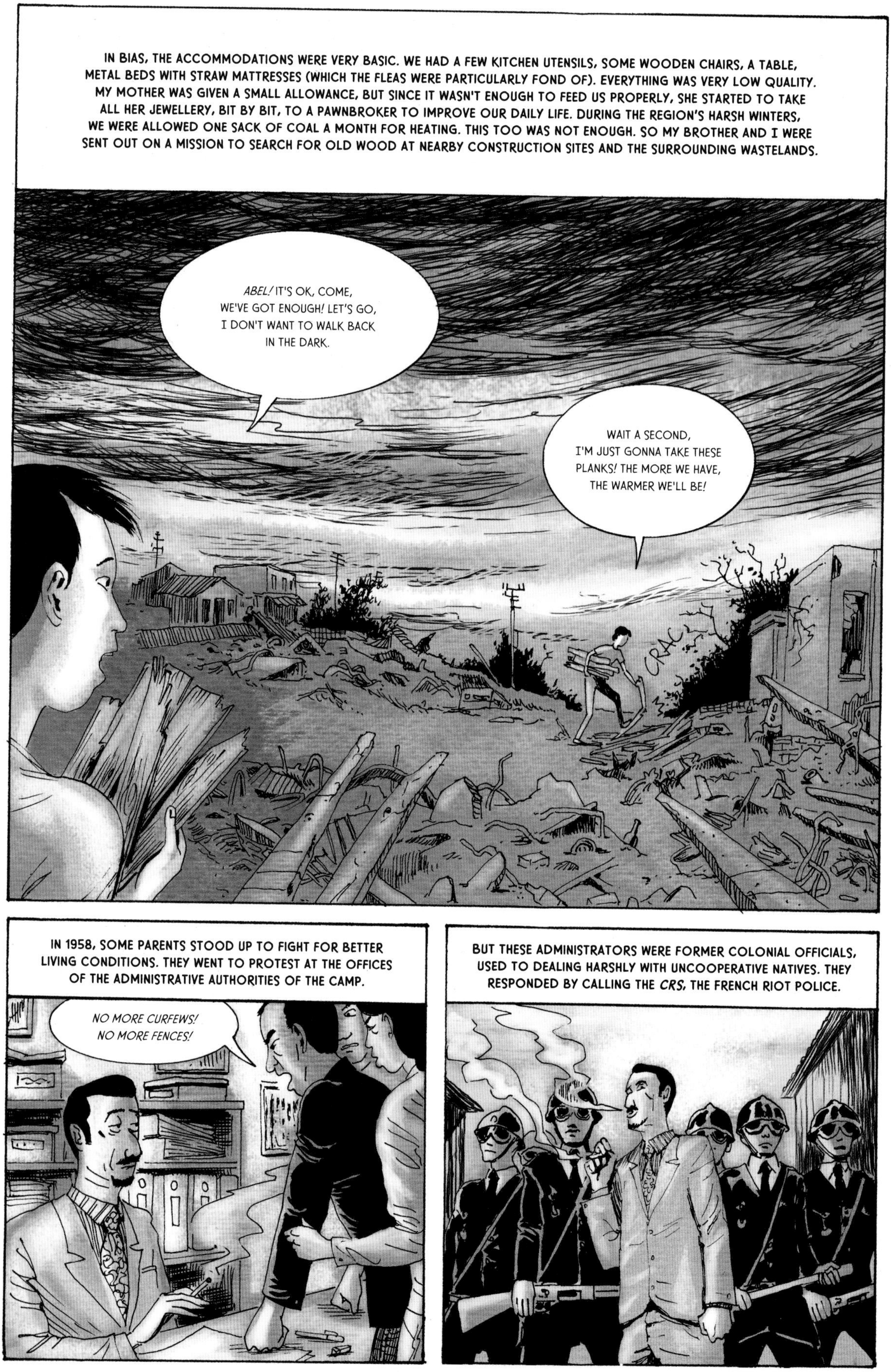
IN BIAS, THE ACCOMMODATIONS WERE VERY BASIC. WE HAD A FEW KITCHEN UTENSILS, SOME WOODEN CHAIRS, A TABLE, METAL BEDS WITH STRAW MATTRESSES (WHICH THE FLEAS WERE PARTICULARLY FOND OF). EVERYTHING WAS VERY LOW QUALITY. MY MOTHER WAS GIVEN A SMALL ALLOWANCE, BUT SINCE IT WASN'T ENOUGH TO FEED US PROPERLY, SHE STARTED TO TAKE ALL HER JEWELLERY, BIT BY BIT, TO A PAWNBROKER TO IMPROVE OUR DAILY LIFE. DURING THE REGION'S HARSH WINTERS, WE WERE ALLOWED ONE SACK OF COAL A MONTH FOR HEATING. THIS TOO WAS NOT ENOUGH. SO MY BROTHER AND I WERE SENT OUT ON A MISSION TO SEARCH FOR OLD WOOD AT NEARBY CONSTRUCTION SITES AND THE SURROUNDING WASTELANDS.
ABEL! IT'S OK, COME, WE'VE GOT ENOUGH! LET'S GO, I DON'T WANT TO WALK BACK IN THE DARK.
WAIT A SECOND, I'M JUST GONNA TAKE THESE PLANKS! THE MORE WE HAVE, THE WARMER WE'LL BE!
CRAC
IN 1958, SOME PARENTS STOOD UP TO FIGHT FOR BETTER LIVING CONDITIONS. THEY WENT TO PROTEST AT THE OFFICES OF THE ADMINISTRATIVE AUTHORITIES OF THE CAMP.
NO MORE CURFEWS! NO MORE FENCES!
BUT THESE ADMINISTRATORS WERE FORMER COLONIAL OFFICIALS, USED TO DEALING HARSHLY WITH UNCOOPERATIVE NATIVES. THEY RESPONDED BY CALLING THE *CRS*, THE FRENCH RIOT POLICE.

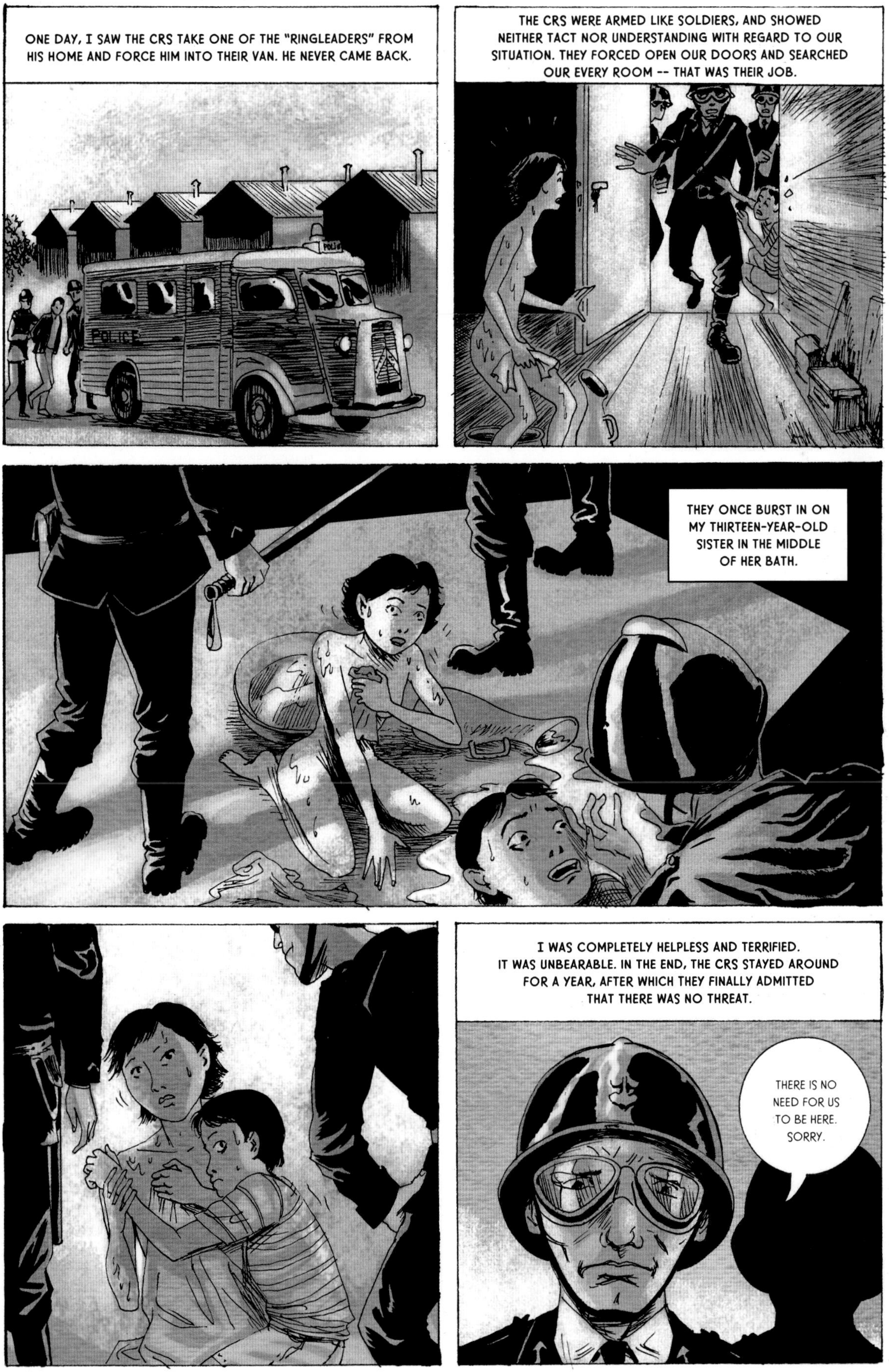
ONE DAY, I SAW THE CRS TAKE ONE OF THE "RINGLEADERS" FROM HIS HOME AND FORCE HIM INTO THEIR VAN. HE NEVER CAME BACK.
POLICE
THE CRS WERE ARMED LIKE SOLDIERS, AND SHOWED NEITHER TACT NOR UNDERSTANDING WITH REGARD TO OUR SITUATION. THEY FORCED OPEN OUR DOORS AND SEARCHED OUR EVERY ROOM -- THAT WAS THEIR JOB.
THEY ONCE BURST IN ON MY THIRTEEN-YEAR-OLD SISTER IN THE MIDDLE OF HER BATH.
I WAS COMPLETELY HELPLESS AND TERRIFIED. IT WAS UNBEARABLE. IN THE END, THE CRS STAYED AROUND FOR A YEAR, AFTER WHICH THEY FINALLY ADMITTED THAT THERE WAS NO THREAT.
THERE IS NO NEED FOR US TO BE HERE. SORRY.

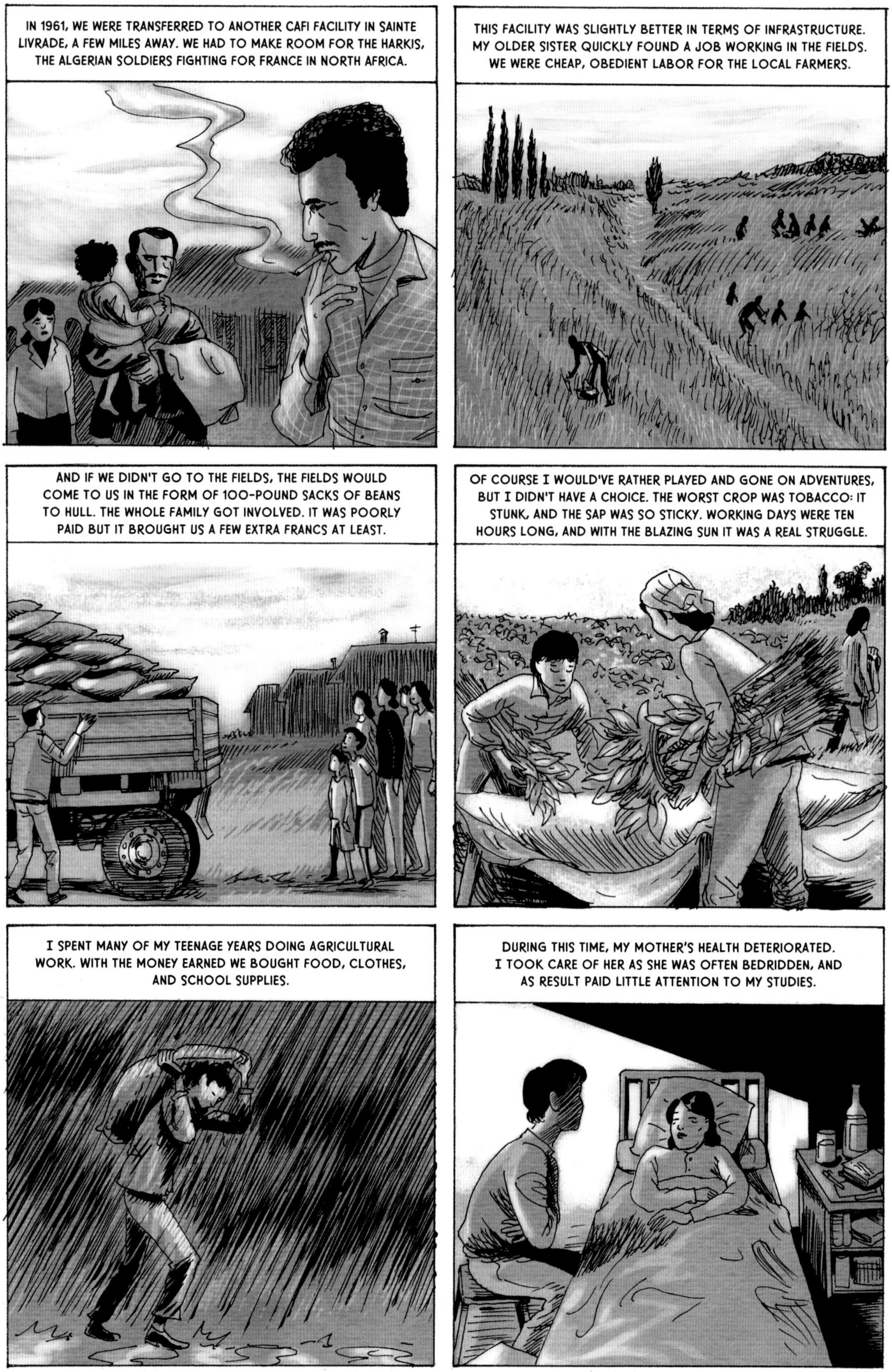
IN 1961, WE WERE TRANSFERRED TO ANOTHER CAFI FACILITY IN SAINTE LIVRADE, A FEW MILES AWAY. WE HAD TO MAKE ROOM FOR THE HARKIS, THE ALGERIAN SOLDIERS FIGHTING FOR FRANCE IN NORTH AFRICA.
THIS FACILITY WAS SLIGHTLY BETTER IN TERMS OF INFRASTRUCTURE. MY OLDER SISTER QUICKLY FOUND A JOB WORKING IN THE FIELDS. WE WERE CHEAP, OBEDIENT LABOR FOR THE LOCAL FARMERS.
AND IF WE DIDN'T GO TO THE FIELDS, THE FIELDS WOULD COME TO US IN THE FORM OF 100-POUND SACKS OF BEANS TO HULL. THE WHOLE FAMILY GOT INVOLVED. IT WAS POORLY PAID BUT IT BROUGHT US A FEW EXTRA FRANCS AT LEAST.
OF COURSE I WOULD'VE RATHER PLAYED AND GONE ON ADVENTURES, BUT I DIDN'T HAVE A CHOICE. THE WORST CROP WAS TOBACCO: IT STUNK, AND THE SAP WAS SO STICKY. WORKING DAYS WERE TEN HOURS LONG, AND WITH THE BLAZING SUN IT WAS A REAL STRUGGLE.
I SPENT MANY OF MY TEENAGE YEARS DOING AGRICULTURAL WORK. WITH THE MONEY EARNED WE BOUGHT FOOD, CLOTHES, AND SCHOOL SUPPLIES.
DURING THIS TIME, MY MOTHER'S HEALTH DETERIORATED. I TOOK CARE OF HER AS SHE WAS OFTEN BEDRIDDEN, AND AS RESULT PAID LITTLE ATTENTION TO MY STUDIES.

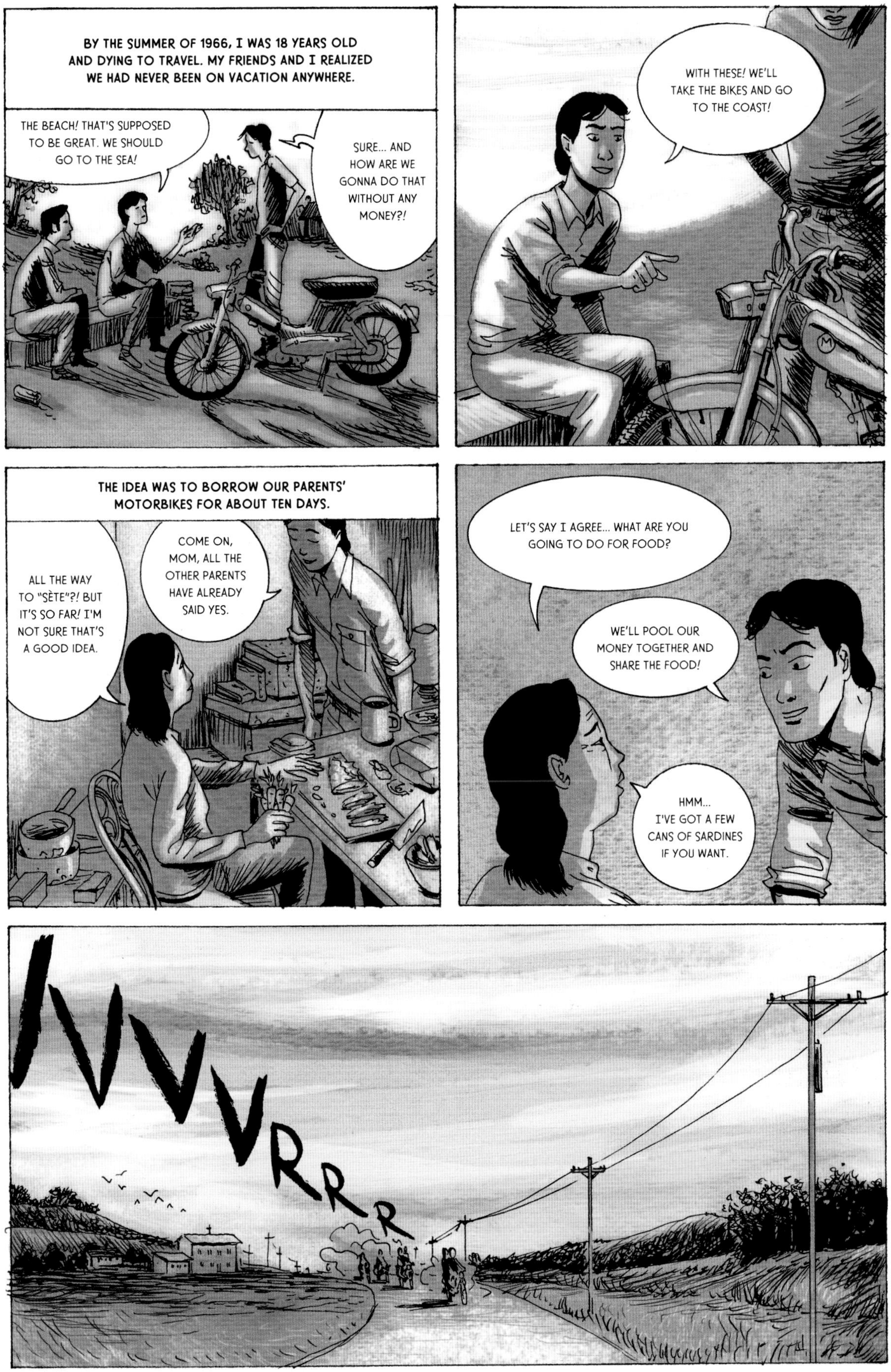
BY THE SUMMER OF 1966, I WAS 18 YEARS OLD AND DYING TO TRAVEL. MY FRIENDS AND I REALIZED WE HAD NEVER BEEN ON VACATION ANYWHERE.
THE BEACH! THAT'S SUPPOSED TO BE GREAT. WE SHOULD GO TO THE SEA!
SURE... AND HOW ARE WE GONNA DO THAT WITHOUT ANY MONEY?!
WITH THESE! WE'LL TAKE THE BIKES AND GO TO THE COAST!
THE IDEA WAS TO BORROW OUR PARENTS' MOTORBIKES FOR ABOUT TEN DAYS.
COME ON, MOM, ALL THE OTHER PARENTS HAVE ALREADY SAID YES.
ALL THE WAY TO "SÈTE"?! BUT IT'S SO FAR! I'M NOT SURE THAT'S A GOOD IDEA.
LET'S SAY I AGREE... WHAT ARE YOU GOING TO DO FOR FOOD?
WE'LL POOL OUR MONEY TOGETHER AND SHARE THE FOOD!
HMM... I'VE GOT A FEW CANS OF SARDINES IF YOU WANT.
NNVRRR

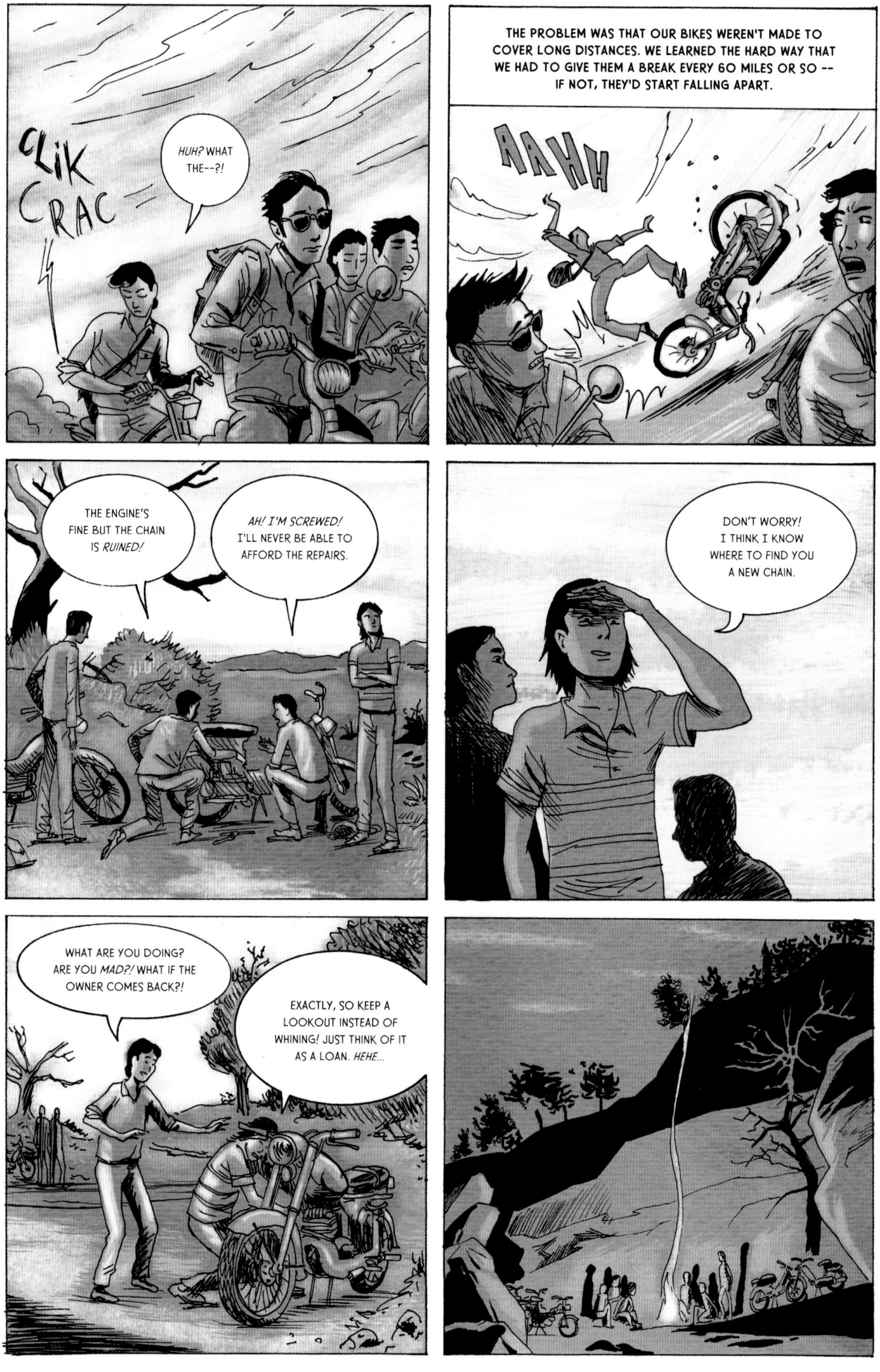
CLIK
CRAC
HUH? WHAT THE--?!
THE PROBLEM WAS THAT OUR BIKES WEREN'T MADE TO COVER LONG DISTANCES. WE LEARNED THE HARD WAY THAT WE HAD TO GIVE THEM A BREAK EVERY 60 MILES OR SO -- IF NOT, THEY'D START FALLING APART.
AAHH
THE ENGINE'S FINE BUT THE CHAIN IS RUINED!
AH! I'M SCREWED! I'LL NEVER BE ABLE TO AFFORD THE REPAIRS.
DON'T WORRY! I THINK I KNOW WHERE TO FIND YOU A NEW CHAIN.
WHAT ARE YOU DOING? ARE YOU MAD?! WHAT IF THE OWNER COMES BACK?!
EXACTLY, SO KEEP A LOOKOUT INSTEAD OF WHINING! JUST THINK OF IT AS A LOAN. HEHE...

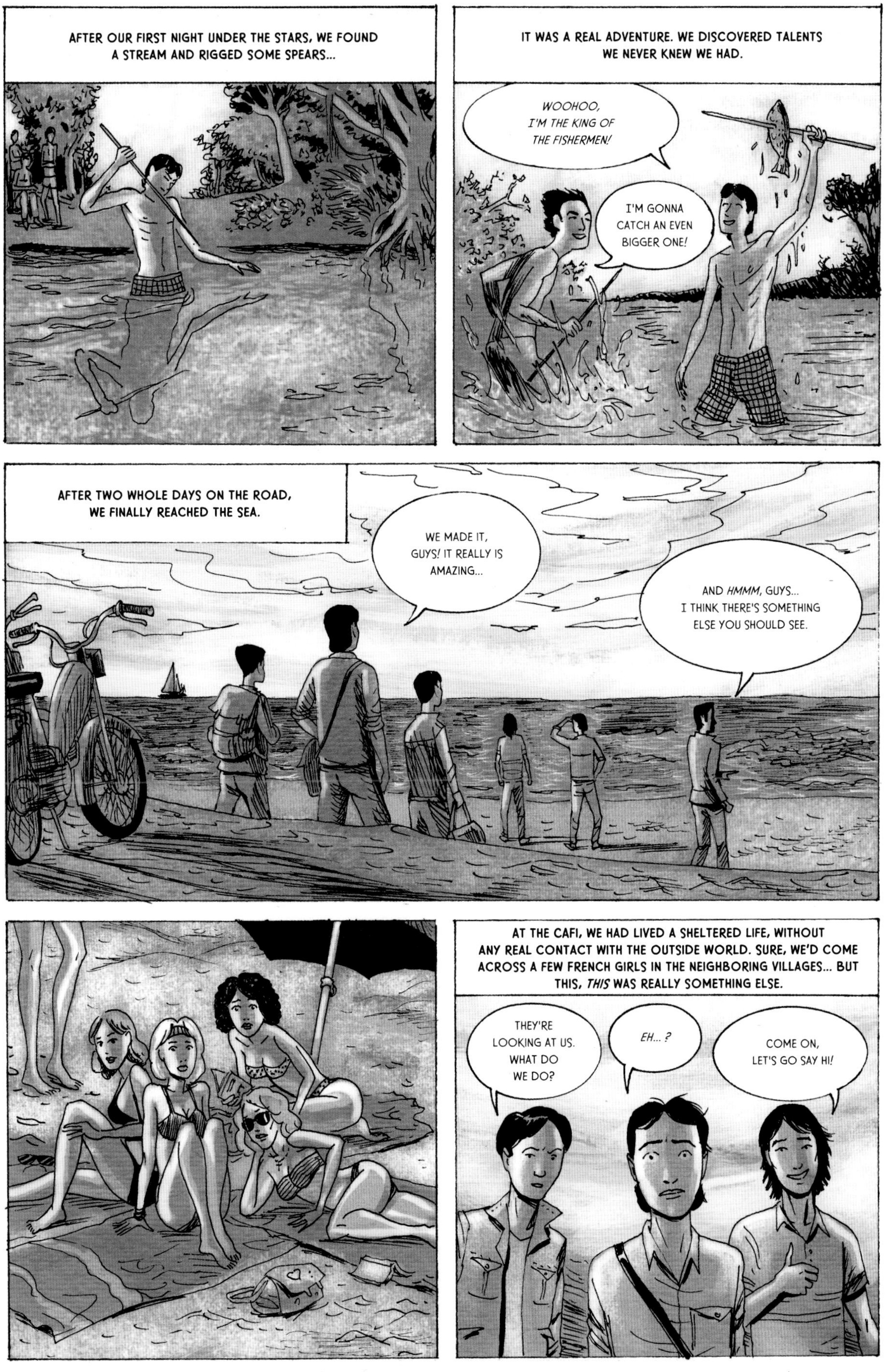
AFTER OUR FIRST NIGHT UNDER THE STARS, WE FOUND A STREAM AND RIGGED SOME SPEARS...
IT WAS A REAL ADVENTURE. WE DISCOVERED TALENTS WE NEVER KNEW WE HAD.
WOOHOO, I'M THE KING OF THE FISHERMEN!
I'M GONNA CATCH AN EVEN BIGGER ONE!
AFTER TWO WHOLE DAYS ON THE ROAD, WE FINALLY REACHED THE SEA.
WE MADE IT, GUYS! IT REALLY IS AMAZING...
AND HMMM, GUYS... I THINK THERE'S SOMETHING ELSE YOU SHOULD SEE.
AT THE CAFI, WE HAD LIVED A SHELTERED LIFE, WITHOUT ANY REAL CONTACT WITH THE OUTSIDE WORLD. SURE, WE'D COME ACROSS A FEW FRENCH GIRLS IN THE NEIGHBORING VILLAGES... BUT THIS, THIS WAS REALLY SOMETHING ELSE.
THEY'RE LOOKING AT US. WHAT DO WE DO?
EH... ?
COME ON, LET'S GO SAY HI!

THE GIRLS WERE OUR AGE AND THEY WERE JUST AS CURIOUS ABOUT US AS WE WERE ABOUT THEM.

ABEL, WE HAVE TO GO. BUT WE WERE THINKING WE COULD MEET UP AGAIN AT THE NIGHTCLUB TONIGHT?

AT THE NIGHTCLUB?

OH NO, NO THANKS. WE ALREADY HAVE PLANS FOR TONIGHT. BYE!

BUT I WANTED TO SEE THEM AGAIN! WHY DID YOU TELL THEM THAT, ABEL?

THINK ABOUT IT! HOW WILL WE AFFORD TO GET INTO THE NIGHTCLUB? OR ANYWHERE ELSE, FOR THAT MATTER?!

LET'S NOT LOSE FACE! WE MIGHT NOT HAVE ANY MONEY BUT WE DO HAVE OUR PRIDE!

THE NEXT DAY, OUR HOPES FROM THE NIGHT BEFORE WERE FULFILLED: THE GROUP OF GIRLS CAME AND JOINED US AT THE BEACH AGAIN.

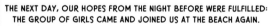

YOU'RE VIETNAMESE? AND YOU'VE COME ALL THIS WAY TO BE HERE? VIETNAM IS NEAR CHINA, RIGHT?

ACTUALLY, WE LIVE IN FRANCE, IN A VILLAGE NEAR AGEN. AND ON PAPER, WE'RE FRENCH JUST LIKE YOU.

WAIT, A WHOLE VILLAGE OF VIETNAMESE PEOPLE? THAT'S CRAZY!

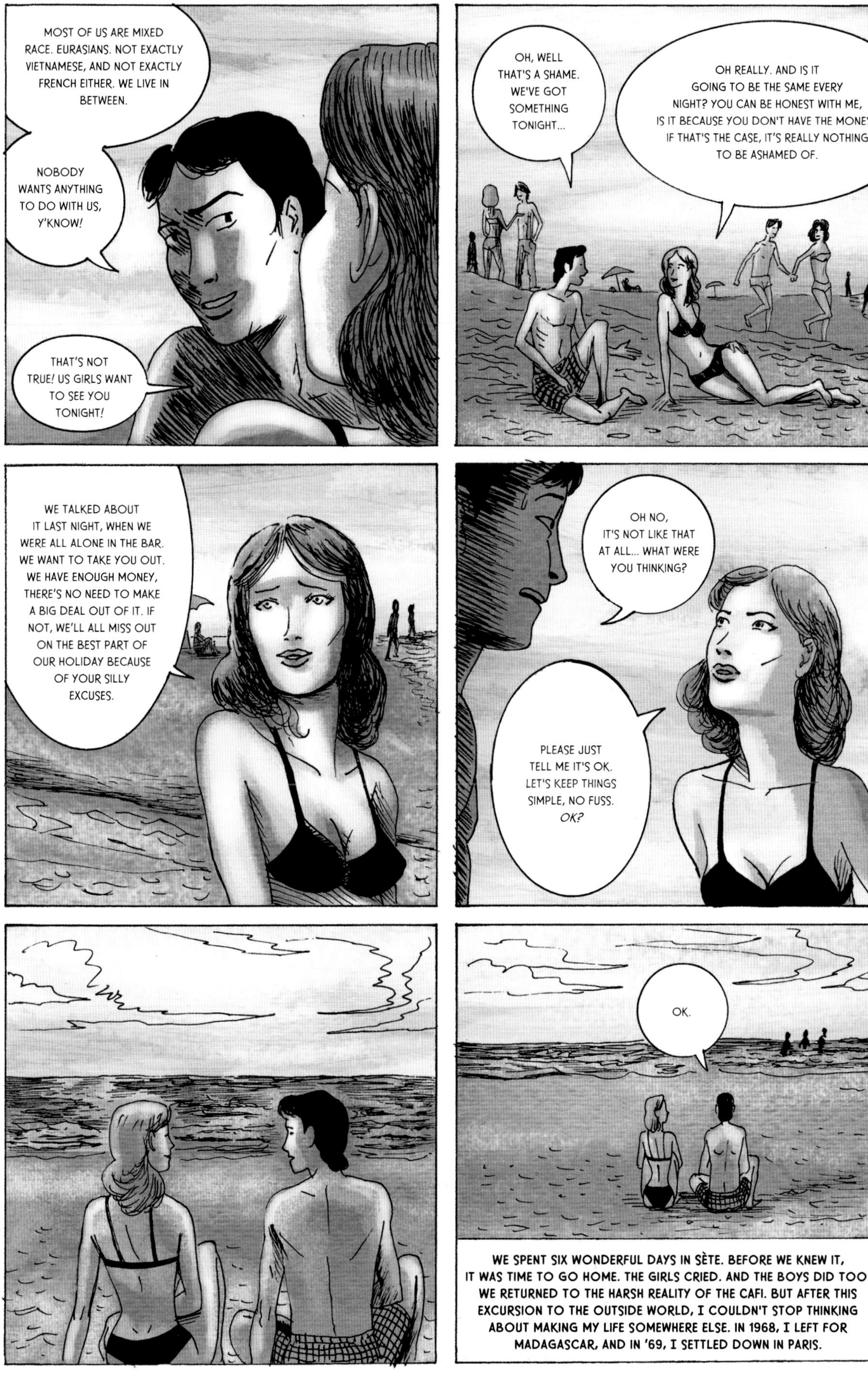

MOST OF US ARE MIXED RACE. EURASIANS. NOT EXACTLY VIETNAMESE, AND NOT EXACTLY FRENCH EITHER. WE LIVE IN BETWEEN.
NOBODY WANTS ANYTHING TO DO WITH US, Y'KNOW!
THAT'S NOT TRUE! US GIRLS WANT TO SEE YOU TONIGHT!
OH, WELL THAT'S A SHAME. WE'VE GOT SOMETHING TONIGHT...
OH REALLY. AND IS IT GOING TO BE THE SAME EVERY NIGHT? YOU CAN BE HONEST WITH ME, IS IT BECAUSE YOU DON'T HAVE THE MONEY? IF THAT'S THE CASE, IT'S REALLY NOTHING TO BE ASHAMED OF.
WE TALKED ABOUT IT LAST NIGHT, WHEN WE WERE ALL ALONE IN THE BAR. WE WANT TO TAKE YOU OUT. WE HAVE ENOUGH MONEY, THERE'S NO NEED TO MAKE A BIG DEAL OUT OF IT. IF NOT, WE'LL ALL MISS OUT ON THE BEST PART OF OUR HOLIDAY BECAUSE OF YOUR SILLY EXCUSES.
OH NO, IT'S NOT LIKE THAT AT ALL... WHAT WERE YOU THINKING?
PLEASE JUST TELL ME IT'S OK. LET'S KEEP THINGS SIMPLE, NO FUSS. *OK?*
OK.
WE SPENT SIX WONDERFUL DAYS IN SÈTE. BEFORE WE KNEW IT, IT WAS TIME TO GO HOME. THE GIRLS CRIED. AND THE BOYS DID TOO. WE RETURNED TO THE HARSH REALITY OF THE CAFI. BUT AFTER THIS EXCURSION TO THE OUTSIDE WORLD, I COULDN'T STOP THINKING ABOUT MAKING MY LIFE SOMEWHERE ELSE. IN 1968, I LEFT FOR MADAGASCAR, AND IN '69, I SETTLED DOWN IN PARIS.

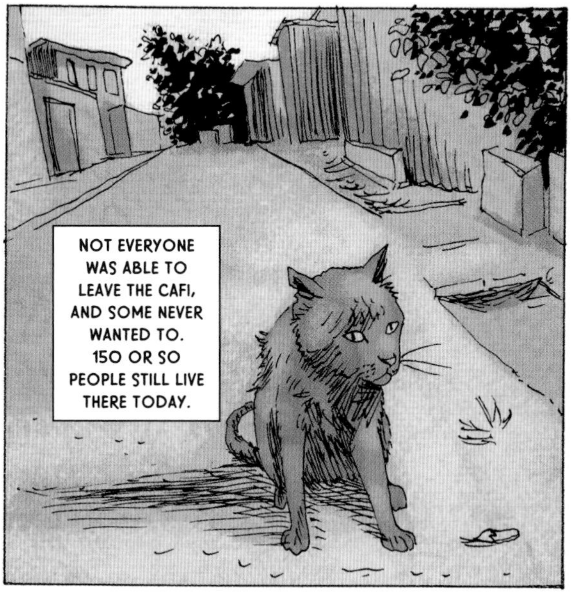
NOT EVERYONE WAS ABLE TO LEAVE THE CAFI, AND SOME NEVER WANTED TO. 150 OR SO PEOPLE STILL LIVE THERE TODAY.

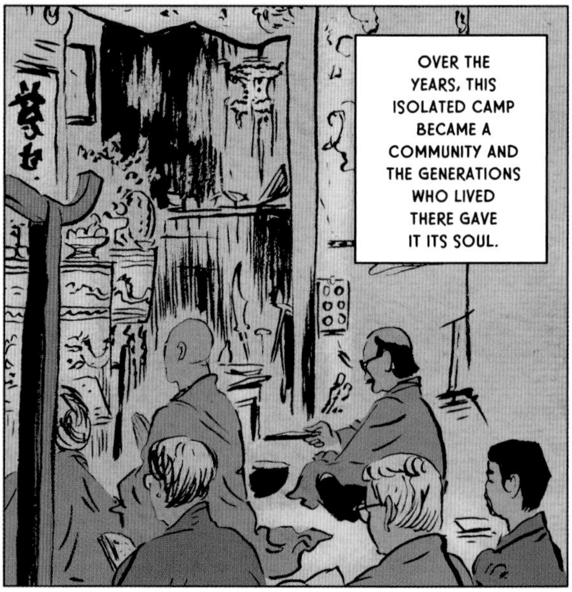
OVER THE YEARS, THIS ISOLATED CAMP BECAME A COMMUNITY AND THE GENERATIONS WHO LIVED THERE GAVE IT ITS SOUL.

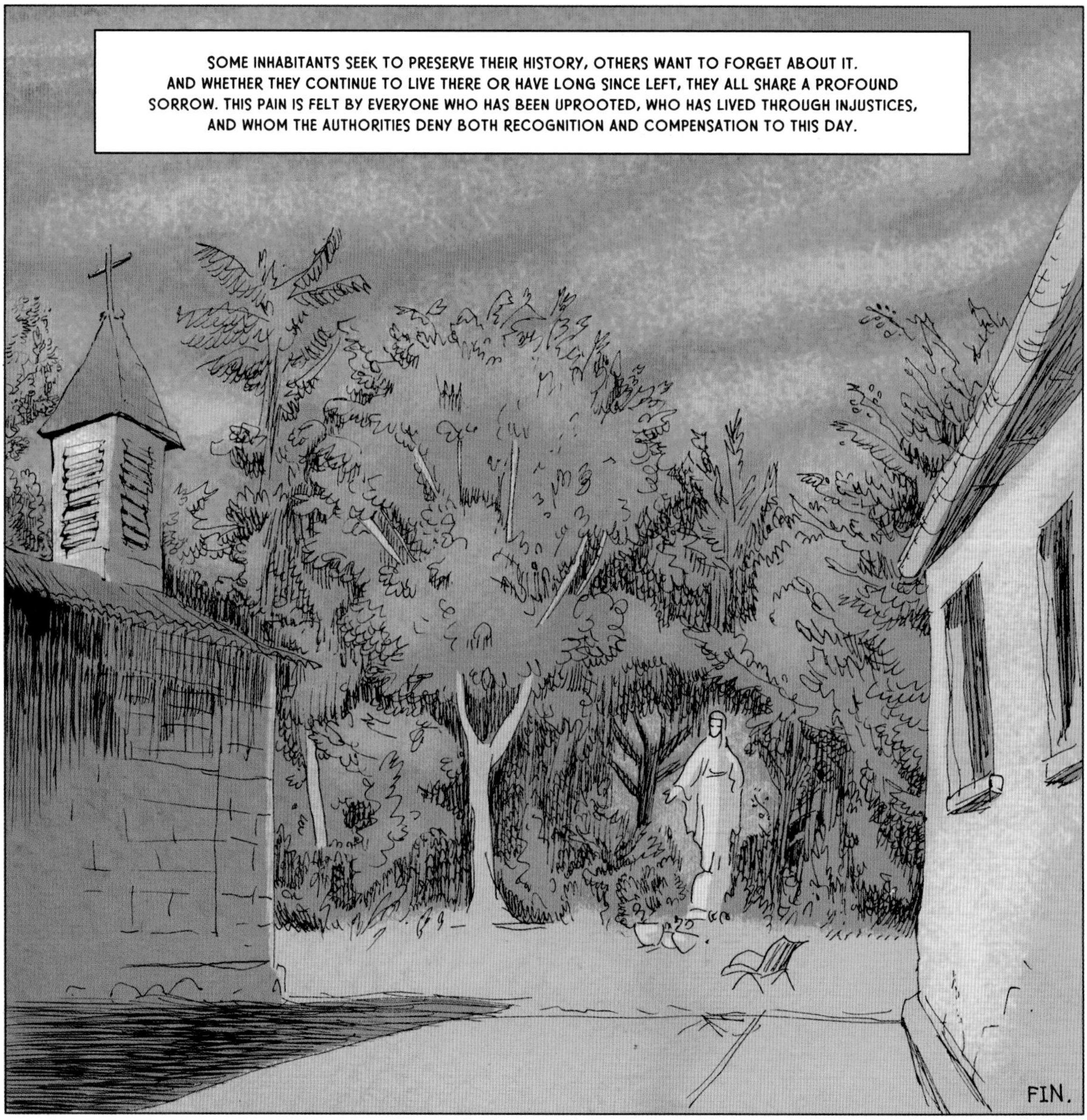
SOME INHABITANTS SEEK TO PRESERVE THEIR HISTORY, OTHERS WANT TO FORGET ABOUT IT. AND WHETHER THEY CONTINUE TO LIVE THERE OR HAVE LONG SINCE LEFT, THEY ALL SHARE A PROFOUND SORROW. THIS PAIN IS FELT BY EVERYONE WHO HAS BEEN UPROOTED, WHO HAS LIVED THROUGH INJUSTICES, AND WHOM THE AUTHORITIES DENY BOTH RECOGNITION AND COMPENSATION TO THIS DAY.
FIN.

LINH THO

THE FORCED IMMIGRANTS

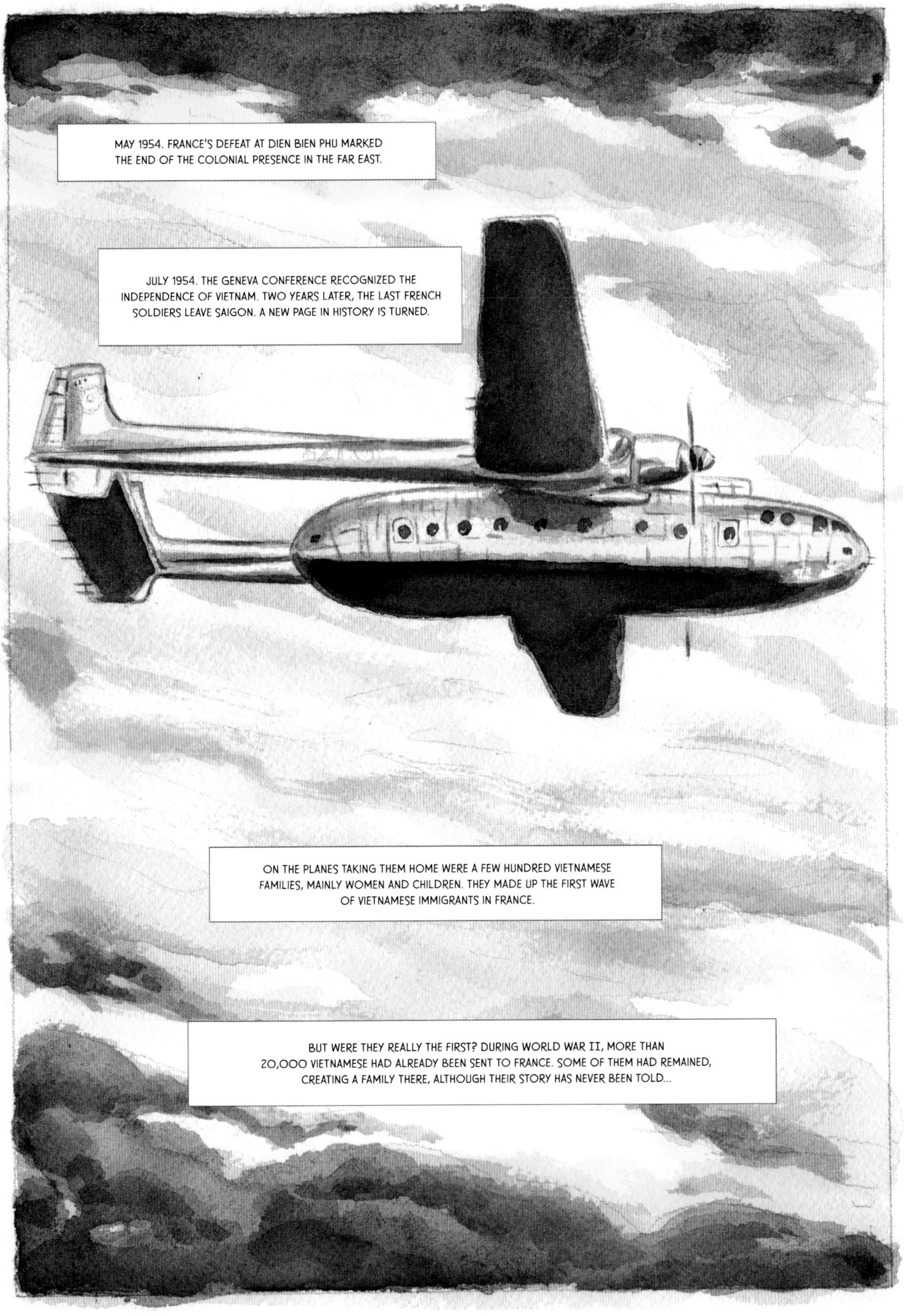
MAY 1954. FRANCE'S DEFEAT AT DIEN BIEN PHU MARKED THE END OF THE COLONIAL PRESENCE IN THE FAR EAST.
JULY 1954. THE GENEVA CONFERENCE RECOGNIZED THE INDEPENDENCE OF VIETNAM. TWO YEARS LATER, THE LAST FRENCH SOLDIERS LEAVE SAIGON. A NEW PAGE IN HISTORY IS TURNED.
ON THE PLANES TAKING THEM HOME WERE A FEW HUNDRED VIETNAMESE FAMILIES, MAINLY WOMEN AND CHILDREN. THEY MADE UP THE FIRST WAVE OF VIETNAMESE IMMIGRANTS IN FRANCE.
BUT WERE THEY REALLY THE FIRST? DURING WORLD WAR II, MORE THAN 20,000 VIETNAMESE HAD ALREADY BEEN SENT TO FRANCE. SOME OF THEM HAD REMAINED, CREATING A FAMILY THERE, ALTHOUGH THEIR STORY HAS NEVER BEEN TOLD...

1. THE PHOTO

OR HOW A JOURNALIST DISCOVERS BY CHANCE A BURIED EPISODE OF WORLD WAR II HISTORY.

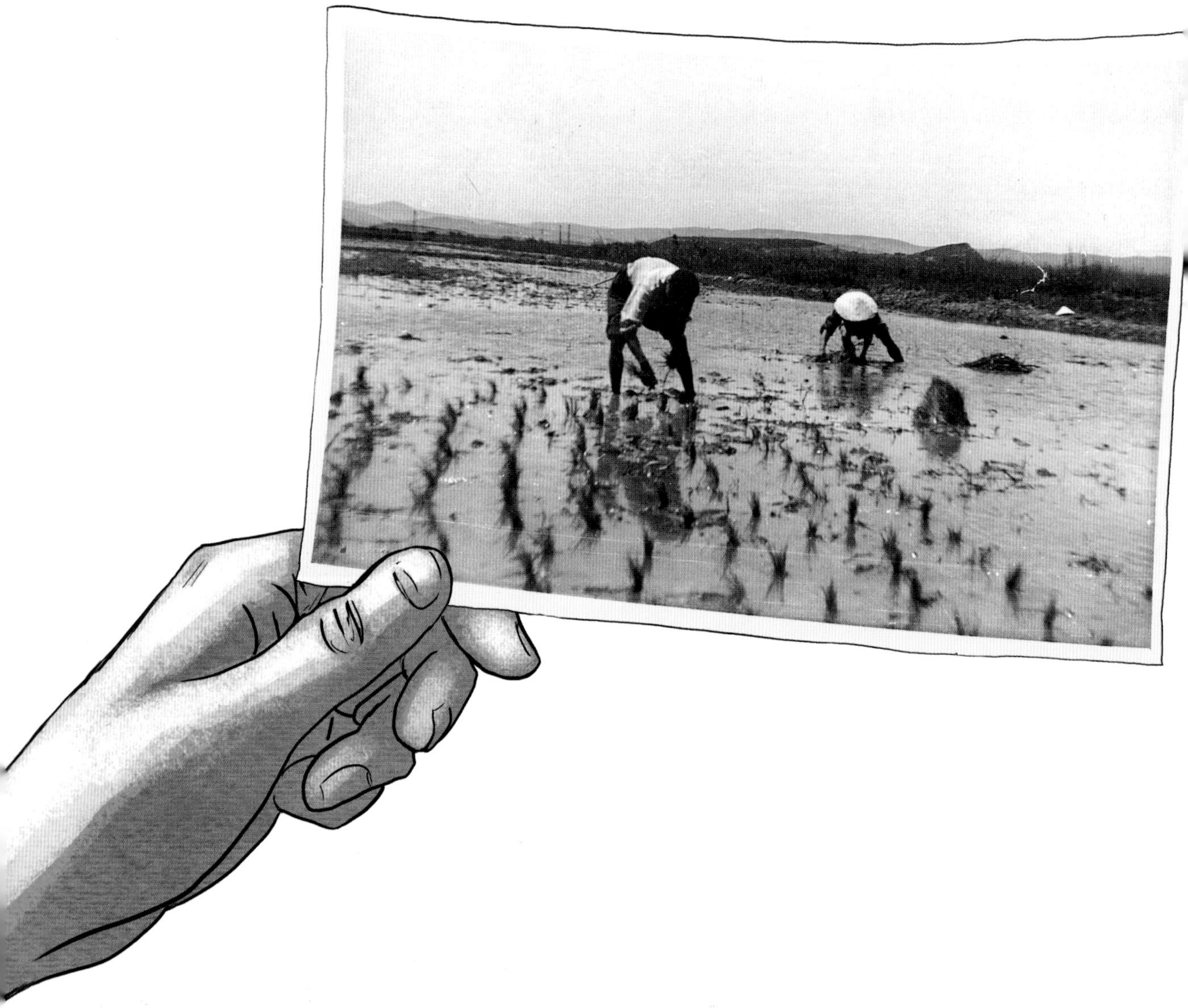

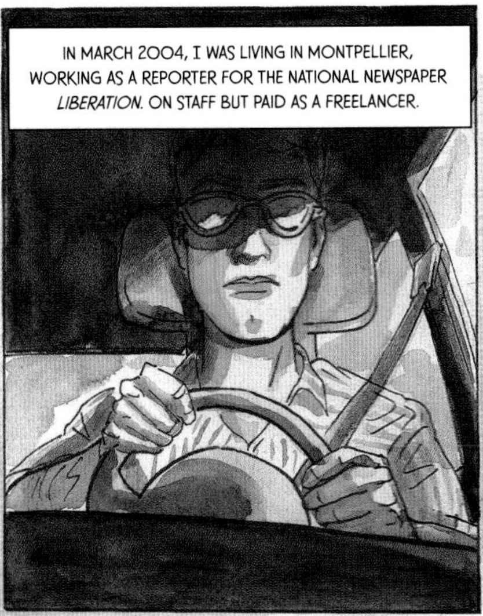
IN MARCH 2004, I WAS LIVING IN MONTPELLIER, WORKING AS A REPORTER FOR THE NATIONAL NEWSPAPER *LIBERATION*. ON STAFF BUT PAID AS A FREELANCER.

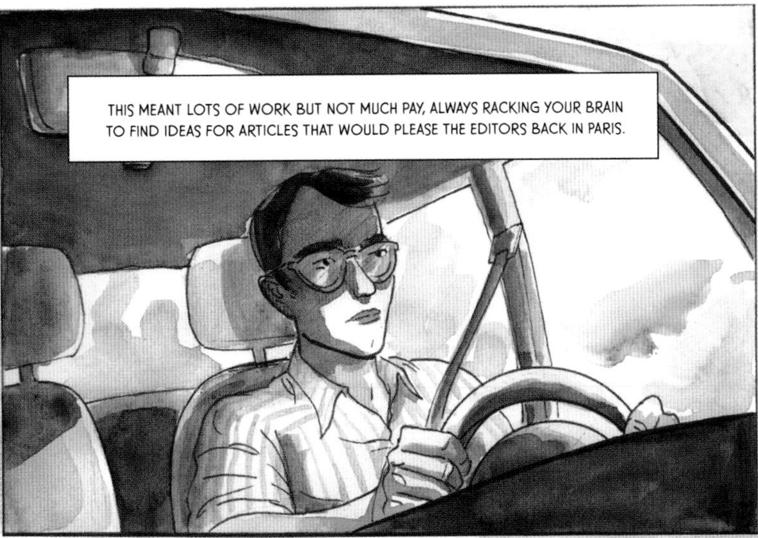
THIS MEANT LOTS OF WORK BUT NOT MUCH PAY, ALWAYS RACKING YOUR BRAIN TO FIND IDEAS FOR ARTICLES THAT WOULD PLEASE THE EDITORS BACK IN PARIS.

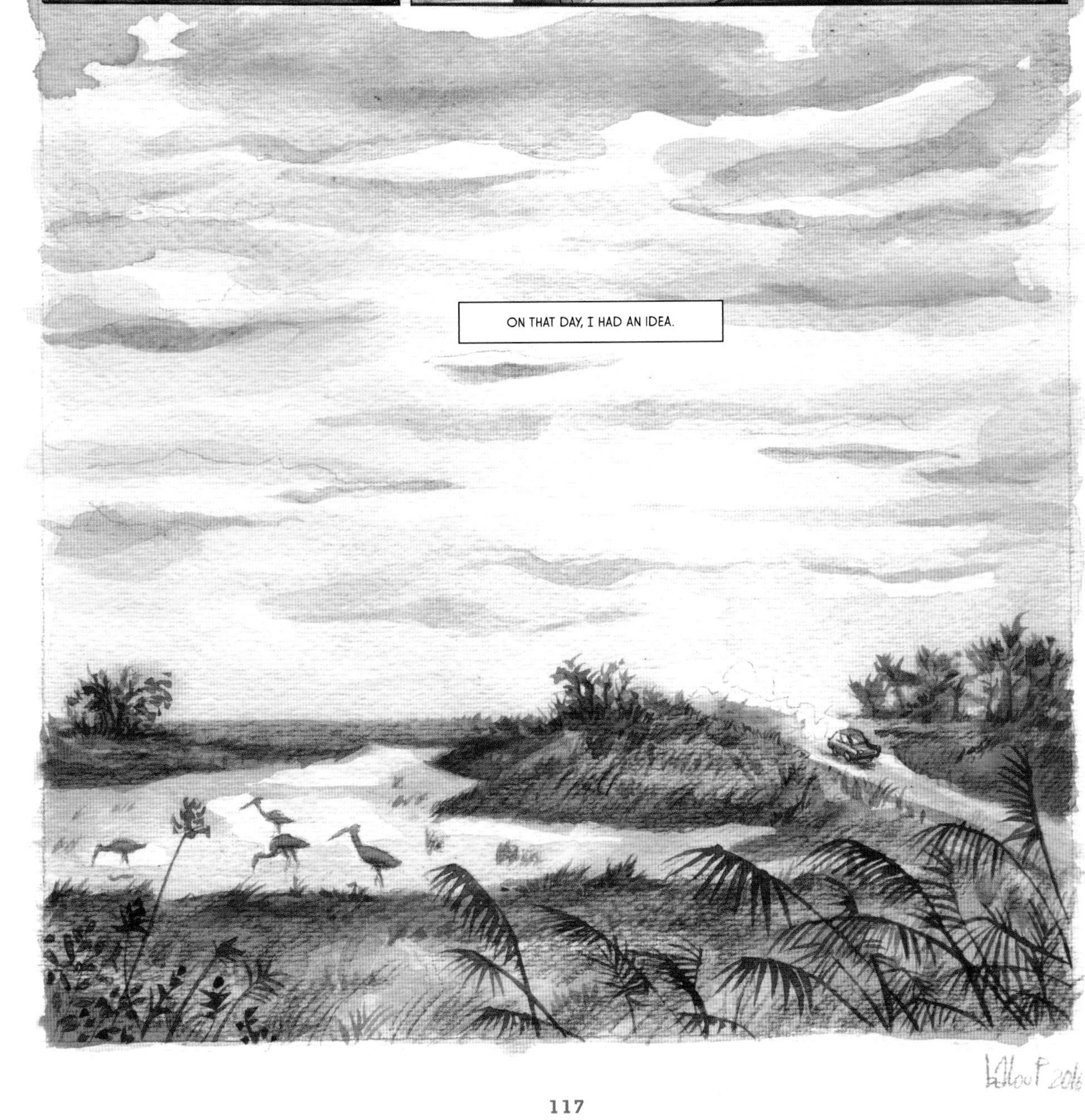
ON THAT DAY, I HAD AN IDEA.

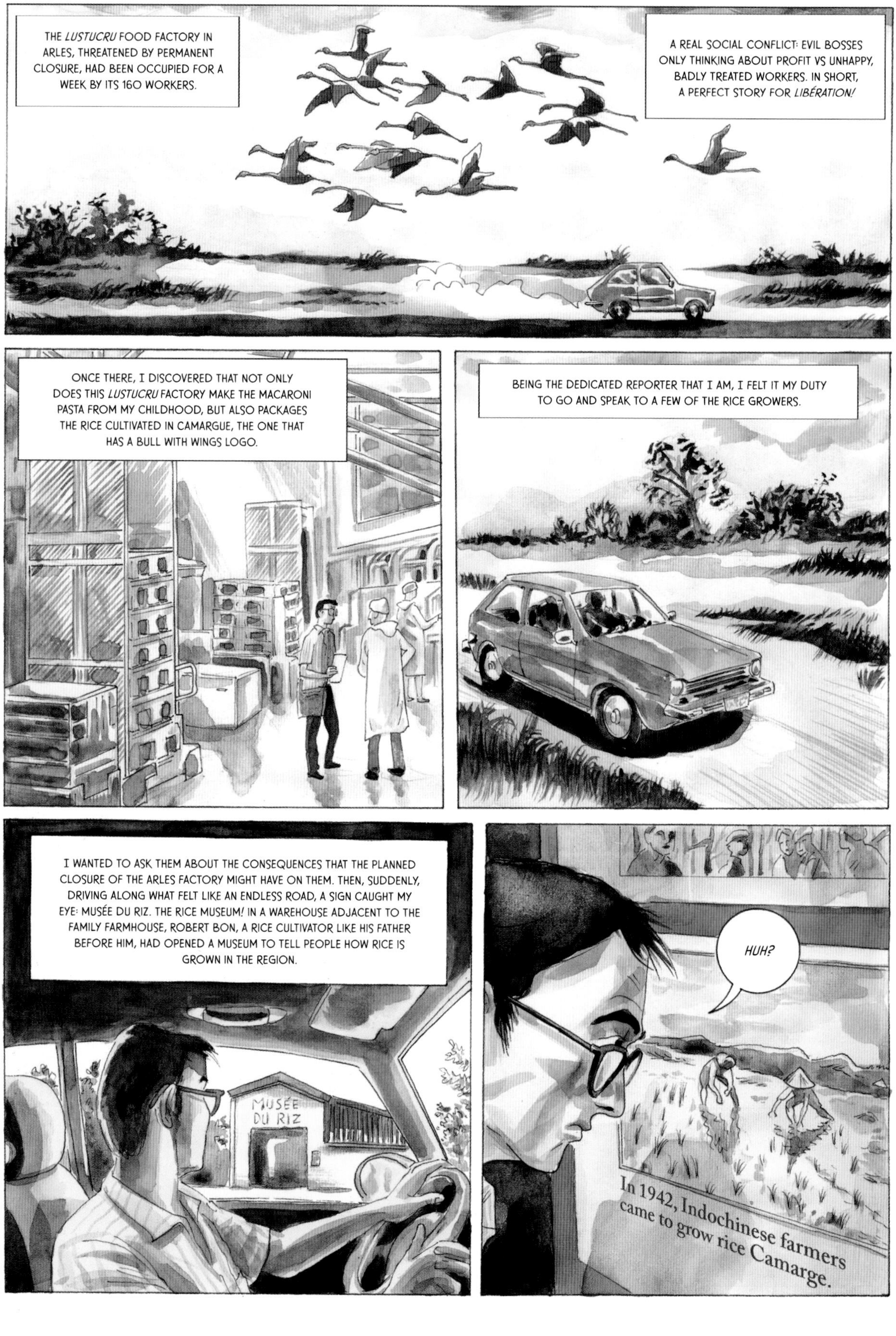
THE *LUSTUCRU* FOOD FACTORY IN ARLES, THREATENED BY PERMANENT CLOSURE, HAD BEEN OCCUPIED FOR A WEEK BY ITS 160 WORKERS.
A REAL SOCIAL CONFLICT: EVIL BOSSES ONLY THINKING ABOUT PROFIT VS UNHAPPY, BADLY TREATED WORKERS. IN SHORT, A PERFECT STORY FOR *LIBÉRATION!*
ONCE THERE, I DISCOVERED THAT NOT ONLY DOES THIS *LUSTUCRU* FACTORY MAKE THE MACARONI PASTA FROM MY CHILDHOOD, BUT ALSO PACKAGES THE RICE CULTIVATED IN CAMARGUE, THE ONE THAT HAS A BULL WITH WINGS LOGO.
BEING THE DEDICATED REPORTER THAT I AM, I FELT IT MY DUTY TO GO AND SPEAK TO A FEW OF THE RICE GROWERS.
I WANTED TO ASK THEM ABOUT THE CONSEQUENCES THAT THE PLANNED CLOSURE OF THE ARLES FACTORY MIGHT HAVE ON THEM. THEN, SUDDENLY, DRIVING ALONG WHAT FELT LIKE AN ENDLESS ROAD, A SIGN CAUGHT MY EYE: MUSÉE DU RIZ. THE RICE MUSEUM! IN A WAREHOUSE ADJACENT TO THE FAMILY FARMHOUSE, ROBERT BON, A RICE CULTIVATOR LIKE HIS FATHER BEFORE HIM, HAD OPENED A MUSEUM TO TELL PEOPLE HOW RICE IS GROWN IN THE REGION.
MUSÉE DU RIZ
HUH?
In 1942, Indochinese farmers came to grow rice Camarge.

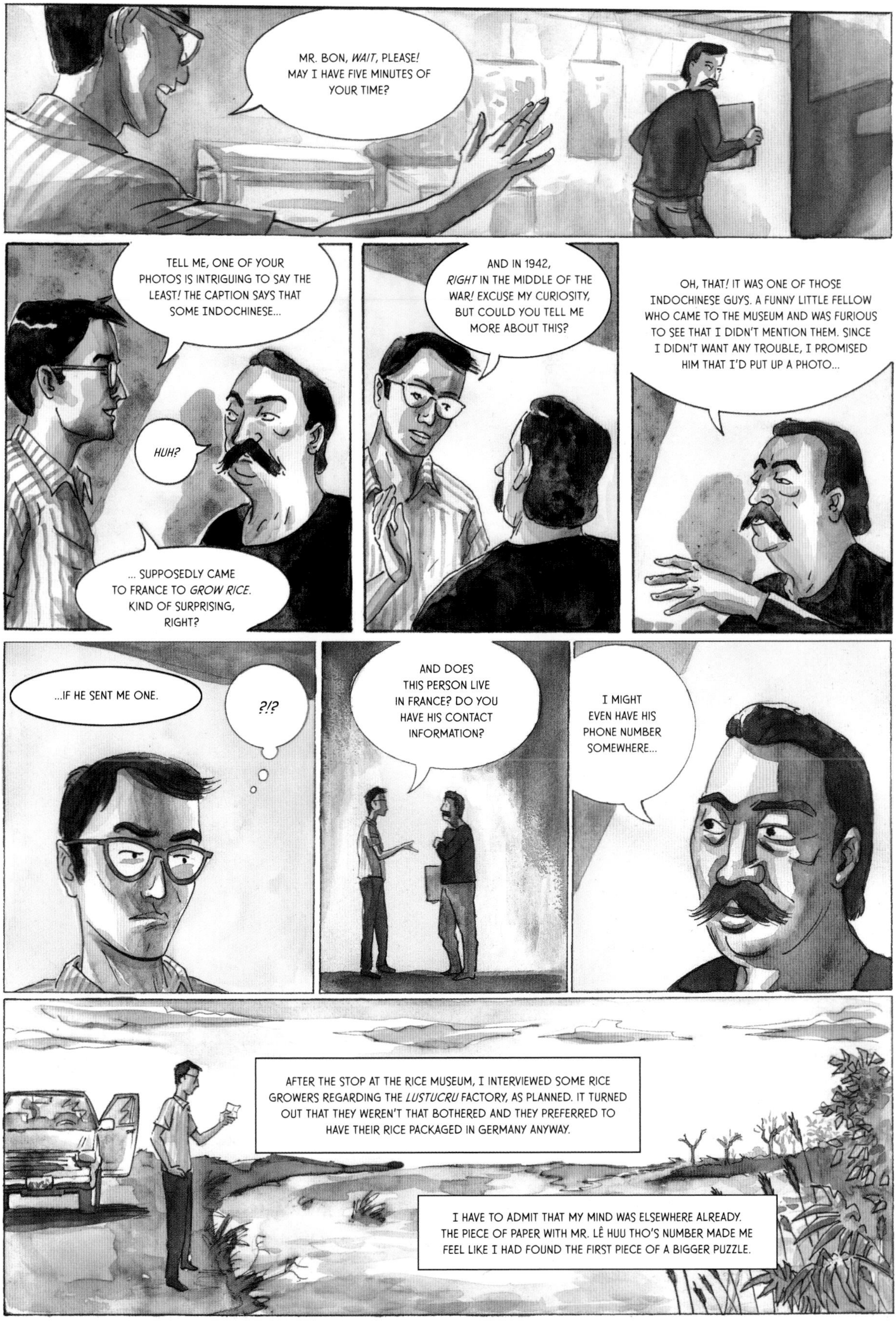
MR. BON, *WAIT*, PLEASE! MAY I HAVE FIVE MINUTES OF YOUR TIME?
TELL ME, ONE OF YOUR PHOTOS IS INTRIGUING TO SAY THE LEAST! THE CAPTION SAYS THAT SOME INDOCHINESE...
HUH?
... SUPPOSEDLY CAME TO FRANCE TO *GROW RICE*. KIND OF SURPRISING, RIGHT?
AND IN 1942, *RIGHT* IN THE MIDDLE OF THE WAR! EXCUSE MY CURIOSITY, BUT COULD YOU TELL ME MORE ABOUT THIS?
OH, THAT! IT WAS ONE OF THOSE INDOCHINESE GUYS. A FUNNY LITTLE FELLOW WHO CAME TO THE MUSEUM AND WAS FURIOUS TO SEE THAT I DIDN'T MENTION THEM. SINCE I DIDN'T WANT ANY TROUBLE, I PROMISED HIM THAT I'D PUT UP A PHOTO...
...IF HE SENT ME ONE.
?!?
AND DOES THIS PERSON LIVE IN FRANCE? DO YOU HAVE HIS CONTACT INFORMATION?
I MIGHT EVEN HAVE HIS PHONE NUMBER SOMEWHERE...
AFTER THE STOP AT THE RICE MUSEUM, I INTERVIEWED SOME RICE GROWERS REGARDING THE *LUSTUCRU* FACTORY, AS PLANNED. IT TURNED OUT THAT THEY WEREN'T THAT BOTHERED AND THEY PREFERRED TO HAVE THEIR RICE PACKAGED IN GERMANY ANYWAY.
I HAVE TO ADMIT THAT MY MIND WAS ELSEWHERE ALREADY. THE PIECE OF PAPER WITH MR. LÊ HUU THO'S NUMBER MADE ME FEEL LIKE I HAD FOUND THE FIRST PIECE OF A BIGGER PUZZLE.

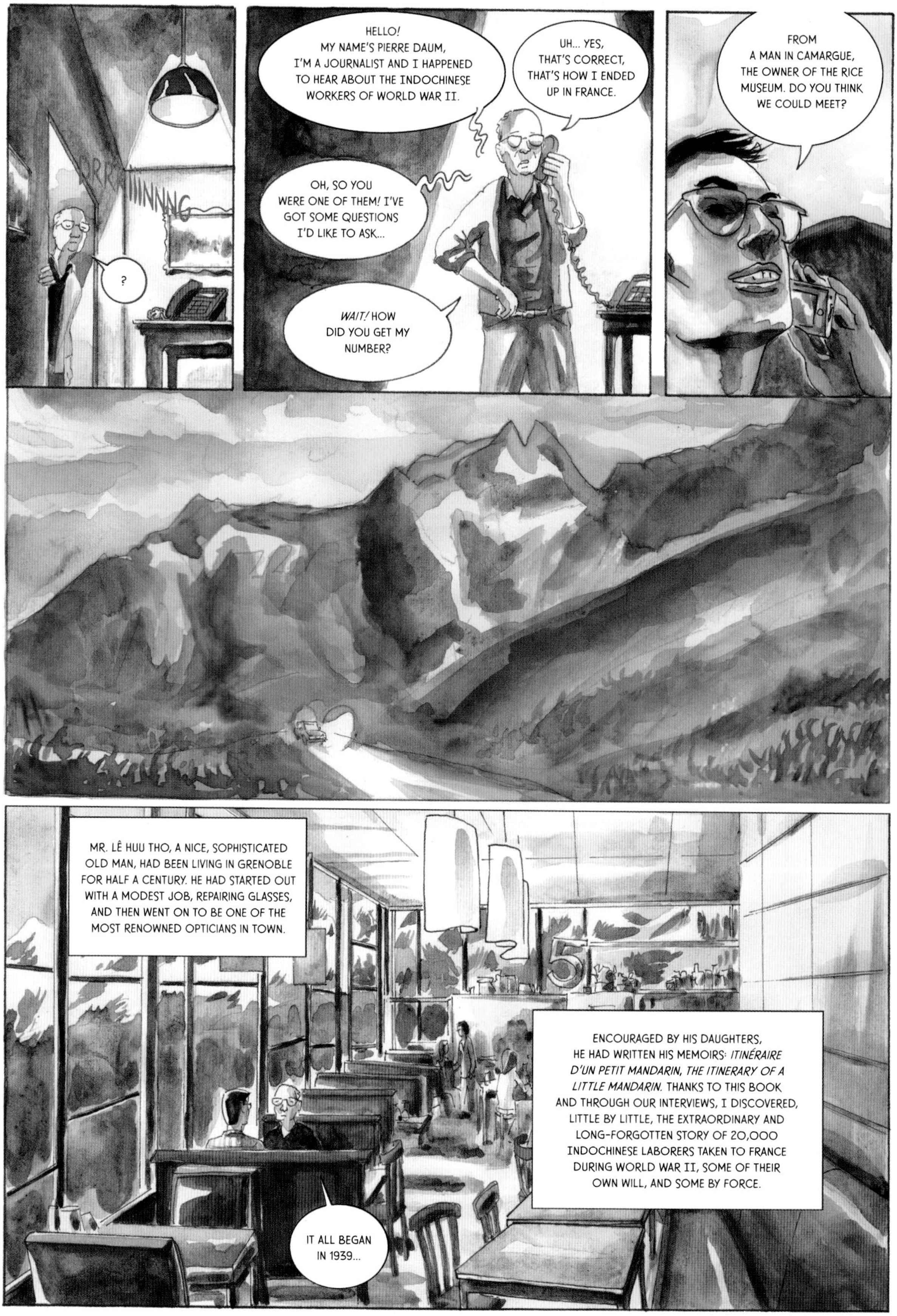
DRRRIIIINNNG
?
HELLO! MY NAME'S PIERRE DAUM, I'M A JOURNALIST AND I HAPPENED TO HEAR ABOUT THE INDOCHINESE WORKERS OF WORLD WAR II.
UH... YES, THAT'S CORRECT, THAT'S HOW I ENDED UP IN FRANCE.
OH, SO YOU WERE ONE OF THEM! I'VE GOT SOME QUESTIONS I'D LIKE TO ASK...
WAIT! HOW DID YOU GET MY NUMBER?
FROM A MAN IN CAMARGUE, THE OWNER OF THE RICE MUSEUM. DO YOU THINK WE COULD MEET?
MR. LÊ HUU THO, A NICE, SOPHISTICATED OLD MAN, HAD BEEN LIVING IN GRENOBLE FOR HALF A CENTURY. HE HAD STARTED OUT WITH A MODEST JOB, REPAIRING GLASSES, AND THEN WENT ON TO BE ONE OF THE MOST RENOWNED OPTICIANS IN TOWN.
ENCOURAGED BY HIS DAUGHTERS, HE HAD WRITTEN HIS MEMOIRS: *ITINÉRAIRE D'UN PETIT MANDARIN, THE ITINERARY OF A LITTLE MANDARIN.* THANKS TO THIS BOOK AND THROUGH OUR INTERVIEWS, I DISCOVERED, LITTLE BY LITTLE, THE EXTRAORDINARY AND LONG-FORGOTTEN STORY OF 20,000 INDOCHINESE LABORERS TAKEN TO FRANCE DURING WORLD WAR II, SOME OF THEIR OWN WILL, AND SOME BY FORCE.
IT ALL BEGAN IN 1939...

LÊ HUU THO, 35TH COMPANY, ID NO. ZAN 208. MET IN GRENOBLE, JUNE 2005.

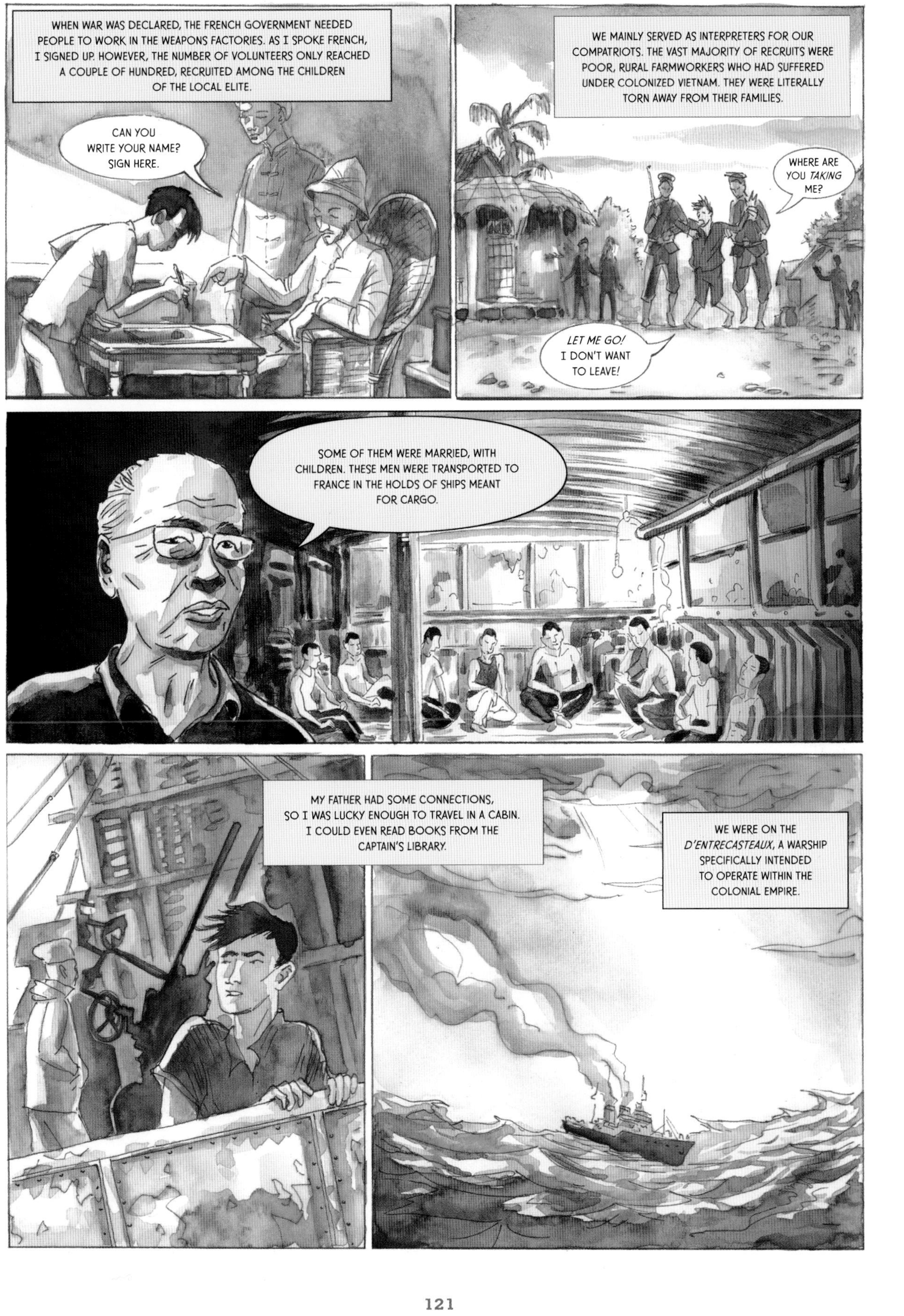

WHEN WAR WAS DECLARED, THE FRENCH GOVERNMENT NEEDED PEOPLE TO WORK IN THE WEAPONS FACTORIES. AS I SPOKE FRENCH, I SIGNED UP. HOWEVER, THE NUMBER OF VOLUNTEERS ONLY REACHED A COUPLE OF HUNDRED, RECRUITED AMONG THE CHILDREN OF THE LOCAL ELITE.
CAN YOU WRITE YOUR NAME? SIGN HERE.
WE MAINLY SERVED AS INTERPRETERS FOR OUR COMPATRIOTS. THE VAST MAJORITY OF RECRUITS WERE POOR, RURAL FARMWORKERS WHO HAD SUFFERED UNDER COLONIZED VIETNAM. THEY WERE LITERALLY TORN AWAY FROM THEIR FAMILIES.
WHERE ARE YOU *TAKING* ME?
LET ME GO! I DON'T WANT TO LEAVE!
SOME OF THEM WERE MARRIED, WITH CHILDREN. THESE MEN WERE TRANSPORTED TO FRANCE IN THE HOLDS OF SHIPS MEANT FOR CARGO.
MY FATHER HAD SOME CONNECTIONS, SO I WAS LUCKY ENOUGH TO TRAVEL IN A CABIN. I COULD EVEN READ BOOKS FROM THE CAPTAIN'S LIBRARY.
WE WERE ON THE *D'ENTRECASTEAUX*, A WARSHIP SPECIFICALLY INTENDED TO OPERATE WITHIN THE COLONIAL EMPIRE.

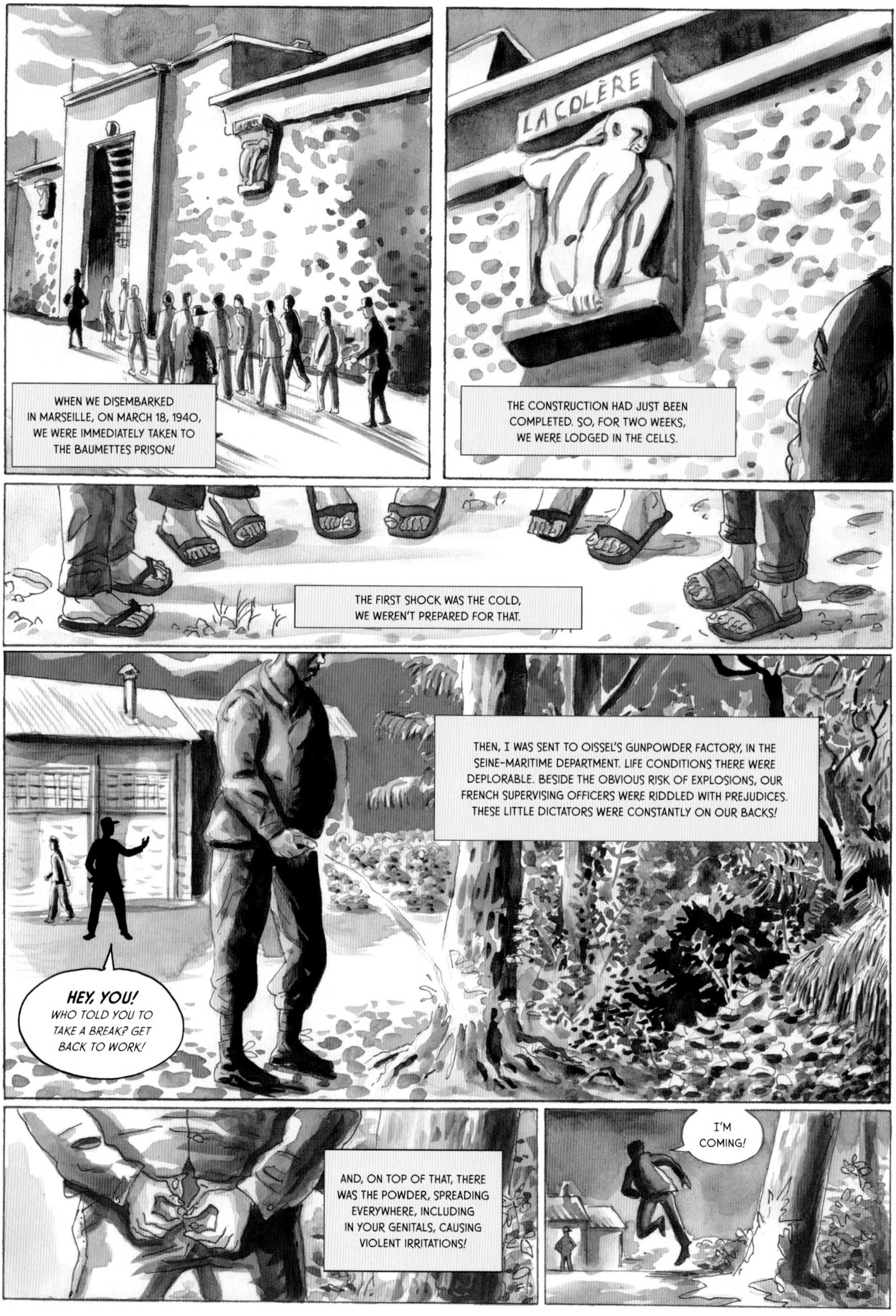

LA COLÈRE
WHEN WE DISEMBARKED IN MARSEILLE, ON MARCH 18, 1940, WE WERE IMMEDIATELY TAKEN TO THE BAUMETTES PRISON!
THE CONSTRUCTION HAD JUST BEEN COMPLETED. SO, FOR TWO WEEKS, WE WERE LODGED IN THE CELLS.
THE FIRST SHOCK WAS THE COLD, WE WEREN'T PREPARED FOR THAT.
THEN, I WAS SENT TO OISSEL'S GUNPOWDER FACTORY, IN THE SEINE-MARITIME DEPARTMENT. LIFE CONDITIONS THERE WERE DEPLORABLE. BESIDE THE OBVIOUS RISK OF EXPLOSIONS, OUR FRENCH SUPERVISING OFFICERS WERE RIDDLED WITH PREJUDICES. THESE LITTLE DICTATORS WERE CONSTANTLY ON OUR BACKS!
HEY, YOU! WHO TOLD YOU TO TAKE A BREAK? GET BACK TO WORK!
AND, ON TOP OF THAT, THERE WAS THE POWDER, SPREADING EVERYWHERE, INCLUDING IN YOUR GENITALS, CAUSING VIOLENT IRRITATIONS!
I'M COMING!

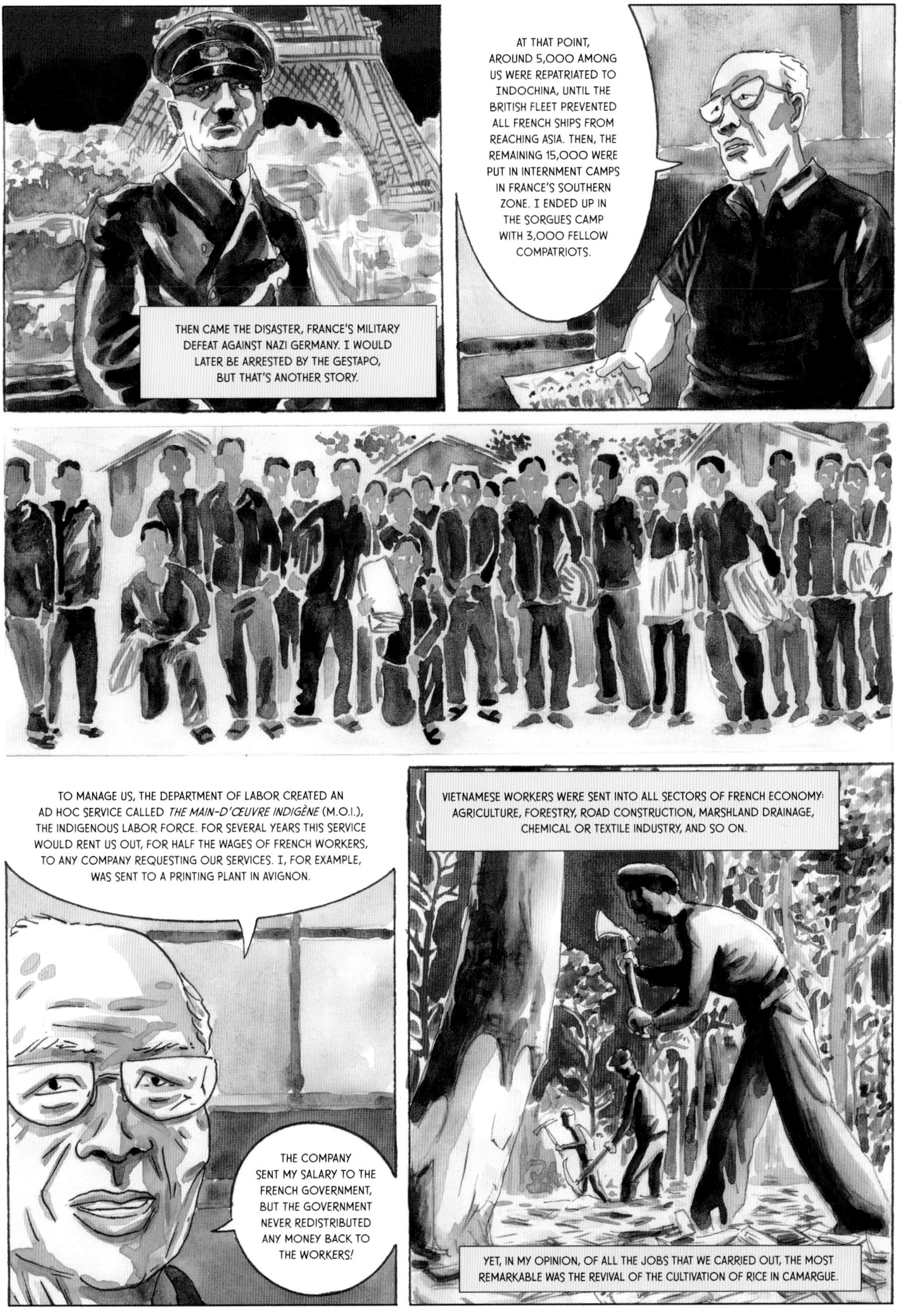
THEN CAME THE DISASTER, FRANCE'S MILITARY DEFEAT AGAINST NAZI GERMANY. I WOULD LATER BE ARRESTED BY THE GESTAPO, BUT THAT'S ANOTHER STORY.
AT THAT POINT, AROUND 5,000 AMONG US WERE REPATRIATED TO INDOCHINA, UNTIL THE BRITISH FLEET PREVENTED ALL FRENCH SHIPS FROM REACHING ASIA. THEN, THE REMAINING 15,000 WERE PUT IN INTERNMENT CAMPS IN FRANCE'S SOUTHERN ZONE. I ENDED UP IN THE SORGUES CAMP WITH 3,000 FELLOW COMPATRIOTS.
TO MANAGE US, THE DEPARTMENT OF LABOR CREATED AN AD HOC SERVICE CALLED *THE MAIN-D'ŒUVRE INDIGÈNE* (M.O.I.), THE INDIGENOUS LABOR FORCE. FOR SEVERAL YEARS THIS SERVICE WOULD RENT US OUT, FOR HALF THE WAGES OF FRENCH WORKERS, TO ANY COMPANY REQUESTING OUR SERVICES. I, FOR EXAMPLE, WAS SENT TO A PRINTING PLANT IN AVIGNON.
THE COMPANY SENT MY SALARY TO THE FRENCH GOVERNMENT, BUT THE GOVERNMENT NEVER REDISTRIBUTED ANY MONEY BACK TO THE WORKERS!
VIETNAMESE WORKERS WERE SENT INTO ALL SECTORS OF FRENCH ECONOMY: AGRICULTURE, FORESTRY, ROAD CONSTRUCTION, MARSHLAND DRAINAGE, CHEMICAL OR TEXTILE INDUSTRY, AND SO ON.
YET, IN MY OPINION, OF ALL THE JOBS THAT WE CARRIED OUT, THE MOST REMARKABLE WAS THE REVIVAL OF THE CULTIVATION OF RICE IN CAMARGUE.

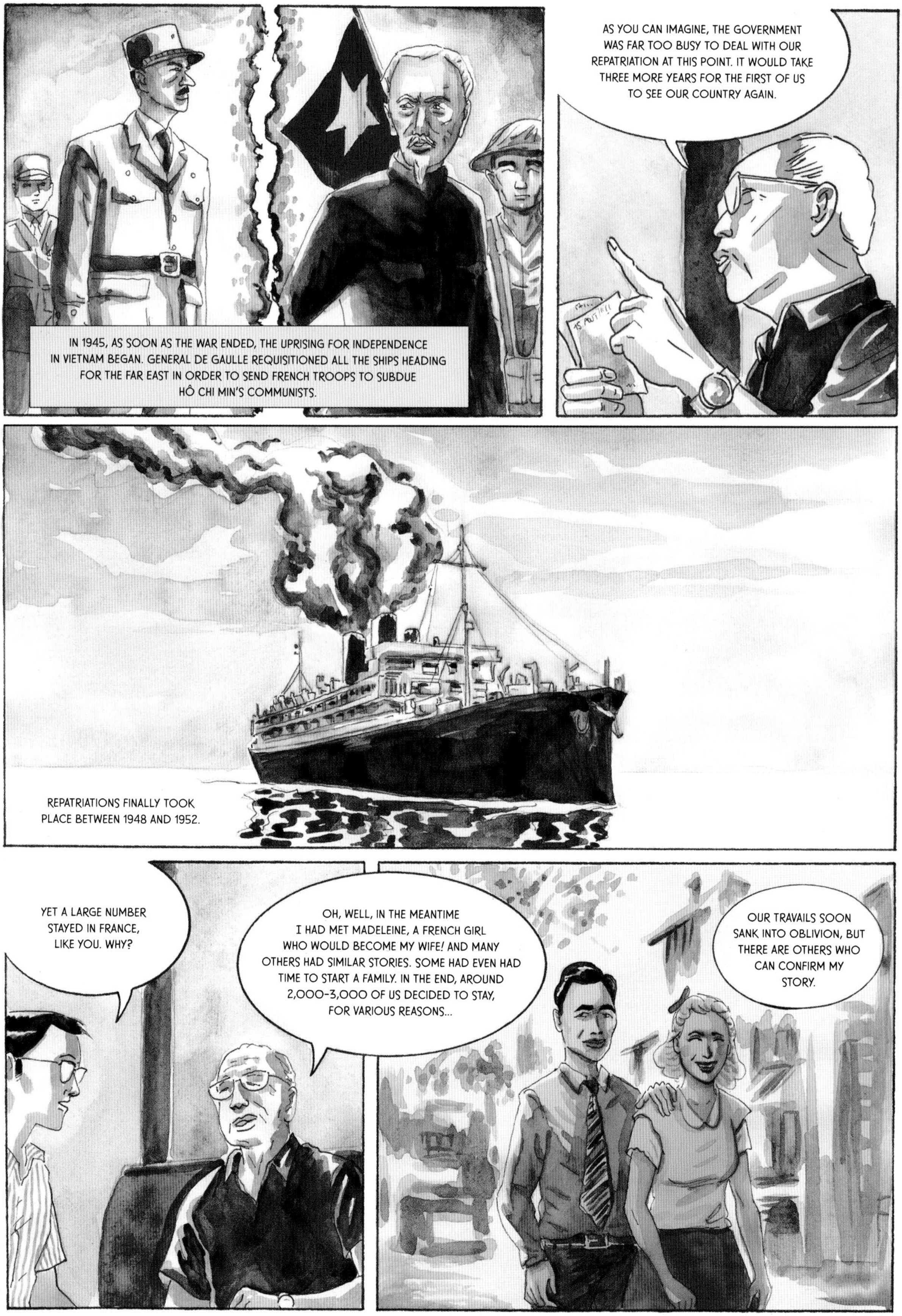

IN 1945, AS SOON AS THE WAR ENDED, THE UPRISING FOR INDEPENDENCE IN VIETNAM BEGAN. GENERAL DE GAULLE REQUISITIONED ALL THE SHIPS HEADING FOR THE FAR EAST IN ORDER TO SEND FRENCH TROOPS TO SUBDUE HÔ CHI MIN'S COMMUNISTS.
AS YOU CAN IMAGINE, THE GOVERNMENT WAS FAR TOO BUSY TO DEAL WITH OUR REPATRIATION AT THIS POINT. IT WOULD TAKE THREE MORE YEARS FOR THE FIRST OF US TO SEE OUR COUNTRY AGAIN.
REPATRIATIONS FINALLY TOOK PLACE BETWEEN 1948 AND 1952.
YET A LARGE NUMBER STAYED IN FRANCE, LIKE YOU. WHY?
OH, WELL, IN THE MEANTIME I HAD MET MADELEINE, A FRENCH GIRL WHO WOULD BECOME MY WIFE! AND MANY OTHERS HAD SIMILAR STORIES. SOME HAD EVEN HAD TIME TO START A FAMILY. IN THE END, AROUND 2,000-3,000 OF US DECIDED TO STAY, FOR VARIOUS REASONS...
OUR TRAVAILS SOON SANK INTO OBLIVION, BUT THERE ARE OTHERS WHO CAN CONFIRM MY STORY.

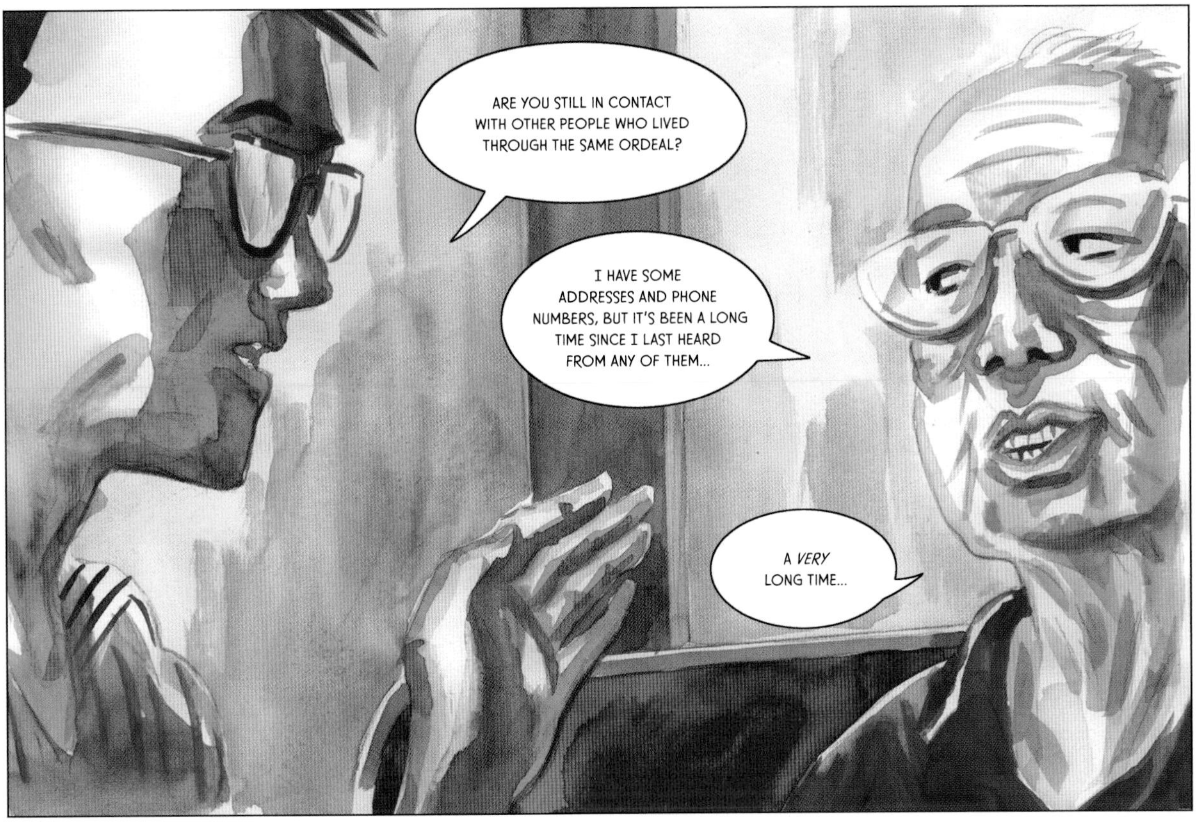
ARE YOU STILL IN CONTACT WITH OTHER PEOPLE WHO LIVED THROUGH THE SAME ORDEAL?
I HAVE SOME ADDRESSES AND PHONE NUMBERS, BUT IT'S BEEN A LONG TIME SINCE I LAST HEARD FROM ANY OF THEM...
A *VERY* LONG TIME...

AFTER THIS FIRST MEETING, I COULD HAVE JUST BEEN CONTENT WITH AN ARTICLE SOLELY BASED ON THE INTERVIEW, BUT THE FACT THAT THERE WERE SO MANY OF THESE FORMER LABORERS, THEN CALLED O.N.S., FOR *OUVRIERS NON SPÉCIALISÉS*, UNSKILLED WORKERS, OUT THERE BOTHERED ME. I KNEW I COULD FIND MORE OF THEM.

THE MORE INFORMATION I GATHERED ON THEM, THE MORE I WAS CONVINCED THAT THE STORY OF THE INDOCHINESE WORKERS DESERVED MORE THAN A SAD PAGE OR TWO IN *LIBÉRATION*...

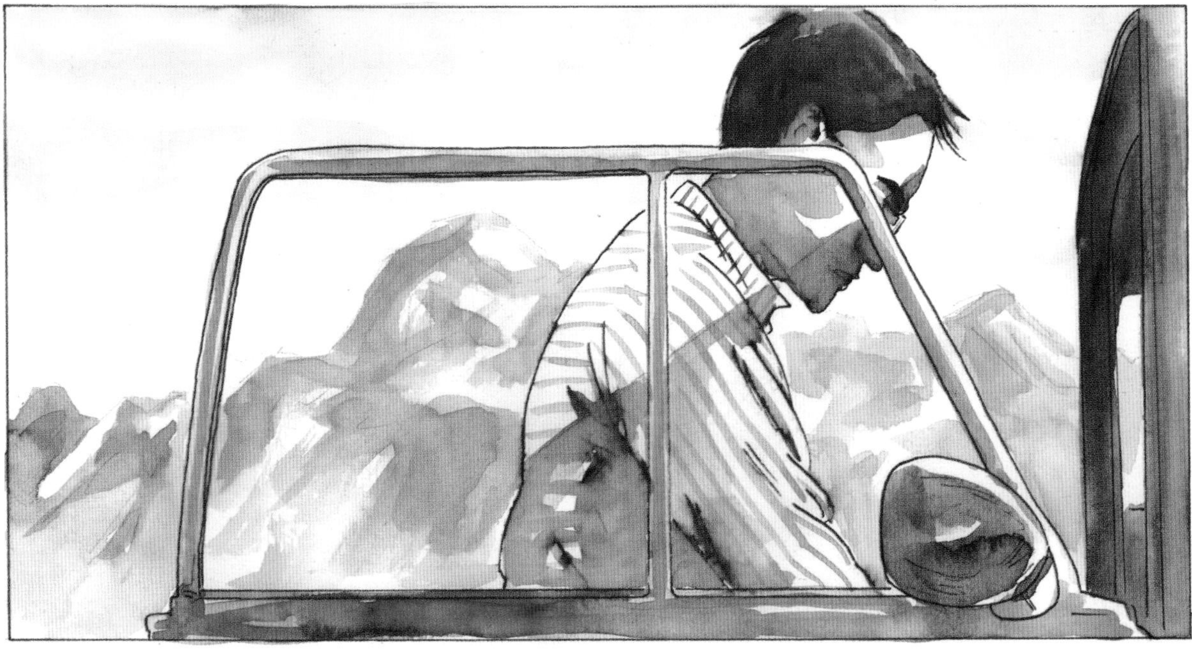

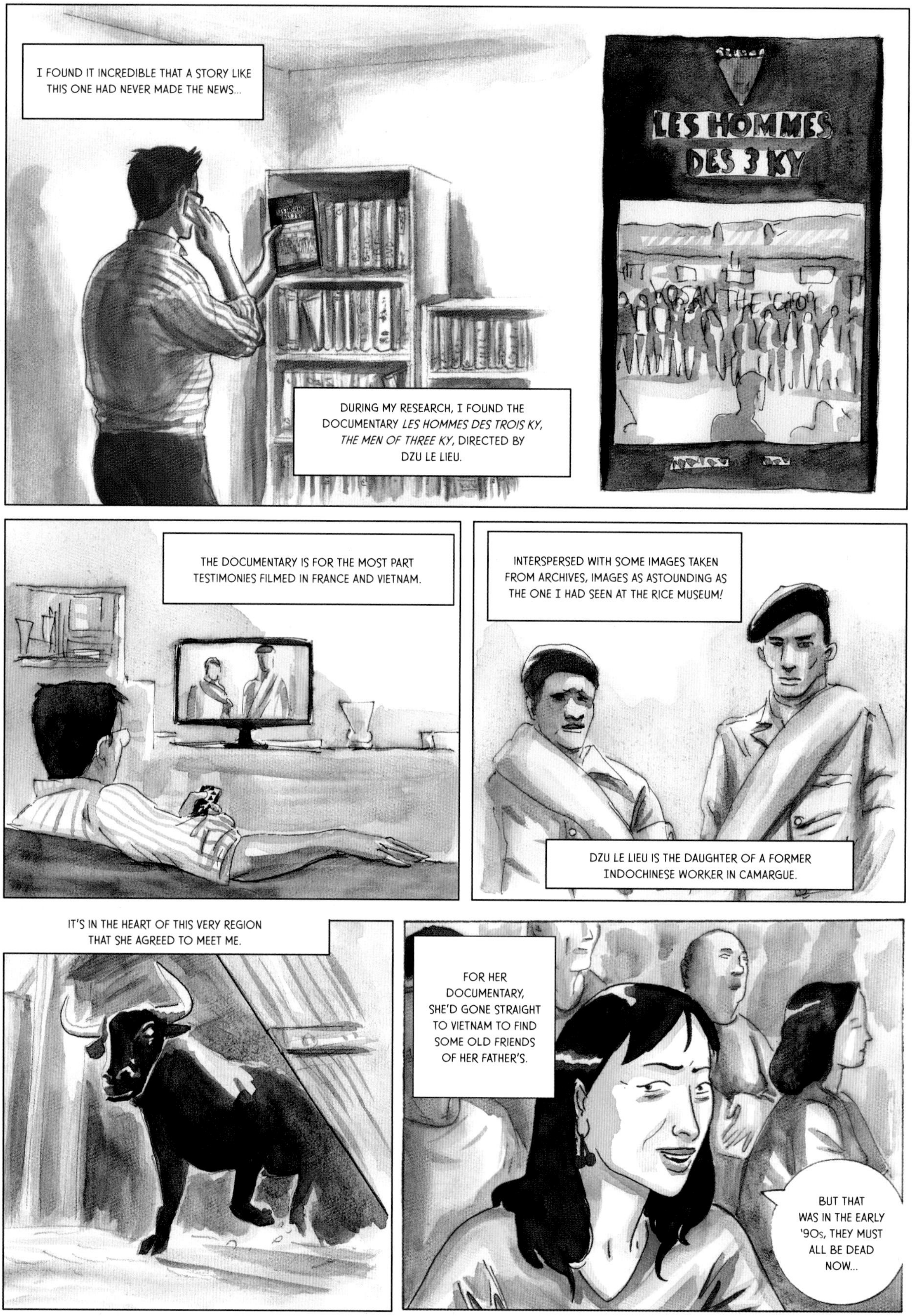
I FOUND IT INCREDIBLE THAT A STORY LIKE THIS ONE HAD NEVER MADE THE NEWS...
LES HOMMES DES 3 KY
DURING MY RESEARCH, I FOUND THE DOCUMENTARY *LES HOMMES DES TROIS KY, THE MEN OF THREE KY*, DIRECTED BY DZU LE LIEU.
THE DOCUMENTARY IS FOR THE MOST PART TESTIMONIES FILMED IN FRANCE AND VIETNAM.
INTERSPERSED WITH SOME IMAGES TAKEN FROM ARCHIVES, IMAGES AS ASTOUNDING AS THE ONE I HAD SEEN AT THE RICE MUSEUM!
DZU LE LIEU IS THE DAUGHTER OF A FORMER INDOCHINESE WORKER IN CAMARGUE.
IT'S IN THE HEART OF THIS VERY REGION THAT SHE AGREED TO MEET ME.
FOR HER DOCUMENTARY, SHE'D GONE STRAIGHT TO VIETNAM TO FIND SOME OLD FRIENDS OF HER FATHER'S.
BUT THAT WAS IN THE EARLY '90s, THEY MUST ALL BE DEAD NOW...

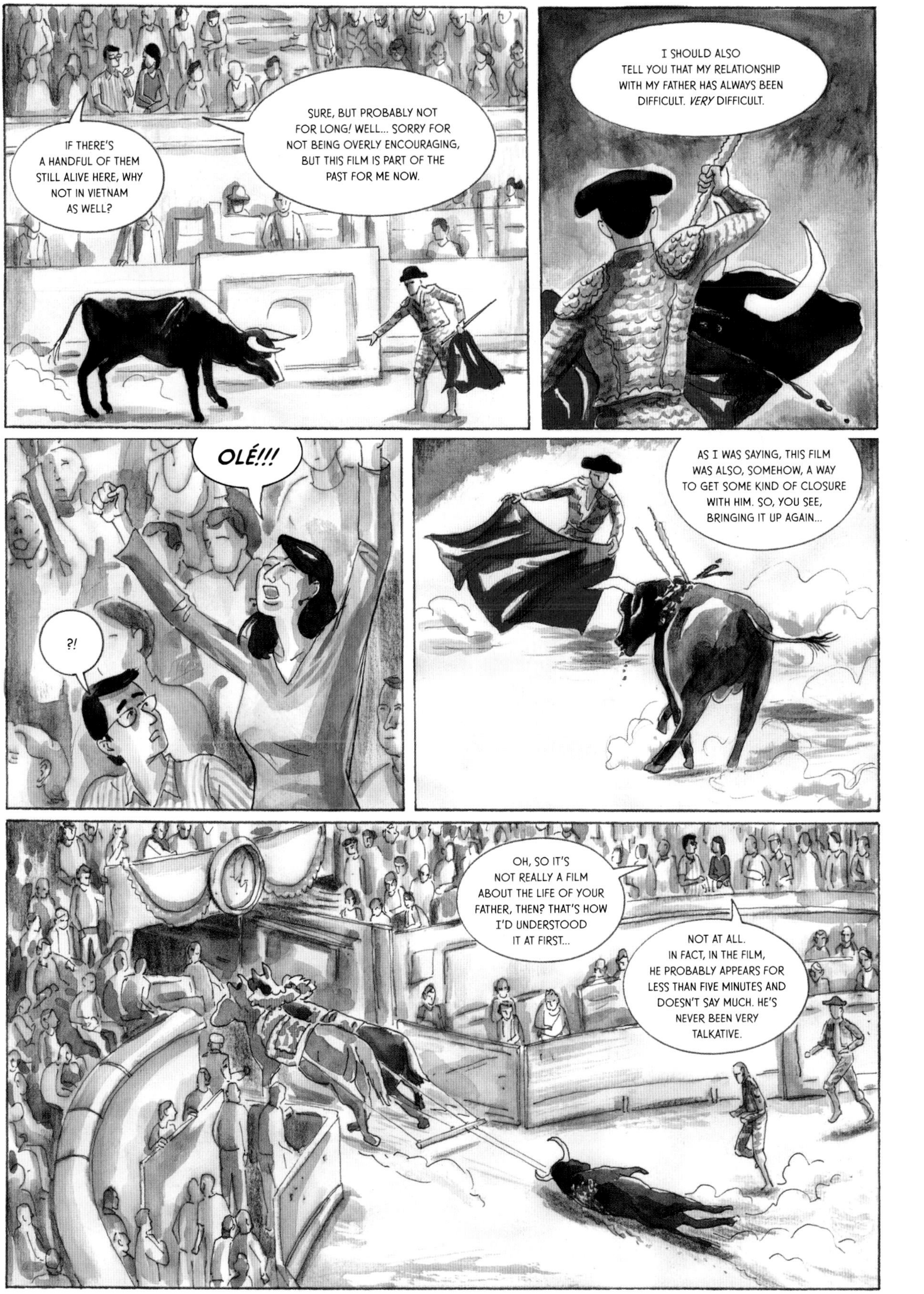
IF THERE'S A HANDFUL OF THEM STILL ALIVE HERE, WHY NOT IN VIETNAM AS WELL?
SURE, BUT PROBABLY NOT FOR LONG! WELL... SORRY FOR NOT BEING OVERLY ENCOURAGING, BUT THIS FILM IS PART OF THE PAST FOR ME NOW.
I SHOULD ALSO TELL YOU THAT MY RELATIONSHIP WITH MY FATHER HAS ALWAYS BEEN DIFFICULT. *VERY* DIFFICULT.
OLÉ!!!
?!
AS I WAS SAYING, THIS FILM WAS ALSO, SOMEHOW, A WAY TO GET SOME KIND OF CLOSURE WITH HIM. SO, YOU SEE, BRINGING IT UP AGAIN...
OH, SO IT'S NOT REALLY A FILM ABOUT THE LIFE OF YOUR FATHER, THEN? THAT'S HOW I'D UNDERSTOOD IT AT FIRST...
NOT AT ALL. IN FACT, IN THE FILM, HE PROBABLY APPEARS FOR LESS THAN FIVE MINUTES AND DOESN'T SAY MUCH. HE'S NEVER BEEN VERY TALKATIVE.

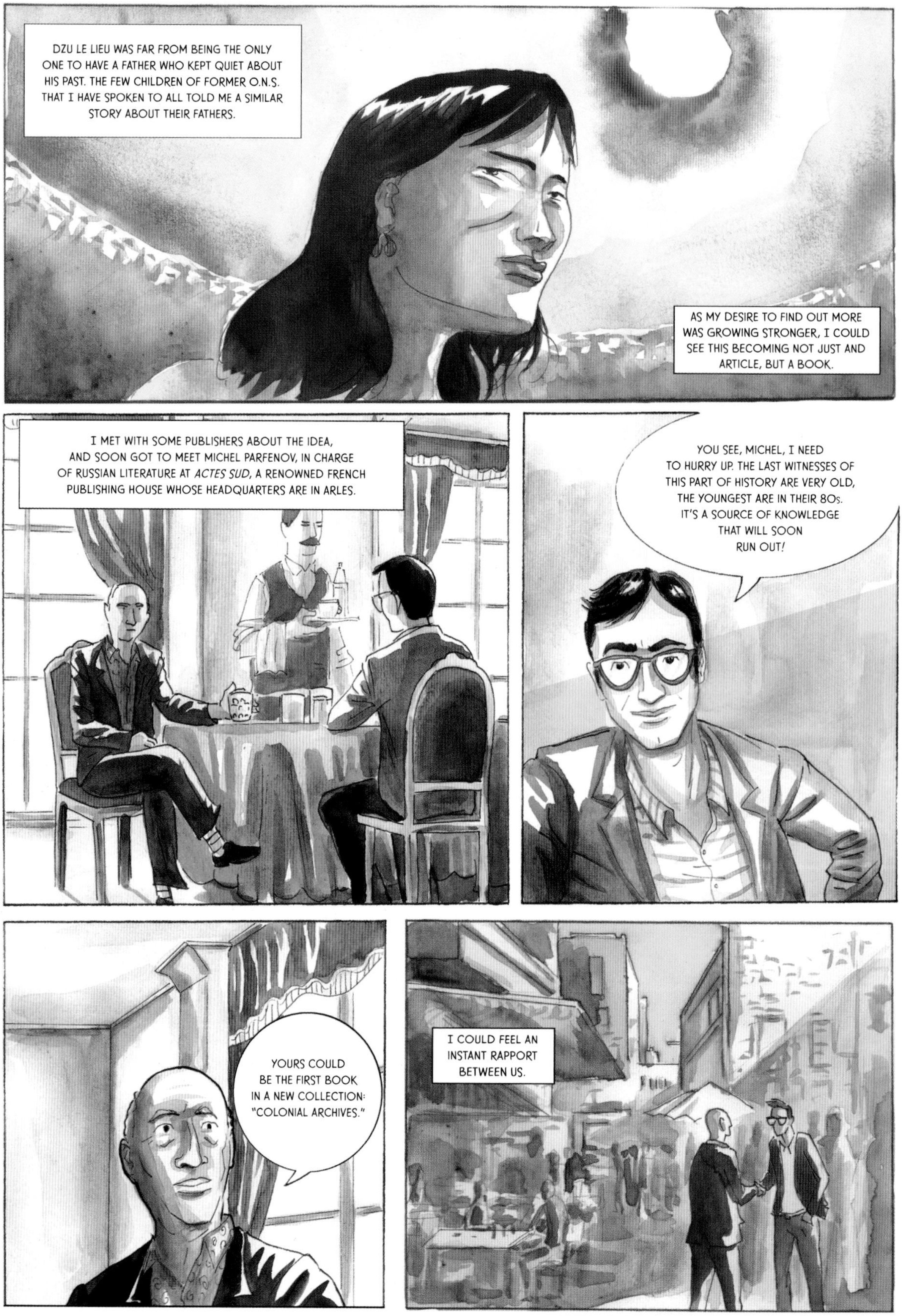
DZU LE LIEU WAS FAR FROM BEING THE ONLY ONE TO HAVE A FATHER WHO KEPT QUIET ABOUT HIS PAST. THE FEW CHILDREN OF FORMER O.N.S. THAT I HAVE SPOKEN TO ALL TOLD ME A SIMILAR STORY ABOUT THEIR FATHERS.
AS MY DESIRE TO FIND OUT MORE WAS GROWING STRONGER, I COULD SEE THIS BECOMING NOT JUST AND ARTICLE, BUT A BOOK.
I MET WITH SOME PUBLISHERS ABOUT THE IDEA, AND SOON GOT TO MEET MICHEL PARFENOV, IN CHARGE OF RUSSIAN LITERATURE AT *ACTES SUD*, A RENOWNED FRENCH PUBLISHING HOUSE WHOSE HEADQUARTERS ARE IN ARLES.
YOU SEE, MICHEL, I NEED TO HURRY UP. THE LAST WITNESSES OF THIS PART OF HISTORY ARE VERY OLD, THE YOUNGEST ARE IN THEIR 80s. IT'S A SOURCE OF KNOWLEDGE THAT WILL SOON RUN OUT!
YOURS COULD BE THE FIRST BOOK IN A NEW COLLECTION: "COLONIAL ARCHIVES."
I COULD FEEL AN INSTANT RAPPORT BETWEEN US.

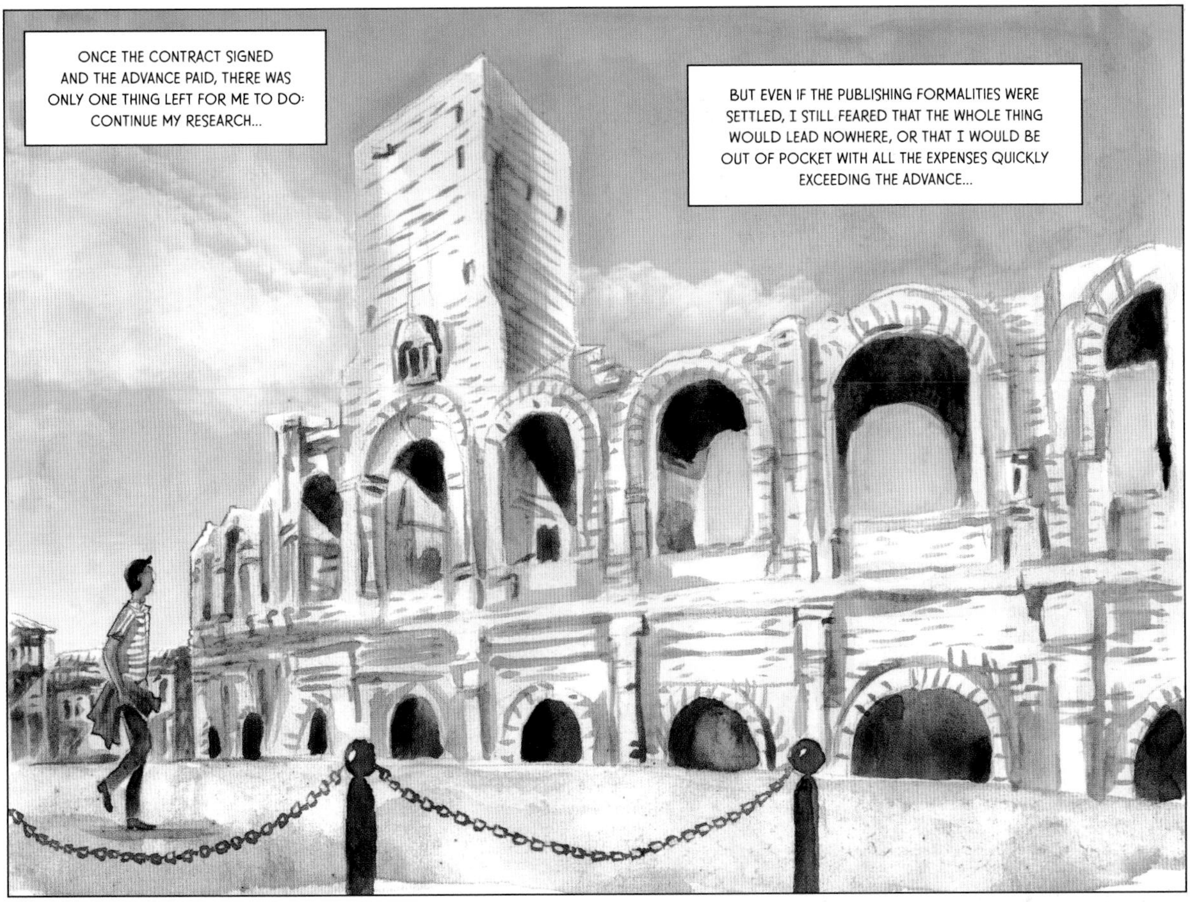
ONCE THE CONTRACT SIGNED AND THE ADVANCE PAID, THERE WAS ONLY ONE THING LEFT FOR ME TO DO: CONTINUE MY RESEARCH...
BUT EVEN IF THE PUBLISHING FORMALITIES WERE SETTLED, I STILL FEARED THAT THE WHOLE THING WOULD LEAD NOWHERE, OR THAT I WOULD BE OUT OF POCKET WITH ALL THE EXPENSES QUICKLY EXCEEDING THE ADVANCE...

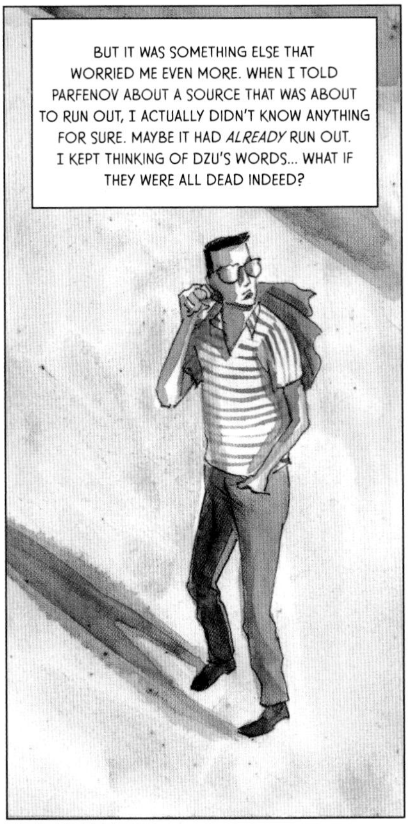
BUT IT WAS SOMETHING ELSE THAT WORRIED ME EVEN MORE. WHEN I TOLD PARFENOV ABOUT A SOURCE THAT WAS ABOUT TO RUN OUT, I ACTUALLY DIDN'T KNOW ANYTHING FOR SURE. MAYBE IT HAD *ALREADY* RUN OUT. I KEPT THINKING OF DZU'S WORDS... WHAT IF THEY WERE ALL DEAD INDEED?

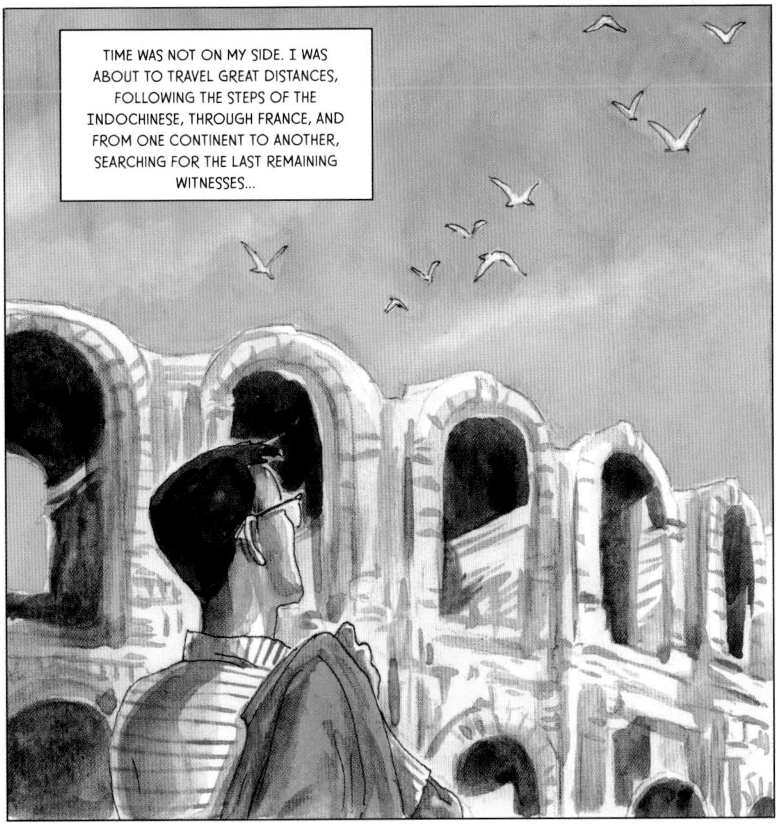
TIME WAS NOT ON MY SIDE. I WAS ABOUT TO TRAVEL GREAT DISTANCES, FOLLOWING THE STEPS OF THE INDOCHINESE, THROUGH FRANCE, AND FROM ONE CONTINENT TO ANOTHER, SEARCHING FOR THE LAST REMAINING WITNESSES...

2. INDOCHINESE IN CAMARGUE

OR THE FATE OF MEN TORN BETWEEN TWO COUNTRIES AND BETWEEN TWO WARS

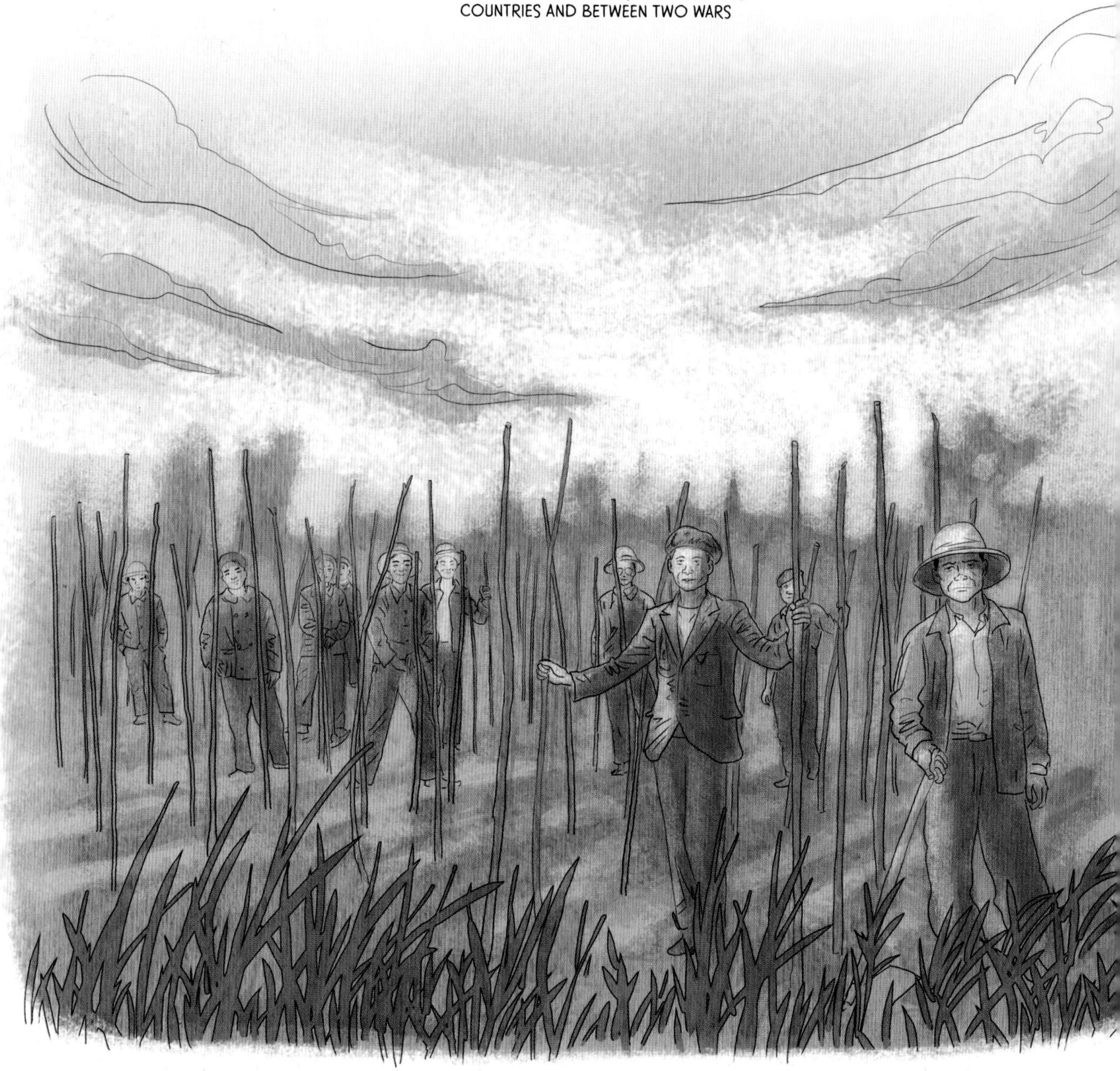

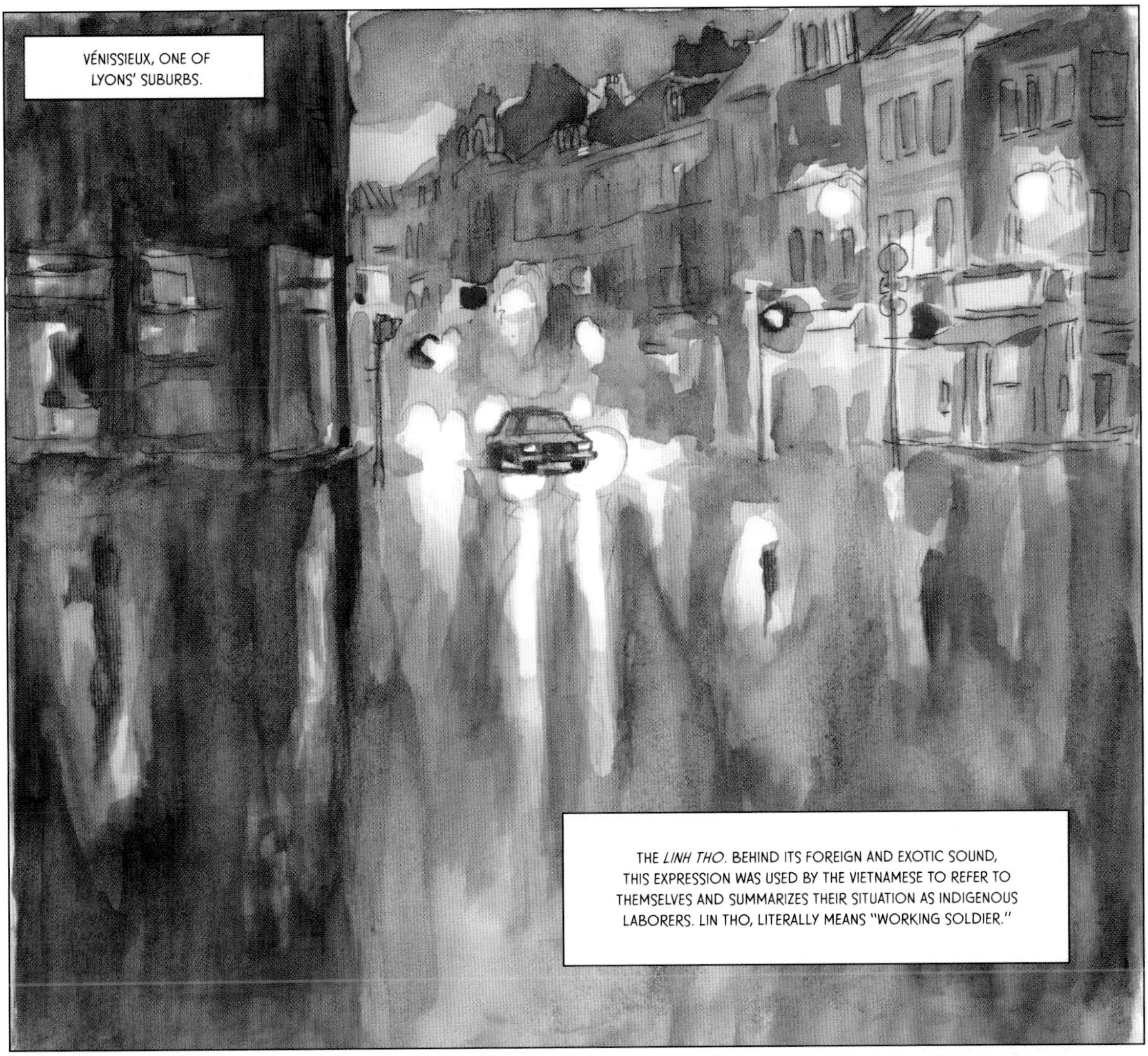
VÉNISSIEUX, ONE OF
LYONS' SUBURBS.
THE *LINH THO*. BEHIND ITS FOREIGN AND EXOTIC SOUND, THIS EXPRESSION WAS USED BY THE VIETNAMESE TO REFER TO THEMSELVES AND SUMMARIZES THEIR SITUATION AS INDIGENOUS LABORERS. LIN THO, LITERALLY MEANS "WORKING SOLDIER."

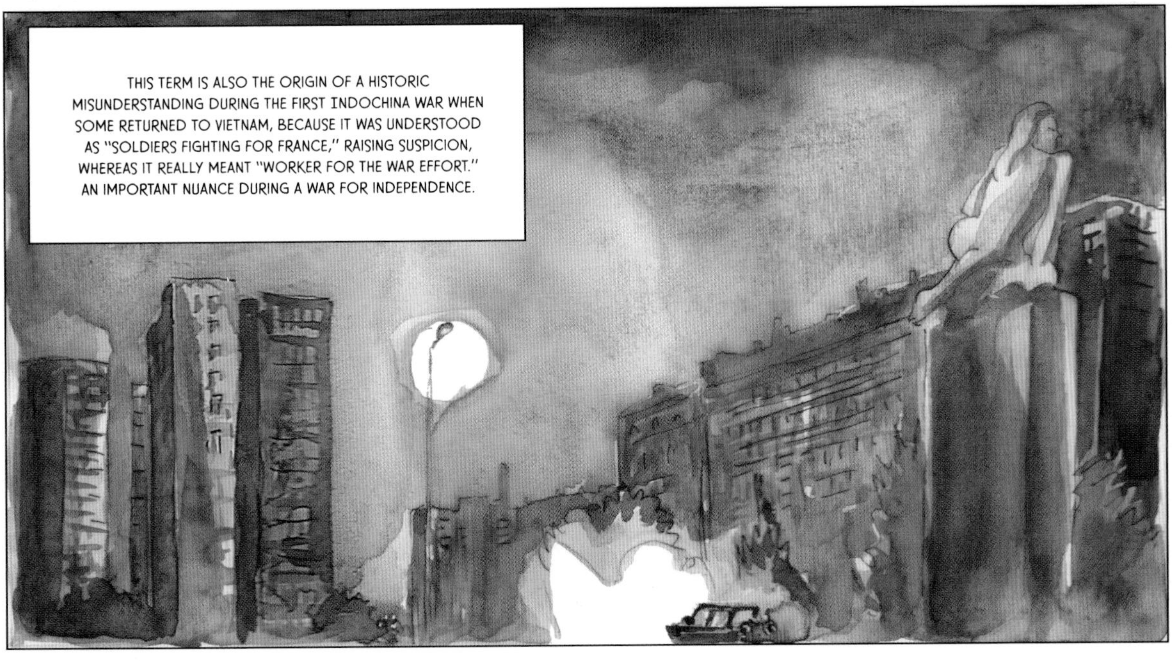
THIS TERM IS ALSO THE ORIGIN OF A HISTORIC MISUNDERSTANDING DURING THE FIRST INDOCHINA WAR WHEN SOME RETURNED TO VIETNAM, BECAUSE IT WAS UNDERSTOOD AS "SOLDIERS FIGHTING FOR FRANCE," RAISING SUSPICION, WHEREAS IT REALLY MEANT "WORKER FOR THE WAR EFFORT." AN IMPORTANT NUANCE DURING A WAR FOR INDEPENDENCE.

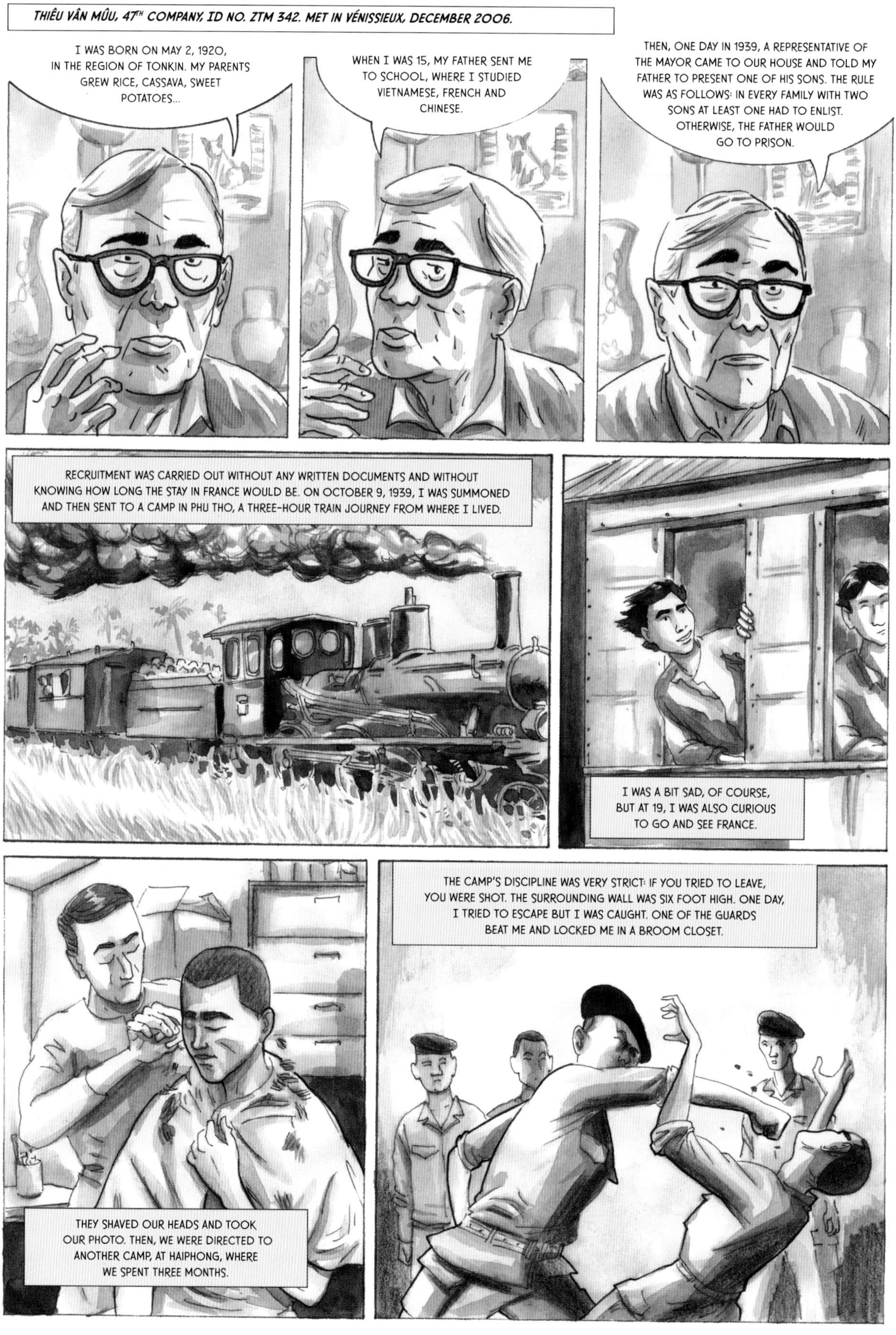
THIÊU VÂN MÛU, 47TH COMPANY, ID NO. ZTM 342. MET IN VÉNISSIEUX, DECEMBER 2006.
I WAS BORN ON MAY 2, 1920, IN THE REGION OF TONKIN. MY PARENTS GREW RICE, CASSAVA, SWEET POTATOES...
WHEN I WAS 15, MY FATHER SENT ME TO SCHOOL, WHERE I STUDIED VIETNAMESE, FRENCH AND CHINESE.
THEN, ONE DAY IN 1939, A REPRESENTATIVE OF THE MAYOR CAME TO OUR HOUSE AND TOLD MY FATHER TO PRESENT ONE OF HIS SONS. THE RULE WAS AS FOLLOWS: IN EVERY FAMILY WITH TWO SONS AT LEAST ONE HAD TO ENLIST. OTHERWISE, THE FATHER WOULD GO TO PRISON.
RECRUITMENT WAS CARRIED OUT WITHOUT ANY WRITTEN DOCUMENTS AND WITHOUT KNOWING HOW LONG THE STAY IN FRANCE WOULD BE. ON OCTOBER 9, 1939, I WAS SUMMONED AND THEN SENT TO A CAMP IN PHU THO, A THREE-HOUR TRAIN JOURNEY FROM WHERE I LIVED.
I WAS A BIT SAD, OF COURSE, BUT AT 19, I WAS ALSO CURIOUS TO GO AND SEE FRANCE.
THEY SHAVED OUR HEADS AND TOOK OUR PHOTO. THEN, WE WERE DIRECTED TO ANOTHER CAMP, AT HAIPHONG, WHERE WE SPENT THREE MONTHS.
THE CAMP'S DISCIPLINE WAS VERY STRICT: IF YOU TRIED TO LEAVE, YOU WERE SHOT. THE SURROUNDING WALL WAS SIX FOOT HIGH. ONE DAY, I TRIED TO ESCAPE BUT I WAS CAUGHT. ONE OF THE GUARDS BEAT ME AND LOCKED ME IN A BROOM CLOSET.

ONCE, MY BROTHER AND MY LITTLE SISTER CAME ALL THE WAY FROM OUR VILLAGE TO SEE ME.

BUT I COULDN'T LEAVE THE CAMP, SO WE HAD TO SPEAK THROUGH A HOLE IN THE WALL.

WE SPOKE LIKE THIS.

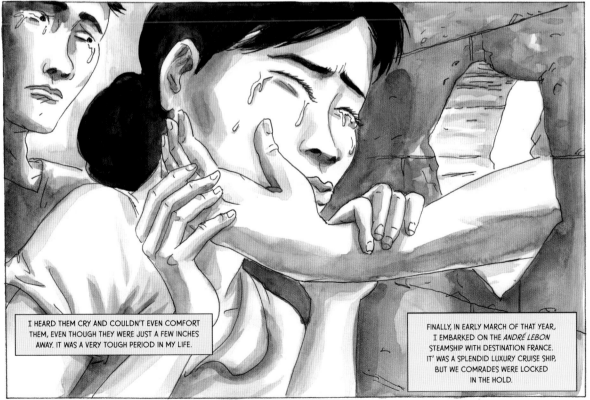

I HEARD THEM CRY AND COULDN'T EVEN COMFORT THEM, EVEN THOUGH THEY WERE JUST A FEW INCHES AWAY. IT WAS A VERY TOUGH PERIOD IN MY LIFE.

FINALLY, IN EARLY MARCH OF THAT YEAR, I EMBARKED ON THE *ANDRÉ LEBON* STEAMSHIP WITH DESTINATION FRANCE. IT' WAS A SPLENDID LUXURY CRUISE SHIP, BUT WE COMRADES WERE LOCKED IN THE HOLD.

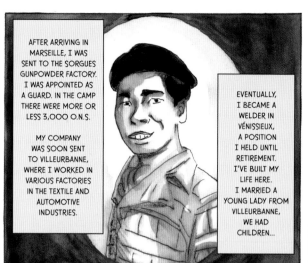

AFTER ARRIVING IN MARSEILLE, I WAS SENT TO THE SORGUES GUNPOWDER FACTORY. I WAS APPOINTED AS A GUARD. IN THE CAMP THERE WERE MORE OR LESS 3,000 O.N.S.

MY COMPANY WAS SOON SENT TO VILLEURBANNE, WHERE I WORKED IN VARIOUS FACTORIES IN THE TEXTILE AND AUTOMOTIVE INDUSTRIES.

EVENTUALLY, I BECAME A WELDER IN VÉNISSIEUX, A POSITION I HELD UNTIL RETIREMENT. I'VE BUILT MY LIFE HERE. I MARRIED A YOUNG LADY FROM VILLEURBANNE, WE HAD CHILDREN...

... AND IN 1976, WHEN I RETURNED TO VIETNAM FOR THE FIRST TIME, MY PARENTS WERE DEAD, AS WELL AS MOST OF MY SIBLINGS. ONLY ONE OF MY SISTERS WAS STILL ALIVE.

ACCORDING TO HIS OWN SON, THIỀU VẨN MỦU HAS ALWAYS SHOWN AN EXTRAORDINARY DESIRE TO INTEGRATE, SO MUCH SO THAT HE DIDN'T SPEAK OF HIS NATIVE CULTURE FOR A LONG TIME AND GAVE HIS CHILDREN WESTERN NAMES.

THEN, LATER ON IN LIFE, HE BEGAN WRITING HIS MEMOIRS, TO TELL HIS CHILDREN WHERE HE'D COME FROM AND WHAT HE'D COME TO DO IN A COUNTRY THAT WAS FOREIGN TO HIM.

NEXT LEG OF MY JOURNEY...

PARIS!

LE BA DANG, 69TH COMPANY, ID NO. ZAE 6. MET IN PARIS, OCTOBER 2006.

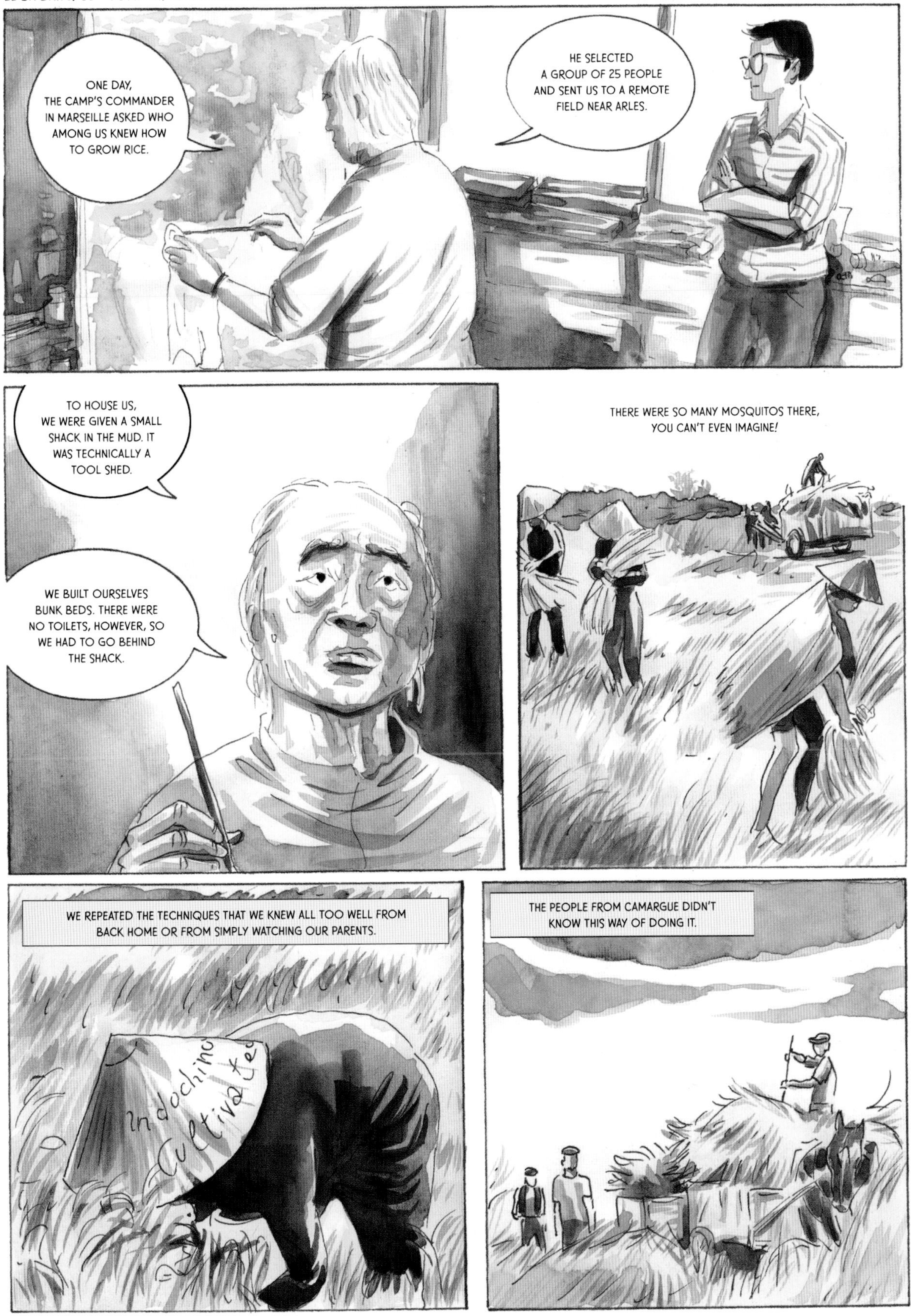
ONE DAY, THE CAMP'S COMMANDER IN MARSEILLE ASKED WHO AMONG US KNEW HOW TO GROW RICE.
HE SELECTED A GROUP OF 25 PEOPLE AND SENT US TO A REMOTE FIELD NEAR ARLES.
TO HOUSE US, WE WERE GIVEN A SMALL SHACK IN THE MUD. IT WAS TECHNICALLY A TOOL SHED.
WE BUILT OURSELVES BUNK BEDS. THERE WERE NO TOILETS, HOWEVER, SO WE HAD TO GO BEHIND THE SHACK.
THERE WERE SO MANY MOSQUITOS THERE, YOU CAN'T EVEN IMAGINE!
WE REPEATED THE TECHNIQUES THAT WE KNEW ALL TOO WELL FROM BACK HOME OR FROM SIMPLY WATCHING OUR PARENTS.
THE PEOPLE FROM CAMARGUE DIDN'T KNOW THIS WAY OF DOING IT.

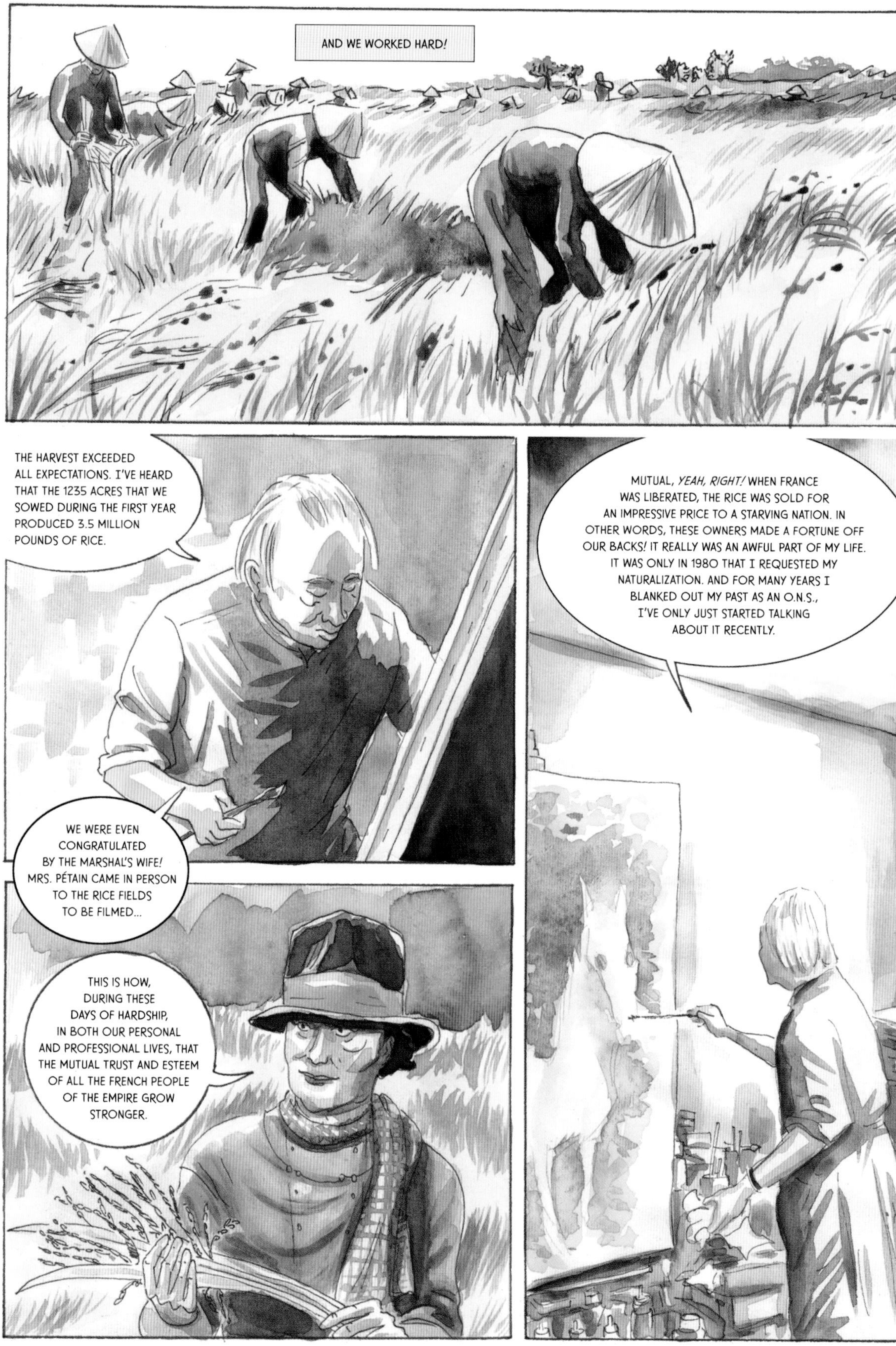
AND WE WORKED HARD!
THE HARVEST EXCEEDED ALL EXPECTATIONS. I'VE HEARD THAT THE 1235 ACRES THAT WE SOWED DURING THE FIRST YEAR PRODUCED 3.5 MILLION POUNDS OF RICE.
WE WERE EVEN CONGRATULATED BY THE MARSHAL'S WIFE! MRS. PÉTAIN CAME IN PERSON TO THE RICE FIELDS TO BE FILMED...
THIS IS HOW, DURING THESE DAYS OF HARDSHIP, IN BOTH OUR PERSONAL AND PROFESSIONAL LIVES, THAT THE MUTUAL TRUST AND ESTEEM OF ALL THE FRENCH PEOPLE OF THE EMPIRE GROW STRONGER.
MUTUAL, *YEAH, RIGHT!* WHEN FRANCE WAS LIBERATED, THE RICE WAS SOLD FOR AN IMPRESSIVE PRICE TO A STARVING NATION. IN OTHER WORDS, THESE OWNERS MADE A FORTUNE OFF OUR BACKS! IT REALLY WAS AN AWFUL PART OF MY LIFE. IT WAS ONLY IN 1980 THAT I REQUESTED MY NATURALIZATION. AND FOR MANY YEARS I BLANKED OUT MY PAST AS AN O.N.S., I'VE ONLY JUST STARTED TALKING ABOUT IT RECENTLY.

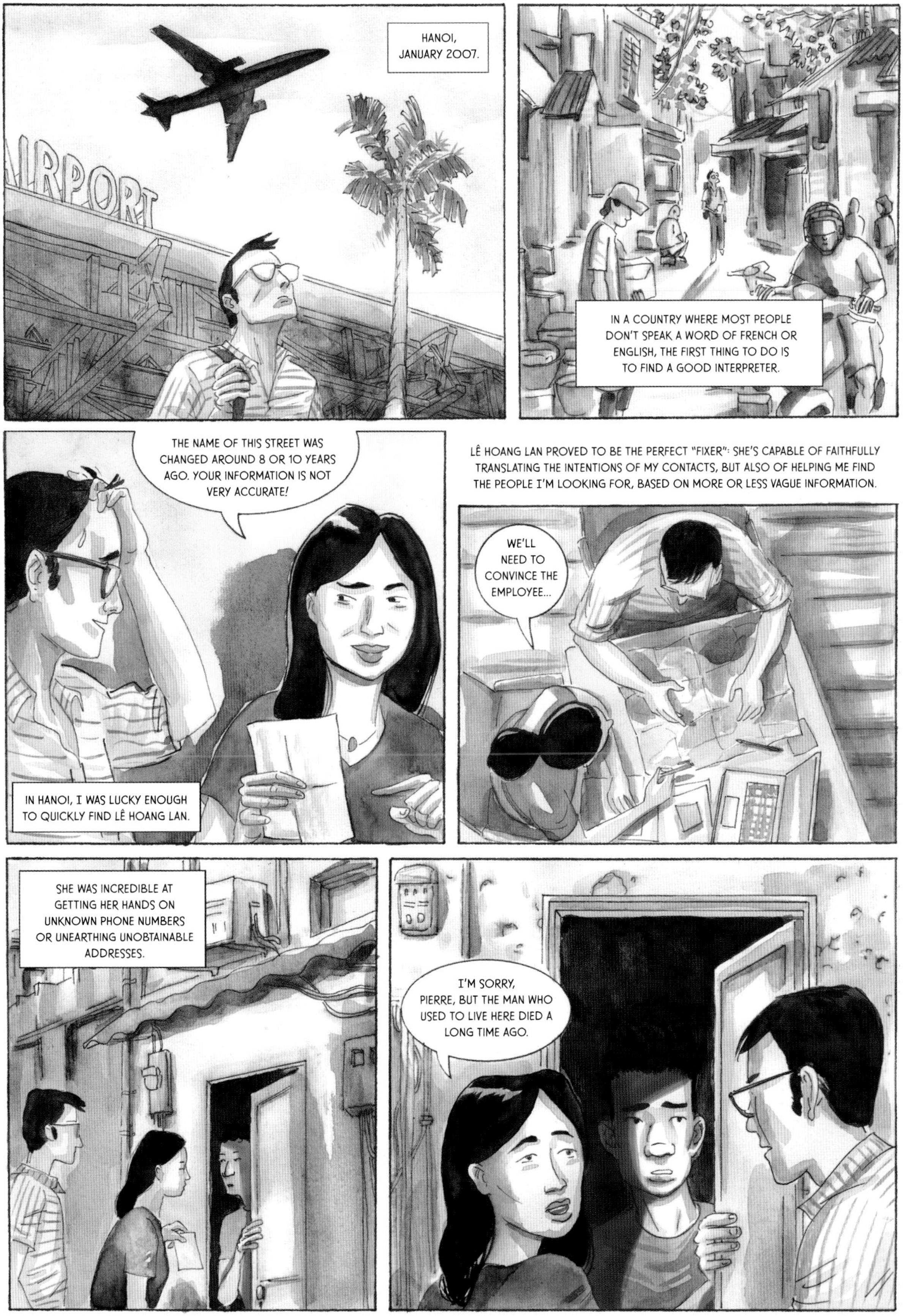
HANOI, JANUARY 2007.
AIRPORT
IN A COUNTRY WHERE MOST PEOPLE DON'T SPEAK A WORD OF FRENCH OR ENGLISH, THE FIRST THING TO DO IS TO FIND A GOOD INTERPRETER.
THE NAME OF THIS STREET WAS CHANGED AROUND 8 OR 10 YEARS AGO. YOUR INFORMATION IS NOT VERY ACCURATE!
IN HANOI, I WAS LUCKY ENOUGH TO QUICKLY FIND LÊ HOANG LAN.
LÊ HOANG LAN PROVED TO BE THE PERFECT "FIXER": SHE'S CAPABLE OF FAITHFULLY TRANSLATING THE INTENTIONS OF MY CONTACTS, BUT ALSO OF HELPING ME FIND THE PEOPLE I'M LOOKING FOR, BASED ON MORE OR LESS VAGUE INFORMATION.
WE'LL NEED TO CONVINCE THE EMPLOYEE...
SHE WAS INCREDIBLE AT GETTING HER HANDS ON UNKNOWN PHONE NUMBERS OR UNEARTHING UNOBTAINABLE ADDRESSES.
I'M SORRY, PIERRE, BUT THE MAN WHO USED TO LIVE HERE DIED A LONG TIME AGO.

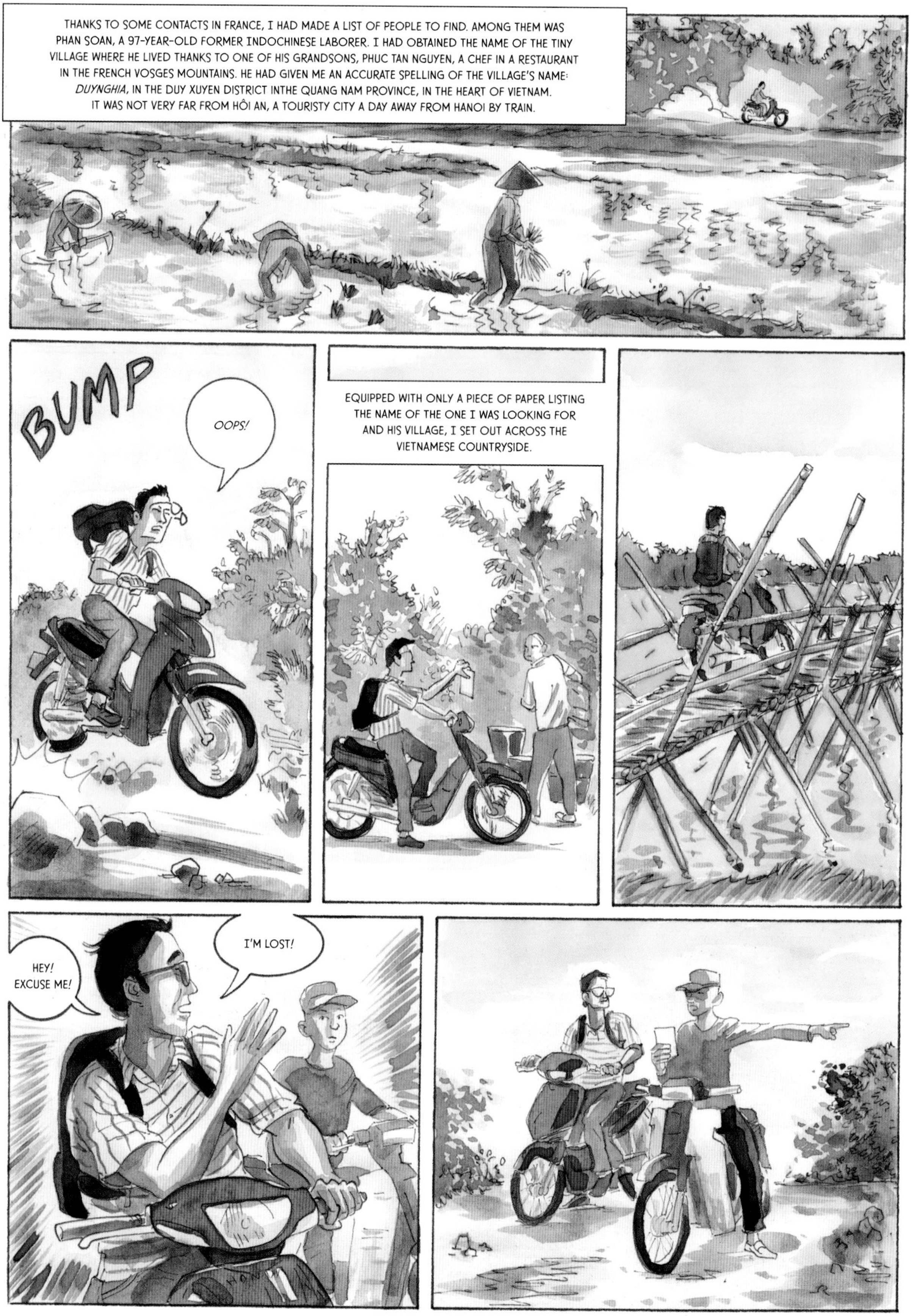
THANKS TO SOME CONTACTS IN FRANCE, I HAD MADE A LIST OF PEOPLE TO FIND. AMONG THEM WAS PHAN SOAN, A 97-YEAR-OLD FORMER INDOCHINESE LABORER. I HAD OBTAINED THE NAME OF THE TINY VILLAGE WHERE HE LIVED THANKS TO ONE OF HIS GRANDSONS, PHUC TAN NGUYEN, A CHEF IN A RESTAURANT IN THE FRENCH VOSGES MOUNTAINS. HE HAD GIVEN ME AN ACCURATE SPELLING OF THE VILLAGE'S NAME: *DUYNGHIA*, IN THE DUY XUYEN DISTRICT INTHE QUANG NAM PROVINCE, IN THE HEART OF VIETNAM. IT WAS NOT VERY FAR FROM HÔI AN, A TOURISTY CITY A DAY AWAY FROM HANOI BY TRAIN.
BUMP
OOPS!
EQUIPPED WITH ONLY A PIECE OF PAPER LISTING THE NAME OF THE ONE I WAS LOOKING FOR AND HIS VILLAGE, I SET OUT ACROSS THE VIETNAMESE COUNTRYSIDE.
HEY! EXCUSE ME!
I'M LOST!

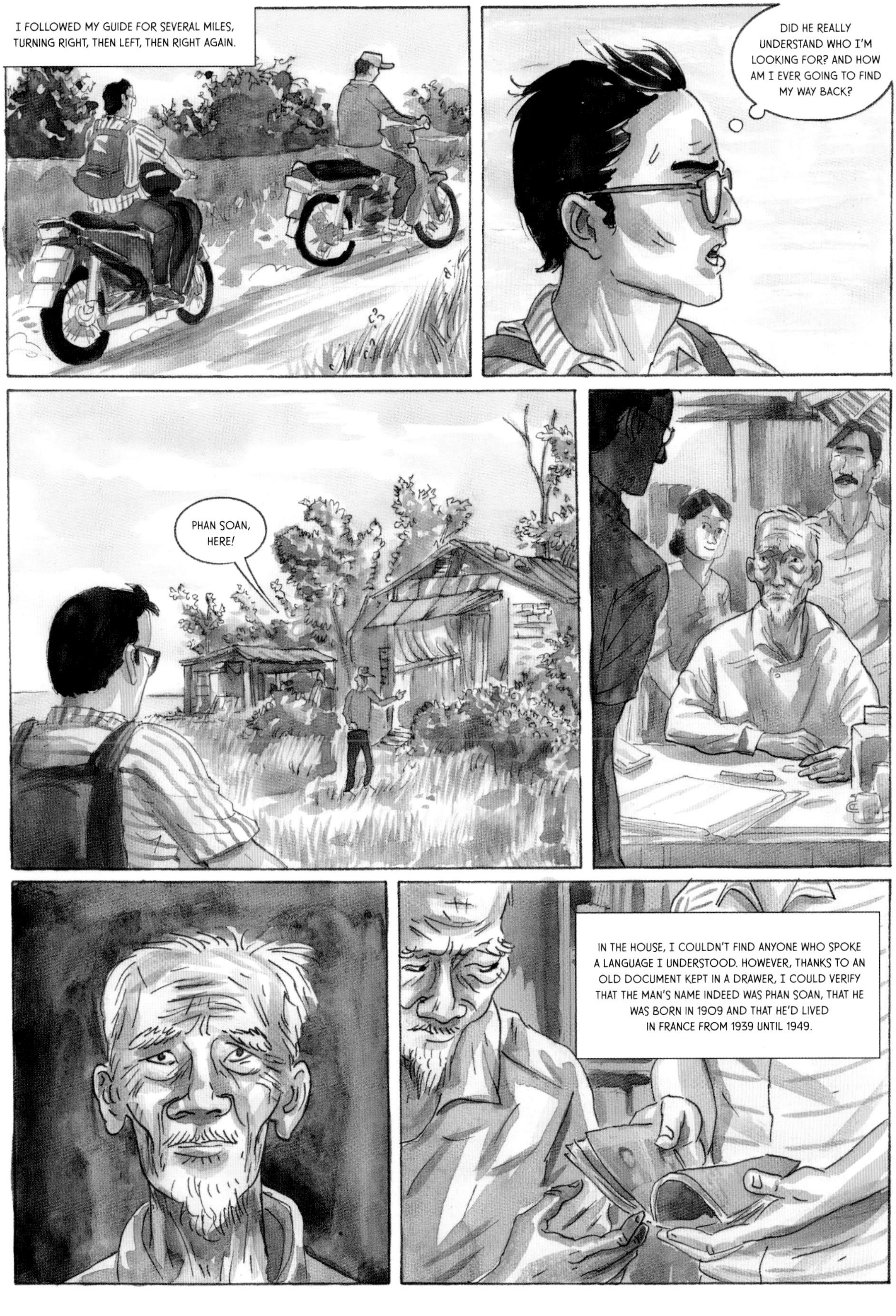
I FOLLOWED MY GUIDE FOR SEVERAL MILES, TURNING RIGHT, THEN LEFT, THEN RIGHT AGAIN.
DID HE REALLY UNDERSTAND WHO I'M LOOKING FOR? AND HOW AM I EVER GOING TO FIND MY WAY BACK?
PHAN SOAN, HERE!
IN THE HOUSE, I COULDN'T FIND ANYONE WHO SPOKE A LANGUAGE I UNDERSTOOD. HOWEVER, THANKS TO AN OLD DOCUMENT KEPT IN A DRAWER, I COULD VERIFY THAT THE MAN'S NAME INDEED WAS PHAN SOAN, THAT HE WAS BORN IN 1909 AND THAT HE'D LIVED IN FRANCE FROM 1939 UNTIL 1949.

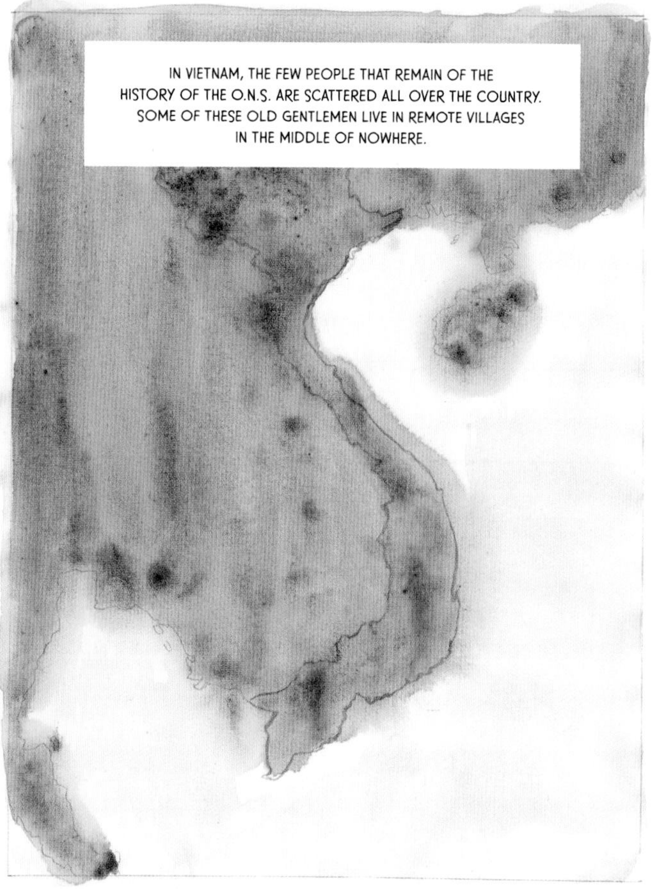
IN VIETNAM, THE FEW PEOPLE THAT REMAIN OF THE HISTORY OF THE O.N.S. ARE SCATTERED ALL OVER THE COUNTRY. SOME OF THESE OLD GENTLEMEN LIVE IN REMOTE VILLAGES IN THE MIDDLE OF NOWHERE.

HERE'S DÔ VI, MET IN VINH DIÊN, JANUARY 2007.

VINH DIÊN LIES INLAND, A FEW MILES FROM HÔI AN, IN THE MIDDLE OF THE COUNTRY. DÔ VI LIVES IN A SMALL VILLAGE ON THE OUTSKIRTS OF VINH DIÊN.

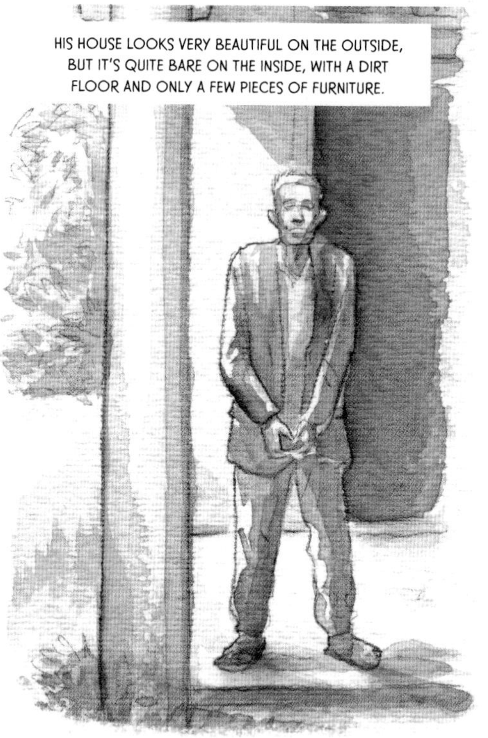
HIS HOUSE LOOKS VERY BEAUTIFUL ON THE OUTSIDE, BUT IT'S QUITE BARE ON THE INSIDE, WITH A DIRT FLOOR AND ONLY A FEW PIECES OF FURNITURE.

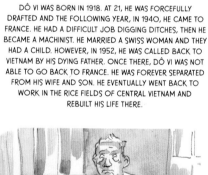

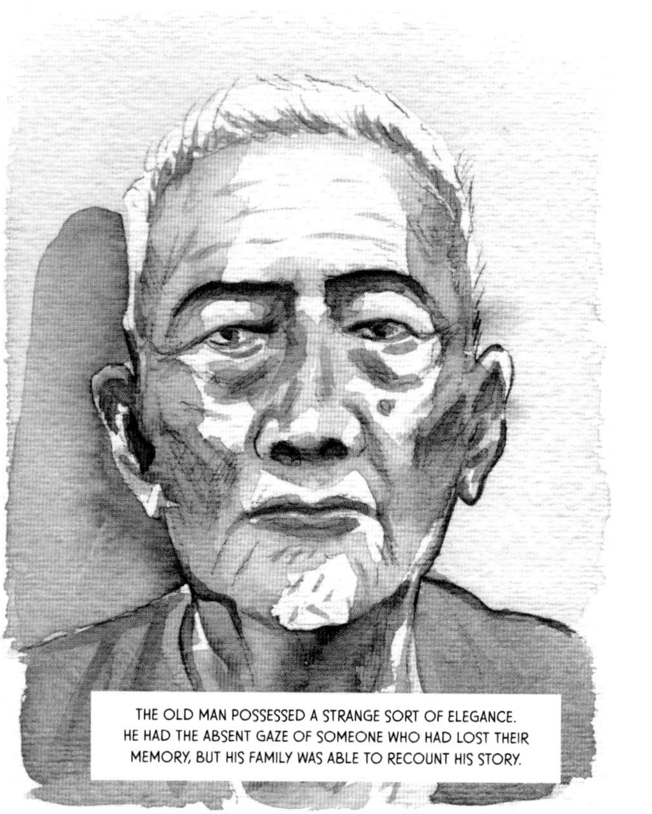
THE OLD MAN POSSESSED A STRANGE SORT OF ELEGANCE. HE HAD THE ABSENT GAZE OF SOMEONE WHO HAD LOST THEIR MEMORY, BUT HIS FAMILY WAS ABLE TO RECOUNT HIS STORY.

DÔ VI WAS BORN IN 1918. AT 21, HE WAS FORCEFULLY DRAFTED AND THE FOLLOWING YEAR, IN 1940, HE CAME TO FRANCE. HE HAD A DIFFICULT JOB DIGGING DITCHES, THEN HE BECAME A MACHINIST. HE MARRIED A SWISS WOMAN AND THEY HAD A CHILD. HOWEVER, IN 1952, HE WAS CALLED BACK TO VIETNAM BY HIS DYING FATHER. ONCE THERE, DÔ VI WAS NOT ABLE TO GO BACK TO FRANCE. HE WAS FOREVER SEPARATED FROM HIS WIFE AND SON. HE EVENTUALLY WENT BACK TO WORK IN THE RICE FIELDS OF CENTRAL VIETNAM AND REBUILT HIS LIFE THERE.

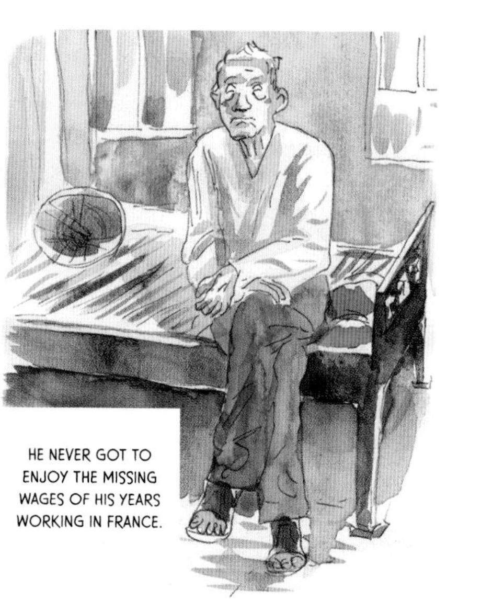
HE NEVER GOT TO ENJOY THE MISSING WAGES OF HIS YEARS WORKING IN FRANCE.

*TRÂN CÔNG GIAO, 58TH COMPANY, ID NO. ZTY 174.
MET IN NAM DINH IN JANUARY 2007.*

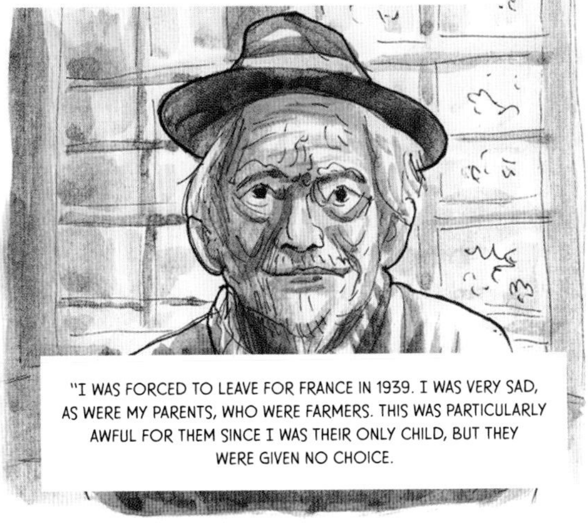
"I WAS FORCED TO LEAVE FOR FRANCE IN 1939. I WAS VERY SAD, AS WERE MY PARENTS, WHO WERE FARMERS. THIS WAS PARTICULARLY AWFUL FOR THEM SINCE I WAS THEIR ONLY CHILD, BUT THEY WERE GIVEN NO CHOICE.

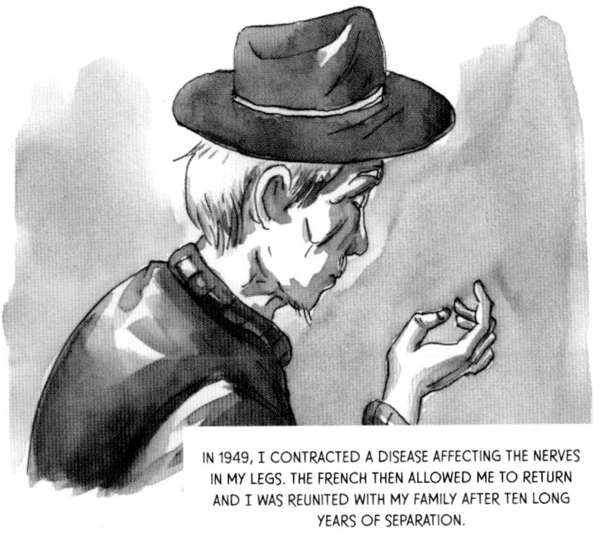
IN 1949, I CONTRACTED A DISEASE AFFECTING THE NERVES IN MY LEGS. THE FRENCH THEN ALLOWED ME TO RETURN AND I WAS REUNITED WITH MY FAMILY AFTER TEN LONG YEARS OF SEPARATION.

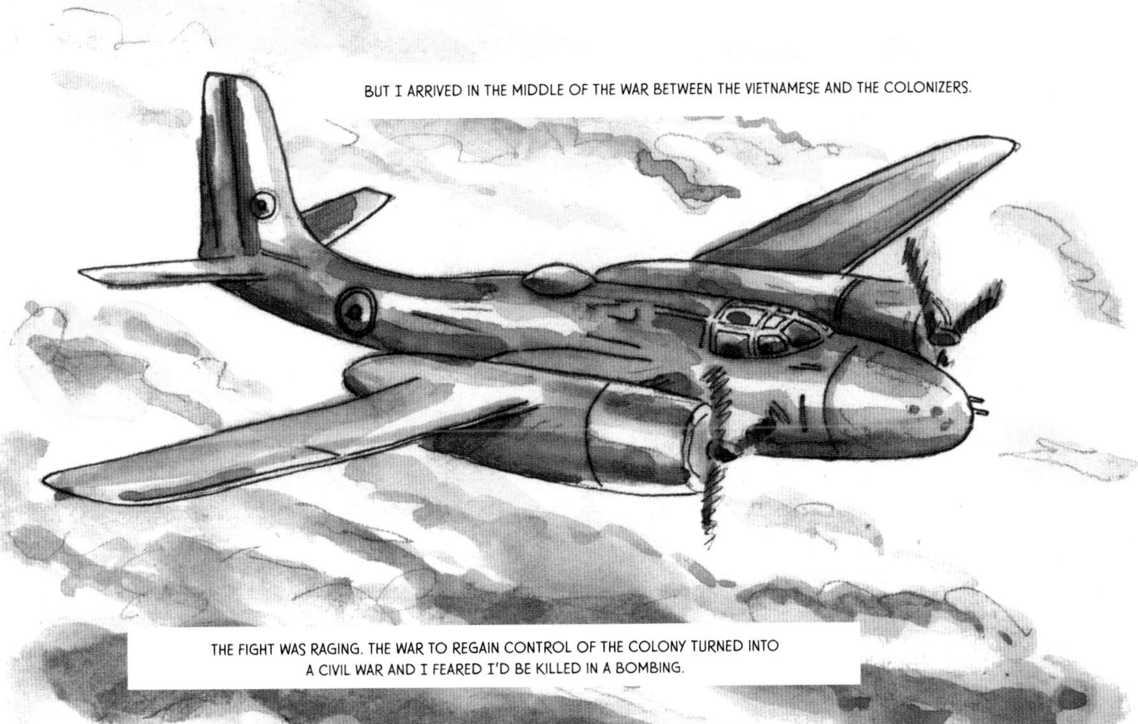
BUT I ARRIVED IN THE MIDDLE OF THE WAR BETWEEN THE VIETNAMESE AND THE COLONIZERS.
THE FIGHT WAS RAGING. THE WAR TO REGAIN CONTROL OF THE COLONY TURNED INTO A CIVIL WAR AND I FEARED I'D BE KILLED IN A BOMBING.

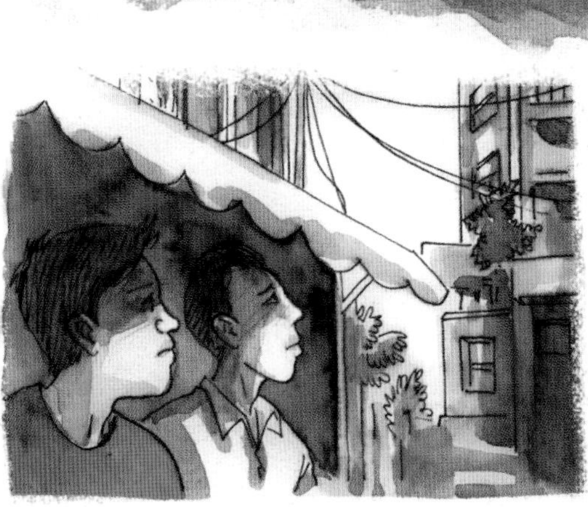

I EVENTUALLY MADE A LIFE FOR MYSELF, HAD CHILDREN, THEN GRANDCHILDREN.

SINCE 1988, I HAVE ASKED THE FRENCH GOVERNMENT FOR A PENSION FOR THE TEN YEARS I SPENT THERE, BUT THEY WANTED DOCUMENTS THAT I DIDN'T HAVE. I EVEN MET PRESIDENT MITTERRAND'S WIFE IN 1991, WHO EXPLAINED TO ME THAT FRANCE HAD SENT 10,555 FRANCS* TO THE VIETNAMESE GOVERNMENT FOR EACHX O.N.S.. BUT, IN ORDER TO CLAIM IT, THE VIETNAMESE GOVERNMENT ALSO ASKED FOR PAPERS THAT I DIDN'T HAVE!"

** ABOUT 9,000 EUROS*

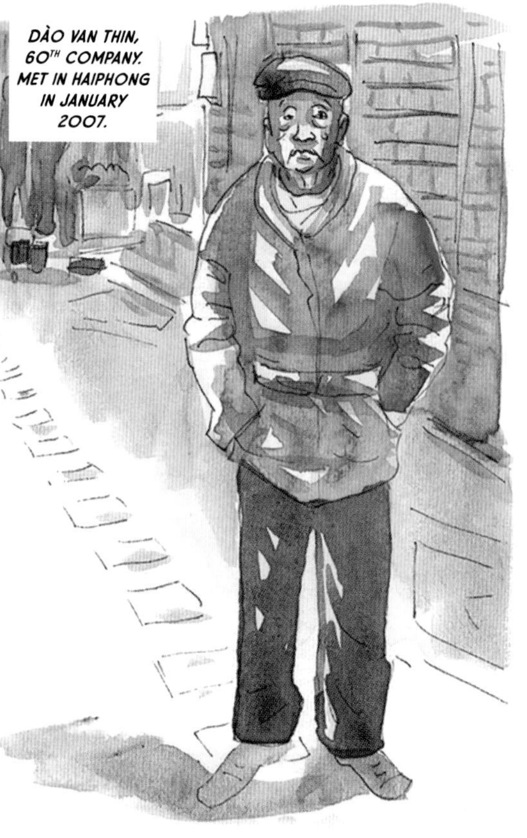
DÀO VAN THIN, 60TH COMPANY. MET IN HAIPHONG IN JANUARY 2007.

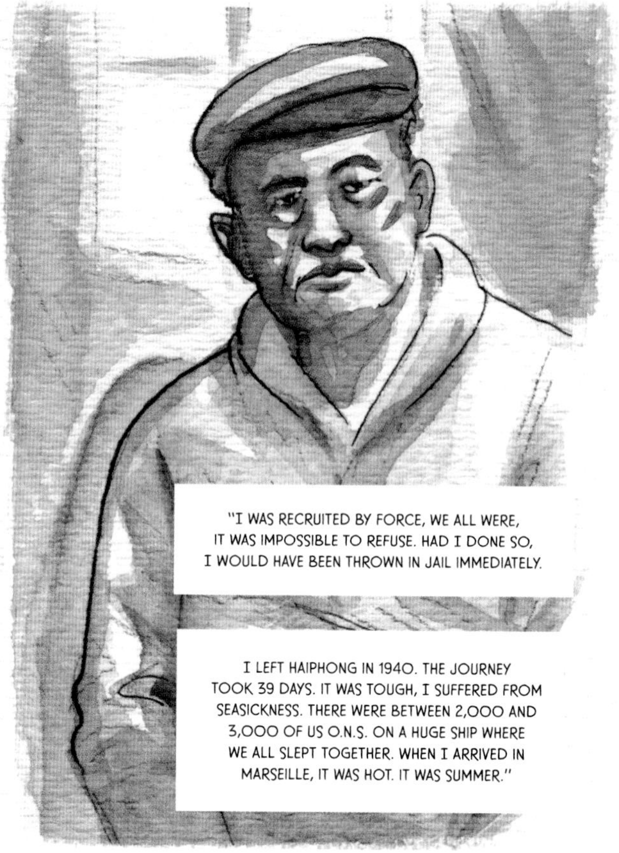
"I WAS RECRUITED BY FORCE, WE ALL WERE, IT WAS IMPOSSIBLE TO REFUSE. HAD I DONE SO, I WOULD HAVE BEEN THROWN IN JAIL IMMEDIATELY.
I LEFT HAIPHONG IN 1940. THE JOURNEY TOOK 39 DAYS. IT WAS TOUGH, I SUFFERED FROM SEASICKNESS. THERE WERE BETWEEN 2,000 AND 3,000 OF US O.N.S. ON A HUGE SHIP WHERE WE ALL SLEPT TOGETHER. WHEN I ARRIVED IN MARSEILLE, IT WAS HOT. IT WAS SUMMER."

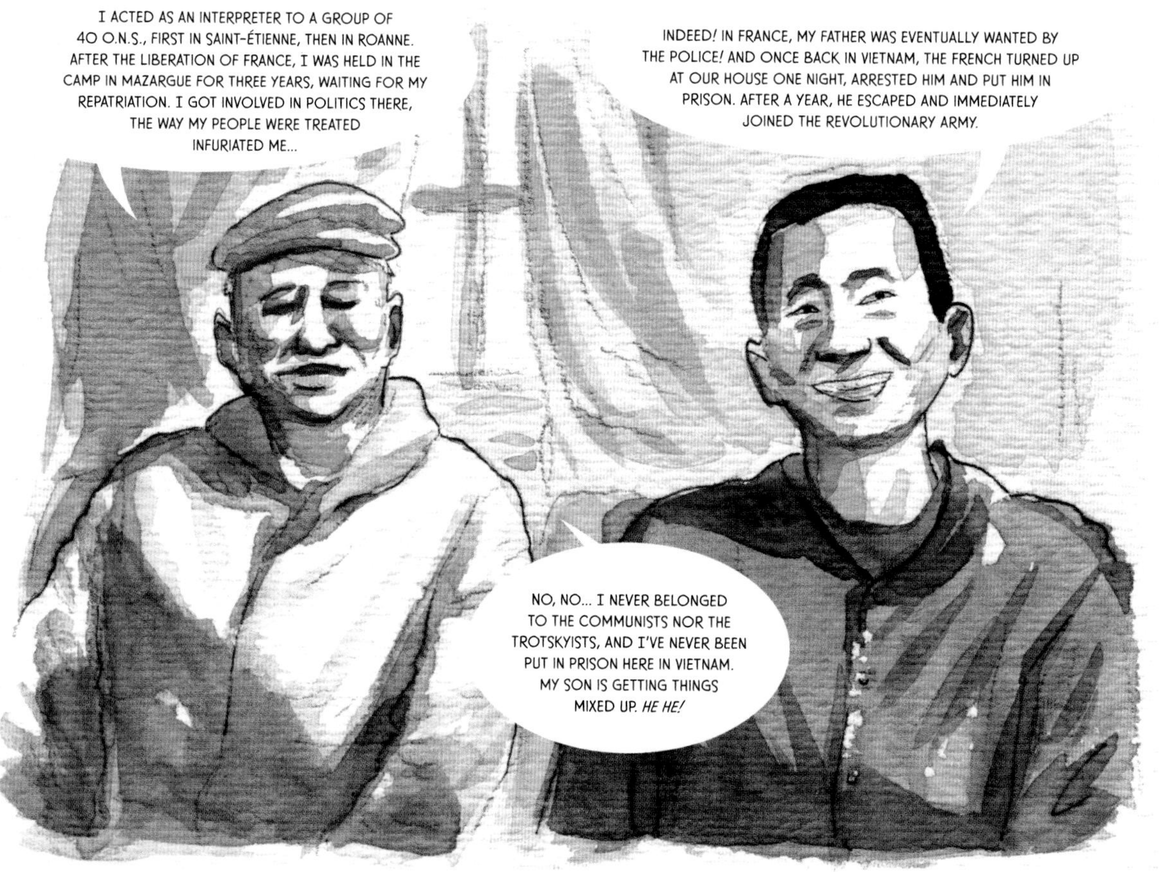
I ACTED AS AN INTERPRETER TO A GROUP OF 40 O.N.S., FIRST IN SAINT-ÉTIENNE, THEN IN ROANNE. AFTER THE LIBERATION OF FRANCE, I WAS HELD IN THE CAMP IN MAZARGUE FOR THREE YEARS, WAITING FOR MY REPATRIATION. I GOT INVOLVED IN POLITICS THERE, THE WAY MY PEOPLE WERE TREATED INFURIATED ME...
INDEED! IN FRANCE, MY FATHER WAS EVENTUALLY WANTED BY THE POLICE! AND ONCE BACK IN VIETNAM, THE FRENCH TURNED UP AT OUR HOUSE ONE NIGHT, ARRESTED HIM AND PUT HIM IN PRISON. AFTER A YEAR, HE ESCAPED AND IMMEDIATELY JOINED THE REVOLUTIONARY ARMY.
NO, NO... I NEVER BELONGED TO THE COMMUNISTS NOR THE TROTSKYISTS, AND I'VE NEVER BEEN PUT IN PRISON HERE IN VIETNAM. MY SON IS GETTING THINGS MIXED UP. *HE HE!*

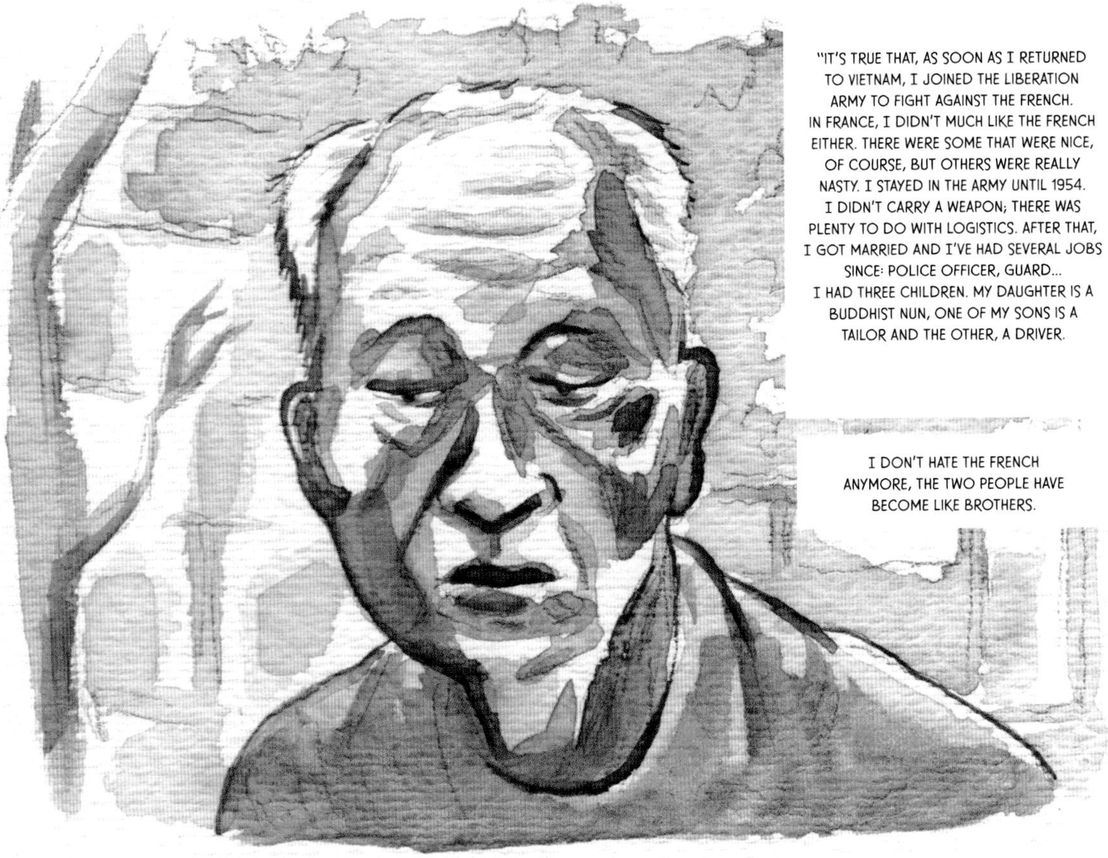
"IT'S TRUE THAT, AS SOON AS I RETURNED TO VIETNAM, I JOINED THE LIBERATION ARMY TO FIGHT AGAINST THE FRENCH. IN FRANCE, I DIDN'T MUCH LIKE THE FRENCH EITHER. THERE WERE SOME THAT WERE NICE, OF COURSE, BUT OTHERS WERE REALLY NASTY. I STAYED IN THE ARMY UNTIL 1954. I DIDN'T CARRY A WEAPON; THERE WAS PLENTY TO DO WITH LOGISTICS. AFTER THAT, I GOT MARRIED AND I'VE HAD SEVERAL JOBS SINCE: POLICE OFFICER, GUARD... I HAD THREE CHILDREN. MY DAUGHTER IS A BUDDHIST NUN, ONE OF MY SONS IS A TAILOR AND THE OTHER, A DRIVER.
I DON'T HATE THE FRENCH ANYMORE, THE TWO PEOPLE HAVE BECOME LIKE BROTHERS.

THERE'S ONE GOOD MEMORY I HAVE KEPT OF THOSE YEARS IN FRANCE. IN 1946, I TRAVELED 500 MILES WITH SOME FRIENDS TO WELCOME HÔ CHI MINH TO PARIS. WE CHEERED HIM AT THE FONTAINEBLEAU CONFERENCE."

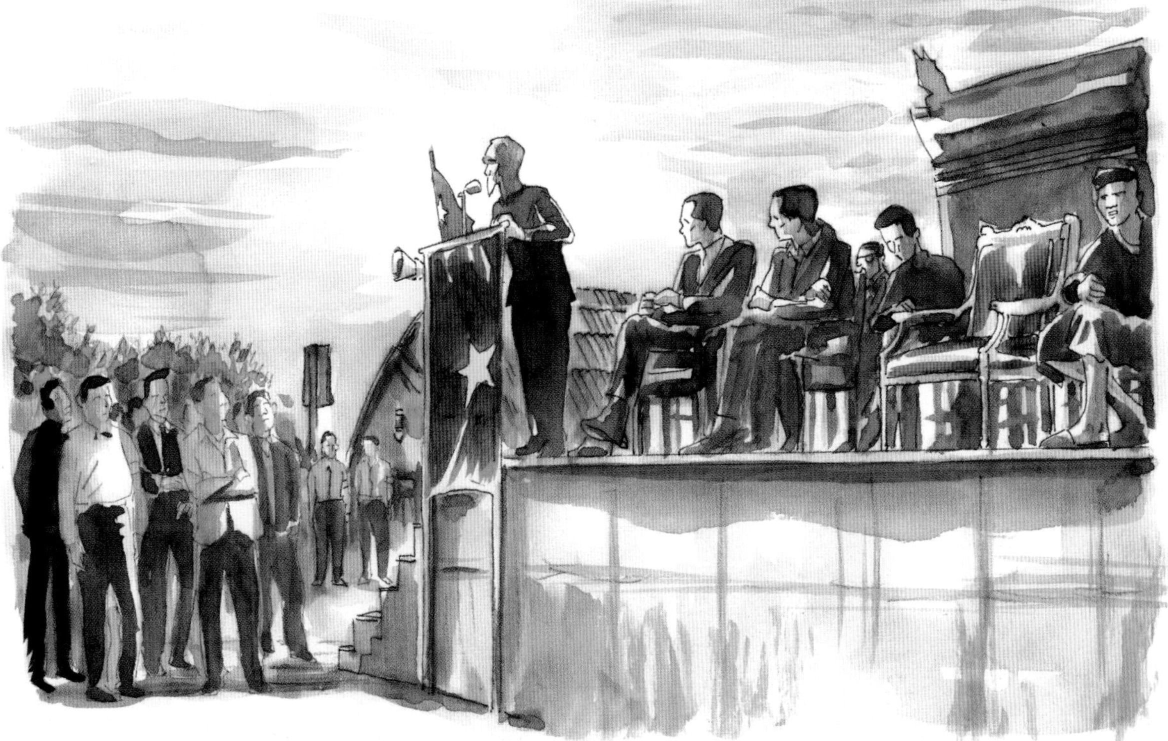

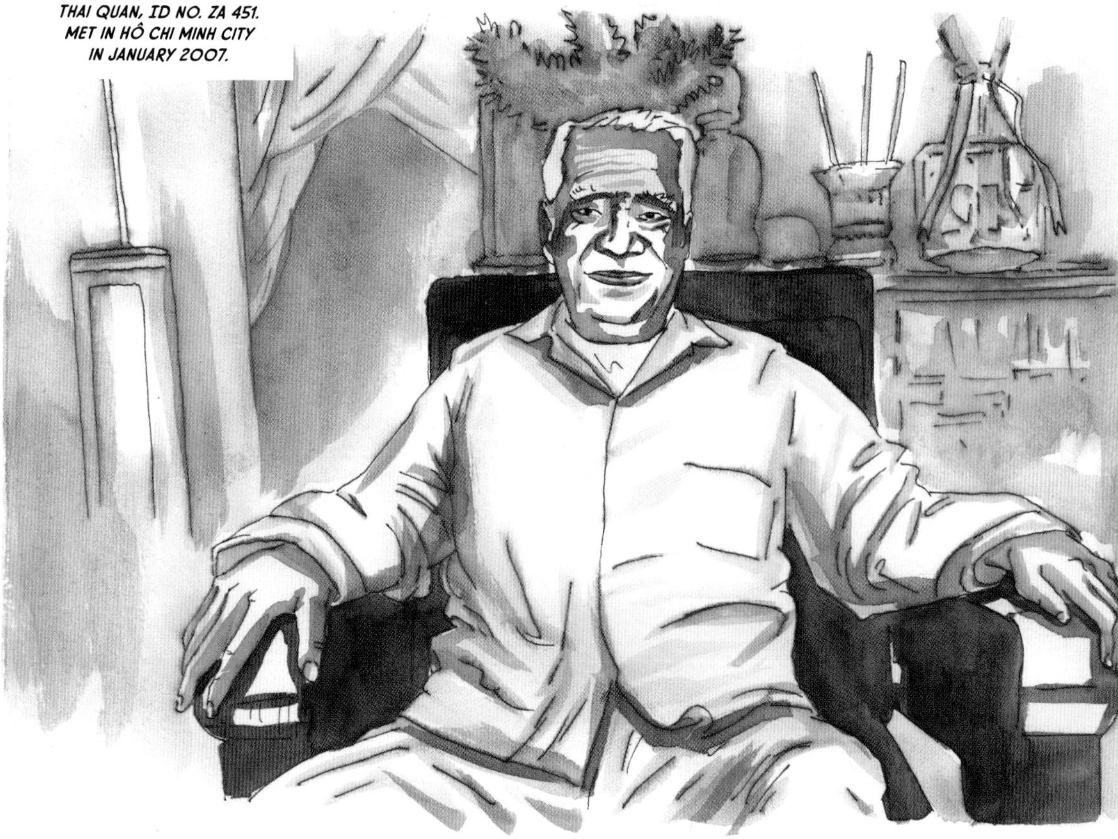
THAI QUAN, ID NO. ZA 451.
MET IN HÔ CHI MINH CITY
IN JANUARY 2007.

THAI QUAN WAS BORN IN 1913 IN SON LONG, A VILLAGE IN THE CENTER OF WHAT WAS THEN KNOWN AS ANNAM. IN 1939, HIS BROTHER WAS SELECTED FOR CONSCRIPTION, BUT BEING A FATHER OF FOUR, SO THAI QUAN TOOK HIS PLACE. IN FRANCE, HIS COMPANY WAS TRANSFERRED HALF A DOZEN TIMES. DURING HIS TIME IN CANNES, THAI QUAN JOINED SIDES WITH THE RESISTANCE TO FIGHT AGAINST HITLER'S ARMIES. AFTER 1946, HE WORKED FOR 6 YEARS AS A TURNER IN THE *PEUGEOT* FACTORY IN ENGHIEN, NEAR PARIS.

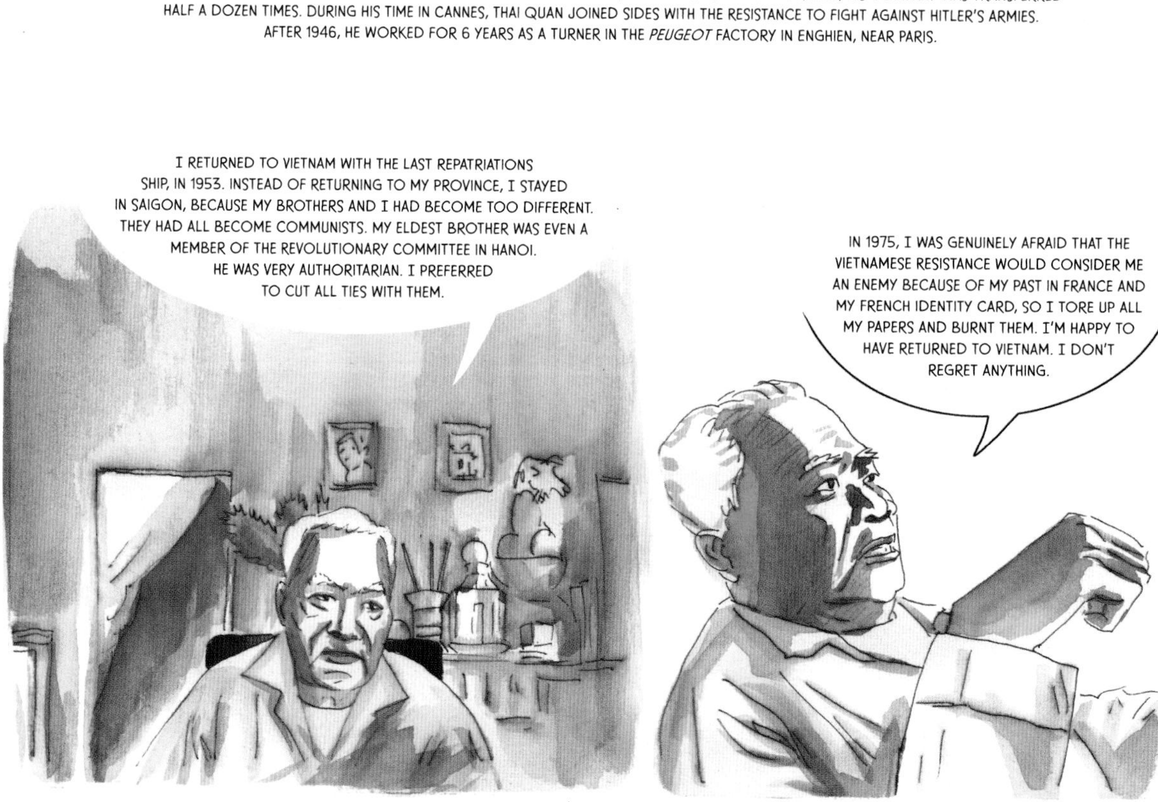
I RETURNED TO VIETNAM WITH THE LAST REPATRIATIONS SHIP, IN 1953. INSTEAD OF RETURNING TO MY PROVINCE, I STAYED IN SAIGON, BECAUSE MY BROTHERS AND I HAD BECOME TOO DIFFERENT. THEY HAD ALL BECOME COMMUNISTS. MY ELDEST BROTHER WAS EVEN A MEMBER OF THE REVOLUTIONARY COMMITTEE IN HANOI. HE WAS VERY AUTHORITARIAN. I PREFERRED TO CUT ALL TIES WITH THEM.
IN 1975, I WAS GENUINELY AFRAID THAT THE VIETNAMESE RESISTANCE WOULD CONSIDER ME AN ENEMY BECAUSE OF MY PAST IN FRANCE AND MY FRENCH IDENTITY CARD, SO I TORE UP ALL MY PAPERS AND BURNT THEM. I'M HAPPY TO HAVE RETURNED TO VIETNAM. I DON'T REGRET ANYTHING.

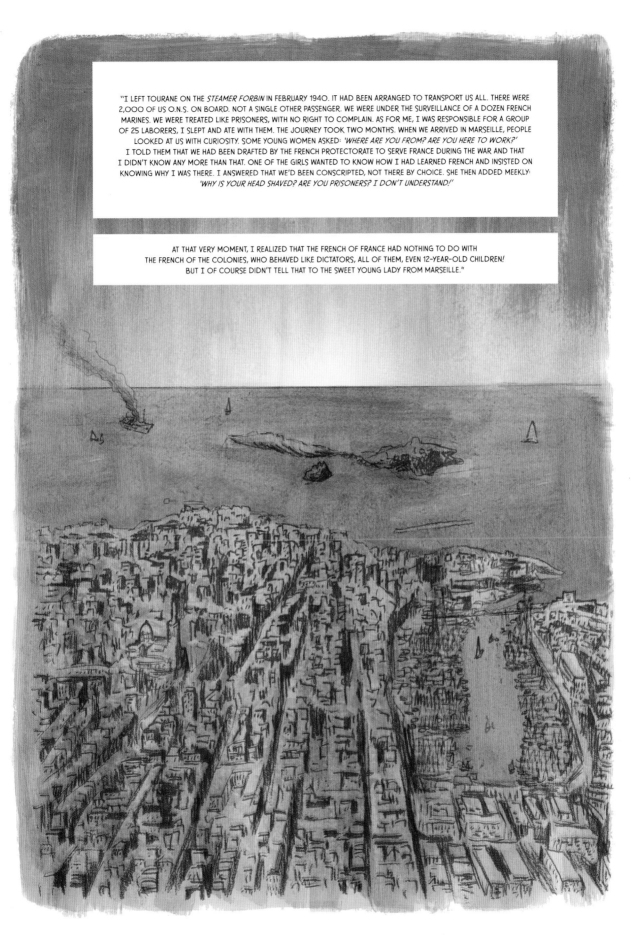

"I LEFT TOURANE ON THE *STEAMER FORBIN* IN FEBRUARY 1940. IT HAD BEEN ARRANGED TO TRANSPORT US ALL. THERE WERE 2,000 OF US O.N.S. ON BOARD. NOT A SINGLE OTHER PASSENGER. WE WERE UNDER THE SURVEILLANCE OF A DOZEN FRENCH MARINES. WE WERE TREATED LIKE PRISONERS, WITH NO RIGHT TO COMPLAIN. AS FOR ME, I WAS RESPONSIBLE FOR A GROUP OF 25 LABORERS, I SLEPT AND ATE WITH THEM. THE JOURNEY TOOK TWO MONTHS. WHEN WE ARRIVED IN MARSEILLE, PEOPLE LOOKED AT US WITH CURIOSITY. SOME YOUNG WOMEN ASKED: *'WHERE ARE YOU FROM? ARE YOU HERE TO WORK?'* I TOLD THEM THAT WE HAD BEEN DRAFTED BY THE FRENCH PROTECTORATE TO SERVE FRANCE DURING THE WAR AND THAT I DIDN'T KNOW ANY MORE THAN THAT. ONE OF THE GIRLS WANTED TO KNOW HOW I HAD LEARNED FRENCH AND INSISTED ON KNOWING WHY I WAS THERE. I ANSWERED THAT WE'D BEEN CONSCRIPTED, NOT THERE BY CHOICE. SHE THEN ADDED MEEKLY: *'WHY IS YOUR HEAD SHAVED? ARE YOU PRISONERS? I DON'T UNDERSTAND!'*

AT THAT VERY MOMENT, I REALIZED THAT THE FRENCH OF FRANCE HAD NOTHING TO DO WITH THE FRENCH OF THE COLONIES, WHO BEHAVED LIKE DICTATORS, ALL OF THEM, EVEN 12-YEAR-OLD CHILDREN! BUT I OF COURSE DIDN'T TELL THAT TO THE SWEET YOUNG LADY FROM MARSEILLE."

LÊ XUÂN THIÊU, 19TH COMPANY.
MET IN HANOI IN JANUARY 2007.

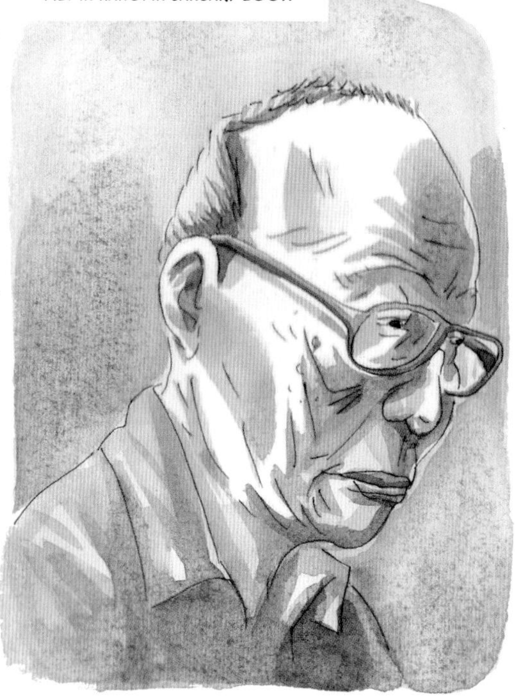

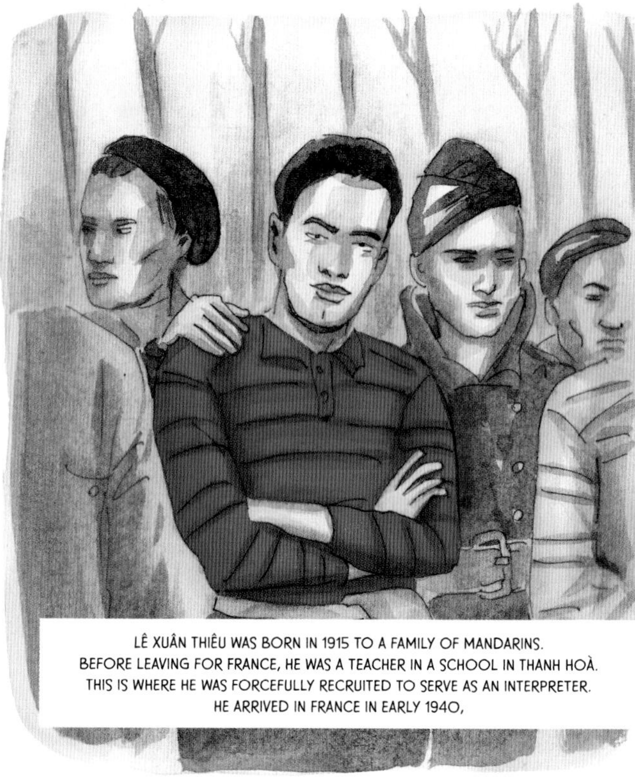
LÊ XUÂN THIÊU WAS BORN IN 1915 TO A FAMILY OF MANDARINS.
BEFORE LEAVING FOR FRANCE, HE WAS A TEACHER IN A SCHOOL IN THANH HOÀ.
THIS IS WHERE HE WAS FORCEFULLY RECRUITED TO SERVE AS AN INTERPRETER.
HE ARRIVED IN FRANCE IN EARLY 1940,

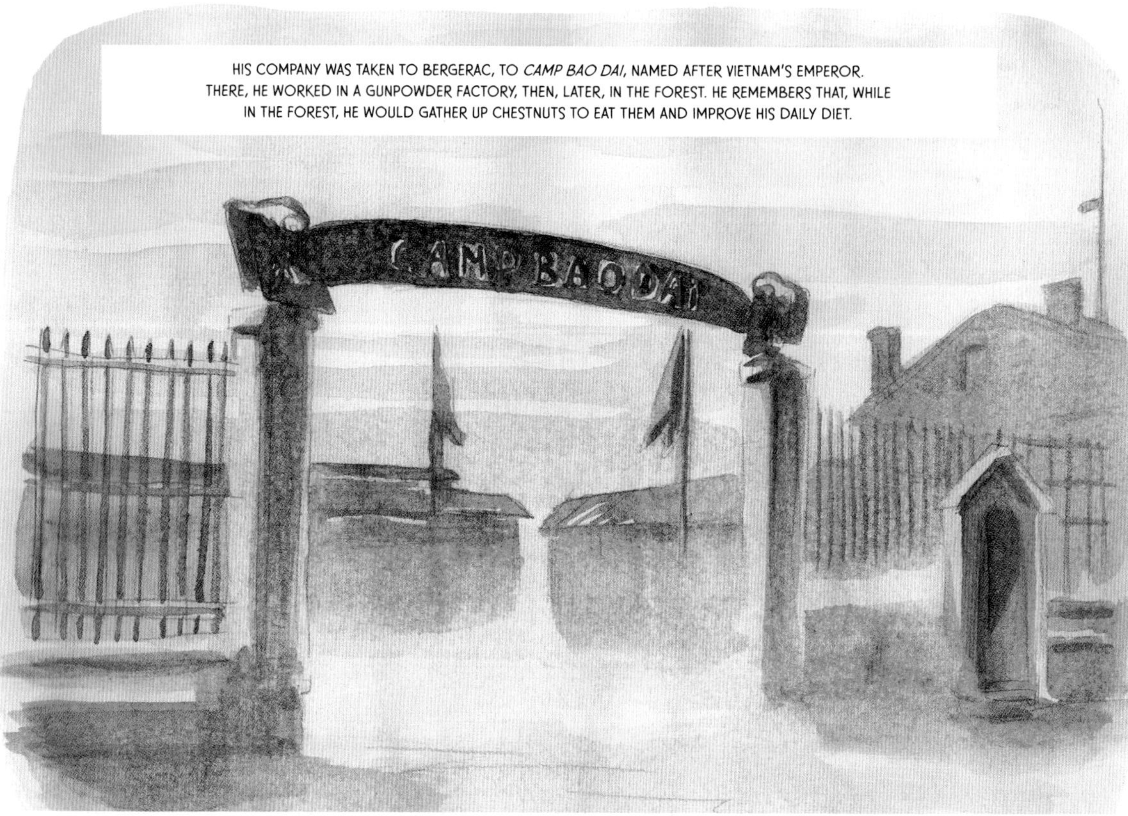
HIS COMPANY WAS TAKEN TO BERGERAC, TO *CAMP BAO DAI*, NAMED AFTER VIETNAM'S EMPEROR.
THERE, HE WORKED IN A GUNPOWDER FACTORY, THEN, LATER, IN THE FOREST. HE REMEMBERS THAT, WHILE
IN THE FOREST, HE WOULD GATHER UP CHESTNUTS TO EAT THEM AND IMPROVE HIS DAILY DIET.
CAMP BAODAI

IN 1945, HE FOUND A JOB IN PARIS AS AN APPRENTICE IN AN AERONAUTICAL FACTORY, THEN HE MOVED ON TO *RENAULT*, FRANCE'S NATIONAL AUTOMOTIVE COMPANY AT THE TIME. WHERE HE WOULD WORK FOR 37 YEARS BEFORE RETIRING. DURING HIS FREE TIME, HE VOLUNTEERED IN AN ASSOCIATION FOR VIETNAMESE PEOPLE IN FRANCE AND, IN 1995, HE DECIDED TO RETURN TO VIETNAM. OUT OF ALL THE FORMER O.N.S. THAT I MET IN VIETNAM, HE'S THE ONLY ONE TO RECEIVE AN ACTUAL PENSION FROM FRANCE, PURELY BECAUSE HE SPENT HIS ENTIRE PROFESSIONAL LIFE THERE.

BUT, IN TRUTH, THE REASON LÊ XUÂN THIÊU STAYED IN FRANCE FOR SO LONG IS THAT HE HAD BUILT A LIFE THERE WITH A FRENCH GIRL HE HAD MARRIED. THEY NEVER HAD CHILDREN. IT WAS SHORTLY AFTER SHE DIED THAT HE DECIDED TO RETURN TO VIETNAM.

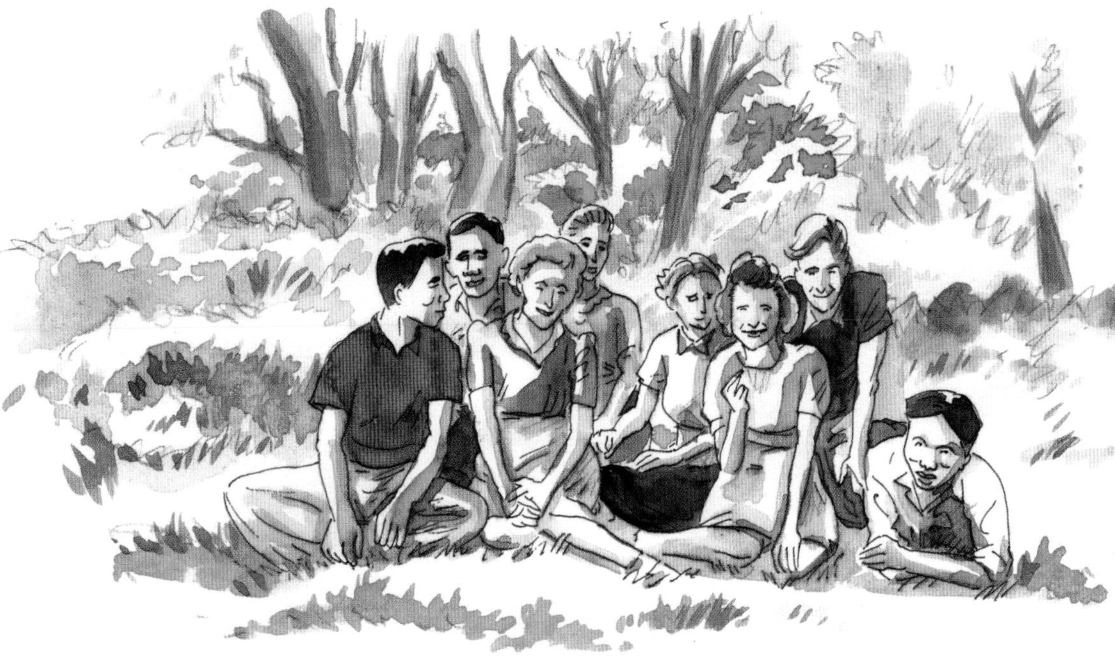

LOVE STORIES OR EVEN SIMPLE FLIRTATIONS BETWEEN INDOCHINESE MEN AND FRENCH WOMEN PLAY A PARTICULARLY IMPORTANT PART IN THE STORIES OF FORMER O.N.S.. THEIR MAIN ASSET WAS THEIR EXOTIC CHARM, AND THE YOUNG FRENCH GIRLS WERE MUCH LESS TIMID THAN THEIR VIETNAMESE COUNTERPARTS.

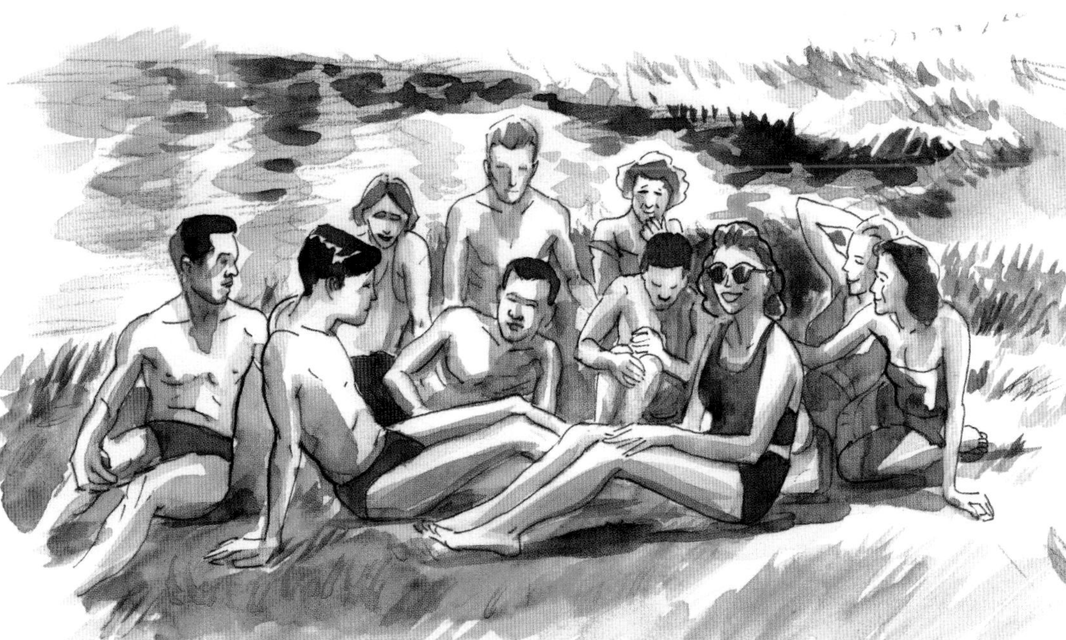

THESE ROMANTIC RELATIONSHIPS STIRRED UP DEEP CONCERN AMONG THE FRENCH POPULATION. A NEWSPAPER ARTICLE FROM 1941 EVEN WARNED YOUNG GIRLS AND THEIR PARENTS OF THE DUPLICITY OF THE INDOCHINESE -- ALL THOUGHT TO BE ALREADY MARRIED --, THE KIND OF INTOLERABLE INDIGENOUS MARRIAGE AWAITING THEM, AND, FINALLY, OF THE INCAPABILITY OF THE INDOCHINESE TO EARN THEIR LIVING DUE TO THEIR FRAIL PHYSIQUE. LOVE, HOWEVER, ALWAYS TRUMPS BIAS AND MANY COUPLES WERE FORMED, SOME SHORT-LIVED, SOME LONG-LASTING. BY MAY 1946, MORE THAN 100 MARRIAGES HAD ALREADY BEEN CELEBRATED AND AROUND A HUNDRED MIXED-RACE BABIES HAD ALREADY STEPPED INTO THE WORLD.

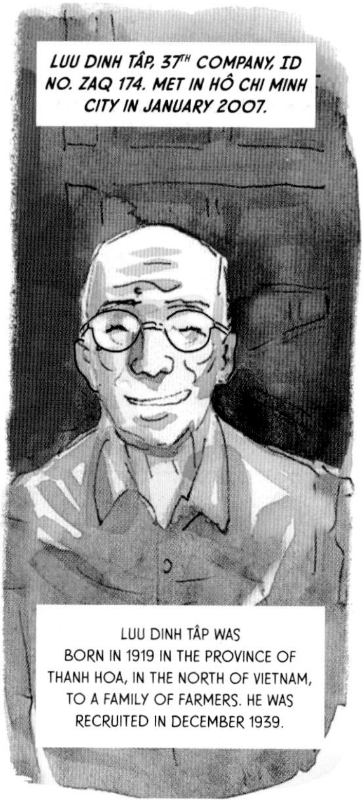
LUU DINH TÂP, 37TH COMPANY, ID NO. ZAQ 174. MET IN HÔ CHI MINH CITY IN JANUARY 2007.
LUU DINH TÂP WAS BORN IN 1919 IN THE PROVINCE OF THANH HOA, IN THE NORTH OF VIETNAM, TO A FAMILY OF FARMERS. HE WAS RECRUITED IN DECEMBER 1939.

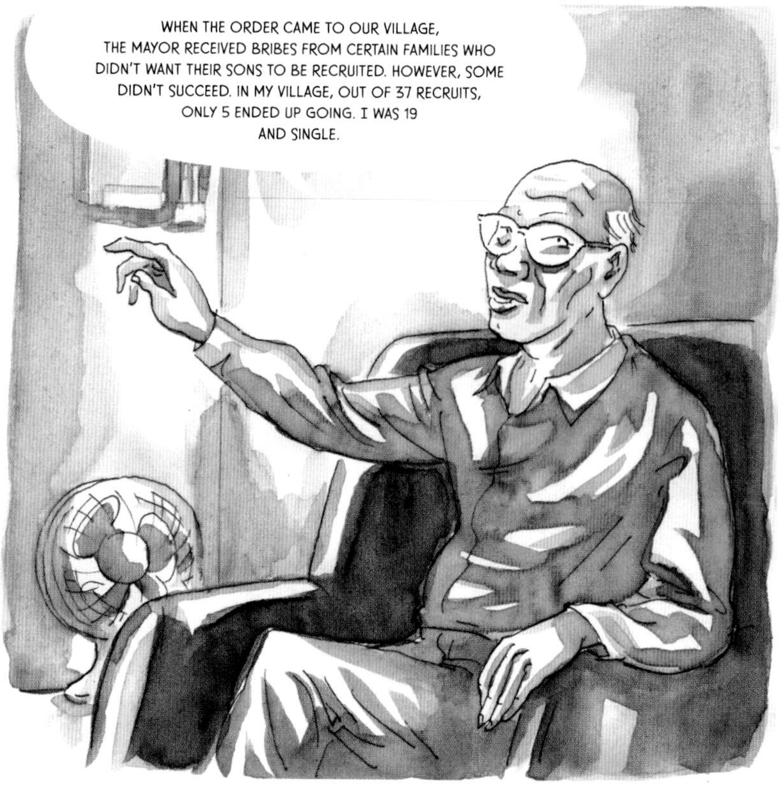
WHEN THE ORDER CAME TO OUR VILLAGE, THE MAYOR RECEIVED BRIBES FROM CERTAIN FAMILIES WHO DIDN'T WANT THEIR SONS TO BE RECRUITED. HOWEVER, SOME DIDN'T SUCCEED. IN MY VILLAGE, OUT OF 37 RECRUITS, ONLY 5 ENDED UP GOING. I WAS 19 AND SINGLE.

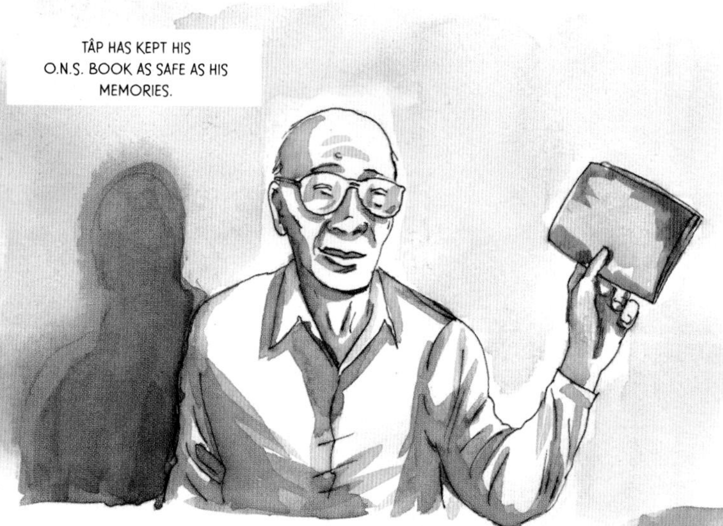
TÂP HAS KEPT HIS O.N.S. BOOK AS SAFE AS HIS MEMORIES.

"I WAS CURIOUS TO DISCOVER FRANCE. WE WERE ONLY LABORERS, WE WEREN'T GOING TO FIGHT ANY BATTLES. BUT AROUND THE SAME TIME, SOLDIERS WERE BEING RECRUITED AS WELL.

EVERYTHING WAS DONE ORALLY, NO WRITTEN CONTRACTS NOR ANY MENTION AS TO THE DURATION. I NAIVELY THOUGHT THAT IT WOULD LAST TWO OR THREE YEARS, BUT I NEVER ASKED. SAME FOR THE MONEY: THEY DIDN'T TELL US ANYTHING.

THE JOURNEY TOOK THREE MONTHS. WE ARRIVED IN FRANCE IN 1940. I REMEMBER THAT WE PASSED THROUGH THE SUEZ CANAL. THE FOOD WAS NOT GOOD, THE MEALS VERY BADLY PREPARED. THERE WERE ABOUT A THOUSAND OF US O.N.S., ALL LODGED IN THE HOLD AND NOT ALLOWED TO ACCESS THE UPPER DECKS.

AT OUR ARRIVAL IN MARSEILLE, WE WERE ORGANIZED INTO COMPANIES. I WAS PUT IN THE 37TH COMPANY.

THE 37TH AND 38TH COMPANIES WERE SENT TO THE RIFFAUT WEAPONRY FACTORY IN ORBEC, IN THE CALVADOS DEPARTMENT. IN THE FACTORY, WE WERE SEATED ON TWO BENCHES ON EITHER SIDE OF A LONG TABLE. WE RECEIVED GUNPOWDER IN THE FORM OF SHEETS. WE HAD TO GRIND IT AND PUT IT IN AN IRON BOX. OTHERS WORKED TO PRODUCE FUSES. I DIDN'T WEAR GLOVES, BUT MY SKIN WAS NOT IRRITATED. ONE OF MY FRIENDS, HOWEVER, DIED DUE TO THE AFTER-EFFECTS. HE WAS TAKEN TO LE DANTEC HOSPITAL, IN MARSEILLE. ONCE YOU WERE ADMITTED TO THAT HOSPITAL, YOU HAD LITTLE CHANCE OF LEAVING IT ALIVE. WE ONLY WORKED THERE FOR 3 MONTHS. THE WORK WASN'T HARD, CHILD'S PLAY REALLY."

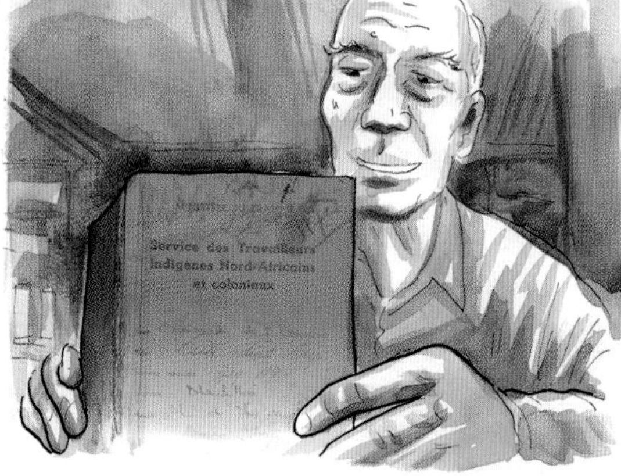
Service des Travailleurs
indigènes Nord-Africains
et coloniaux

"WHEN MARSHAL PÉTAIN SIGNED THE ARMISTICE, THE FACTORY WAS DESTROYED. WE RECEIVED ORDERS TO WITHDRAW TOWARDS THE SOUTH. THE MAIN THING WAS TO GET OUT OF THE ZONE OCCUPIED BY NAZI GERMANY. WE ENDED UP IN SAINT CHAMAS, SORGUES, MARSEILLE, WHERE THEY HAD US CHOP WOOD.

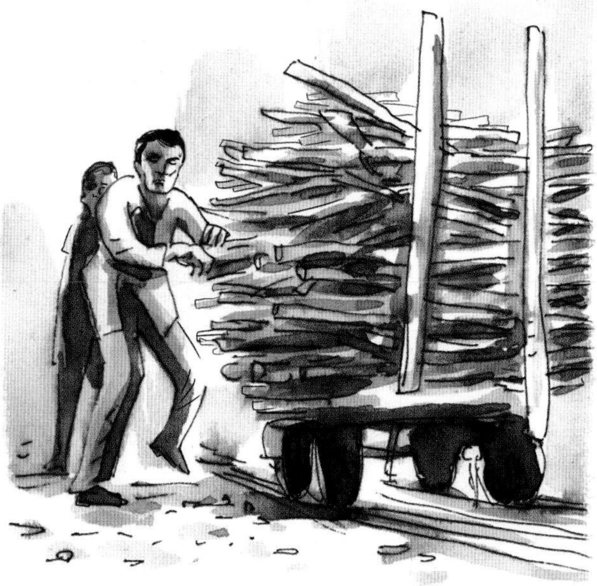

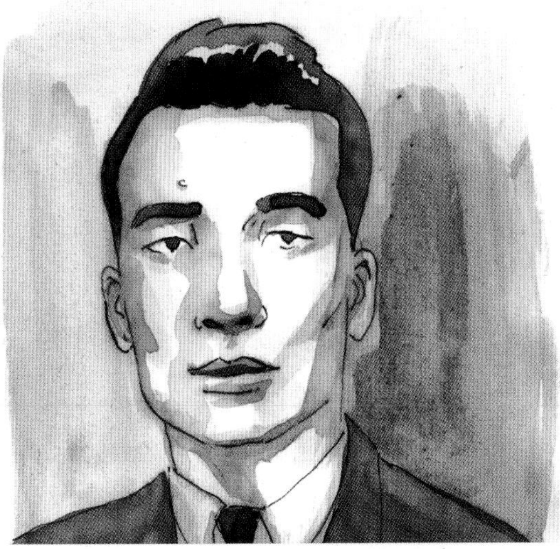

WHEN VIETNAM DECLARED ITS INDEPENDENCE IN 1945, WE CREATED AN ASSOCIATION IN FRANCE. WE RAISED MONEY TO SEND TO VIETNAM. I WAS ONE OF THE REPRESENTATIVES OF THE ASSOCIATION. I WAS A TROTSKYIST AND FOUGHT FOR THE REVOLUTION.

AFTER THE LIBERATION, I WAS IN CHARGE OF THE PUBLICATION OF A NEWSPAPER CALLED *SOLDAT OUVRIER*, 'THE WORKING SOLDIER.' THE O.N.S. WERE FORCED TO RETURN TO VIETNAM, BUT I DIDN'T WANT TO. I WANTED TO STAY WITH A GROUP OF FRIENDS WHO ALSO WISHED TO REMAIN IN FRANCE, SO I ESCAPED. IN PARIS, I GOT TO KNOW A FAMILY WITH THREE DAUGHTERS. I HAD DINNER AT THEIR HOME EVERY WEEKEND. ONE OF THE GIRLS WAS IN LOVE WITH ME AND, HAD I STAYED IN FRANCE, I WOULD HAVE MARRIED HER.

I TOOK PART IN MANY DEMONSTRATIONS IN FRANCE. I WAS EVEN ARRESTED ONCE AND RELEASED THE FOLLOWING DAY. THE THREE SISTERS WERE WITH ME. WE DENOUNCED THE WAR IN VIETNAM AND SHOUTED SLOGANS LIKE *'DOWN WITH BAO DAI!'* THIS IS THE LIFE I LED IN PARIS FROM 1949 UNTIL 1952. I LIVED WITH A FRIEND, AN ENGINEER WHO WROTE POEMS AGAINST BAO DAI.

I WORKED AT THE MINH-TÂN BOOKSHOP AND PUBLISHING HOUSE AS A TYPOGRAPHER. I WAS IN CHARGE OF THE *TIÊNG THO* NEWSPAPER, THE VOICE OF THE WORKERS. FIVE PEOPLE WORKED ON THE EDITION OF THE WEEKLY PAPER AND IT WAS SENT TO THE O.N.S STAYING IN THE CAMPS.

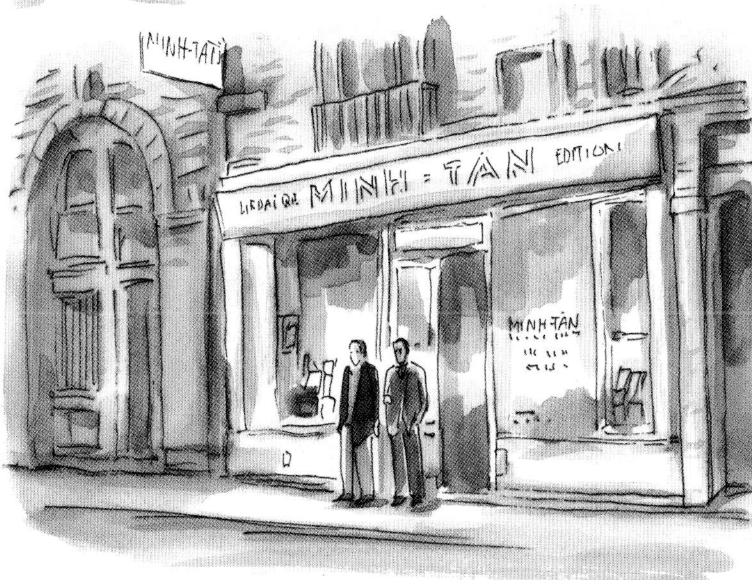
MINH-TÂN
MINH-TÂN

IN 1952, I FINALLY RETURNED TO VIETNAM. IT WAS THE LAST CHANCE GIVEN BY THE FRENCH ADMINISTRATION TO TRAVEL BACK WITHOUT PAYING FOR THE TRANSPORT. WHEN I DISEMBARKED AT CAP SAINT JACQUES, VIETNAM WAS DIVIDED IN TWO. THE SOUTH WAS IN THE HANDS OF THE FRENCH AND, AFTER THEM, THE AMERICANS. IN ORDER TO COMMUNICATE WITH MY FAMILY, WHO LIVED IN THE NORTH, I HAD TO SEND MY LETTERS TO FRANCE, WHO FORWARDED THEM TO NORTH VIETNAM. I DIDN'T SEE MY BROTHERS AND SISTERS UNTIL 1975. MY MOTHER AND FATHER, I NEVER SAW AGAIN..."

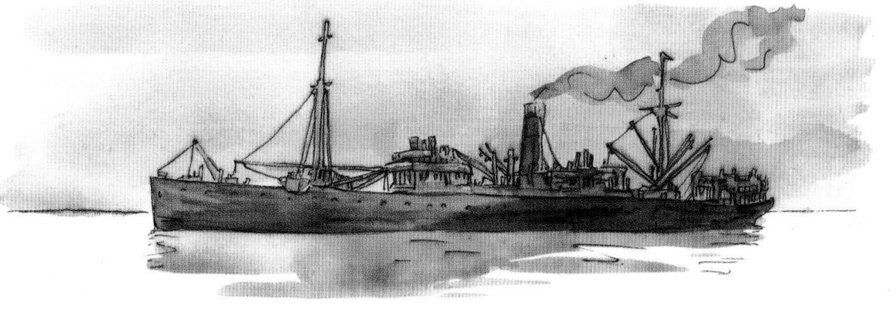

CHU VAN NGÀN, 36TH COMPANY.
MET IN NGHÊ AN, IN FEBRUARY 2007.

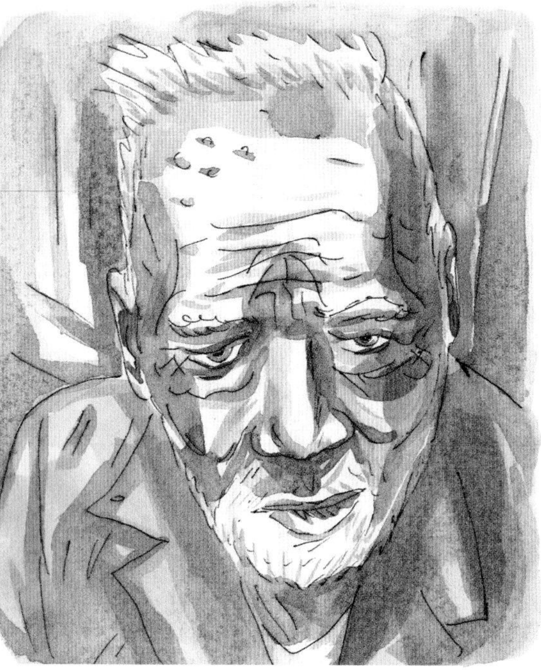

BORN IN THE VILLAGE NEXT TO THE ONE HE'S LIVING IN TODAY, CHU VAN NGÀN WAS FORCEFULLY RECRUITED IN 1939.

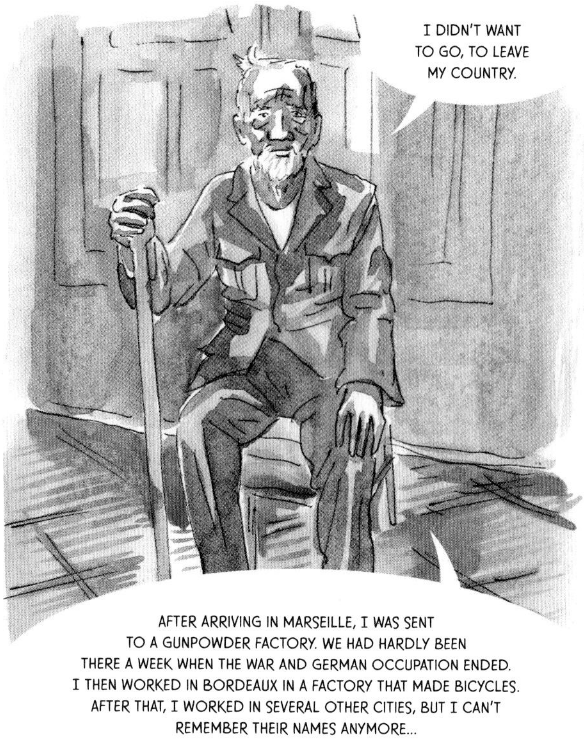

I DIDN'T WANT TO GO, TO LEAVE MY COUNTRY.
AFTER ARRIVING IN MARSEILLE, I WAS SENT TO A GUNPOWDER FACTORY. WE HAD HARDLY BEEN THERE A WEEK WHEN THE WAR AND GERMAN OCCUPATION ENDED. I THEN WORKED IN BORDEAUX IN A FACTORY THAT MADE BICYCLES. AFTER THAT, I WORKED IN SEVERAL OTHER CITIES, BUT I CAN'T REMEMBER THEIR NAMES ANYMORE...

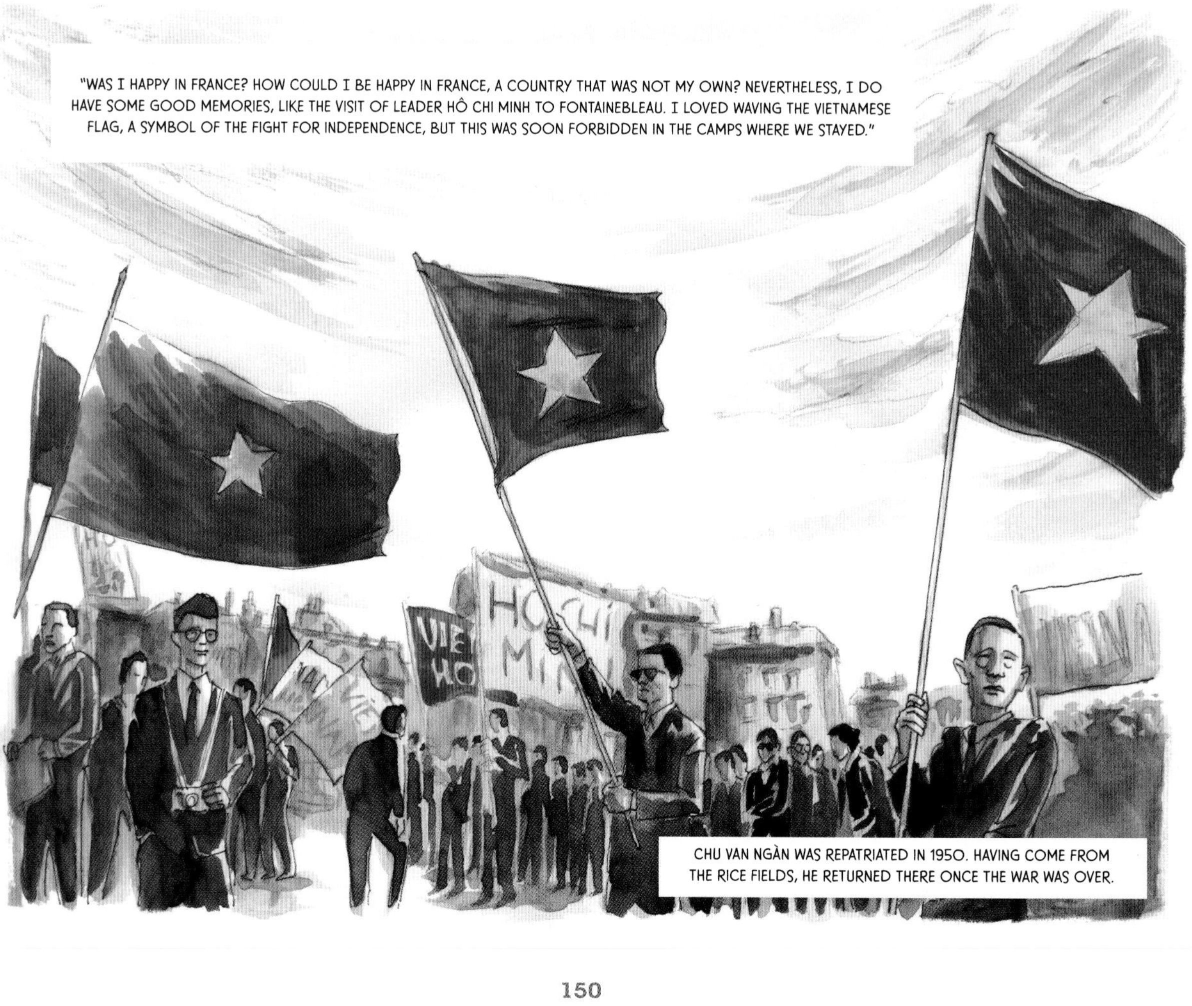

"WAS I HAPPY IN FRANCE? HOW COULD I BE HAPPY IN FRANCE, A COUNTRY THAT WAS NOT MY OWN? NEVERTHELESS, I DO HAVE SOME GOOD MEMORIES, LIKE THE VISIT OF LEADER HÔ CHI MINH TO FONTAINEBLEAU. I LOVED WAVING THE VIETNAMESE FLAG, A SYMBOL OF THE FIGHT FOR INDEPENDENCE, BUT THIS WAS SOON FORBIDDEN IN THE CAMPS WHERE WE STAYED."
CHU VAN NGÀN WAS REPATRIATED IN 1950. HAVING COME FROM THE RICE FIELDS, HE RETURNED THERE ONCE THE WAR WAS OVER.

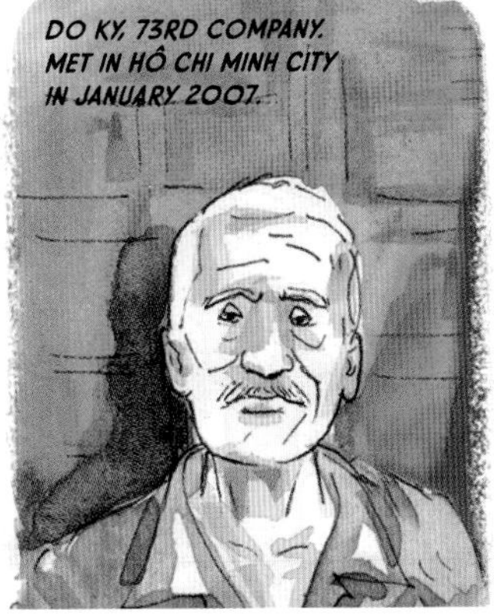
DO KY, 73RD COMPANY.
MET IN HÔ CHI MINH CITY
IN JANUARY 2007.

"I HAD BARELY FINISHED MY EDUCATION WHEN THE RECRUITMENT FOR O.N.S. STARTED. SINCE YOU HAD TO BE 18, WE MADE FALSE PAPERS SO THAT I COULD GO. I WANTED TO SEE OTHER PLACES! MY FAMILY DIDN'T HAVE ENOUGH TO PROVIDE FOR ALL OF US. SOME OF US NEEDED TO GO AND EARN THEIR BREAD ELSEWHERE.

IN 1948, IN MAZARGUE'S CAMP, KY GOT INVOLVED IN THE AFFAIR THAT THE NEWSPAPERS NICKNAMED "THE INDOCHINESE ST. BARTHOLOMEW'S DAY MASSACRE." A FIGHT BROKE OUT BETWEEN STALINISTS AND NON-STALINISTS. THERE WERE CASUALTIES ON BOTH SIDES.

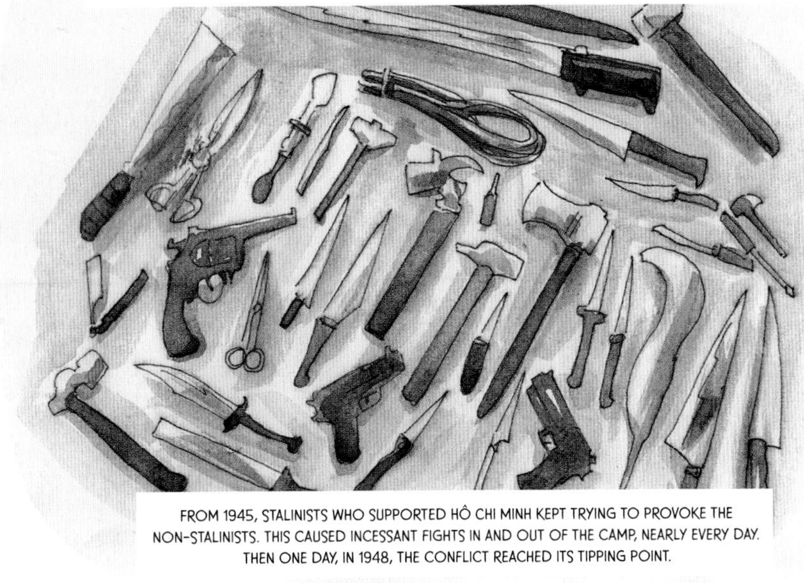
FROM 1945, STALINISTS WHO SUPPORTED HÔ CHI MINH KEPT TRYING TO PROVOKE THE NON-STALINISTS. THIS CAUSED INCESSANT FIGHTS IN AND OUT OF THE CAMP, NEARLY EVERY DAY. THEN ONE DAY, IN 1948, THE CONFLICT REACHED ITS TIPPING POINT.

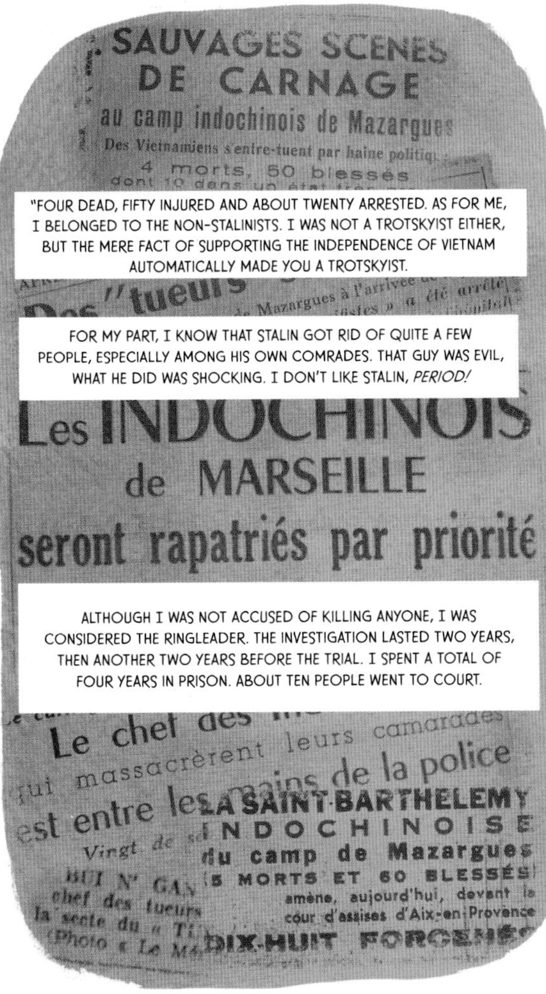
SAUVAGES SCENES
DE CARNAGE
au camp indochinois de Mazargues
Des Vietnamiens s'entre-tuent par haine politiq
4 morts, 50 blessés
"FOUR DEAD, FIFTY INJURED AND ABOUT TWENTY ARRESTED. AS FOR ME, I BELONGED TO THE NON-STALINISTS. I WAS NOT A TROTSKYIST EITHER, BUT THE MERE FACT OF SUPPORTING THE INDEPENDENCE OF VIETNAM AUTOMATICALLY MADE YOU A TROTSKYIST.
tueurs
Mazargues à l'arrivée
FOR MY PART, I KNOW THAT STALIN GOT RID OF QUITE A FEW PEOPLE, ESPECIALLY AMONG HIS OWN COMRADES. THAT GUY WAS EVIL, WHAT HE DID WAS SHOCKING. I DON'T LIKE STALIN, *PERIOD!*
Les INDOCHINOIS
de MARSEILLE
seront rapatriés par priorité
ALTHOUGH I WAS NOT ACCUSED OF KILLING ANYONE, I WAS CONSIDERED THE RINGLEADER. THE INVESTIGATION LASTED TWO YEARS, THEN ANOTHER TWO YEARS BEFORE THE TRIAL. I SPENT A TOTAL OF FOUR YEARS IN PRISON. ABOUT TEN PEOPLE WENT TO COURT.
Le chef des
massacrèrent leurs camarades
est entre les mains de la police
LA SAINT-BARTHELEMY
INDOCHINOISE
du camp de Mazargues
(5 MORTS ET 60 BLESSÉS)
amène, aujourd'hui, devant la
cour d'assises d'Aix-en-Provence
DIX-HUIT FORCENÉS

I ACTED AS THE INTERPRETER FOR MY FRIENDS, FIRST BEFORE THE INVESTIGATING JUDGE, AND THEN AT THE CRIMINAL COURT LATER ON.

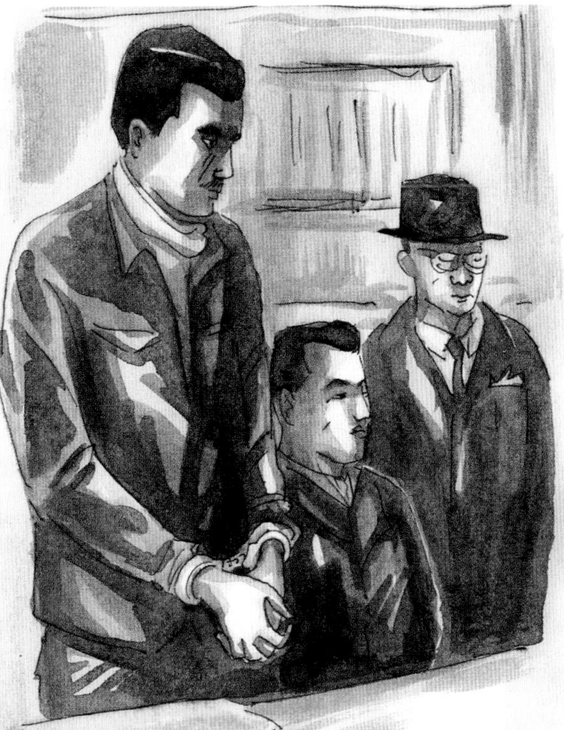
A VERDICT WAS REACHED IN 1952, SENTENCING US ALL TO FOUR YEARS, WHICH COVERED THE TIME WE'D SPENT IN PRISON ALREADY. UPON MY RELEASE, I WAS EXTRADITED BY THE PREFECT OF THE BOUCHES-DU-RHÔNE DEPARTMENT AND I WAS PUT ON A BOAT HOME."

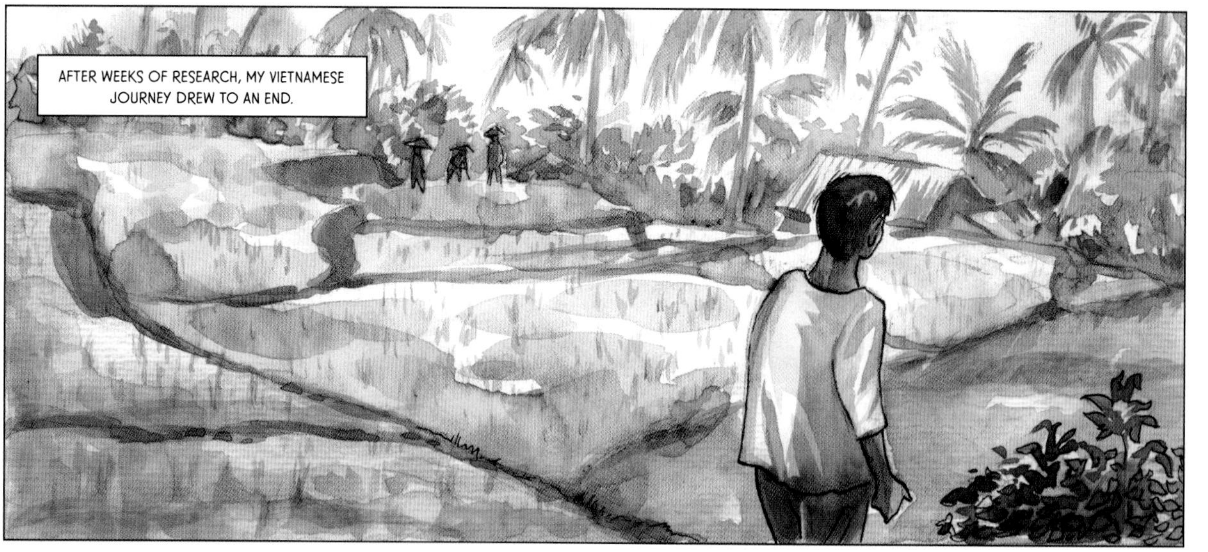
AFTER WEEKS OF RESEARCH, MY VIETNAMESE JOURNEY DREW TO AN END.

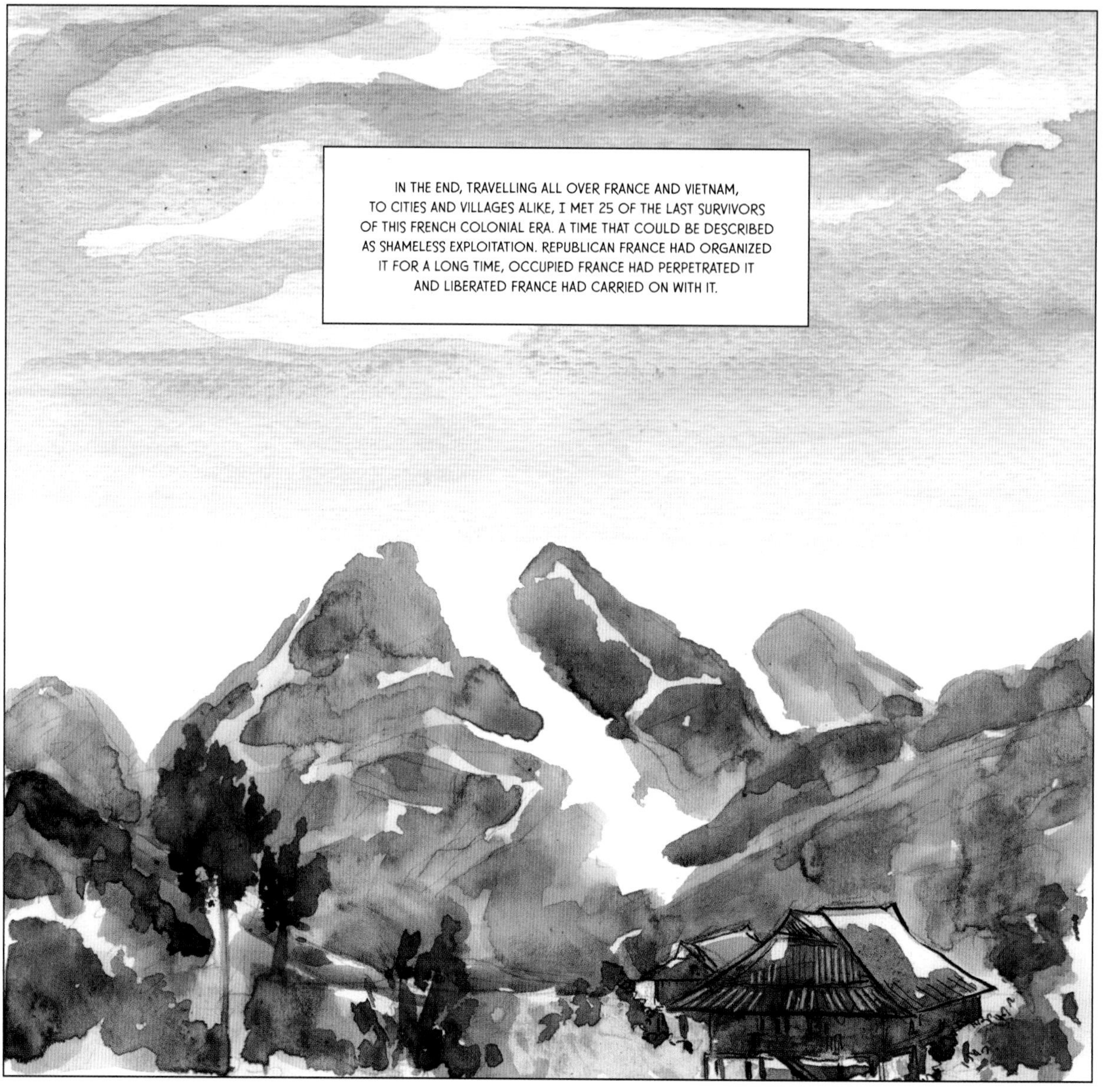
IN THE END, TRAVELLING ALL OVER FRANCE AND VIETNAM, TO CITIES AND VILLAGES ALIKE, I MET 25 OF THE LAST SURVIVORS OF THIS FRENCH COLONIAL ERA. A TIME THAT COULD BE DESCRIBED AS SHAMELESS EXPLOITATION. REPUBLICAN FRANCE HAD ORGANIZED IT FOR A LONG TIME, OCCUPIED FRANCE HAD PERPETRATED IT AND LIBERATED FRANCE HAD CARRIED ON WITH IT.

3. THE DUTY TO REMEMBER

WHERE THE INDOCHINESE WORKERS'
PLACE IN HISTORY IS DISCUSSED

MY RESEARCH TOOK THREE YEARS, COMPRISING BOTH SPEAKING TO WITNESSES AND SPENDING HOURS BURIED IN ARCHIVAL MATERIAL. THE BOOK "FORCED IMMIGRANTS" CAME OUT OF ALL THIS WORK AND WAS PUBLISHED IN MAY 2009.

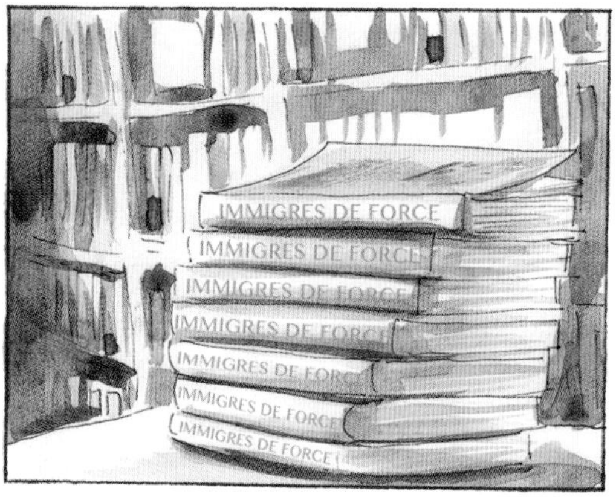
IMMIGRES DE FORCE
IMMIGRES DE FORCE
IMMIGRES DE FORCE
IMMIGRES DE FORCE
IMMIGRES DE FORCE
IMMIGRES DE FORCE
IMMIGRES DE FORCE

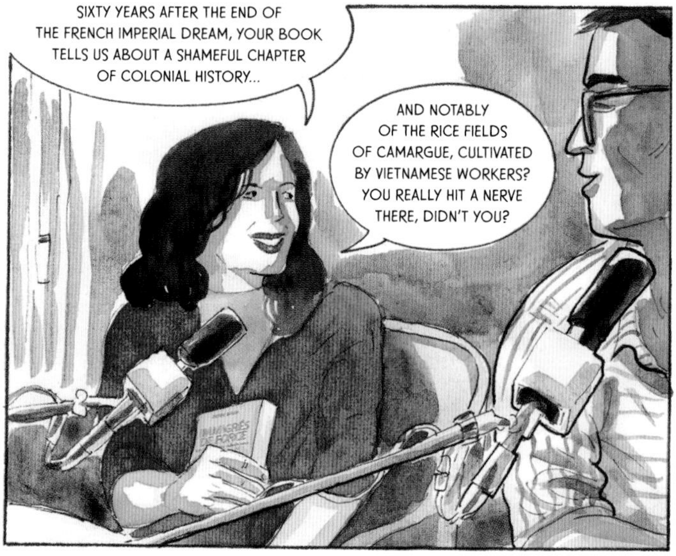
SIXTY YEARS AFTER THE END OF THE FRENCH IMPERIAL DREAM, YOUR BOOK TELLS US ABOUT A SHAMEFUL CHAPTER OF COLONIAL HISTORY...
AND NOTABLY OF THE RICE FIELDS OF CAMARGUE, CULTIVATED BY VIETNAMESE WORKERS? YOU REALLY HIT A NERVE THERE, DIDN'T YOU?

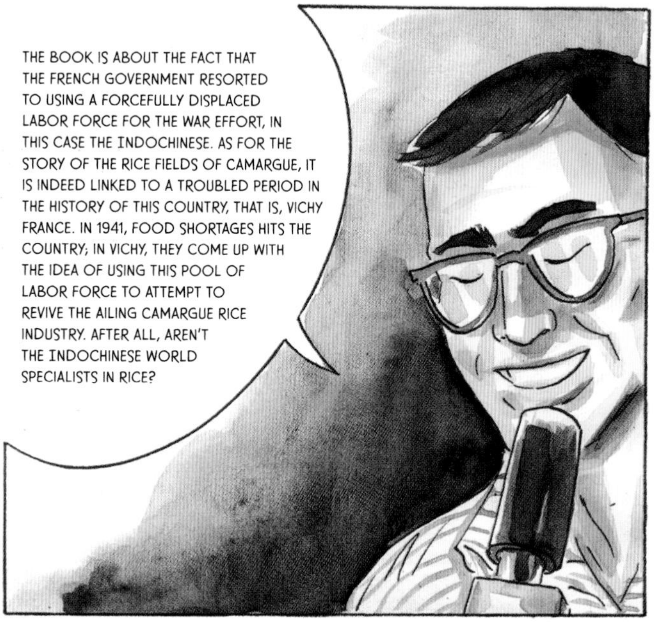
THE BOOK IS ABOUT THE FACT THAT THE FRENCH GOVERNMENT RESORTED TO USING A FORCEFULLY DISPLACED LABOR FORCE FOR THE WAR EFFORT, IN THIS CASE THE INDOCHINESE. AS FOR THE STORY OF THE RICE FIELDS OF CAMARGUE, IT IS INDEED LINKED TO A TROUBLED PERIOD IN THE HISTORY OF THIS COUNTRY, THAT IS, VICHY FRANCE. IN 1941, FOOD SHORTAGES HITS THE COUNTRY; IN VICHY, THEY COME UP WITH THE IDEA OF USING THIS POOL OF LABOR FORCE TO ATTEMPT TO REVIVE THE AILING CAMARGUE RICE INDUSTRY. AFTER ALL, AREN'T THE INDOCHINESE WORLD SPECIALISTS IN RICE?

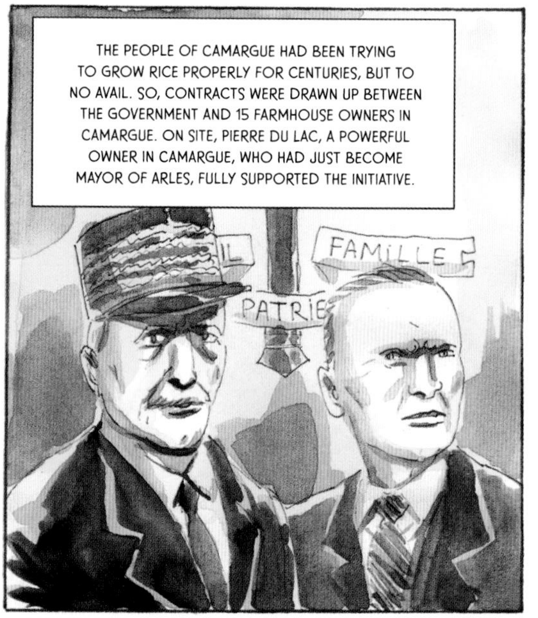
THE PEOPLE OF CAMARGUE HAD BEEN TRYING TO GROW RICE PROPERLY FOR CENTURIES, BUT TO NO AVAIL. SO, CONTRACTS WERE DRAWN UP BETWEEN THE GOVERNMENT AND 15 FARMHOUSE OWNERS IN CAMARGUE. ON SITE, PIERRE DU LAC, A POWERFUL OWNER IN CAMARGUE, WHO HAD JUST BECOME MAYOR OF ARLES, FULLY SUPPORTED THE INITIATIVE.
FAMILLE
PATRIE

OTHER NOTABLE LOCALS WERE IN FAVOR OF THIS PROJECT, SUCH AS EDMOND CLAUZEL, LANDOWNER AND AGRICULTURAL ENGINEER. OTHERS FACILITATED THE PROJECT. JEAN DE VALLIÈRES, DEPUTY PREFECT OF ARLES, WAS THE GODSON OF MARSHAL PÉTAIN AND THE FAMILY OF THE MARSHAL'S WIFE OWNED A FARMHOUSE IN PORT-SAINT-LOUIS-DU-RHÔNE.

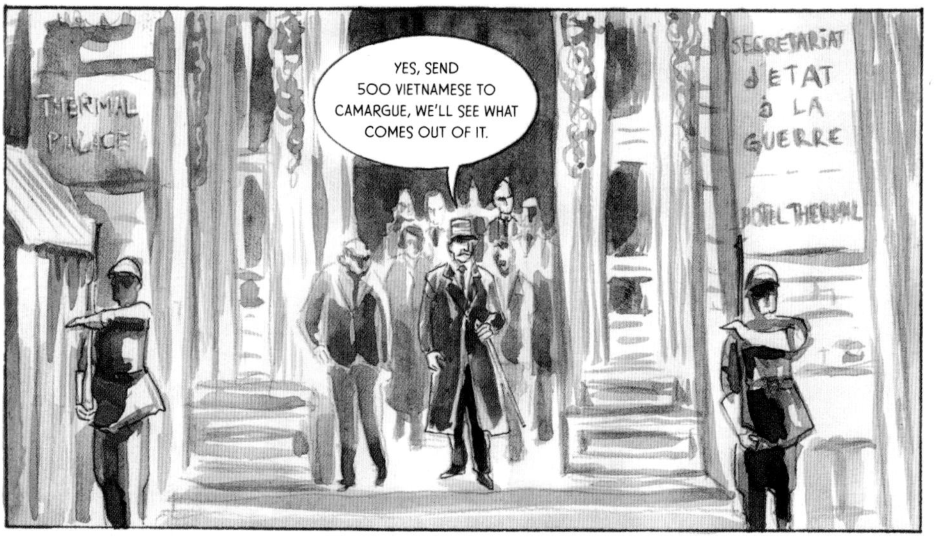
YES, SEND 500 VIETNAMESE TO CAMARGUE, WE'LL SEE WHAT COMES OUT OF IT.
THERMAL PALACE
SECRETARIAT D'ETAT À LA GUERRE
HOTEL THERMAL

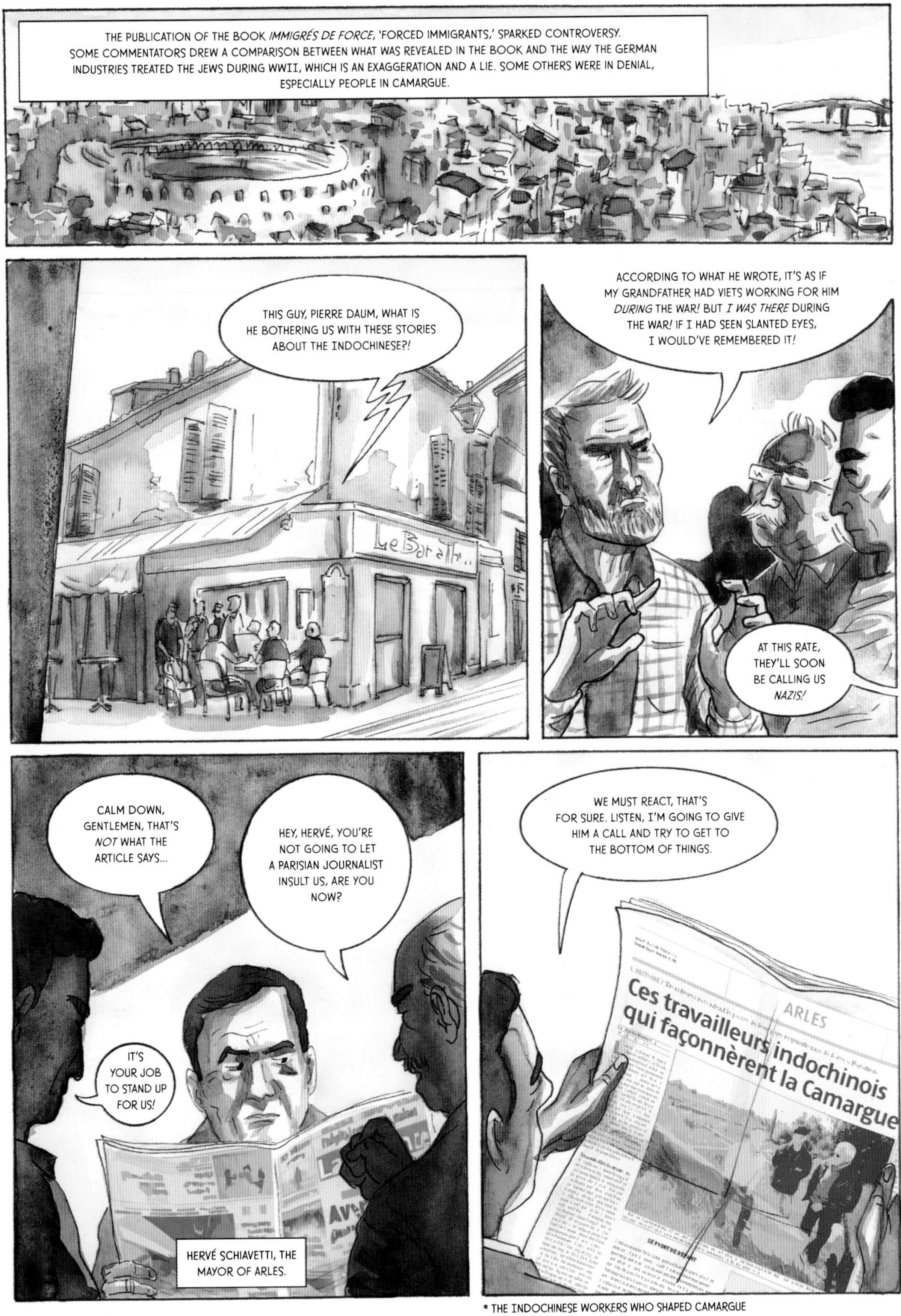
THE PUBLICATION OF THE BOOK *IMMIGRÉS DE FORCE*, 'FORCED IMMIGRANTS,' SPARKED CONTROVERSY. SOME COMMENTATORS DREW A COMPARISON BETWEEN WHAT WAS REVEALED IN THE BOOK AND THE WAY THE GERMAN INDUSTRIES TREATED THE JEWS DURING WWII, WHICH IS AN EXAGGERATION AND A LIE. SOME OTHERS WERE IN DENIAL, ESPECIALLY PEOPLE IN CAMARGUE.
THIS GUY, PIERRE DAUM, WHAT IS HE BOTHERING US WITH THESE STORIES ABOUT THE INDOCHINESE?!
ACCORDING TO WHAT HE WROTE, IT'S AS IF MY GRANDFATHER HAD VIETS WORKING FOR HIM *DURING* THE WAR! BUT *I WAS THERE* DURING THE WAR! IF I HAD SEEN SLANTED EYES, I WOULD'VE REMEMBERED IT!
AT THIS RATE, THEY'LL SOON BE CALLING US *NAZIS!*
CALM DOWN, GENTLEMEN, THAT'S *NOT* WHAT THE ARTICLE SAYS...
HEY, HERVÉ, YOU'RE NOT GOING TO LET A PARISIAN JOURNALIST INSULT US, ARE YOU NOW?
IT'S YOUR JOB TO STAND UP FOR US!
HERVÉ SCHIAVETTI, THE MAYOR OF ARLES.
WE MUST REACT, THAT'S FOR SURE. LISTEN, I'M GOING TO GIVE HIM A CALL AND TRY TO GET TO THE BOTTOM OF THINGS.
ARLES
Ces travailleurs indochinois qui façonnèrent la Camargue

* THE INDOCHINESE WORKERS WHO SHAPED CAMARGUE

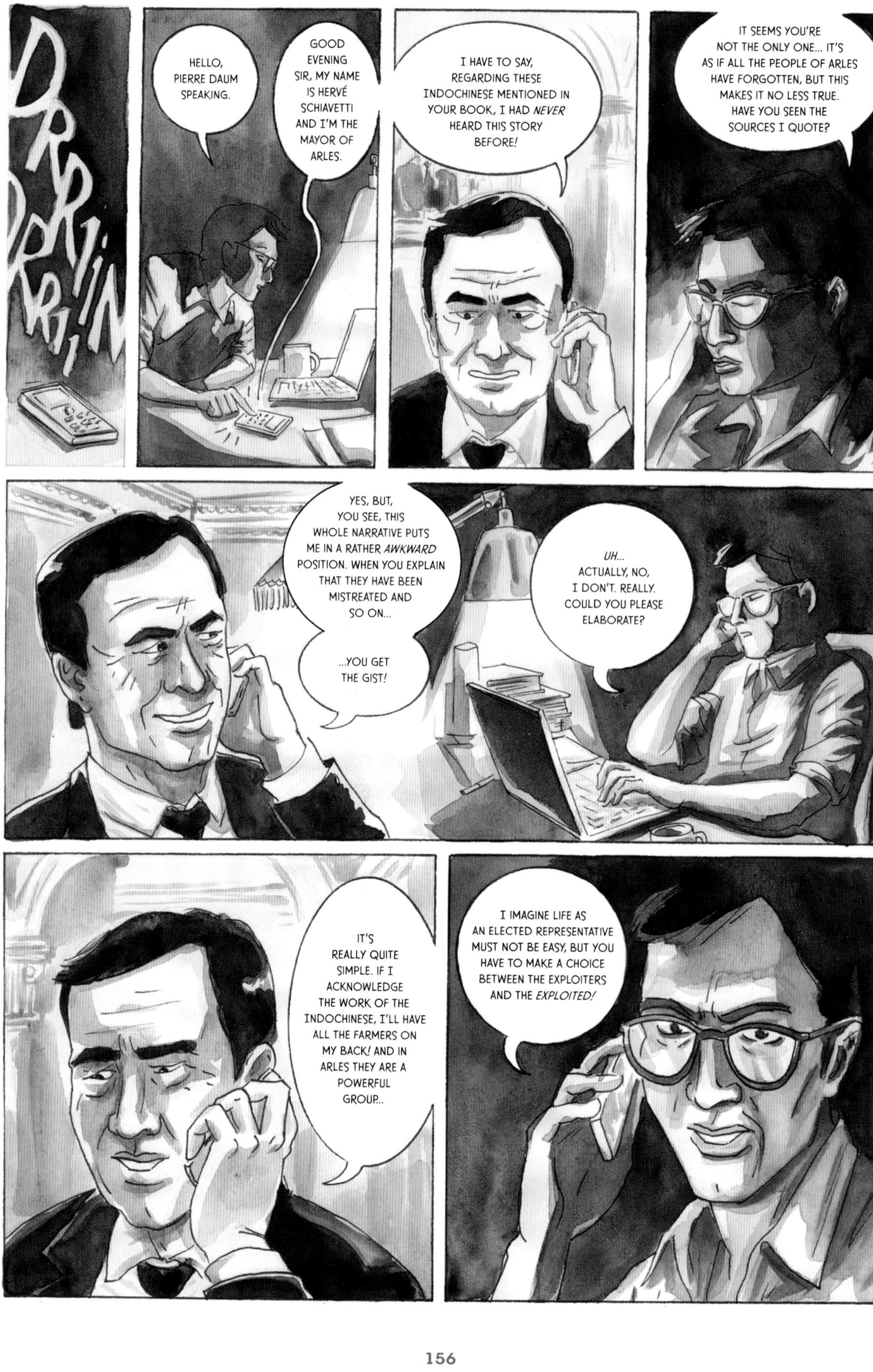
HELLO, PIERRE DAUM SPEAKING.
GOOD EVENING SIR, MY NAME IS HERVÉ SCHIAVETTI AND I'M THE MAYOR OF ARLES.
I HAVE TO SAY, REGARDING THESE INDOCHINESE MENTIONED IN YOUR BOOK, I HAD *NEVER* HEARD THIS STORY BEFORE!
IT SEEMS YOU'RE NOT THE ONLY ONE... IT'S AS IF ALL THE PEOPLE OF ARLES HAVE FORGOTTEN, BUT THIS MAKES IT NO LESS TRUE. HAVE YOU SEEN THE SOURCES I QUOTE?
YES, BUT, YOU SEE, THIS WHOLE NARRATIVE PUTS ME IN A RATHER *AWKWARD* POSITION. WHEN YOU EXPLAIN THAT THEY HAVE BEEN MISTREATED AND SO ON...
...YOU GET THE GIST!
UH... ACTUALLY, NO, I DON'T. REALLY. COULD YOU PLEASE ELABORATE?
IT'S REALLY QUITE SIMPLE. IF I ACKNOWLEDGE THE WORK OF THE INDOCHINESE, I'LL HAVE ALL THE FARMERS ON MY BACK! AND IN ARLES THEY ARE A POWERFUL GROUP...
I IMAGINE LIFE AS AN ELECTED REPRESENTATIVE MUST NOT BE EASY, BUT YOU HAVE TO MAKE A CHOICE BETWEEN THE EXPLOITERS AND THE *EXPLOITED!*

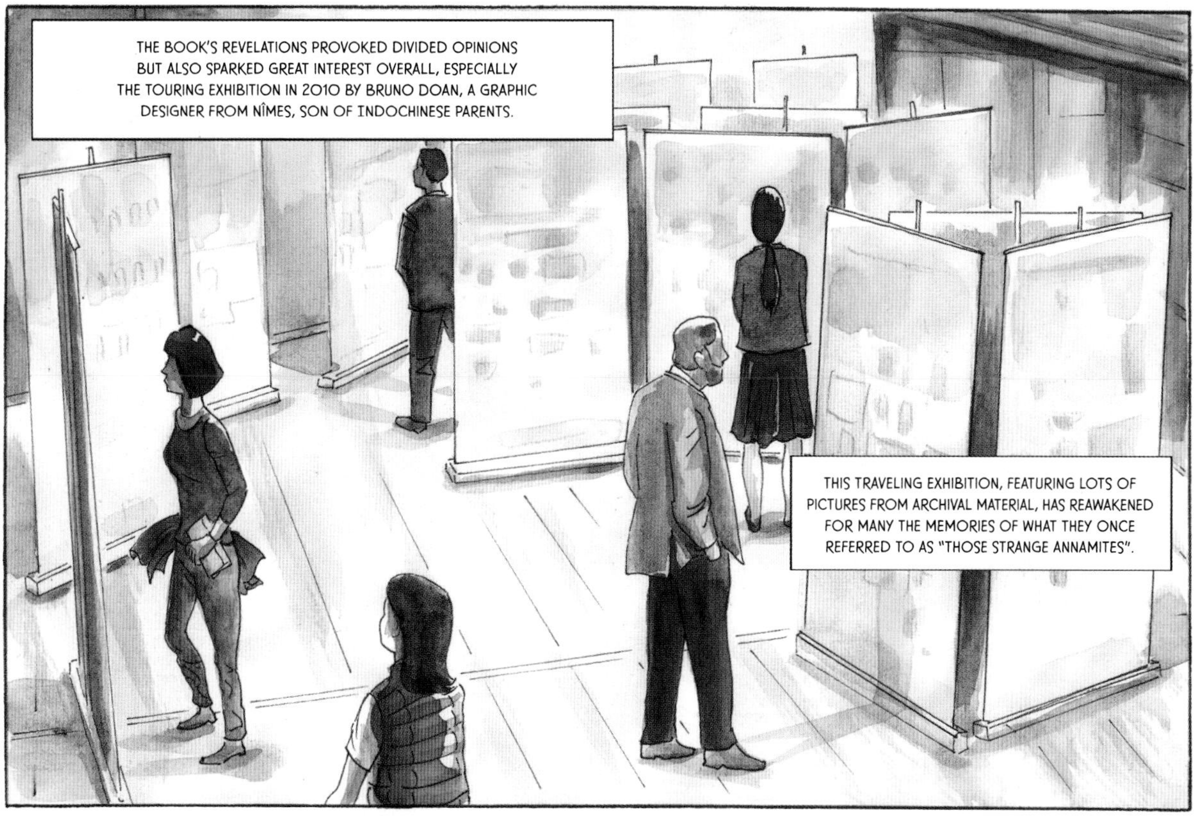
THE BOOK'S REVELATIONS PROVOKED DIVIDED OPINIONS BUT ALSO SPARKED GREAT INTEREST OVERALL, ESPECIALLY THE TOURING EXHIBITION IN 2010 BY BRUNO DOAN, A GRAPHIC DESIGNER FROM NÎMES, SON OF INDOCHINESE PARENTS.
THIS TRAVELING EXHIBITION, FEATURING LOTS OF PICTURES FROM ARCHIVAL MATERIAL, HAS REAWAKENED FOR MANY THE MEMORIES OF WHAT THEY ONCE REFERRED TO AS "THOSE STRANGE ANNAMITES".

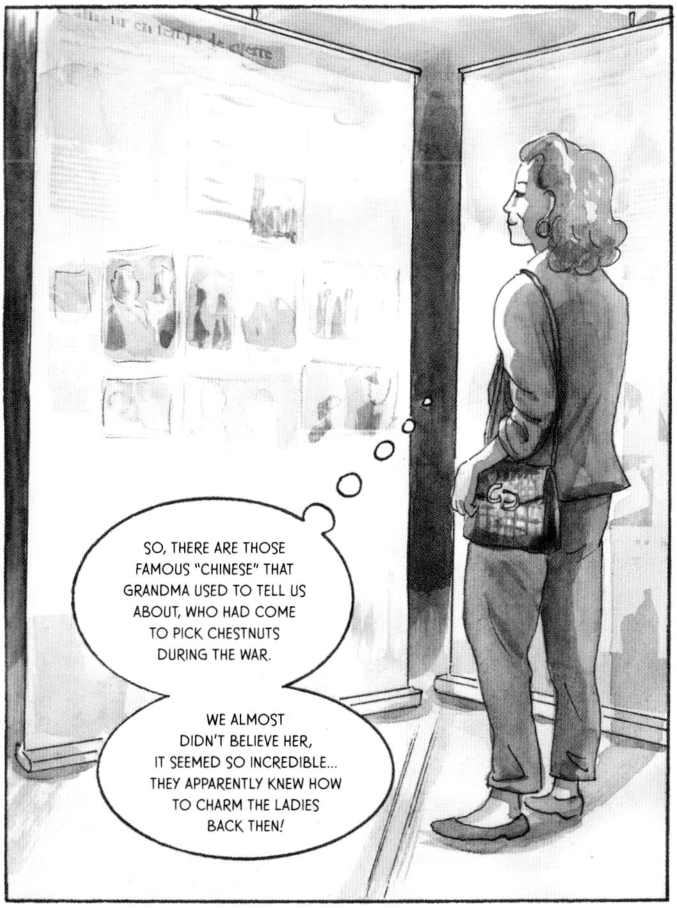
SO, THERE ARE THOSE FAMOUS "CHINESE" THAT GRANDMA USED TO TELL US ABOUT, WHO HAD COME TO PICK CHESTNUTS DURING THE WAR.
WE ALMOST DIDN'T BELIEVE HER, IT SEEMED SO INCREDIBLE... THEY APPARENTLY KNEW HOW TO CHARM THE LADIES BACK THEN!

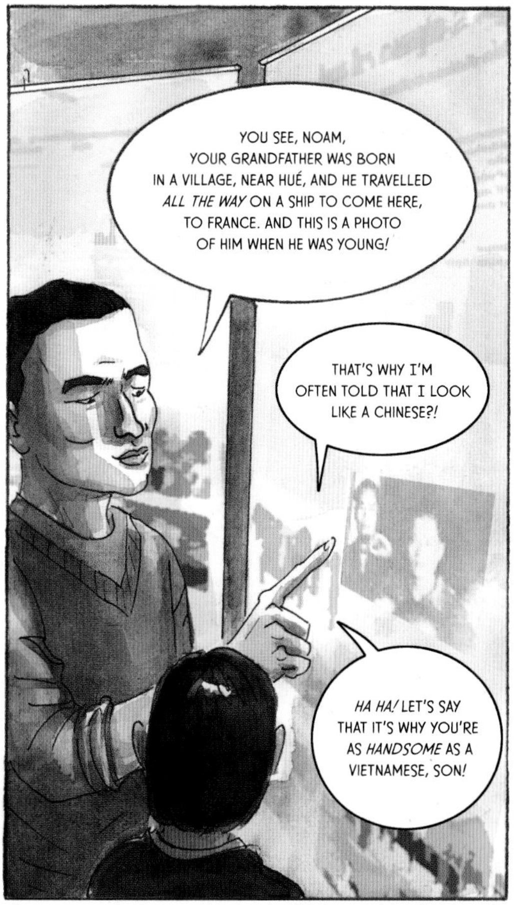
YOU SEE, NOAM, YOUR GRANDFATHER WAS BORN IN A VILLAGE, NEAR HUÉ, AND HE TRAVELLED *ALL THE WAY* ON A SHIP TO COME HERE, TO FRANCE. AND THIS IS A PHOTO OF HIM WHEN HE WAS YOUNG!
THAT'S WHY I'M OFTEN TOLD THAT I LOOK LIKE A CHINESE?!
HA HA! LET'S SAY THAT IT'S WHY YOU'RE AS *HANDSOME* AS A VIETNAMESE, SON!

ABOVE ALL, THE BOOK'S RELEASE HAS CREATED A RAISED AWARENESS, ESPECIALLY AMONG THE DESCENDANTS -- CHILDREN AND GRANDCHILDREN -- OF THE FORMER O.N.S. WHOSE SHARED HISTORY IS DESCRIBED.

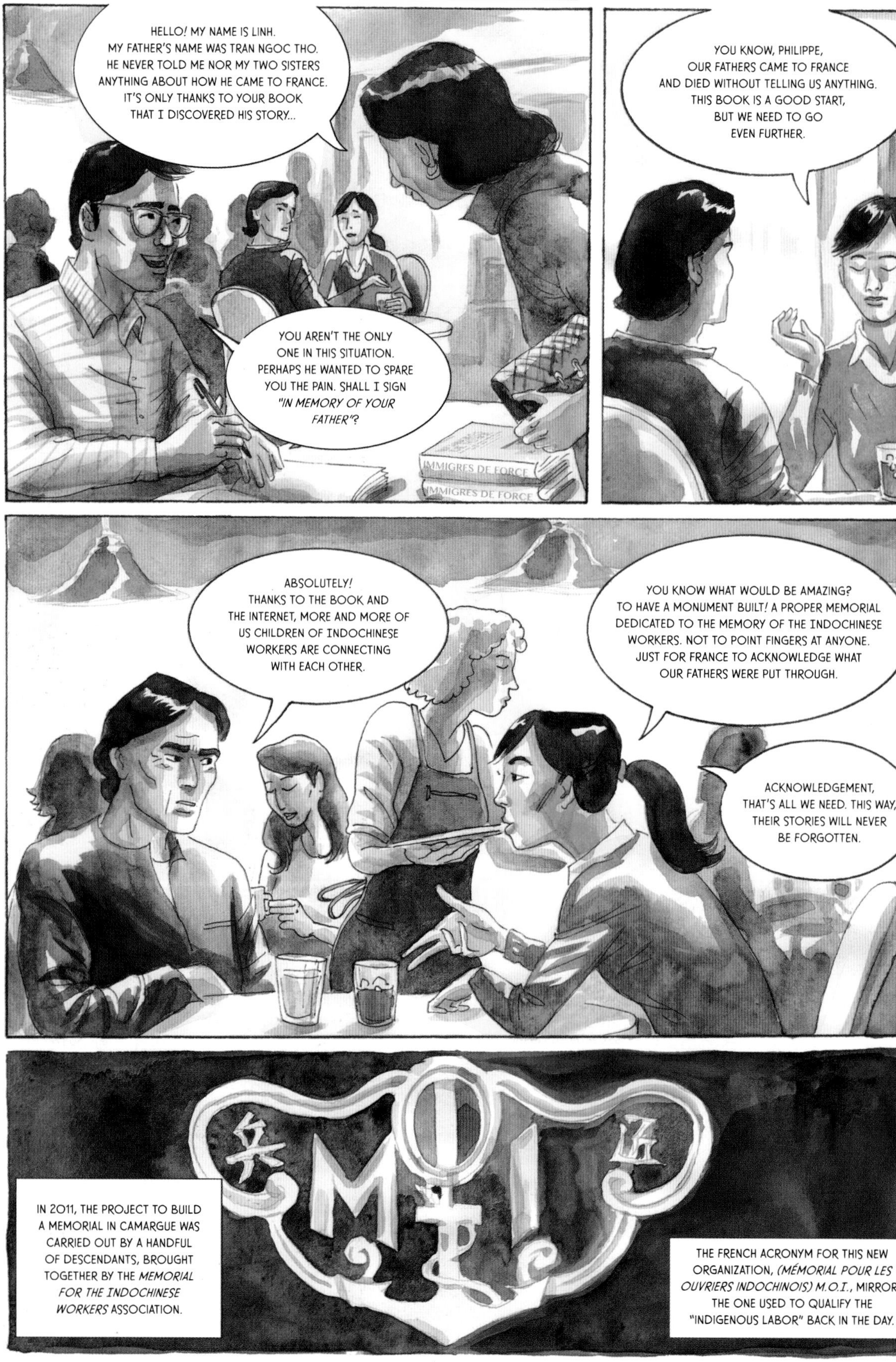
HELLO! MY NAME IS LINH. MY FATHER'S NAME WAS TRAN NGOC THO. HE NEVER TOLD ME NOR MY TWO SISTERS ANYTHING ABOUT HOW HE CAME TO FRANCE. IT'S ONLY THANKS TO YOUR BOOK THAT I DISCOVERED HIS STORY...
YOU AREN'T THE ONLY ONE IN THIS SITUATION. PERHAPS HE WANTED TO SPARE YOU THE PAIN. SHALL I SIGN *"IN MEMORY OF YOUR FATHER"*?
IMMIGRES DE FORCE
IMMIGRES DE FORCE
YOU KNOW, PHILIPPE, OUR FATHERS CAME TO FRANCE AND DIED WITHOUT TELLING US ANYTHING. THIS BOOK IS A GOOD START, BUT WE NEED TO GO EVEN FURTHER.
ABSOLUTELY! THANKS TO THE BOOK AND THE INTERNET, MORE AND MORE OF US CHILDREN OF INDOCHINESE WORKERS ARE CONNECTING WITH EACH OTHER.
YOU KNOW WHAT WOULD BE AMAZING? TO HAVE A MONUMENT BUILT! A PROPER MEMORIAL DEDICATED TO THE MEMORY OF THE INDOCHINESE WORKERS. NOT TO POINT FINGERS AT ANYONE. JUST FOR FRANCE TO ACKNOWLEDGE WHAT OUR FATHERS WERE PUT THROUGH.
ACKNOWLEDGEMENT, THAT'S ALL WE NEED. THIS WAY, THEIR STORIES WILL NEVER BE FORGOTTEN.
IN 2011, THE PROJECT TO BUILD A MEMORIAL IN CAMARGUE WAS CARRIED OUT BY A HANDFUL OF DESCENDANTS, BROUGHT TOGETHER BY THE *MEMORIAL FOR THE INDOCHINESE WORKERS* ASSOCIATION.
MOI
THE FRENCH ACRONYM FOR THIS NEW ORGANIZATION, *(MÉMORIAL POUR LES OUVRIERS INDOCHINOIS)* M.O.I., MIRRORS THE ONE USED TO QUALIFY THE "INDIGENOUS LABOR" BACK IN THE DAY.

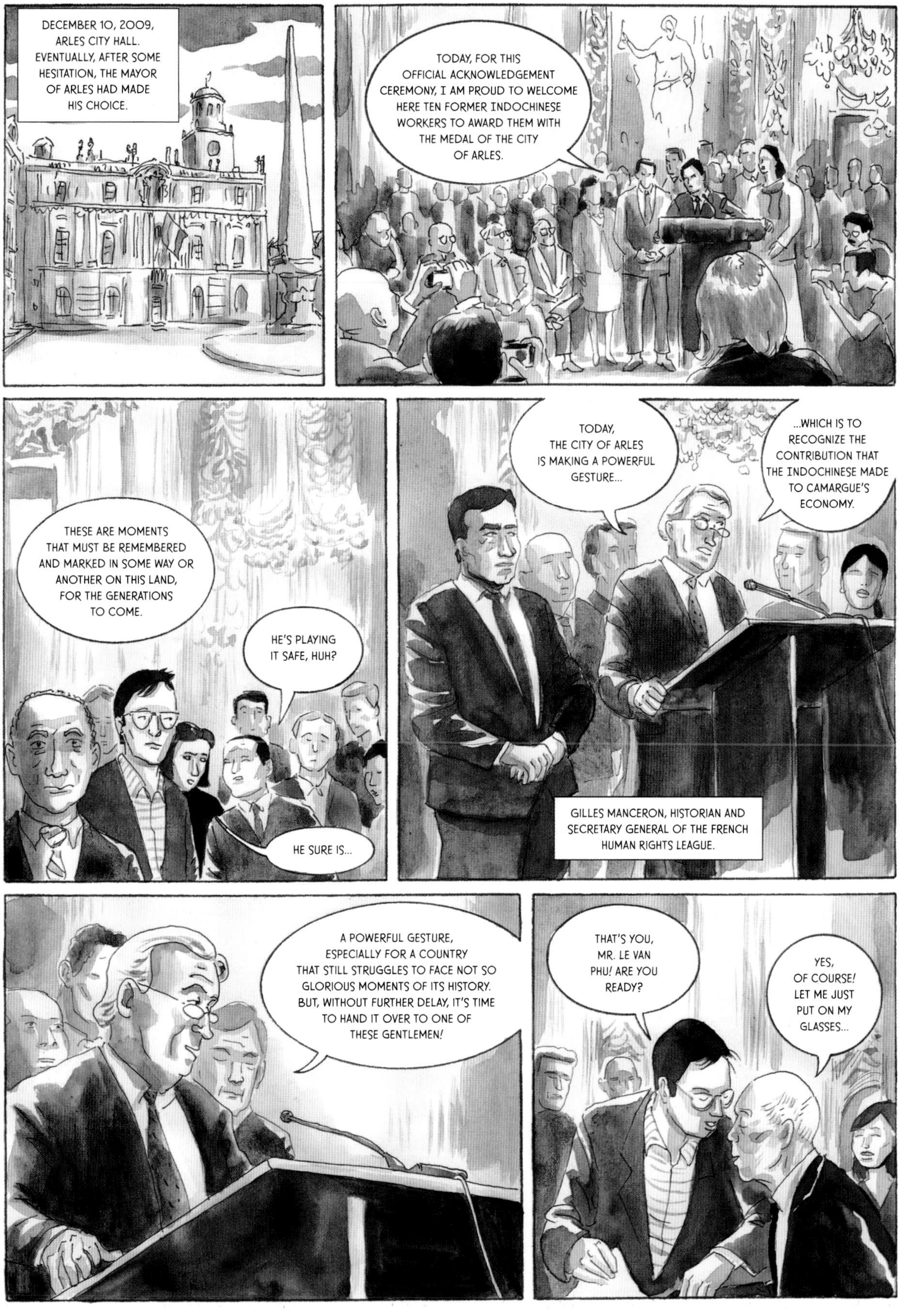
DECEMBER 10, 2009, ARLES CITY HALL. EVENTUALLY, AFTER SOME HESITATION, THE MAYOR OF ARLES HAD MADE HIS CHOICE.
TODAY, FOR THIS OFFICIAL ACKNOWLEDGEMENT CEREMONY, I AM PROUD TO WELCOME HERE TEN FORMER INDOCHINESE WORKERS TO AWARD THEM WITH THE MEDAL OF THE CITY OF ARLES.
THESE ARE MOMENTS THAT MUST BE REMEMBERED AND MARKED IN SOME WAY OR ANOTHER ON THIS LAND, FOR THE GENERATIONS TO COME.
HE'S PLAYING IT SAFE, HUH?
HE SURE IS...
TODAY, THE CITY OF ARLES IS MAKING A POWERFUL GESTURE...
...WHICH IS TO RECOGNIZE THE CONTRIBUTION THAT THE INDOCHINESE MADE TO CAMARGUE'S ECONOMY.
GILLES MANCERON, HISTORIAN AND SECRETARY GENERAL OF THE FRENCH HUMAN RIGHTS LEAGUE.
A POWERFUL GESTURE, ESPECIALLY FOR A COUNTRY THAT STILL STRUGGLES TO FACE NOT SO GLORIOUS MOMENTS OF ITS HISTORY. BUT, WITHOUT FURTHER DELAY, IT'S TIME TO HAND IT OVER TO ONE OF THESE GENTLEMEN!
THAT'S YOU, MR. LE VAN PHU! ARE YOU READY?
YES, OF COURSE! LET ME JUST PUT ON MY GLASSES...

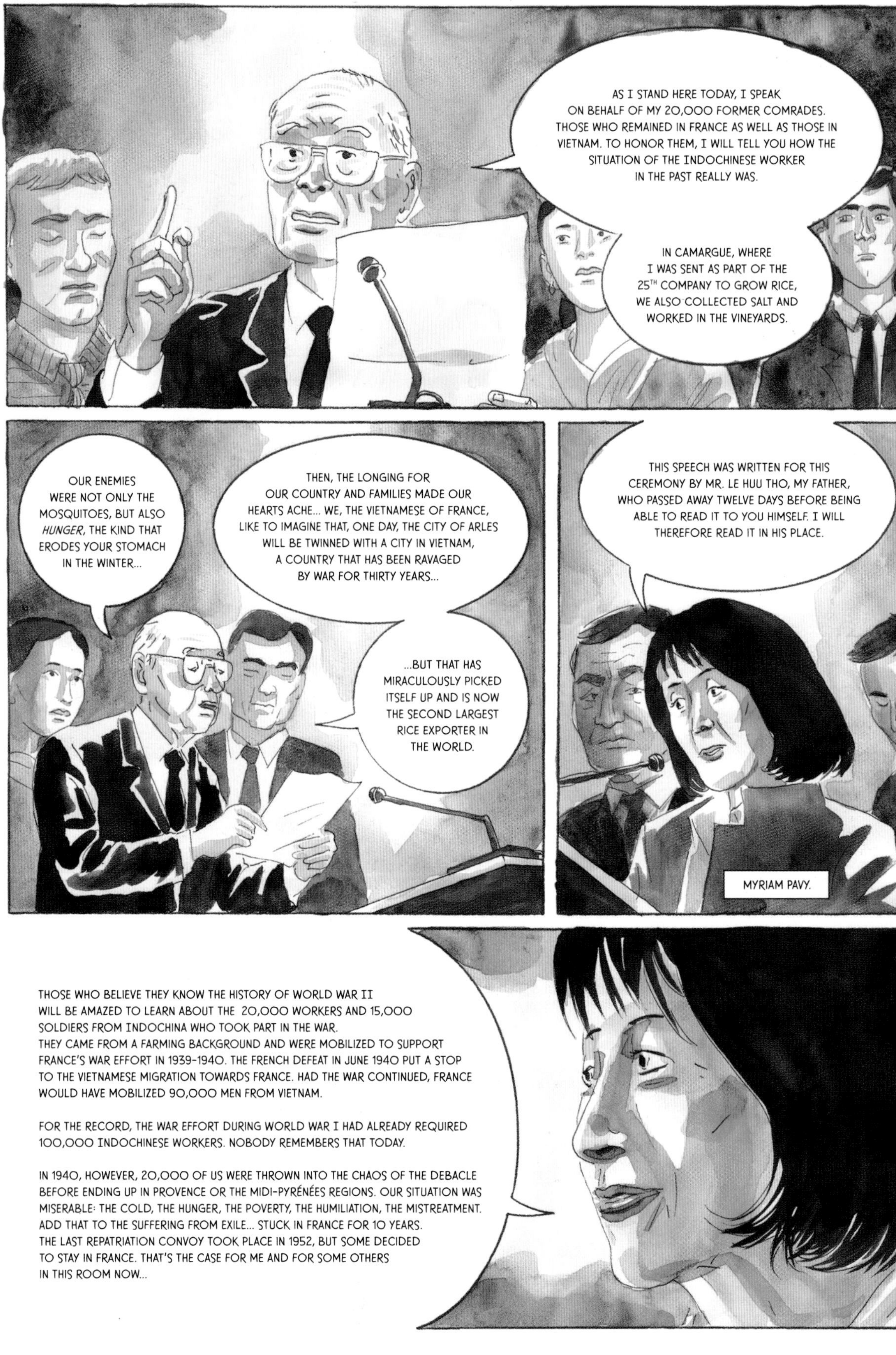
AS I STAND HERE TODAY, I SPEAK ON BEHALF OF MY 20,000 FORMER COMRADES. THOSE WHO REMAINED IN FRANCE AS WELL AS THOSE IN VIETNAM. TO HONOR THEM, I WILL TELL YOU HOW THE SITUATION OF THE INDOCHINESE WORKER IN THE PAST REALLY WAS.
IN CAMARGUE, WHERE I WAS SENT AS PART OF THE 25TH COMPANY TO GROW RICE, WE ALSO COLLECTED SALT AND WORKED IN THE VINEYARDS.
OUR ENEMIES WERE NOT ONLY THE MOSQUITOES, BUT ALSO *HUNGER*, THE KIND THAT ERODES YOUR STOMACH IN THE WINTER...
THEN, THE LONGING FOR OUR COUNTRY AND FAMILIES MADE OUR HEARTS ACHE... WE, THE VIETNAMESE OF FRANCE, LIKE TO IMAGINE THAT, ONE DAY, THE CITY OF ARLES WILL BE TWINNED WITH A CITY IN VIETNAM, A COUNTRY THAT HAS BEEN RAVAGED BY WAR FOR THIRTY YEARS...
...BUT THAT HAS MIRACULOUSLY PICKED ITSELF UP AND IS NOW THE SECOND LARGEST RICE EXPORTER IN THE WORLD.
THIS SPEECH WAS WRITTEN FOR THIS CEREMONY BY MR. LE HUU THO, MY FATHER, WHO PASSED AWAY TWELVE DAYS BEFORE BEING ABLE TO READ IT TO YOU HIMSELF. I WILL THEREFORE READ IT IN HIS PLACE.
MYRIAM PAVY.
THOSE WHO BELIEVE THEY KNOW THE HISTORY OF WORLD WAR II WILL BE AMAZED TO LEARN ABOUT THE 20,000 WORKERS AND 15,000 SOLDIERS FROM INDOCHINA WHO TOOK PART IN THE WAR. THEY CAME FROM A FARMING BACKGROUND AND WERE MOBILIZED TO SUPPORT FRANCE'S WAR EFFORT IN 1939-1940. THE FRENCH DEFEAT IN JUNE 1940 PUT A STOP TO THE VIETNAMESE MIGRATION TOWARDS FRANCE. HAD THE WAR CONTINUED, FRANCE WOULD HAVE MOBILIZED 90,000 MEN FROM VIETNAM.
FOR THE RECORD, THE WAR EFFORT DURING WORLD WAR I HAD ALREADY REQUIRED 100,000 INDOCHINESE WORKERS. NOBODY REMEMBERS THAT TODAY.
IN 1940, HOWEVER, 20,000 OF US WERE THROWN INTO THE CHAOS OF THE DEBACLE BEFORE ENDING UP IN PROVENCE OR THE MIDI-PYRÉNÉES REGIONS. OUR SITUATION WAS MISERABLE: THE COLD, THE HUNGER, THE POVERTY, THE HUMILIATION, THE MISTREATMENT. ADD THAT TO THE SUFFERING FROM EXILE... STUCK IN FRANCE FOR 10 YEARS. THE LAST REPATRIATION CONVOY TOOK PLACE IN 1952, BUT SOME DECIDED TO STAY IN FRANCE. THAT'S THE CASE FOR ME AND FOR SOME OTHERS IN THIS ROOM NOW...

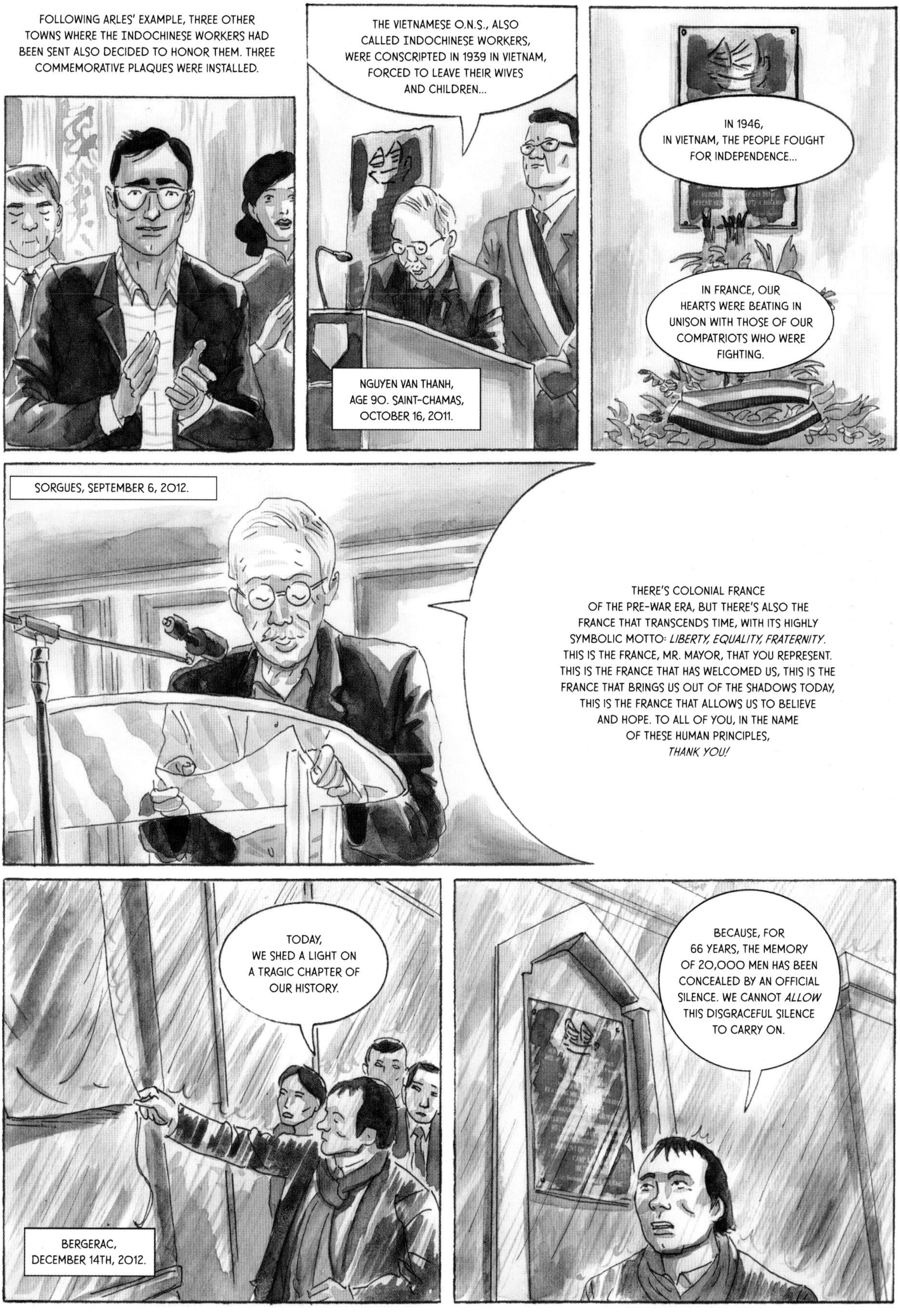
FOLLOWING ARLES' EXAMPLE, THREE OTHER TOWNS WHERE THE INDOCHINESE WORKERS HAD BEEN SENT ALSO DECIDED TO HONOR THEM. THREE COMMEMORATIVE PLAQUES WERE INSTALLED.
THE VIETNAMESE O.N.S., ALSO CALLED INDOCHINESE WORKERS, WERE CONSCRIPTED IN 1939 IN VIETNAM, FORCED TO LEAVE THEIR WIVES AND CHILDREN...
NGUYEN VAN THANH, AGE 90. SAINT-CHAMAS, OCTOBER 16, 2011.
IN 1946, IN VIETNAM, THE PEOPLE FOUGHT FOR INDEPENDENCE...
IN FRANCE, OUR HEARTS WERE BEATING IN UNISON WITH THOSE OF OUR COMPATRIOTS WHO WERE FIGHTING.
SORGUES, SEPTEMBER 6, 2012.
THERE'S COLONIAL FRANCE OF THE PRE-WAR ERA, BUT THERE'S ALSO THE FRANCE THAT TRANSCENDS TIME, WITH ITS HIGHLY SYMBOLIC MOTTO: *LIBERTY, EQUALITY, FRATERNITY*. THIS IS THE FRANCE, MR. MAYOR, THAT YOU REPRESENT. THIS IS THE FRANCE THAT HAS WELCOMED US, THIS IS THE FRANCE THAT BRINGS US OUT OF THE SHADOWS TODAY, THIS IS THE FRANCE THAT ALLOWS US TO BELIEVE AND HOPE. TO ALL OF YOU, IN THE NAME OF THESE HUMAN PRINCIPLES, *THANK YOU!*
TODAY, WE SHED A LIGHT ON A TRAGIC CHAPTER OF OUR HISTORY.
BERGERAC, DECEMBER 14TH, 2012.
BECAUSE, FOR 66 YEARS, THE MEMORY OF 20,000 MEN HAS BEEN CONCEALED BY AN OFFICIAL SILENCE. WE CANNOT *ALLOW* THIS DISGRACEFUL SILENCE TO CARRY ON.

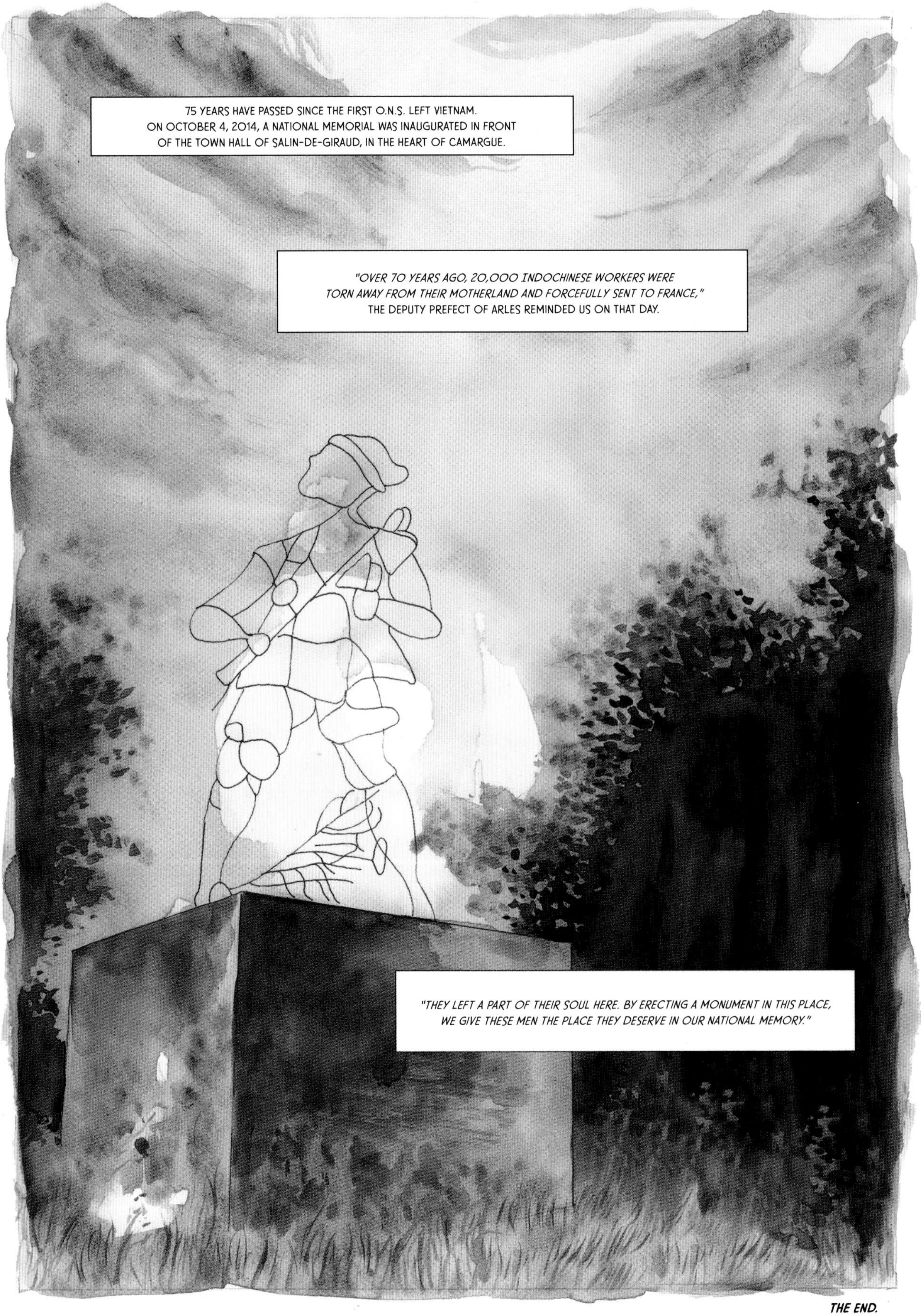
75 YEARS HAVE PASSED SINCE THE FIRST O.N.S. LEFT VIETNAM. ON OCTOBER 4, 2014, A NATIONAL MEMORIAL WAS INAUGURATED IN FRONT OF THE TOWN HALL OF SALIN-DE-GIRAUD, IN THE HEART OF CAMARGUE.
"OVER 70 YEARS AGO, 20,000 INDOCHINESE WORKERS WERE TORN AWAY FROM THEIR MOTHERLAND AND FORCEFULLY SENT TO FRANCE," THE DEPUTY PREFECT OF ARLES REMINDED US ON THAT DAY.
"THEY LEFT A PART OF THEIR SOUL HERE. BY ERECTING A MONUMENT IN THIS PLACE, WE GIVE THESE MEN THE PLACE THEY DESERVE IN OUR NATIONAL MEMORY."

THE END.

FROM JOURNALISM TO COMICS JOURNALISM, PIERRE DAUM'S JOURNEY

The tale you've just read in the second part of this book is based on a true story. Pierre Daum's 4-year investigation, published as a non-fiction novel under the name *Immigrés de Force* ("Forced Immigrants," Éditions Actes Sud, 2009) and chronicling the fate of 20,000 Indochinese workers displaced during World War 2, triggered an incredible memory awakening, followed by a major call to action. Following publication of the book, many villages and cities of France started to restore and honor the memory of those long-forgotten immigrants, as well as their own role in this chapter of French history. In addition, an exhibit as well as three documentaries on the subject were created and widely attended.

En 1942, des paysans in[...] sont venus planter du ri[...] Camargue.

In the meantime, Pierre Daum has distanced himself from *Libération* and pure news reporting to concentrate on deep investigative journalism. His works have found a new home in specialty outlets such as *Le Monde Diplomatique*. He has also published more books on France's colonial past, this time focusing on France's role in Algeria: *Ni valise ni cercueil, les Pieds-noirs restés en Algérie après l'indépendance*, ("Neither Suitcase nor Coffin: the Pieds-Noirs Who Stayed in Algeria After Its Independence, Éditions Actes Sud, 2012), and *Le dernier tabou, les 'harkis' restés en Algérie après l'indépendance* ("The Last Taboo: Harkis Who Stayed in Algeria After 1962," Éditions Actes Sud, 2015).

After hesitating for years, the Vietnamese authorities have finally granted I*mmigrés de Force* the right to be published in Vietnam. Translated in 2014, the book has been renamed: *Lính Thợ Đông Duong O Pháp* (1939-1952).

Further information on the subject and on Pierre Daum can be found at www.immigresdeforce.com.

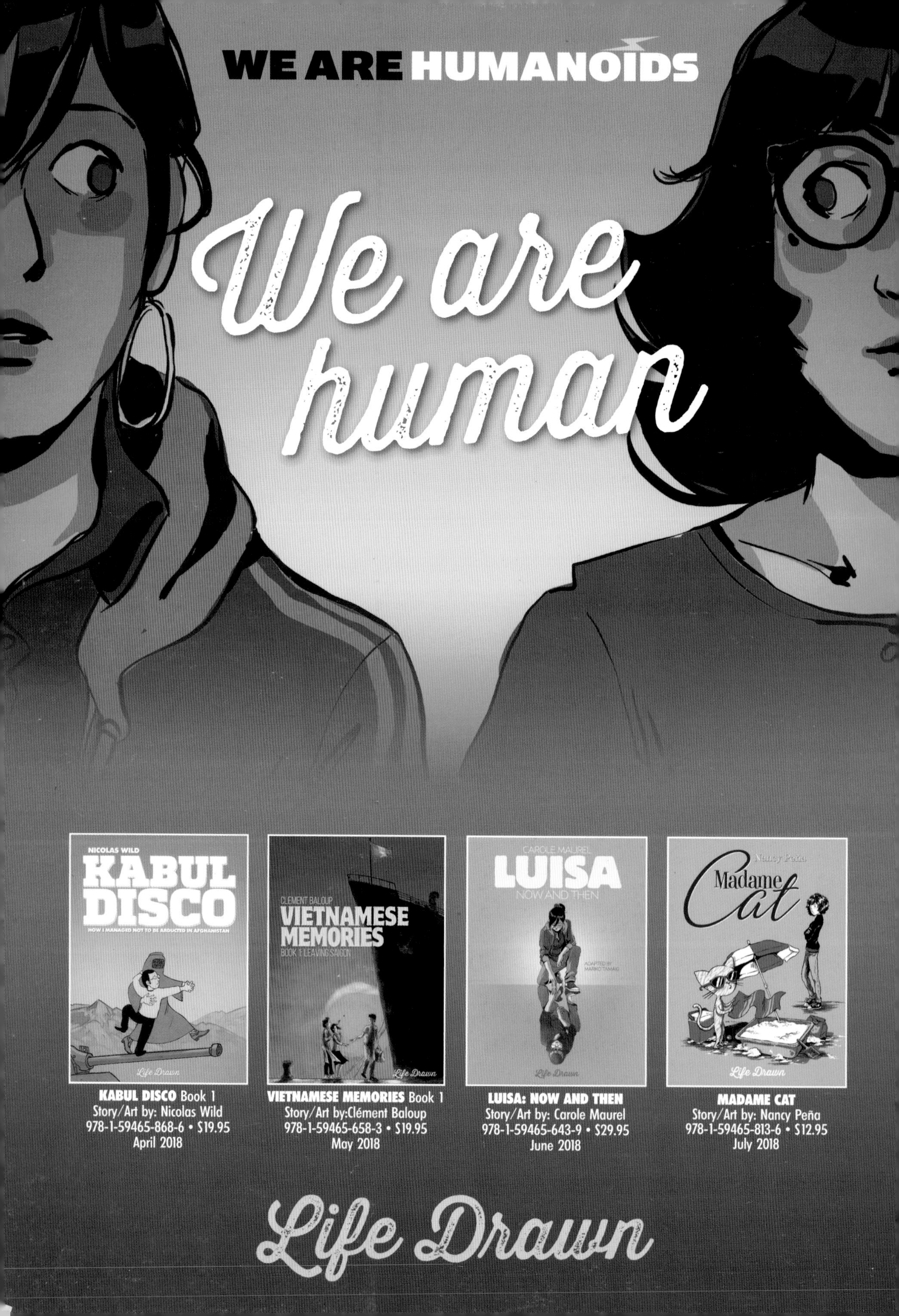

WE ARE HUMANOIDS
We are human
NICOLAS WILD
KABUL DISCO
HOW I MANAGED NOT TO BE ABDUCTED IN AFGHANISTAN
Life Drawn
CLEMENT BALOUP
VIETNAMESE MEMORIES
BOOK 1: LEAVING SAIGON
Life Drawn
CAROLE MAUREL
LUISA
NOW AND THEN
Life Drawn
Nancy Peña
Madame Cat
Life Drawn
KABUL DISCO Book 1
Story/Art by: Nicolas Wild
978-1-59465-868-6 • $19.95
April 2018
VIETNAMESE MEMORIES Book 1
Story/Art by:Clément Baloup
978-1-59465-658-3 • $19.95
May 2018
LUISA: NOW AND THEN
Story/Art by: Carole Maurel
978-1-59465-643-9 • $29.95
June 2018
MADAME CAT
Story/Art by: Nancy Peña
978-1-59465-813-6 • $12.95
July 2018
Life Drawn